FOUR GREAT STORIES FROM SILHOUETTE

THE TWELFTH MOON by Kathleen Eagle

Sergeant Luke Tracker h
expecting to find the pr
always characterized rese
Hope Spencer, who spen
children the ways of the
nights teaching Luke the far
the heart.

EIGHT NIGHTS by Brooke Hastings

Rebecca's children had suffered enough from workaholic parents. She couldn't allow it to happen again,
no matter how drawn she was to her hard-driving boss,
David. Besides, neither she nor David could find time
for loving when they worked eight days a week. Until
the eight nights of Hanukkah offered them a
miracle....

CHRISTMAS MAGIC by Annette Broadrick

For Natalie Phillips, returning home revived painful
memories. It was in Portland, years ago, that she lost
Tony D'Angelo, the only man she'd ever loved. But
fate—or was it the magic of Christmas?—helped heal
old wounds as Natalie and Tony discovered a new love
that was so powerful that every day was a holiday!

MIRACLE ON I-40 by Curtiss Ann Matlock

To reconcile with her folks back East and give her kids
grandparents for Christmas, truck-stop waitress Lacey
Bryant arranged transportation with her steadiest
customer. Little did she know she'd hitched a ride with
Scrooge! Eighteen hundred miles confined with
scowling Barry Cooper would feel endless...unless
Lacey miraculously changed his "Bah Humbug" to
"Barry Christmas!"

Dear Reader:

1988 marks our third volume of Silhouette Christmas Stories. You've been tremendously supportive, and for that we all thank you. Each year we try to bring you something new and different. We showcase some of our most popular authors who create memorable characters in stories that express all the joy, warmth and love that are so much a part of the holiday season.

This year we have something very special for you—our first Hanukkah story. Written by Brooke Hastings, "Eight Nights" is the story of David, who learns to get his priorities straight as he balances work, family and love. In "The Twelfth Moon" by Kathleen Eagle, you'll read about some of the wonderful Indian traditions surrounding Christmas in South Dakota. For Lacey Bryant, the heroine of Curtiss Ann Matlock's "Miracle on I-40," Christmas is a time of reconciliation, love—and puppies! Christmas *is* magic in Annette Broadrick's heartwarming story, "Christmas Magic," when Natalie is reunited with the man she loved and thought she lost long ago.

I dare you to read these stories without a Kleenex!

We wish you the happiest of holidays and hope you'll enjoy reading this collection as much as we enjoyed preparing it for you.

Karen Solem
Vice President
Editorial Director

Silhouette Christmas Stories 1988

Kathleen Eagle
Brooke Hastings
Annette Broadrick
Curtiss Ann Matlock

Silhouette Books.

Published by Silhouette Books New York
America's Publisher of Contemporary Romance

SILHOUETTE BOOKS
300 E. 42nd St., New York, N.Y. 10017

Silhouette Christmas Stories 1988
Copyright © 1988 by Silhouette Books

ISBN: 0-373-48215-9

First Silhouette Books printing November 1988

The publisher acknowledges the copyright holders of
the individual works as follows:

The Twelfth Moon
Copyright © 1988 by Kathleen Eagle

Eight Nights
Copyright © 1988 by Deborah H. Gordon

Christmas Magic
Copyright © 1988 by Annette Broadrick

Miracle on I-40
Copyright © 1988 by Curtiss Ann Matlock

America's Publishers of Contemporary Romance

Printed in the U.S.A.

CONTENTS

THE TWELFTH MOON

Kathleen Eagle

DANGER DAVE

Artwork by David Eagle

Prologue

The long Greyhound topped the rise and dropped Luke Tracker's stomach over the hill ahead of the rest of him. For at least the tenth time since he'd left Fort Leonard Wood, Missouri, he asked himself why he'd taken the bus. The answer that came back was, That's part of coming home, remember? Jets flew over Wakpala, South Dakota, but passengers saw nothing except the winding white scar of a river and maybe the lights of Mobridge, ten miles away.

Luke sat up and peered over the top of the seat in front of him. The town of Mobridge sprawled across the flat below, with the Missouri River throwing a cozy loop around it on the south and west. The Mobridge he remembered wasn't much of a town, either. The old Brown Palace Hotel was the dominant building on Main Street, and it only stood three stories high. Main Street itself looked like a movie set for a Western, with its row of storefronts and its tacky saloons gathered at the west end. Jets flew over Mobridge, too, and freight trains rumbled through without stopping, but there was a bus stop here. Luke wasn't sure he actually wanted to get off, but he'd damn sure be glad when the bus came to a stop.

He settled back to watch the fields fly past the window as the bus drew near the edge of town. Golden stubble poked through a crusty, bright snow shell. It was always hard to tell how much snow they'd got-

ten, because the wind seldom let it pile up. The sky out
here was high, wide and handsome, and the winter sun
bounced its brightness off the white ground cover, reminding Luke that nature had a practical reason for
endowing his race with hooded eyes and high cheek-
bones.

The bus pulled up in front of the Brown Palace.
Luke's own reflection in the window superimposed itself over the assortment of faces that looked up from
the street below. He dismissed the fuzzy Scotch caps
with earflaps and the black felt cowboy hats as he
searched the crowd. Then he caught a glimpse of
Frankie's blue-black hair, done up in a fashionable
French braid, and he smiled.

Her eyes brightened when she saw that he'd finally
picked her out of the crowd. She sank her chin into the
pile collar of her bright red down-filled jacket, happily puffing out mist as she flashed a row of white
teeth. She was such a pretty sight, it made Luke's heart
swell. He grabbed his green overcoat and his dress cap
from the aisle seat and stepped off the bus to greet his
sister.

"Damn it, Frankie, if you don't look just like a
woman." He grinned as he dropped an arm around
her shoulders and edged her away from the crowd.
Even after three years there would be no showy public embrace from Luke and no delighted shrieks from
his younger sister. Certainly not here in an off-
reservation town. He gave her braid a sly tug, a gesture subtle enough to be shared on the street as they
stood aside and waited for the luggage to be removed
from the bus's underbelly.

"Don't call me that, Luke," she pleaded, although she knew she had little chance of shedding the nickname with her oldest brother. "It's Frances."

"Or Miss Frances? Or, better yet, *Miss* Tracker?" He gave the shoulder under his hand a quick squeeze. "I can't believe you're a teacher now."

"Why not? Anybody can be a teacher," she reminded him with a smile. They were his words. All of them. "All you have to do is finish high school, go to four years of college—"

"And practice your BIA—Bossing Indians Around," he finished with a laugh. It was their old joke on the Bureau of Indian Affairs.

"I'm glad you wore your uniform," she said. "Daddy loves to see you in it." She watched him step forward to claim his army green duffel bag. He hitched the canvas strap over his shoulder, and she pointed across the street. "That's my car."

He heard the note of pride in her voice. The little blue hatchback was the first car she'd bought nearly new. "Nice," he said. He looked up and down the street as he stepped off the curb. "You know, this place looks just the same."

"It isn't. They've opened a new restaurant and at least two new grocery stores." She took two short steps for each of his long strides as they crossed the street together. "It's been seven years since you were home, Luke. Things *have* to change some in that much time."

"It's only been three since I've seen the family." He had to get that in. Seven years sounded pretty negligent.

"But that was in Vermillion, when you came to my graduation. You haven't been *home* in seven years." She unlocked the hatchback, and he tossed his duffel bag into the car. "Mama's at home, cooking to beat the band, and Daddy wanted to come with me, but Mama said it wouldn't be fair, because she couldn't come. So my instructions were to take the shortcut to get you home."

They wanted him home. That was the worst of it. It wasn't as though he were the black sheep of the family who stayed away because he wasn't welcome. He stayed away because nothing ever changed. Except him. He'd changed, and he was sure he wouldn't fit in anymore. When he'd first enlisted, he used to come home a couple of times a year. He'd wanted to see Monica then. When it became obvious that Monica would never leave home, not for him or for anyone else, his visits had dwindled to once a year—Christmas, for sure. Then *maybe* Christmas. He was good about calling, and he even wrote once in a while. But he'd left the Reservation, and he wasn't anxious to return.

"I'll bet *you're* good at bossing Indians around." Once she had her brother's attention, Frances handed him her car keys. "Or anybody else, for that matter. You look one-hundred-percent government issue." And he wore it well, she thought. He was the right man for the uniform. The shiny black brim of his dress cap pulled down low over his brow gave him an eagle-eyed look, and his square jaw was the perfect complement to his square shoulders.

"I don't suppose you'll take orders from me anymore, now that you're a big teacher." He smiled. "You've gotten so damn pretty, Frankie. I think I oughta teach you a little self-defense."

"Are you kidding? I grew up the same place you did, remember? I learned that long ago." It surprised her when he opened the car door for her. It wasn't something she'd seen him do for anyone except their mother.

"So tell me, little sister, what's new in Wakpala?"

Frances gave him a mysterious little smile as he pushed the driver's seat back from the wheel. "You'll have to find out for yourself. I will tell you this. Your parents are getting old, and they shouldn't have to wait so long between visits from their oldest son. And—" She turned her attention to the windshield "—your ex-girlfriend moved to Billings with some truck driver."

"She did, huh?" He turned the key in the ignition, and the little car's engine roared. Luke chuckled. More power to her. She'd turned out to be stronger than he'd thought. "You sure you want me to drive this thing across the river?"

"Sure I'm sure. The ice is thick enough." She raised a challenging eyebrow his way. "You're not chicken, are you?"

Luke grinned. "Baby sister, we are taking the shortcut."

Chapter One

"Ho-ho-ho!"

The initial "Ho" sent the table knife flying out of Hope Spencer's hand. She grabbed the oblong cake pan before it toppled over the edge of her desk and clattered the way of the knife. A tentative giggle rippled through the group of nine-year-olds that had gathered for chocolate cake, but there were several faces registering such wide-eyed, gap-toothed awe that Hope hesitated to crane her neck toward the doorway.

"Mer-ry Christmas!"

Two small hands latched on to Hope's belt. She laid her hand on the quaking shoulder, holding her first two fingers straight out to avoid smearing chocolate frosting on little Carol Two Horses' sweater. "It's okay, Carol," she said softly as she turned her head toward the classroom door. "It's Santa Claus."

Hope's friend, Frances Tracker, had delivered the man with the booming voice to the door. He did look like Santa Claus. Sort of. The plush red suit had obviously been in storage for twelve months, and it was a little short for a man his size. The tall black combat boots were an interesting touch. Hope wondered how soon the children would notice the contrast between his white beard and his thick black eyebrows.

"Here he is!" Frances announced. From the gleam in her eyes, she might have brought some hot screen star. "Santa brought treats for everybody. My second graders are sure enjoying theirs."

Santa looked the group over and scowled. "What sort of boys and girls are *these*, Miss Tracker?" He gave Frances a dramatic over-the-shoulder look. "Are they *good* boys and girls?" Again he surveyed the group, huddling closer now behind the teacher's desk. "Or are they *naughty* boys and girls?"

"You'll have to ask Miss Spencer that, Santa. They're probably a little of each," Frankie said.

"A little of each, hmm?" Santa raised one eyebrow and stepped into the room. In each hand he carried a flowered pillow case that presumably contained the promised treats. "Guess I'll have to find out for myself which is which."

"I have to get back to my bunch," Frances said, smiling so hard her face must have hurt. "Have fun, Miss Spencer."

Most of the children were jostling for position behind Hope. Only a few brave souls stood their ground and watched as the tall man approached. Feeling a little wary and childlike herself, Hope quickly licked the sweet chocolate from her fingers.

"I think what Miss Tracker meant, Santa, was that they've all had good days and bad." Hope shrugged as she offered a tentative smile. "Don't we all?"

"We definitely do," Santa agreed. "I have them myself."

A stubby arm clamped itself around her waist, and she reached down to smooth Courtney Brown Bear's mop of hair. "I think we're all wondering, uh, which it might be today, Santa."

He turned his rich, deep laughter into a Ho-ho-ho, then said, "I've come a long way, and I'm very tired.

Will you bring your chair out here for me, Miss Spencer?'' He patted the saggy stuffing under his wide plastic belt, then pointed to the array of small chairs throughout the classroom. ''I certainly can't sit in one of *those* little things.''

''Of course.'' It took some maneuvering to give herself room to do the job. ''Excuse me, Carol. Courtney, here, just let me...'' Courtney dove under the desk as Hope lifted the chair and used it to clear a path. ''I'm not going anywhere, Patty. Santa needs to sit down so he can—''

As she broke free of the cluster, one of the braver youngsters grasped her by the wrist. ''What is it, Cowboy?''

''That ain't no Santa Claus,'' the boy confided quietly. ''I saw Santa Claus at the Ben Franklin store in Mobridge, and you can just tell this one's a fake.''

She knew she shouldn't ask, but it slipped out. ''How can you tell?''

''Well, he's not white.''

Hope's face reddened, while Santa Claus enjoyed a belly-shaking laugh. On the heels of the laughter he asked, ''What makes you think I always have to be white, Cowboy?''

''Well, every time *I* see you...''

''Have you ever seen me after I just got back from down south?'' Santa boomed. ''I just made a run down to Brazil. Gotta see those kids down there, too, you know. Don't you get darker in the sun?'' Now as wide-eyed as the rest of the children, Cowboy nodded. ''So do I,'' Santa said. ''I tan real easy. It's summertime in Brazil.'' He kept his eyes on Cowboy as he reached for the big armless oak chair. ''Or didn't you know that, Cowboy? Haven't you been doing your geography homework?"

"We haven't gotten to South America yet," Hope put in.

"You haven't, huh?" Santa made a production of seating himself with a weary groan, settling his sacks on either side of the chair and planting his hands on his knees. "Bunch of real nice kids down there in Brazil," he said absently. Then he pointed a white-gloved finger in Hope's direction. "You be sure and teach these little guys all about South America, Miss Spencer."

"Yes, I . . . I certainly will."

"Now." Santa slapped both knees at once as he eyed the crowd. "I want each and every one of you children to come over here, sit on old Santa's knee— whichever one you want—and introduce yourself properly so I know whether to give you something from this bag—" he nodded to the right "—or this other one. Who wants to be first?"

There were no volunteers.

Hope stepped closer to the formidable visitor from the North Pole via Brazil. "Santa, maybe I could just help you distribute the gifts—"

"Nope." The bell on the point of his cap jingled as Santa shook his acrylic white wig. "I came here to shake hands with each and every person in this room, including that one." He pointed at the big brown eyes that were peeking out from under the desk. They vanished immediately. "And that's just what I'm gonna do." He lifted a challenging eyebrow as he turned his face up at Hope. "Maybe we should start with the teacher."

The children's giggles seemed encouraging. "Shake hands?" she said. "Why, of course." She extended hers, and it was lost in his white glove. She felt the strength in the warm hand beneath the velvety fabric.

"So tell me your name," he demanded.

"I . . . I'm Hope Spencer, Santa Claus."

"Very nice name." He planted his feet wide apart on the floor and hooked his hands at his hips. "Well?"

Hope blinked. "Well, what?"

"Which knee do you prefer, Hope Spencer?"

Hope stepped up close to Santa's side and lowered her voice. "I really don't think that's necessary, Santa. I'm a pretty big girl."

"They say there's a kid in all of us at Christmas." He turned his head to the side and muttered from the corner of his mouth, "Do you want these kids to play the game or not?"

Hope stared at the red-clad thighs. They were long and looked completely sturdy. "Did Miss Tracker sit on your lap, Santa?"

"'Course she did. She's getting a new typewriter for Christmas, too, so sit right down here, Miss Spencer." His eyes danced as he slapped his thigh. "Let's see what ol' Santa can do for you."

Hope stepped between his knees and seated herself gingerly, as though his thigh might be connected to the radiator along the wall. He cupped his hand lightly at her waist, smiled and then let loose with a Ho-ho-ho that didn't begin to express his utter delight with the situation.

"I think that if you'd tone that down," Hope muttered with a forced smile, "you might have better results."

"I think I'm getting pretty damn good results," he mumbled back. "How do you like it so far?" Before she could answer, he Ho-ho-hoed again, and Hope just rolled her eyes toward the ceiling. "Are you a good girl, Hope Spencer?" Santa demanded.

"I try hard to be, Santa."

"I'm trying hard to be Santa," he mumbled into his beard. "You just try hard not to look so terrified." Then, in his stage voice, he announced, "I'll bet you do. I'll bet you're a very good teacher. *But...*" He raised his white-gloved index finger. "Do you eat your vegetables?"

"I love vegetables," she managed evenly. She was beginning to enjoy this man.

"Of course you do." He glanced at the children, who were gradually venturing forth from the stockade of the teacher's desk. "That wasn't a fair test, was it, you guys? She's an adult. Adults *all* love vegetables. Most of their taste buds have died." There were some nods, some shaking heads and some giggles. "*So*, Hope Spencer. Do you make your bed every morning?"

"Yes, well...most of the time."

"With the blanket tucked tight enough so I could bounce a quarter on it?"

"I don't know." She frowned and then shrugged. "I've never tried bouncing—"

"And what about your desk over there?" He held his hand in front of her face, and his challenge rumbled deep in his chest. "If I ran this glove over that desk, would I find dust?"

"Probably," she confessed.

"Hmm. Two demerits so far." He tapped his fingers against his thigh as he weighed the evidence. *"Now,"* he barked, "let me see your shoes."

"What?"

He waggled his fingers above her knees, which were covered demurely by a drapy Christmas-green skirt. By this time the children were laughing easily. "Get 'em up here. Let me see how long it's been since you polished your shoes."

She turned slightly and stretched one leg out in front of her. "You sound like a drill sergeant," she muttered, and he answered with a chuckle. She saw that his visual inspection took in her calf, her ankle and finally her black pump.

"Pretty dull," he judged, and he noticed a little stiffening in her back as she lowered her leg. "Didn't you use any spit?"

"I used the stuff that comes in the can."

"The stuff in the can, huh?" he nodded thoughtfully. "I don't know, Hope Spencer. I'd say you're a *pretty* good girl." He reached for the pillowcase on the right. "But when I come back next year, I expect to hear that you've made some improvements." He pulled a small, gaily-wrapped box from his sack and handed it to her. "I expect to see some shine on those shoes. That stuff in the can, that's not good enough. You've gotta use a little spit."

She lifted her toe into the air again and studied the shoe. "Doesn't eating my vegetables count for anything?" she wondered.

"'Course it does. 'Course it does. That's why your gift came from the *good* sack. Now tell me what else is on your wish list." Hope opened her mouth to speak and felt his hand tighten at her waist as he leaned closer, his eyes dancing. "Whisper your wishes into Santa's ear, Miss Spencer."

With a look that told him she could handle the challenge, she cupped one hand around his ear, lifted her chin and shared her Christmas wishes. Then she leaned back and smiled. Just when she was getting comfortable, he roared another "Ho-ho-ho" that made her spring off his lap. He looked up at her, somewhat regretfully. Santa had been getting comfortable, too.

By the time Santa left, he'd gotten all of the children, including Courtney, to shake his hand, sit on his lap and tell him their Christmas wishes. Everyone got something from the *good* sack, which left them to wonder, after he'd disappeared down the hall with a parting "Ho-ho-ho," what the *bad* sack had contained. Hope dutifully admired every trinket and sweet that had come from Santa and had so enlivened the class Christmas party. Through it all she couldn't quite rid her mind of the burning question for the day. Who *was* that bearded man?

Hope loaded a box of gifts into the back of her car, and Frances heaved Hope's suitcase over the tailgate. "I let my brother use my car today, but it's just as well. You'd never find our place by yourself."

"You must really have the Christmas spirit, Frances. I thought you said you never let anyone else drive your car."

"Oh, well, Luke's different. Luke's my older brother."

"The one who's in the army?" Hope shut the tailgate and adjusted her sunglasses as she sorted mentally through the gifts she'd brought. When Frances had invited her to spend Christmas vacation at the Tracker ranch, Hope had begun to make subtle inquiries about brothers and sisters and their ages and interests. It was easy to choose gifts for children, especially the younger ones whom she knew from school, but Frances hadn't known which of the older siblings might be home. Hope had brought a couple of generic gifts, just in case.

"The one who's finally come home for Christmas after seven long years." Frances grabbed Hope's arm as she started for the driver's side. "You want me to drive? It's mostly gravel roads."

"I need the practice," Hope said.

"Yeah, but . . ."

The two friends looked at each other, black eyes searching blue, and Hope finally handed the keys over with a laugh. "I don't guess we want to spend Christmas in the hospital."

"You *are* getting better," Frances admitted, grateful for the keys. They'd hit a washboard several weeks ago when Hope had been driving them out to meet with the parents of one of her students, and they'd had to flag down a pickup to pull them out of the ditch. "You've got such a great car, but these roads take some getting used to."

Hope's four-wheel-drive wagon had been a gift from her father, who had insisted she leave Connecticut with a vehicle built for the wilderness. He was certain she was headed for the ends of the earth, but, as always, he bought her something grand and wished her well. He had his younger second family to worry about, and, as he often marveled whenever he saw Hope, she'd "suddenly become a young woman" when his back was turned. Since Hope's mother had married a widower with three children, Hope didn't really consider herself a part of any family. The family she'd once thought she belonged to had disintegrated in divorce.

Perhaps it was because both her parents had been so completely unhappy with each other that she'd been their only child. She'd been shipped off to prep school when she was thirteen, and each of her parents had begun fashioning new lives. She'd fashioned her own. She'd been teaching for five years, but this was her first year in South Dakota. Her interest in Native American culture had prompted her to apply for the position in the tiny town of Wakpala on the Standing Rock Sioux Indian Reservation. Because so many of the children lived in remote areas, St. Elizabeth's Mission provided dormitories where the children stayed during the winter months while they attended the public school in town. Hope's apartment at St. Elizabeth's, some five miles from the school, was provided in return for her counseling and tutoring services.

The peacefulness of the countryside was one of the many pleasant aspects of Hope's new situation. Fall had become winter without the fanfare of color to which she was accustomed, but the brown prairie had been blanketed quickly, and the rolling white landscape was as soothing to the eye as endless sea. She liked its timelessness. The network of gravel roads did little to insult the land, and it was easy to drive ten, even twenty miles without seeing a house. Maybe that was why people seemed so willing to include each other in their lives out here. The Trackers were a family of twelve by Hope's count, but Frances had assured and *re*assured her that they were anxious to have one more for the holidays.

"You never did tell me who Santa Claus was," Hope reminded her friend as they approached a two-story white house flanked on the north by a stand of cottonwood trees and chokecherry bushes.

Frances grinned. "What do you mean? Santa Claus was Santa Claus."

"He was quite a character. He nearly scared the wits out of the kids when he first came in."

"Those department-store Santa Clauses are no fun. No sense of humor. Did you sit on his lap?" Frances asked.

"Didn't you?"

Frances shut the engine off and handed Hope the keys with a mischievous smile and a shake of her head. "He told you I did?"

"Yes. I thought it was part of the tradition."

With a merry laugh Frances threw the car door open and hopped out. "I think Santa likes you. What'd you ask for?"

"Snow on Christmas Eve." Hope shut the door on her side. "And something else. Something I used to ask for every year when I was a kid. Nobody ever took me seriously."

"Really? Maybe you never asked the right Santa."

"My father thinks he's the world's greatest Santa." The curtains moved in an upstairs window, and a small face appeared. Hope smiled and waved, absently adding, "But I never got what I asked for."

Frances took Hope's luggage, while Hope carried her gifts. "I see my car's not back yet," Frances noted. "I wonder what Luke's up to."

Hope greeted George and Emma Tracker, Frances's parents, and a succession of children whose ages ranged from eight to eighteen. A couple of the older siblings were missing at the moment. Everyone seemed to have a nickname, like Sweetie and Tom Tom and Beaver. After Hope had deposited her gifts under the tree, Frances took her upstairs to deposit her luggage. They were to share a room. Hope saw only four bedrooms upstairs, and she was sure the rest of the family would be crowded, but Frances said that her mother would see that everyone had a place to sleep.

Both women turned their heads toward the sound of the opening of the front door and the mighty "Ho-ho-ho!" that followed. Hope's eyes widened as she noted the familiar mischief in Frances's smile.

"I should have guessed."

"He was one of the few people we were sure the kids wouldn't recognize," Frances explained. "Last year we hired a Santa with a German accent, and the kids thought he was Lawrence Welk. Altogether too tame."

"Your brother can't be accused of that. Well—" she remembered being seated on that sturdy thigh, and she turned quickly as she felt her face redden "—let's go see what he looks like without the beard."

Two of the younger children were relieving Luke of several packages, while a third stripped him of his brown-leather bomber jacket and ran to put it away. Luke wiped his black boots on the mat one more time for good measure and then looked up to the top of the stairs at the two women.

The man who had been Santa made jeans and a blue chambray shirt look like a uniform, Hope thought. His black hair was closely cut, stylish by chance and practical by design. His clothes were crisply ironed, and they skimmed his trim body as though they'd been tailored for him. He was startlingly handsome, but he gave the impression that he would permit only regulation handsomeness. Even so, there was nothing regulation about his slow, easy smile and the glint in his eyes that hinted that he shared some secret with the woman who followed his sister down the stairs.

"Hello, Hope Spencer. Have you recovered from your ordeal with Santa Claus?"

"I wouldn't call it an ordeal," she protested as she reached the foot of the stairs and accepted his proffered handshake. "I'd say it was a learning experience. I take it the 'jolly old elf' image doesn't make it out West."

"Unless things have changed drastically since I was a kid, my version of Santa was a pussycat compared to what's in store."

"I haven't told Hope much about what she's in for," Frances put in. "But I'll let you both in on one secret. If the weather's good, Daddy promised to take the bobsled out Christmas Eve."

"Is that old thing still around?" Luke asked.

"Daddy's not about to give up his team, Luke. You know that."

Luke shook his head in amazement. "He's getting too old to be fooling around with those Percherons, especially in the winter."

"After a blizzard he's able to get feed out to the stock before most people get their tractors started." In the back of her mind Frances forgave her brother for being so out of touch with his memories. He well knew how little heavy equipment their father used in keeping their small cattle operation going. They had a small tractor with a few attachments, but the summer haying was accomplished largely because the family had so many hands.

"Your dad uses a team to pull a *bobsled*?" Hope asked. "Doesn't it just sail down the hill on its own steam?"

Luke looked at Frances, and they both laughed. "In the Olympics, maybe," Luke said, "but not in Wakpala."

"See, you take the wheels off the wagon box," Frances explained, going through the motions with her hands. "And you put runners on it. It's kind of a sleigh."

"Only we call it a bobsled," Luke added. Yes, *we*, he thought. He remembered how excited the mere mention a bobsled ride had once made him. Even now, he liked the thought of hearing the jingle of the harness again and knowing his father held the reins. He reminded himself to hold the sentimentality down to a minimum, and he changed the subject. "So who helps Dad take care of the stock?" he asked Frances. "Gorgeous?"

"Imagine Gorgeous George being any help." Frances laughed. "He works when Mama tells him no work, no supper." She turned to Hope. "Gorgeous is my other older brother. His birth certificate says he's twenty-seven years old, but he's still trying to find himself."

"He never had much trouble finding himself in the mirror. Give me a few weeks with him in boot camp. I'll help him find himself." Luke sniffed the air. "Is that coffee I smell? And maybe frybread?"

"It is," Frances said. "And we'll probably be able to have some if you promise Mama you'll be nice to Gorgeous when and *if* you see him."

"If? I haven't been home in seven years," Luke pointed out as he led the way to the kitchen.

"And your brother's visits are no more predictable than yours, although they're certainly more frequent." Frances tossed Hope a conspiratorial wink and continued. "Who's to say whether you can be worked into his busy schedule?"

"Busy my a—"

"Luke!" Emma Tracker—short, graying and clearly accustomed to being in charge of her children—turned from her crackling skillet. "Mind your mouth. I don't want our guest thinking I raised any boys who cuss all the time."

"Yes, ma'am," Luke responded with a smile as he took a chair at the long table. "I always tell recruits I was born to whip them into shape. Raised by the original female drill sergeant."

"Then you *are* a drill sergeant," Hope said as she joined him at the table.

"Drill instructor," he corrected. "A teacher, like yourself."

Frances set three mugs on the table and poured the coffee. "I wish I could get my second graders to jump to attention," she said as she put a carton of milk in front of Hope. "Maybe if I told them I was a specialist in martial arts and I'd been a Green Beret like my brother..."

"Go ahead and tell them," Luke teased. "I'll vouch for you, Frankie."

Frances laughed. "You had enough trouble getting them to believe you were Santa Claus."

"The uniform didn't fit right. Get me in parade dress and I'll have your little darlings saluting smartly and saying 'yes, ma'am' before you can recite the Pledge of Allegiance.''

Hope shook her head as she tried to imagine the scene. ''If you came into my class and started barking orders, I have a feeling there'd be eighteen children fighting for space under the teacher's desk.''

Frances readily agreed. She had never regarded her oldest brother as anything less than a hero, and the worshipful eyes of a child still glowed in her womanly face when she looked at him. Emma treated the three to hot frybread and persistently shooed the younger children away to give them this time to visit. She knew she had Frances to thank for convincing Luke to come home for Christmas. Luke was the son who had to leave home as soon as he had come of age, and Frances was the daughter who had to bring her education home to the children who needed her. But there had always been a special bond between the two.

Decorating the church for Christmas was a community project. After supper the Trackers crowded into all available vehicles and headed for the old church at St. Elizabeth's Mission. Hope's car was packed with excited children, who scattered when they arrived, while the adults set about trimming the church. The arrangement was time-honored, and it was clearly important to recall exactly the way it had been done in previous years. There were real poinsettias for the altar, as well as plastic blooms that were saved from year to year and tacked to the pews. Red candles, white linen and gold garland brightened the church's dark wood. A spruce tree rose to the ceiling in the center of the basement parish hall, its green needles gradually disappearing as decorators piled on the multi-colored lights and silver tinsel.

Hope enjoyed watching the activity as much as being part of it. She was a coffee fetcher, a tack hander, a bow tier. It was nice to be included. She was also an observer, and during her break from handing Frances tacks, she sat in a pew at the back of the church and listened to the rhythm of the women's voices as they exchanged stories, mainly in English. Some of the older people spoke with one another in Lakota, but few of the young adults knew the language. Even so, Lakota words and phrases would slip into the conversation, and there were local expressions of unknown origin that enriched these people's English with a special spice. Listeners encouraged the storyteller with an occasional *"E'n it?"* which roughly meant, "Really?" Or, if the story became totally incredible, the comment might be *"Dwah-lay!"*

A steaming Styrofoam cup appeared at Hope's shoulder. She looked up as she accepted it with a smile and slid over, hoping that Luke would join her. She sipped the coffee and wondered where he had found creamer in this land of drinkers of strong black coffee.

"How would you be spending Christmas if you weren't in Wakpala?" he asked as he sat down beside her.

Hope's indifferent shrug said a great deal about how little it had mattered. "I'd have to pay a visit to each of my parents at some point, and I'd probably have dinner with friends." She considered his expression and realized that, after seven years, he'd become an observer here, too.

"Married friends?"

She nodded. "Usually. I like to watch the kids."

"Me, too. It's probably the only time of year when I miss all this—" he gestured, cup in hand "—togetherness stuff."

"So how have you been spending Christmas for the last seven years?"

"Dinner in the mess hall," he told her. "It's good for morale. And, you know...friends." His voice drifted, echoing in the hollowness of the years. "'Course, in the military, they come and go. You don't get too attached."

"If I had a family like yours, I'd come home every Christmas." It was a spontaneous comment, born of a wish, but she knew once she'd said it that it sounded like a judgment.

Surprisingly he gave her a one-sided smile. "You would, huh? Just drop everything on the twenty-third or so and trot right home?"

"I'd try." His eyes unnerved her. They were too dark, too deep and too compelling. "I really think I would, unless something came up and I just couldn't get away."

He chuckled, appreciating the fact that she'd decided to give him an out. "The longer you put it off, the harder it gets," he confessed. "After a while all it takes is an ingrown toenail, and you can't get away."

"But don't you miss them?"

"Sure, I miss them." He looked around at the familiar arched windows of one of the oldest buildings in the area. "I even miss the town sometimes, which scares me. When I was growing up my one goal was to get out of here any way I could. Nothing ever changes here. Nothing ever will."

His goal was understandable. Hope knew how little employment there was on the reservation, and how much poverty. "But your family's here," she reminded him. "Pictures of you are hanging all over your parents' house. Frances thinks you could fight off an invasion single-handedly."

He smiled as he caught a glimpse of his sister ducking behind the bishop's chair with a dust cloth. "Frankie's a dreamer."

"She tells me you helped put her through college."

"Did what I could." He tossed off the recognition of his efforts with a shrug. "She made damn good grades. I wish she'd take her dreams and get out of here. Go someplace bright and pretty, where it's Christmas all year long."

"Don't send her to Connecticut," Hope admonished with a smirk.

"Missouri, either." He thought for a moment, then shook his head. "I've been to Texas, South Carolina, New Jersey, Germany. Didn't find Christmas all year long in any of those places."

There was a buzzing of voices up front, and Frances's laughter rang out from behind the big wooden chair. "Maybe once a year is enough for her, Luke."

"I guess it's better than once in seven years."

His smile stirred a warmth inside her that gave new meaning to her own idea of Yuletide spirit. She glanced away and remembered the job she'd been given when she saw the two plastic wreaths she'd set on the pew. "I guess I'm shirking my duty," she said as she reached for the wreaths. "I'm living in the dormitory apartment just across the way, but I confess I haven't used the church facilities that much. I'm supposed to tack these up on the bathroom doors, but I can't find the bathrooms."

Luke tipped his head back and laughed as heartily as Frances just had. He set his cup down and took Hope by the hand. "Get your coat, Hope Spencer. The bathrooms are out back."

Chapter Two

It was the first time in his life that Luke remembered being impressed by brown hair. Black hair, of course, was beautiful, especially when it was long and thick like Frankie's. And he'd done a double take a time or two when a sunlit head of yellow hair had crossed his path. As he lifted Hope's coat over her shoulders, she swept her pretty brown hair up in her hand and dropped it over her collar, and he was captivated. The color was mink rich, and he could smell the floral fragrance of her shampoo. She turned a glittering blue-eyed smile on him as she clamped a set of fur earmuffs over her head. Real mink. Just a shade darker than her hair, and they rivaled each other for shine. Luke was looking forward to this hayride.

"Hey, Luke." Ten-year-old Crystal turned worshipful eyes up at her brother. "Can I sit next to you?"

"No, me!" little Sweetie demanded, cuing a chorus of pleas from children who stretched to their full height like puppies clamoring to be picked from the litter.

Luke had to think fast. "We have to put all you little guys in the middle of the box, so you won't bounce out. Big guys around the outside." He turned to Hope. "Ever been on a bobsled?"

"No, I haven't. This is so exci—"

"Listen, you guys, Hope's never been on a bobsled, and she's pretty nervous." With a face full of concern, he laid a hand on each of two little shoulders. "I think I'd better sit by her, just in case. After all, she's our guest."

"In case what?" Hope asked.

Luke's smile reminded Hope of Frances's. They both had Fourth of July sparklers in their eyes when they teased. "You never know," he told her. "Wolves, thin ice. Full moon tonight. Anything can happen."

"But I haven't been on a bobsled, either," Sweetie insisted as she tugged on Luke's leather sleeve.

He swung the little girl up in his arms. "Yeah, but you're a cowboy. Hope's just a dude. Boy, you've gotten big, Sweetie."

"They grow a lot in three years." Emma came from the kitchen with two large Thermos bottles. "If you had children of your own, you'd know that. Here, take these," she ordered, thrusting the supply of coffee into the arms of one of the older children.

The Tracker matriarch obviously lacked enthusiasm for this Christmas Eve outing, but she hadn't spelled out her objections to her husband. Instead, she grabbed, shoved, stomped around and grumbled. "A woman my age should have grandchildren," she muttered, looking Luke's way. When she got nothing but an impertinent chuckle from her eldest offspring, she pulled her plaid wool scarf down tightly over her head and whipped it into a knot under her sagging chin. "A woman my age should ride to church in a car," she grumbled as she threw the door open. "Tell Frances to hurry up with the rest of the blankets. Sissy," she ordered over her shoulder as she headed out into the night, "go help her."

Long-legged Sissy leaped into action, taking the steps two at a time. In another moment the two sisters descended the steps, each bearing an armload of quilts and blankets. "This is it," Frances announced. "Some of us will have to share."

Luke took part of Sissy's load and gave Hope a slow smile.

It was impossible to believe that the moon didn't produce its creamy brilliance on its own. Hanging like a medallion on the sky's black velvet breast, it brightened the crusted snow. What had seemed like such a crowd of people within the confines of the house became only a small group of travelers surrounded by endless land, sky and night.

George Tracker held the reins of his two-horse team as two of his sons helped their mother climb into the seat beside him. The box of their buckboard had been removed from its wheels and set on runners for winter use. It was filled with loose hay.

"Climb aboard." His eager tone hinted that he was about to share something wonderful with his family. "The cats chased all the mice out of the hay," he promised.

Emma grumbled something to her husband, but no one paid attention. There was too much excitement. The younger children took their blankets and dove into the hay in the center of the wagon. Dolly and Beaver, who were well into their upper teens and, like their mother, preferred cars—though for speed rather than comfort—sat together behind the driver's seat with a cache of potato chips. Sixteen-year-old Lana sat beside her mother, and Tom Tom, who couldn't decide whether he was really ready for encroaching adolescence, opted for childhood and took to the center of the box, where the best wrestling matches would take place. At the tailgate Luke was comfortably flanked by two women—his favorite sister and the friend he predicted he would know much better by the end of the night.

"Your mother doesn't seem to be a fan of hay-rides," Hope suggested as Frances took pains to pack hay around their hips.

"This was the only transportation we had for a long time," Luke told her. "Frances and I grew up going to church in the bobsled or the buckboard. For Mom, it's like going back to the washboard after you've had a ringer washer."

"Washboard? You mean, for doing laundry?" Hope had used a ringer washer for the first time in the laundry room at the Mission. Fully automatic washing machines couldn't withstand the corrosive effects of the artesian-well water, which was used only for washing. Drinking water had to be hauled in. But washboards and horse-drawn wagons seemed far-fetched, given how young Frances was.

"Where've you been hiding yourself, Hope Spencer? Connecticut?" Luke chuckled. "What would you use a washboard for in Connecticut?"

"We tried to find one for a jug band once when I was in college," she said innocently. "We found kazoos, but no washboards."

"Welcome to Wakpala, South Dakota."

"Oh, Luke," Frances protested, "most people have cars now. Daddy uses the bobsled to feed the stock when the weather gets bad, but he never takes us to church in it anymore. This is Sweetie's first ride in it, and she's already eight."

"So we've made progress."

"I don't think you should ever give this up," Hope said happily. "It's a beautiful night, and it's Christmas Eve, and I can't think of anything more perfect." She smiled at Luke. "I'm having fun already."

The light in her eyes illuminated her pretty face and kicked Luke's metabolism into high gear. "So am I," he admitted as he unfurled his woolen army blanket. "The trick is to keep warm, so if both of you scoot in, I'll share my blanket with your legs."

"You notice he gets the best of the deal," Frances pointed out as she scooted over and ducked her head under his arm. "He's in the middle."

"My mama didn't raise no fool," he quipped. He moved more gradually to bracket Hope's shoulders, and she slid more cautiously than Frances had. When she'd aligned her thigh against Luke's, he urged her to lean into his side with the steady, gentling pressure of his strong right arm. She looked up and saw the pleasure he was taking in her company in the soft expression on his face.

The Trackers were among the last to arrive, but no one seemed to be worried about starting at a certain hour. The socializing was well underway in the church basement, and supper would be served when people were hungry. The coats were piled high on a bench near the wall. George headed for the coffeepot, and Emma sought the consolation of her sisterhood of friends, who would understand what a trial life with a "crazy old Indian" could sometimes be. The young children's anticipation became tangible energy as they raced, tussled and teased in every corner of the large basement room.

Except for the tinsel and colored lights, it was a stark room, with its bare gray floor and whitewashed walls. There was a small kitchen alcove with a stove, but there was no running water. An old fuel-hungry furnace provided a background roar. The air was blue with smoke, but heat was too precious to be vented into the night through an open window.

Hope had been part of the community for several months, but the only social event she'd attended had been school-sponsored. This was different, certainly interesting—and a little scary. She felt a need to stay close to Frances and Luke, to belong here with some-one. When someone asked Frances to take charge of the cigarette bowl for a while, Hope flashed a quick look of alarm at Luke, and he responded with the soft expression she'd seen earlier. He would be with her. Standing at her side, he found it easy to give her hand a subtle squeeze.

"What's the cigarette bowl?" Hope asked.

"They fill a bowl with cigarettes, and the girls offer it around all night," Luke explained. "At a celebration like this, no one ever has to bum a cigarette."

"How, um...how thoughtful." She looked up at him and made a squinty face. "I guess."

He laughed. "We have an ancient love affair with tobacco. It's one vice we can't blame on you guys." When Frances offered him the bowl, Luke shook his head. "I've quit. I was tired of getting winded twenty minutes into a workout."

"You should see his karate moves," Frances said. "Poetry in motion."

Hope looked up and caught his quick frown. "So you really are a martial-arts expert."

Luke shoved his hands into the pockets of his jeans. "The army spreads the term 'expert' around pretty freely."

"I wouldn't call black belts in jujitsu and karate anything less than expert," Frances insisted with pride. "Luke's an instructor."

He tugged at her long black braid as she turned to walk away. "Big mouth," he teased. "What, are you trying to sell me or something? Why don't you just let her count my teeth?"

"Because she wouldn't be impressed," Frances tossed back when she was safely out of range. "I knocked one out with a well-aimed rock when you were fourteen years old."

"You really know how to ruin a guy, Frankie." With a dramatic sigh, Luke rolled his eyes toward the ceiling. "Yes, I really do have a false tooth. So I guess in order to save face, I have to confess that she's right about my karate moves." He grinned, knowing that Hope was trying to figure out which tooth it was. He gave her a wink. "Pure poetry."

Suddenly a booming "Ho-ho-ho" filled the stairwell and echoed through the room. Hope had never seen so many children take cover so quickly. They scurried behind folding chairs that were occupied by comfortably familiar adults, or dove underneath the benches along the walls.

Hope looked up at Luke, who raised his hands, as if empty palms somehow proved his innocence. "That didn't come from me."

"This is the strangest reaction to jolly old Saint Nick I've ever seen," she murmured.

"You oughta hear some of the ghost stories they tell us as kids," he whispered as they watched a genuinely rotund Santa descend the bottom step, set two white sacks on the floor, settle his gloved hands on his ample hips and survey the room. He could have been

Matt Dillon bringing instantaneous order to the Long Branch Saloon.

"Boy, when you say, 'You'd better watch out, you'd better not cry...'"

"We mean the man is not about to tolerate any pouting or sniveling," Luke concluded for her. "It's part of the game, just like the ghost stories. Part of growing up."

"Were you scared, too?"

"Damn right." He jerked his chin toward a heavy wooden table in the far corner. "That was my favorite spot."

"Don't you guys got any kids in here?" Santa roared. "I thought I heard kids' voices down here."

"Looks like they don't want any Christmas presents, Santa," said one smirking parent.

"Guess not," another chimed.

"I do!"

"Shh, quiet!" warned a voice from under a bench.

"But I want—"

"Get out there, then. Go on!"

"I'm not scared." A six-year-old in bib overalls scrambled from his hiding place. "I want a Christmas present, Santa."

"And I want that kid in another twelve years," Luke whispered. "He'll make a hell of a soldier."

By twos and threes, the children came out of hiding, and, while their parents looked on, each was given a gift. Most of the children anticipated little more in the way of material gains at Christmas than this gift, but the level of excitement that was reached as they tore into red-and-green paper was contagious. It combined with the smell of food to add a festive luster to the barren walls and the most sober elder face.

Santa never completely abandoned his gruff guise, and his parting "Ho-ho-ho" was as formidable as his greeting.

When it was time to eat, the older people took to the head of the line, along with many of the men, who, traditionally, were served first. Hope noticed that people had brought their own plates and utensils, and Frances distributed those the Trackers had brought. Luke waited with Hope until the line dwindled, and then they took their place with the next wave.

"Have you been to a feed yet?"

Hope shook her head.

"You gonna try everything?" he asked, watching her eye the kettles on the table ahead of them.

"Of course," she said brightly. "I'm really hungry, and it smells—" She breathed deeply as she searched for a word. There was something boiled and beefy, but there was no identifiable spice. Kind of fatty. A little fruity. "—Interesting," she decided.

Luke nodded. "I haven't eaten any *taniga* in a long time. Might be interesting for me, too."

She recognized the frybread and *wojapi*, the thickened boysenberry soup that was delicious when you dunked your bread in it. Emma stood behind one of the kettles wielding a long fork and a butcher knife. "Just like sausage," she told Hope as she fished in the steaming kettle, speared something tubular and grayish and whacked a piece off with her knife. "You like sausage, don't you?"

"Oh, yes." Hope's words were more positive than the tone of her voice as she watched the "something" drop onto her plate.

"You want the book?" the lady at the next kettle asked. Hope raised a questioning look over her shoulder at Luke.

"That's what they call—" he gestured toward the pot with slightly puckered lips "—that stuff."

From her kettle the woman had hooked something that looked sort of meaty, sort of leafy and altogether strange. The strong odor was not enticing. Hope glanced around and realized that a number of people were listening for her answer. Either this was a test, or she was holding up the line. "Sure." Whack! "Not too much," she added after the fact. The stuff quivered as it plopped onto her plate. As she moved on, she heard Frances's throaty chuckle.

The lady at the last kettle stood with her ladle poised over steaming broth. "Soup?"

Hope smiled gratefully as she offered up her speckled blue tin cup. "Yes, I'd love some."

Juggling her supper on her lap, Hope sat between Luke and Frances within a large circle of folding chairs. She probed at the strange meats with her fork. "I don't suppose you'll tell me what this really is until I taste it," she said, glancing from Frances's smirk to Luke's.

"I don't suppose we should," Frances said.

Hope tasted the "sausage" first; it bore some resemblance to sausage, but it wasn't spicy. The "book" was blubbery, and nearly impossible to swallow. "All right. Now drop the bombshell."

"It's just tripe," Luke said.

Frances couldn't leave it at that. "Cow intestines and stomach."

"Geez, Frankie, you didn't have to give her the anatomical details."

"Thoroughly cleaned, of course," Frances hastened to add.

"Of course." It occurred to Hope that Frances's information was harder to digest than the food itself.

"You don't have to eat it," Frances assured her.

"It's an acquired taste," Luke added, "and I think I may have unacquired it." He studied his plate. "I remember when it used to taste really good. Either I've changed, or they just don't make it like they used to."

"Try the soup, Hope," Frances suggested.

Although she would have added salt, more vegetables and a few spices, Hope found that the soup passed over her tongue quite easily and warmed her insides.

"They're not still using puppy in the soup, are they?" Luke asked casually between bites.

"Puppy?" Hope's hand froze holding a spoonful of soup as she slid her gaze toward Frances.

"Nobody had any around that were fat enough," she said easily, as if he'd asked about a pig or a calf. "We had to go with beef."

"Puppy's usually pretty greasy." Luke was studying the contents of his cup as if he weren't totally convinced.

"You...don't...eat puppies."

Luke exchanged a look with Frances. "Tell you what we don't eat," he offered. "Horsemeat. I was halfway through a meal once when I was in Germany, and somebody told me I was eating horsemeat. I thought I was going to be sick."

"But you don't *really* eat puppies," Hope insisted. "Tell me I'm not eating a puppy."

"We used to."

"But we don't anymore."

"Hardly ever."

Hope joined in the laughter only after Luke had assured her, "You're not eating a puppy."

When "seconds" were announced, Hope went back to the serving line for more frybread and *wojapi*.

After the meal the men began to line their chairs against the wall, tip them back on two legs and light up cigarettes. Then the relaxed mood was shattered by a sudden yelp. A tiny flame shot up from old Gabe Red Horse's bushy white head as though he had a butane lighter hidden in his hair. A quick-thinking friend threw a coat over Gabe's head. When he was uncovered, Gabe's wrinkled face was ashen, and his hair was singed.

"Who did that?" Gabe demanded, wide-eyed with shock. "Which one of you guys, huh?" Still clutching the coat in both hands, he peered from face to face, repeating, "Who did that?"

"Geez, I'm sorry, Gabe." Beaver Tracker's unlit cigarette dangled from the corner of his mouth as he held up a headless wooden match. "I struck it on my thumbnail, and the head just went flying."

"George Tracker!" Gabe roared as he rubbed the top of his head. "You'd better teach this boy of yours to light a match before you let him start smoking."

Across the room, Luke grumbled, "Kid's only eighteen. What's he doing with matches?"

"Lighting cigarettes," Frances informed him. "Just like you did when you were *fifteen*."

Laughter—old Gabe's included—drowned out Luke's vow to make sure his younger brother never looked at another cigarette.

The women had supper cleaned up in time for the midnight mass. The service was a combination of English and Lakota, with familiar carols sung in both languages. Hope found herself giving voice to the phonetically spelled Lakota almost as easily as the English verses. It was Christmas Eve, and all roads converged in the timelessness of such a night. All traditions blended. All voices harmonized, and all good things became one splendor. It happened in Wakpala, as it happened everywhere, because it was Christmas Eve.

"Come outside," a deep voice entreated near Hope's ear. "I have something to show you."

Luke had disappeared right after the service, and Hope had found herself wondering where he'd gone. Obviously the men had little to do with packing things up and getting ready to go. His voice made her heart flutter, and she turned to find that he was dragging his jacket zipper up to his chin.

"You're probably going to have to carry some of these kids out to the sled," she told him. She pointed to Sweetie and Crystal, who were curled up in a pile of coats.

"I will. This'll just take a minute." He reached for her hand. "Come on."

He helped her with her coat and pulled her out into the night. There had been a gathering of soft white clouds while they were inside, and now a flurry of flakes whirled through the quiet night like ice dancers. Luke held Hope's hand tightly as he brought her away from the church so they could look back at it. The cross on the steeple was illuminated with blue lights, which made it visible for many miles in any direction across the prairie. At night it didn't matter that the old church needed another coat of white paint. It was a scene that could well have graced a postcard.

"First wish granted," Luke said. His voice was roughened around the edges, as though the role of wish granter might take some getting used to. "Snow for Christmas Eve."

"You must have some pull somewhere. There wasn't a cloud in the sky when we got here."

"Here's your second wish." He reached under his jacket and pulled out a bundle he'd made from his own muffler. It mewed as he handed it over.

"A kitten!" She drew the muffler back and discovered two doleful eyes. It didn't occur to her to claim that she had been kidding when she'd sat on his lap and whispered to him that she wanted a kitten for Christmas. "Oh, Luke, I used to ask for one every Christmas when I was a little girl." In those days it had been too simple and heartfelt a wish for Santa to grant.

Luke buried his hands in his jacket pockets. "You didn't say whether you wanted a boy or a girl."

"Well, I wanted a—" She peeked inside the bundle again and clucked at the fuzzy little face. "What have we here? Hmm?"

"It's a girl."

She saw how boyish her gift giver suddenly looked, and her heart melted. "I always wanted a girl. I can't believe you turned out to be such a softie, Sergeant Tracker."

"Neither can I. I hope it's your color. You know, the right size and everything." It was a lame attempt at off-handed humor. He couldn't remember ever having done anything so sentimental.

"I know she's perfect." Hope was having none of his easy humor. She had been given bicycles and doll houses, jewelry and cars, but no one had remembered her wish for something live and soft and warm. "I wish I could give you something half this good."

"Be careful with those wishes, Hope."

While they were standing there smiling at each other like two Christmas elves, the church door opened and the voices of the community permeated the stillness with low laughter and sleepy goodbyes. Luke carried his youngest sister to the bobsled. Little Sweetie slept on as the others bundled around her in the bed of hay. Those who were still awake claimed turns at holding Hope's kitten while the adults loaded up the gifts and dishes. Luke offered to help with the driving, but his father fervently swore that he was good for the duration and that no one could handle his team the way he did. Frances disappeared into the hay with the younger children, and Hope agreed with Luke that two bodies under one blanket would generate more heat than two bodies using separate blankets.

It had stopped snowing. The moon dimmed briefly as a gossamer cloud slid past. Sitting on the tailgate, Luke and Hope surveyed the territory they'd already traveled. They listened as the horses' hooves broke through the crusted snow and the bells on the horse collars jingled. The distant buttes were contoured shadows, dark mysteries at the edge of a lustrous white blanket that rippled over the plains. The soft night wind stirred the topmost branches of a lone cottonwood tree as they passed it.

"It's quiet," she said.

"Mmm-hmm."

"There's no place on earth as quiet as this."

"No place this stark."

"No place this beautiful," she said. Beneath the blanket he slid his hand to the top of her arm and pulled her closer. She felt beautiful. The air she breathed made her nose feel frosty, making it seem all that much warmer under the blanket. They had made a nest for themselves in the sweet-smelling alfalfa hay, and they'd spread a quilt over their legs and tucked it around their hips. "Such a gorgeous moon," Hope added, thinking that all this beauty must be noted.

"In the old days December was called the Twelfth Moon," he told her quietly, "but it had other names, too. It was the Moon of Frost Inside the Tipi." He felt her shiver, and he nuzzled her mink earmuff, adding, "But it was warm beneath the buffalo robes."

"Mmm, I can imagine."

"It was also called the Moon of Horns Dropping Off, because deer lose their horns then." His nose reached the edge of the fur and found her temple.

"How about the Moon of Frostbitten Noses?" she whispered. "Yours is cold."

"So is your cheek."

She grinned at the white moon, riding high in the sky. "I'm cold in some places, warm in others."

"Close to me, you're warm."

His lips brushed the side of her face so lightly that his breath made a more distinct contact. More warmth. Deep, deep inside her.

"Yes. Close to you, I'm warm."

"Put your hand inside my jacket."

Hope gave him a doubtful look. Luke drew his jacket zipper down to half mast. He found her hand and guided it through the opening, where her hesitant fingers discovered a ball of fur. She smiled. "I thought the children had her."

"They passed her around and gave her back. You know how kids are."

Petting the sleeping kitten gave Hope an excuse to keep her hand where it was. Her eyes were level with Luke's lips. She knew that if she tipped her head back it would be an invitation. It felt delicious to think about it and wait. She responded to his comment only because it was her turn.

"Fickle."

"But you're not fickle . . . are you, Hope?"

She closed her eyes to whisper, "No," and lifted her chin on a shaky breath. His kiss was not an order but a tentative, tenderly phrased request. She slid her hand past the slumbering kitten and around his back, flattening her palm and pressing her fingers into his woollen sweater. The catch in his breath reached her ears alone as he tilted his head to kiss her again, to explore the warmth of her mouth and tease her cheek with the cool tip of his nose.

He lifted his head, feeling as dazed as she looked.

So this is shell shock, she thought.

So this is moonstruck, he realized.

He gave her part of a smile, and she gave him the rest of it. "Merry Christmas, Luke," she whispered.

"I think you just got that third wish. That was every bit as good as a kitten."

Chapter Three

Christmas Eve had left a covering of frost feathers on every tree branch and every stalk of prairie grass that poked above the snow. From Frances's upstairs bedroom window, Christmas morning looked crisp, still and fairyland white. Frances reached across to the other twin bed and shook Hope's shoulder.

"Hope! Wake up and look outside."

Hope burrowed her face in the pillow and groaned before she lifted her head, trying to get her bearings as she squinted up at Frances. What had happened to the pretty little sleigh with the flashy silver runners she and Luke had been riding in a moment ago? Frances was kneeling on her pillow and holding onto the brass headboard with one hand as she drew her arm back from Hope's shoulder and gestured toward the window above the beds. Hope wondered whether this was just part of the dream and Frances was passing the sleigh in her chariot.

"Look what a gorgeous Christmas morning this is," Frances said.

Hope ruffled her sleep-flattened hair with one hand and pulled herself up on the brass rail with the other, imitating Frances's stance. Bright morning roused her sleepy brain. "Wow," she murmured as she surveyed the frosted trees in the shelter belt and the whitened strands of barbed wire that were part of a hilltop fence. "When did that happen?"

"Probably sometime between your wish and Luke's." Hope flashed Frances a look that was suddenly fully awake. "I guarantee I'm the only one who heard. The rest of the crew was sound asleep." Grinning at Hope's reddening cheeks, Frances shook her head. "I couldn't believe he actually got you a *kitten.* Luke! He never gives anybody anything more personal than a card with money in it."

"I'm sure he meant it as...kind of a joke. That was the other thing I asked for when he came to my classroom, besides snow, and I think he was just being funny." Hope didn't think anything of the kind. It was a precious gift. She hadn't even wanted to leave the kitten in the box Emma had provided in the kitchen, but, as a guest, she'd had no right to protest.

"I don't think he was being funny at all," Frances insisted. "I think he was being cute, and, believe me, I never imagined Luke actually trying to be cute." She lifted an eyebrow in Hope's direction. "So what do you think?"

Hope saw the empty bobsled standing in the yard below, and her heart yearned for another night like last night. "I think...it was a very sweet thing for him to do," she said quietly.

"Ohhh," Frances sighed dramatically as she flopped on her back. "Luke being sweet. Stony-faced Luke. I love it."

"He's not at all stony-faced." Hope sat on the edge of the bed and slid her feet into her scuffs. "He just looks that way because he's so lean and muscular."

Frances jackknifed to a sitting position with a teasing grin. "Lean and muscular. This gets better and better."

"You're the one who mentioned his expertise in self-defense, Frances. I'm simply making an observation. He looks very military, but inside he's very..." A knowing smile spread into Hope's eyes as she recalled his kiss. "Very sweet." She frowned quickly. "And don't you dare tell him I said that."

"If you keep smiling like that, I won't have to." Frances leaned over to give Hope's knee a friendly smack. "Let's grab the bathroom before the kids get up. Mama always has caramel rolls on Christmas morning."

The kitchen was filled with the smell of caramelized brown sugar and cinnamon. The turkey was in the oven, the rolls were on the table, and almost all was right in Emma's world.

"That cat's been underfoot all morning," Emma grumbled without looking up from her wrestling match with a balloon of white bread dough.

"Oh, I'm sorry," Hope said as she scooped the little ball of calico fur up from the floor. "I wonder if anything's open today. I'll have to buy some cat food."

"It likes turkey liver," Emma said flatly. "Cooked and chopped up fine."

Hope muttered a shy "Thank you," and she was sure she caught a spark of kitten-weakness in Emma's eye as the older woman nodded toward the refrigerator. "I put the rest of it in there. Should be enough for a couple of days."

"No creature goes hungry in Emma Tracker's kitchen." Three faces turned toward the doorway and were treated to Luke's smile and cheery, "Good morning, ladies. The kids are up. I told them to stay out of the kitchen until I scouted it out."

"The caramel rolls are ready," his mother reported. "You guys better help yourselves before they disappear."

Hope's heartbeat had shifted into high gear, and she wondered whether it showed. Considering the fact that she hadn't taken her eyes off Luke since he appeared in the doorway, she figured it did. He hadn't stopped looking at her, either. He wore jeans and a white T-shirt, and she could smell the soap he'd just used in the shower. She held the kitten against her breast and stroked its head with her fingertips.

"Merry Christmas." Luke left only a few inches between them. Somehow he found the top of the kitten's head with his thumb without looking for it with his eyes. He rubbed the soft fur, thinking his caress was within temptingly close range of the sensitive flesh he would much rather touch. He made the kitten purr, and his smile promised Hope that he could do the same for her. "Did you sleep well?"

"Sort of," she managed with a dry throat. Somewhere in the periphery she heard Emma complain that she hadn't slept well, either, after being out in the cold half the night, and she heard Frances's giggle. A child's voice asked about caramel rolls, and something clattered in the sink. Hope's feet were rooted to the center of the kitchen floor as she searched for something intelligent to say. "Did you see the frost?"

"Inside the tipi?"

She gave her head a quick shake. "Outside."

"I think that was last month."

"It's ... it's outside now. It's beautiful."

"Wake up and smell the coffee, you two." They turned toward the aroma and found Frances offering two steaming mugs and a saucy grin. "And help yourselves to caramel rolls, or else it'll be next Christmas before you get another chance."

Hope, Luke and Frances were on their way to the living room with coffee and rolls when they encountered the hungry pack. Six pairs of ravenous eyes fastened on the huge confections on their plates. It occurred to Hope that most children would have been eyeing the gifts under the tree on Christmas morning, but the Tracker children held Emma's caramel rolls in high esteem.

"Have at it," Luke suggested, and all the living room chairs were suddenly vacant. He gestured with his plate. "Sit anywhere, ladies. Either of you up for a little trail ride this morning?"

Hope appeared to concentrate on the sticky task of uncoiling the roll with her fingers. The last time she'd ridden a horse, she'd been tossed into a patch of poison ivy. In the twelve years since Camp Kekekabic, she had made a point of depriving any horse of the opportunity to humiliate her again.

"I think I'd better help with dinner," Frances said, adding quickly, "but you go ahead, Hope. I'll keep the kitten out from under Mama's feet."

"Oh, no, I want to do my share."

"I'll give you your share to do," Luke promised. "Dad says there's fence to fix. He told me to take Beaver, but then I'd feel compelled to give him a lecture on the hazards of smoking, and I don't want to do that on Christmas."

Hope didn't want to get poison ivy on Christmas, either. Frost inside the tipi notwithstanding, she knew darn well there was a patch of it waiting for her somewhere along the trail if she got on a horse. But Luke wasn't giving her a choice. Between sips of coffee he was getting Frances's advice on which horses to take.

There were gifts to be opened after breakfast. Not many, Hope noted. This family wasn't "making a haul" at Christmas. The children's toys had come from Santa Claus the night before, and the family gifts were both modest and practical. Luke's gifts were the most lavish, but they were still practical. He provided warm parkas, cowboy boots, jeans that had not been worn by an older brother or sister, a coat for his mother and seatcovers for his father's old pickup. The typewriter for Frances was a big hit.

Hope pushed the thought of mounting a horse aside for a moment as she watched Luke unwrap the gift she'd bought before they met. The clerk at the cosmetics counter had told her it was the most popular brand this year, but Hope was now certain he'd never use it.

"Ah." His eyes were alight as he spun the cap open. "Smell-good, huh?" Cute expression, Hope thought as she breathed a little more easily. He took a whiff of the men's cologne, then splashed some on his smooth cheeks. "Nice stuff."

Tom Tom leaned over and made a production of sniffing his older brother's face. "Whoo-ee! That'll make 'em come to attention."

Luke took the teasing as good-naturedly as he gave it out. He helped clean up the mess, pointedly noting the three gifts left unopened beneath the tree.

"He'll be here for dinner," Frances promised quietly. "Gorgeous George can smell turkey for a hundred miles."

Luke shrugged. "Better hide my smell-good, then. He's liable to use the whole damn bottle."

Hope decided she was anxious to meet Gorgeous George.

"Well, Hope—" Luke flashed her a smile that was no less than gorgeous in itself "—it's time to saddle up."

Her heart took a nosedive and landed in her stomach. She was anxious to view the morning landscape with Luke, but not from the top of a horse. She decided that there was anxiousness and then there was anxiety. She carried the combination like a set of barbells as she mounted the stairs to change her clothes.

"I know he looks big," Luke admitted as he pulled the cinch tight around the black horse's fuzzy belly. "And he *is*. He's half Percheron. But he's the gentlest horse you'll ever meet. You can put three or four little kids on his back and he'll take care of them just like a baby-sitter."

He extended a leather-gloved hand to Hope, who hung back several feet for safety's sake. She had estimated the length of the huge beast's hind leg and gave herself a few extra feet. "I don't think I can get up there, Luke. He's much too—"

"I'm going to put you up there. Come on."

She didn't want to look like a sissy. He'd called her a dude the night of the hayride, and she'd had the urge to do something to earn herself a better title. She couldn't think of anything that might elevate her from dude to cowboy, the quintessential South Dakota compliment, that didn't involve horses. Lord help her, she thought as she took a step toward the proverbial carrot, which was Luke's hand.

"I'm not much of a rider," she said.

"We'll fix that. We'll take you out on maneuvers. Up you go." He lifted her as easily as he spoke the words, and she grabbed the saddle horn. Her gloves were too slippery, she thought. She wanted a better grip. But to remove the gloves, she would have to let go of the horn. One dilemma was enough. She didn't need the additional one he was trying to hand her.

"Your reins, ma'am."

How could he smile so easily? Hope summoned her nerve and grabbed for the reins.

"You, uh...you aren't scared, are you?"

"No, no." Hope took a stab at smiling. "This is a pretty big animal, but I'm...I'm not scared."

"Good girl. Ride him around the corral a few times while I saddle that sorrel and get the tools." He patted the horse's rump, and the big black obliged with a couple of steps. Hope's eyes widened as she jerked the reins and pulled them as taut as a bowstring. The black laid his ears back.

"Like hell you're not scared," Luke mumbled as he moved quickly toward the horse's head. "Whoa, boy. Just drop the reins, Hope. Hold on to the saddle and let go of the reins."

She did as he told her, and he took charge of the reins before the black could execute the move his ears had forecast. Luke touched Hope's thigh with a soothing hand. "You okay?" She nodded quickly. "I forgot to ask whether you liked horses."

"I do. It's just that they don't like me." She gave a small apologetic smile. "One threw me once."

"You give old Blackie a chance. He'll change your mind, but not if you haul up on his mouth like that. A horse'll rear up if you do that."

"I'm sorry. He started to go before I was ready."

He rubbed her knee a little and squinted up at the bright sky and the nervous woman. "Should we take the pickup?"

She wanted to get over this foolish fear. "Not if you'd rather ride. I . . . I think I can—"

"Tell you what. I'll get the wire stretcher, and we'll try riding double—with you in the saddle. Think you can handle that?" She nodded. "Okay, then, just sit there for a minute." He wrapped the reins loosely around the saddle horn. "He won't go anywhere," Luke promised.

Hope was grateful when the horse made good on Luke's guarantee. With Luke sitting behind her and the reins in his right hand, Hope found that she was able to relax somewhat. They followed a gravel road, then a cow path across the pasture. The first time Luke dismounted to open a gate, Hope grew tense again, but by the third gate she'd developed some faith in "old Blackie."

"So what happened to you when you got thrown?" Luke asked. "Were you hurt bad?"

"A sprained wrist, scratches, bruises, but the worst was the poison ivy."

"The old nag picked his spot, then."

Hope laughed. "That's what I thought."

"A couple of boys in my platoon got into some poison oak last summer," he said. "One of them really had it bad. I didn't let him know it, but there were a few days there when I did ease up on him some."

"That was kind of you," she allowed.

"Hey, careful with those insults. No drill instructor ever wants to be accused of kindness. If you coddle those kids like . . . like a teacher would, they'll wash

out. Or somewhere down the road they'll get themselves killed and take a whole squad with them."

"Did I hear a critical inflection on the word
'teacher'?"

"Uh-uh." He tightened his left arm around her. "I
like teachers. Kindness is great in the third grade. You
go right ahead and be kind, Hope."

"You're not in the third grade," she reminded him.

"Yeah, but I'm off duty." He patted his left hand
against her side. "Kindly take off this glove and stow
it in your pocket."

"Your glove?" She felt him nod near the side of her
face, and she did as he asked.

He slid his hand under the bottom of her jacket and
curled it around her right side. She shivered. "Is it
cold?" She nodded. "You'll warm it for me." He
liked the feel of her angora sweater. "Just want to
make sure I've got a good grip on you."

"It's not as scary this way, with you holding the
reins," she noted. "It's . . . *hardly* scary at all now."

"You're not scared of me, are you?"

"Not really."

"Not really." He chuckled behind her earmuff.
"This tickles my nose."

"The mink? They're a little extravagant, I know,
but they're nice and warm."

"Not as nice as your hair." He nuzzled the back of
her head. "Not as pretty, either."

She smiled at the distant point where the sky
touched the earth. She wondered whether they might
be headed for that, or points beyond. "Do you *really*
have fence to fix out here?"

"Mmm-hmm. Probably wouldn't have taken more
than a couple of hours if we'd taken two horses."

"But—"

"But I'm off duty," he reminded her. "I'm on Indian time. No clocks."

"You probably don't get many chances to ride at Fort Leonard Wood."

"Not many," he agreed.

"And you probably wanted a chance to really ride this morning."

"I wanted a chance to be with you."

It was an admission that echoed in the crisp, clear morning air. Like the mist from their breath, it made a mark—something warm that changed the shape of things entirely. The frost seemed to glitter more, and the icy sheen across the flat seemed brighter.

"I was afraid I wouldn't be able to come," she confessed. "You're to be commended for getting me up here. I'll bet you're very good at what you do. Boot camp must be as scary as horses for those recruits."

"I don't ride double with them, you can be sure of that. Ride herd on 'em, maybe. Crack the whip on 'em, definitely."

"I don't believe you're all that hard, Sergeant Tracker. Not after that kitten."

"Let's keep that a secret."

She laughed. "You'd better tell that to your sister."

"You're right," he said with a groan. "Frankie'll ruin me. It'll be another seven years before I show up around here again."

"Why did you wait so long?" she asked quietly. The question brought silence, and she wondered whether she'd just put a damper on their good time.

Finally he said, "The longer you put it off, you know, the harder it gets. Pretty soon you don't want to face them because you have to come up with some kind of an explanation, and you realize you haven't got one." He sighed. "The simple fact is that I love my family, but I don't like coming home."

"But they don't seem to expect any apologies, Luke. They're just glad to have you home."

"Yeah, maybe." That kernel of truth didn't help. "It's this place, Hope. It holds people down. They get to thinking they can't make it anywhere else. I see a lot of kids from reservations wash out of the army because they want to go home. If they make it through the first year, they're the best soldiers in the world, but, God, that first year. It's like the world's too big for them."

"It's that way for a lot of people," she said.

"There's nothing here for them," he insisted. "No jobs. Plenty of nothing. Plenty of poverty."

"Plenty of people who think the world of Luke Tracker. If I went home I'd have to decide whether I wanted to be a guest in my mother's house or my father's house. So I guess there's really no home for me to go back to. It's all different, and I don't belong."

"You can come back to Wakpala any time and find the same dog lying on the post office steps. *Nothing* changes. And I don't belong, either." He spotted the place where the fence was down, and he laid the reins against the black's neck and tapped the horse's flank with his heel. "I'd like to see Frankie get out of here before she gets stuck," he said. "I hate the idea of her being stuck here."

"She told me about your girlfriend Monica."

"She did, huh?" Luke retrieved his glove from Hope's pocket. "Monica was part of another life. I don't even think about her anymore." He handed

Hope the reins and dismounted with the grace of a gymnast.

"But once you wanted to marry her and take her away from all this."

"I suppose I did." As he spoke he removed the wire stretcher and the small bag of tools from the saddle without looking up. "At the time she didn't want to leave home. Now I hear she's moved to Montana with some guy." He shrugged. "Who can figure it?"

"She's older now," Hope ventured.

"So am I. Older and wiser." He looked up, shutting one eye against the bright sun. "I suppose you want to get down."

Hope tried to imagine swinging her leg over the horse and sliding to the ground. "Well, I guess what I wanted to point out to you is that . . . I think Frances is doing what she wants to do. I don't think she feels that she's stuck here."

"Uh-huh." He grinned. "You wanna come down here and explain all this to me? I'm interested."

"I'm not sure." She gripped the saddle horn and eyed the ground. Her legs felt as though they'd been through a taffy pull. "I think I'm the one who's stuck."

With a laugh, Luke tossed the tools to the ground. "Come on. Let me give you a hand."

"I might not be able to get back up here."

"Yes, you will." He reached for her, and she managed to swing her leg over the horse's neck and slide into Luke's arms.

"That is the widest horse . . ."

"You're doing fine," he said as he pulled her closer.

"My legs feel like mush." She decided not to mention the fact that the way he was looking at her put her stomach in the same condition.

"Mine, too. I think a kiss may help."

"I think a kiss might—" The words *make it worse* were never uttered. They were negated by the warmth of his lips, the delicate stroking of his tongue, the strength of his embrace. The spicy scent of the cologne she'd given him added zest to the cold air. In the bundle of puffy jackets and gloves, only their lips and cheeks and noses could touch, but it was enough to make their senses soar. And the kiss made all things, for the moment, better.

They returned to the house in time for dinner and the arrival of Luke's much-discussed brother, Gorgeous George. Hope saw the physical resemblance between Luke and George, but noted that self-indulgence threatened to mar George's good looks. At the age of twenty-seven his physical condition had already begun to deteriorate, with the effects of an eat-drink-and-be-merry life-style showing in his puffy face and potbelly.

"So how's Uncle Sam treating you, Sarge?" The jovial tone of the question was a thin veneer, and the handshake was tentative. Luke was the man of the hour. George stood in his brother's shadow and shivered imperceptibly for lack of sunshine.

"Can't complain," Luke said. "I like what I'm doing. How about you?"

"I like what I'm doing, too." George laughed nervously and glanced around for someone to join in. "Which is as little as possible. Right, Frankie?"

"You're still just gorgeous, George," Frances chimed.

Luke clapped his hand on his brother's back and offered a smile. The action seemed to release a pressure valve. "Looks like you're getting fed pretty well, boy." He gave George's spare tire a friendly pat.

"But I'm still good-looking," George insisted, returning the grin.

"Still gorgeous," Luke echoed. "Where've you been keeping yourself?"

George gave a quick shrug. "I've got a girlfriend. Takes good care of me. Real good cook." He stepped back to admire his brother's trim figure. "You're eating too much army chicken, Sarge. Look at you. Skinny as you were when you first left here."

Luke gave George's chin a playful clip with his knuckles. "Wanna go a couple rounds, boy? Don't worry. If I get too rough on you, Frankie'll go running for Dad, like she always did."

George's smile faded, and he turned away. "Let's just see who can put away the most turkey. I think that's a competition I can beat you in."

Luke saw the curious look in Hope's eyes and the plea in his sister's. He reached for George's shoulder. "We're about even in our old age, brother. Everybody's a winner at Christmastime."

Chapter Four

Hope tucked the blanket under the corner of the mattress, then smoothed one hand over the woolly surface as she reached for the pink chenille bedspread with the other. Suddenly a quarter flopped on the blanket in the middle of the bed. She looked up, smiling. Luke leaned against the doorjamb and smiled back. Hope saw nothing in those gray sweats and running shoes that could possibly be termed underdeveloped.

"It's supposed to bounce," Luke said.

Hope flipped the quarter in the air. It glinted as it rose past the sunlit window, and she opened her hand to catch it. Luke snatched it out of the air and slapped it on the back of his wrist. "Call it," he said.

"What's at stake?"

"A date for New Year's Eve. I win, I take you to the party. You win, *you* take *me*."

"Does everyone come out a winner on New Year's, too?"

The glint in his eye reminded her of the quarter. "Call it," he repeated.

"Tails."

He took a peek, then grinned down at her. "You win, lucky lady. Good thing, too, since I don't have a car here." He glanced down the hall, then beckoned her with a jerk of his head.

She went to him with a saucy swing in her step. "I win, huh? All week long you've been *letting* me help you with *your* chores." She laid her hands on his chest as he dropped the quarter into her breast pocket and took hold of her shoulders. His sweatshirt was damp, and she felt the hard muscles beneath it. "Like feeding oats to the horses."

"Which gave me a chance to steal a few kisses behind the barn." He decided it was a good time to steal another one.

His kiss was brief, but it left her tingling. "And I helped you pitch hay," she said quietly.

"And I kissed you behind the haystack."

"While somebody pitched a forkful of hay on top of our heads."

"Beaver," he said, his eyes twinkling as he recalled the way he'd caught her by surprise, and then, from the top of the haystack, his brother had surprised them both. "I owe him one."

"If we're not careful, we'll get caught again," she whispered. "Every time you kiss me, the woodwork giggles."

"Why don't *you* try kissing *me*?"

She could only let him hold her gaze for a moment before she lowered her eyes and stared at her own hands. They had spent the week with each other. In the Tracker home, surrounded by his family, Luke and Hope had been together except when they went to their separate beds at night. Each morning she'd wasted no time in getting up and dressed, because she always found him waiting for her with a suggestion for something they could do together. Usually some of the children were included in Luke's plans, which made for both fun and tantalizing frustration. They got closer with each day they spent together, and they talked about everything but what that closeness might mean.

It meant such headiness that when he compounded the feeling by standing this close, Hope couldn't make sense of her thoughts. She saw herself drawing him across the threshold, closing the door and peeling his damp sweatshirt away. If she didn't keep talking, she was afraid she might try something crazier than kissing him.

"What have you been up to?" she asked, because it was all she could think of. "You're all wet."

"Sweaty," he corrected. "I've been running."

She glanced up. "Every day?"

"Every morning. Early." He smiled, because he was still holding her, and even though it wasn't enough, it was something. "Before you got up."

"I could have gotten up earlier."

He'd needed to run to keep his head on straight. For the last week she'd been the last image in his mind before he went to sleep and the first to enter his head when his subconscious alarm clock woke him before daybreak. Being with her had become each day's only priority. Even if half a dozen other people were in the same room, he was with her. When she was helping to get a meal on the table and he was telling his father a story, he'd made it a point to catch her eye and be with her. Some nights, after everyone had gone to bed, he would run and then take a long shower, letting the water run over him until it got cold because he knew she had gone to bed, and he wanted to be with her there, too.

"I didn't know you were a runner," he said.

"I could be." She smiled. "I have a pair of sneakers."

His hands moved over her shoulders, and she became lost in his dark eyes and his promise. "Just say the word, and I'll take you with me."

Yes, take me with you. "No, I'll take you," she promised quietly. "To this party, wherever it is."

"Such blind trust. It's at the Mission. Haven't you noticed? Everything happens at the Mission."

"I'll tell you what I've noticed," she said. "You enjoy being home, whether you want to admit it or not. You like being part of all this."

Then it is time to go, he thought. If it showed that much, the next thing he knew, he'd be thinking about coming back. Or staying. He'd taken to claiming that the army was his home, but even if he'd been kidding himself on that score, he had to remember that the army was his future. This was no time to get sentimental about home and family, even if it was Christmas. Even if this woman had kindled a strong need for something his career could never give him, he had to remember that it came down to choices. He'd made his. All he had to do was get back on the bus. Until then, maybe he could indulge in Christmas sentimentality, home fires and family ties. He could enjoy being with Hope every waking minute before the bus pulled out. But once he got on that bus, he would leave all the binding ties behind him.

"I think you enjoy it, too," he told her. "For whatever reasons. I'm sure this will be a far cry from your customary New Year's Eve party."

"It *is* the first time I've won a date."

"You'll have to take me in my uniform. For the, uh...sake of the ceremony, I promised my dad I'd wear it."

"What ceremony?"

"You'll see." At the sound of footfalls on the stairs, he stole another quick kiss. "I need a shower. And that bed needs more work, Spencer."

"That's a civilian bed," she told him as he drew away from her. "It's fine the way it is."

The New Year's Eve celebration at St. Elizabeth's Mission began in the church. Supper in the parish hall followed the services, and Hope knew her way around the buffet this time. She helped herself to frybread, politely refused the *taniga* and headed directly for the soup kettle. This time she enjoyed a feeling of confidence in knowing what was on her plate as she wended her way to the group of folding chairs Frances had staked out.

Hope covered her lap with a cotton bandanna, which she'd had the forethought to bring. Because it was New Year's Eve, she had worn a dress. It was nothing fancy, she told herself—just a winter white knit with a full skirt that flirted when she twirled. She was counting on dancing, and she was wearing one of the few dresses in the room. Frances had warned her that she might feel out of place if she dressed up, but Hope had dressed for her date. Her date had dressed to please his father, but when he turned from the serving table in his crisp green dress uniform, it was Hope's heart that swelled with pride. He searched the room only for her.

There was little conversation as they ate together. Luke's uniform brought him lingering looks from the young women and admiration from the men, and he was uncomfortable with the attention. A part of him belonged here with these people, and that part of him wanted the years to drop away so that he could be home. The other part of him didn't fit anymore, and the uniform seemed to him to be a visible sign of that fact. Hope in her soft white dress and he in his green uniform with his flashy ribbons and stripes—they both stood out like a pair of sore thumbs.

But they were a pair, and Luke liked that.

After the food was cleared away, the party moved to the gym, which was part of the dormitory complex. There, several women, including Emma and her older daughters, loaded tables with quilts, appliquéd pillows, beading and other handwork. Five men gathered around a big bass drum. Hope anticipated more instruments, but the drum stood alone. Her vision of floating about the dance floor in Luke's arms faded as his father summoned Luke with an imperious gesture.

"Let's get this over with," Luke mumbled as he guided Hope toward what had been established as the front of the room. Hope joined Luke's brothers and sisters while Luke stood between his parents in front of the tables laden with goods. First in Lakota, then in English, George Tracker extolled his oldest son's talents and virtues. He explained that Luke served his country by training young men to be soldiers, and that the ribbons and stripes on his uniform represented wonderful military accomplishments. Luke's stance was formally at ease, but his mind raced as he stared straight ahead. He'd deliberately stayed away, and he didn't want to be honored for it. It had been a matter

of self-preservation. Self-defense. His father was explaining how good he was at that.

George Tracker knew the meaning of every decoration his son wore, and the deep timbre of the old
man's voice was bright with pleasure as he performed
an ancient ritual in its modern form. The people listened, and the men nodded their approval, but Luke
wondered what they were thinking. His father called
him son, warrior, Lakota, but what kind of Lakota
deserted the people he'd grown up with? What kind of
warrior feared the welcoming of family and friends?
What kind of a son stayed away from home for seven
years?

"This is a son to be proud of," George announced.
"My family celebrates this night with a giveaway because our brother, our son, is home for a visit, and we
are glad."

It was that simple. The questions were swept away
as Luke turned and basked in the light in his father's
eyes. Luke's vision was cloudy, but his mind was clear
as he reached blindly for the old man's handshake. No
complaints, no excuses, no apologies. They were glad
he was here, and that was enough.

Then came the giveaway. Names were called—respected elders, friends, Luke's boyhood buddies—and
the recipients of the Trackers' gifts moved down the
line, shaking hands with each member of the family.
It is our pleasure to give, was the unspoken message.
We share your joy, came the wordless reply. Thanks
were not appropriate.

When Hope's name was called, she felt a flush of
excitement. She had taken a chair near the front of the
room to watch the proceedings, and now she was to be
included. Emma displayed the quilt with its star

bursting in bright primary colors, then folded it carefully and laid it over Hope's arm. Following the example of those who had gone before, Hope smiled, shook Emma's hand and moved to George. She saw that the old man expected solemnity from her, and she behaved accordingly. Luke was next in line, and her pulse suddenly thudded in her temples as she took his hand.

She longed to embrace him as no one else had done, and she lifted her eyes to let him see her longing. She wouldn't, not here, but the need was there. The black brim of his dress cap sheltered his eyes, which were flooded with emotion. He held her hand for more than a handshake. It was his night, and she was part of it. "Stand here beside me," he said quietly. "You've been part of the family since my sister brought you to...us."

One member of the Tracker family was missing. Gorgeous George had not arrived, although everyone speculated that he would. After the giveaway there was an honor song. Flanked by his parents and followed by the rest of the family, Luke led the circular procession in a slow hesitation step. The five singers chanted in a high pitch and pounded a steady beat on the bass drum. The other members of the community took their places behind the family to honor Luke Tracker, who had come home.

And now there would be dancing. Hope could feel it in the air. The teenage girls flocked together and cast hopeful looks at the boys, whose lanky arms and legs struck various postures calculated to be an expression of "cool." Battered black speakers were brought in, along with a microphone and a couple of guitars.

"Ho-ho-ho!"

The gym became quiet as all eyes turned toward the door. "Santa Claus?" Hope muttered. "What's he doing here?" Luke smiled and brought his finger to his lips.

Once again the children took cover as the man in red stalked through the door. He circled the room, peered menacingly at the children who stood behind the older people's legs and roared, "Happy New Year!" When he came to Luke, Santa Claus stood at attention and offered a smart salute.

"You don't salute sergeants, Santa," Luke said, smiling.

Santa's big belly was a natural protrusion, but he stood at attention like an experienced soldier. "I salute *you*, Sergeant Tracker."

Luke nodded and returned a snappy salute. He knew of no enclave in the country that held its sons who soldiered in such high esteem.

"Ho-ho-ho!"

Hope looked to the doorway again. "Another one?"

Luke offered the saluting Santa a quick handshake. "You guys make this quick, huh, Santa? I wanna dance with my girl."

"I don't blame you." Santa backed away as his rival Santa approached. "But I've got my pride to think of, same as you. I'm not going down easy."

"What's going on?" Hope asked as she and Luke joined the others, who had backed up to widen the circle. "Two Santas?"

"The old year Santa and the new year Santa," Luke explained.

"Shouldn't it be old Father Time and a baby?"

Luke slipped his arm around Hope's shoulders. "Welcome to Wakpala," he said with a chuckle.

She looked up at him and smiled. "Thank you."

While the crowd cheered them on, the two Santas circled each other like professional wrestlers. They tapped each other's bellies, then circled again in the opposite direction. Suddenly the new Santa lunged for the old, and the tussle was on. The old Santa's age and the new Santa's robust youth were part of the act, but when it came to tumbling on the floor or making a quick dash across the room, both exhibited equal measures of awkwardness and agility. When the new Santa tweaked the old one's beard, the elastic snapped, and old Santa howled. Finally, to the special delight of the children, the new Santa gave the old one a dramatic boot out the door, emitted a triumphant "Ho-ho-ho" and disappeared into the night himself.

"It's enough to make you think twice about sitting on Santa's lap."

"Really?" Luke took Hope's hand as the band struck up a slow country-and-western tune. "How about dancing with him?"

"I'll dance with *you*, Sergeant Tracker." She put her arms around his neck as she had wanted to do earlier, and he pulled her close, so that every breath she drew was scented with his spicy cologne. She rested her chin lightly on his strong shoulder, which was crisply upholstered in clean square military style. The buttons on his jacket pressed against her ribs, and she could feel his hard belt buckle.

The quality of the sound didn't matter as they moved with the music from one song to the next. The overhead lights cast everything in bright, garish tones. Most of the younger children were by now nestled in piles of coats and quilts, and the older ones were venturing out on the dance floor. Among the adults there were as many women dancing together as mixed couples. Hope couldn't have been happier surrounded by candlelight and a fairy-tale king's courtiers, and Luke firmly believed he held royalty in his arms.

"Let's go for a walk," he suggested near her ear as he guided her off the floor.

She pushed back his sleeve and turned his wrist up to check his watch. "But it's almost—"

"I know. Let's get your coat." As an afterthought he added, "Better put your boots on, too."

The lack of wind made it a warm night for midwinter in South Dakota. They walked away from the bright yard lights with their hearts set only on a moment of privacy under a starry winter sky.

"How many more minutes?" she asked. Even her soft voice was startling in the silence of the night.

"Four or five minutes until January," he told her. "The Tree Popping Moon."

"Why do they call it that?"

"You'll know when you get a real cold snap. It gets so cold here it makes trees split open."

She shoved her hands deep into the pockets of her coat. "Is there a Sioux term for New Year's Eve?"

"In the old days, the year began in April—the Moon of the Birth of Calves."

"For someone who was so anxious to get away from the reservation, you seem to know a lot about its traditions." She looked up at him as they strolled along the wide gravel driveway that led past the mission's little collection of buildings. With a knowing smile she asked, "Why do you suppose that is?"

"I read a lot," he said. "Try to put what the anthropologists say together with the stories I heard as a kid." He lifted one shoulder. "It's kind of interesting."

"The ceremony tonight was . . . kind of interesting."

He saw that there was no point in trying to bluff his way through this conversation. "I've been dreading that for days, you know. Standing up there in front of everybody like you're some kind of hero, when you never really wanted to come back in the first place. . . . But then I listened to my father, and I felt . . ." Grinning at the moon, he put his arm around her shoulders and squeezed with the exuberance of remembered warmth. "I felt like everything was okay. Like they understood that I can't live here anymore, but I'm still . . ."

"You're still part of them, Luke. They're just glad to have you home, even for a little while."

"I know." *Even for a little while.* A short holiday, he thought. A brief hint of what having someone to share life with could be like. He wanted more than a hint. Don't be a fool, he told himself. You'll drive yourself crazy with that kind of thinking.

"What will they do in there at midnight?" she asked. "Sing 'Auld Lang Syne' and go around kissing everybody?"

"Oh, there'll be 'Auld Lang Syne,' all right, country-style. Lots of hand shakes. You won't see too much public hugging and kissing. The lovers like us will have to slip away for a kiss."

She looked at him cautiously, as though she wasn't sure she'd heard right. Was it just an expression? Was it a casual term? His unfaltering gaze told her there was nothing casual about the word he'd chosen.

"Is it okay?" he asked quietly.

"I think it's true," she said. "For me."

They stood near a bluff overlooking the frozen river. He took her in his arms, and she looked up, waiting, loving the heated way he looked at her and the cool white moonlight in his hair.

"I'll be leaving in a couple of days," he said.

It was a subject they'd carefully avoided. "I know."

"I don't know when I'll be back."

"I don't know how long I'll be working here."

"It's midnight," he whispered, his voice hoarse as he lowered his head to take her mouth with his. The night receded as the kiss consumed them both. They strained the limits of the act itself, nipping, pressing, seeking, luring, trading tongues and titillation and groaning with the need for more contact. Hunger became an urgency that threatened to shatter all reason. They drew apart on the strength of what little resistance they'd left each other.

He gripped her shoulders. "If this ground wasn't frozen . . ."

"We could go—"

"Don't say it, Hope, because if you say it, we'll do it, and it's crazy."

"It is," she admitted. "It's crazy. You'll be leaving."

"So let's go back inside where it's safe. Where everybody's watching."

"We can dance," she suggested, remembering what bittersweet torture that had been.

"Yeah." He gave her a tender kiss on her forehead. "We sure can dance."

As they walked back to the gym, a car came up from behind and cruised by slowly. The window on the passenger's side rolled down, and Gorgeous George flashed an even row of white teeth. His tone was suggestive. "What are you guys doing out here?"

"Walking," Luke told his brother. "Where have you been?"

"Celebrating. Why? Did I miss something?" The car rolled to a stop on the end of George's question, which was clearly rhetorical. George knew he had missed a great deal.

"Depends on your viewpoint," Luke said. He felt a squeeze of encouragement on his left hand, and he turned to find that encouragement in Hope's eyes. Make peace for the women's sake, his father had always told him. As he extended his hand, he knew it was for his own sake, as well. "Happy New Year, brother."

George's eyes brightened as he grabbed Luke's hand. "Hey, same to you, brother. Same to you." George reached for Hope's hand as he muttered, "Happy New Year, Hope. What do you think of this brother of mine, huh? He's a hell of a soldier, I'll tell you." Before she could reply, George turned to Luke again. "I couldn't handle it, you know. They've still got my picture hanging on the wall at home beside yours, the one they took after basic training. I wish they'd take that damn thing down." His anguished look said that he felt unworthy, even unwelcome. "I didn't know if you'd want me there tonight, Luke. That's why I stayed away."

"I didn't know if I wanted *me* there." Luke's attempt at a chuckle fell short. "I thought I'd feel kind of foolish, standing up in front of everybody like that, in my uniform and all."

"Did you?"

"No," he admitted. "The only part of it I minded was that somebody was missing."

George's eyes glistened as he smiled. "Next time," he promised quietly.

"Hell, I'm not doing an encore." Luke clipped George's arm with a playful hand. "Next time you get the limelight. Give the girls a thrill."

"Yeah." One word and a tight-lipped grin were all George could manage.

"You going in?" Luke asked.

"Nah, they're probably mad." George drew himself back into the car like a turtle. The unseen driver muttered something, and George said, "Yeah, we gotta get on down the road. I left the ol' lady home, so she's probably mad, too." He stuck his head out again, in need of confirmation. "You're really not mad, though, are you, Luke?"

"I'm really not mad."

"I'll see you before you leave?" Luke nodded. "Well, happy New Year, then."

Luke stared after the car as it disappeared over the hill.

"He was in the army, too?" Hope reclaimed his attention with the question.

"Yeah, he joined up just like I did—soon as he was old enough. He made it through basic, but, God, he was a screw-up." He slipped his arm around her, and they started walking again. "George Tracker, Jr. spent most of his short hitch in the guardhouse. He was dishonorably discharged after he stole a jeep and drove it through the wall of the Officers' Club at Fort Dix."

"Oh, no."

"Oh, yes. His exploits were legendary."

"And embarrassing to his older brother?"

He glanced at her and nodded slowly. "It's time I put that aside, isn't it?"

"Sounds like he couldn't live up to your image, so he created one of his own."

"I went my own way," Luke insisted. "Nobody asked him to follow."

"Nobody had to. He wanted to be like you, Luke."

"Then it's time he put *that* aside."

"Hey, Luke!" They turned their attention toward the gym door. One of the musicians was on his way out with a snare drum. "Your dad said to tell you they had to get the kids home. Frances left her car for you."

"Is the dance over?" Luke asked.

"Everybody's packing up."

Luke glanced down at Hope. "Damn. I was looking forward to one more dance."

"Me, too. Walk me over to my apartment?"

He surveyed the dark array of buildings. "You sure you want to stay here tonight? Looks pretty deserted."

"The students will start coming back tomorrow," she told him. "School starts again on the second."

They went back to the gym to get her quilt, his cap and her shoes, and then he walked with her in silence to her back door. She had stopped in earlier to turn the heat up and bring her kitten home, but the mission had had many visitors that night, and Luke insisted on checking her apartment for safety's sake. When he brought her luggage in from her car, he smelled coffee. She came around the kitchen island in stockinged feet and began unbuttoning his overcoat. He covered her hands with his.

"I can't stay, Hope."

"Just for coffee."

He shook his head. "I haven't the slightest desire for coffee."

"Something else, then. I think I have—"

"You know damn well what I want." The look in her eyes said she would postpone his leavetaking at all cost. She raised her chin just a fraction of an inch. "I can't even kiss you again," he said softly. "I can't kiss you now and walk away. And I have to walk away."

"Why?"

Because she was so beautiful, and his heart would tether itself to her, and he would never be able to stand on his own two feet again. He held both her hands in one of his and reached to touch her cheek with the backs of his fingers.

"I can't stay," was the only explanation he could give.

Chapter Five

Hope had made the coffee because she had felt like having a cup. The fact that she'd made twice as much as she intended to drink was—yes, okay, it was irritating. She felt a little foolish about it. She told herself that anticipating a man's wants was probably bad business for a woman. A trap to be cautiously avoided. If she'd made the coffee before she was sure he wanted some, then she deserved what she got—a second cup that would either go to waste or keep her awake the rest of the night.

Something small and soft slid past Hope's ankle. Tears burned in her eyes as she stooped to scoop up the kitten. "Do you have time for a cup of coffee, sweetheart? You can stay, can't you? Or do you have to be off doing kitty things?"

She held the kitten's tricolored velvet body next to her flaming cheek, hoping to be soothed. A tear slid into the feline fur. "Oh, I'm sorry," Hope whispered into the cat's tiny face. "You don't like to be wet, do you?" She petted the damp spot while the cat cast her own hazel-eyed bid for sympathy up at Hope.

"We spent a nice holiday, together, that's all." She took a swipe at another tear with the side of her hand. "He's a soldier, and we all know about soldiers. I'm just lucky he didn't give me some song and dance about being shipped off to the front in the morning." She cuddled the kitten to her breast and promised, "I wouldn't have fallen for it. He thinks he's cornered the market on self-control, but I've got news for—"

A sudden knock brought her head up. She stared at the back door. "—him. He didn't really leave," she whispered as she slid the bolt on the door. "He just went to get his tap shoes."

He looked cold and humble standing out there on the step with his collar turned up. She decided to let him stand there until he said something.

"I, uh . . . I couldn't get the damn car started."

"Funny," she said, ignoring the cold air that rushed into her kitchen. "Frances hasn't had any trouble with that car. Do you think it's gotten that cold out?"

"Yeah, I do. I think it's pretty cold."

She had turned the porch light on. His face was dimly lit. "I still have coffee."

"I'd like some."

She turned, hugging the kitten, and walked quickly toward the stove. As she prepared the cups with one hand she gauged his every move by sound. The door clicked shut. His coat slid off his shoulders and was draped over the back of a kitchen chair. His jacket followed. He took four steps across the linoleum and stood beside the counter.

She worked slowly, deliberately, because she dreaded facing him. She blinked and blinked, but the stinging tears wouldn't stay back, and she wasn't sure why. Was it because he'd left or because he'd come back?

She took a deep breath and tried her voice. "What do you think is wrong with the car?"

"I flooded it."

Laughter bubbled behind the tears, and she couldn't deal gracefully with either. She kissed the kitten and put her on the floor.

"Don't laugh. I feel dumber than hell."

"Dumber than hell," she marveled quietly, her back still to him as she fitted her fingers into the handles of the two mugs and braced herself to face him.

"And don't tell Frankie. I'll be able to hear the two of you laughing at me all the way to... Hope?" She was holding two cups of coffee in unsteady hands, and her face was pink and sweet with tears. "Honey, you're not crying, are you?"

"No." It was a raspy answer.

He took the cups, set them aside and folded his arms around her. They sighed together as they clung to each other tightly, relieved by the stay in the execution of his plans. He could have been gone, but he wasn't. Not yet.

"Don't cry," he whispered. The tears were like silk bonds, making him hurt, making him hold her tighter. He was afraid of them, but he wanted them on his shirt, on his skin, in his soul. They gave him power and made him feel helpless all at once. "Please don't cry, honey."

"I'm really not," she insisted. She wasn't sure what this was. She never cried.

"Okay." He kissed the top of her hair and rubbed her back. "Tell me why you're not crying, then."

"Because you're not leaving yet."

"I can take another shot at it."

"No." Her arms tightened around his middle. "I mean, you're not leaving town yet. I mean, you don't *have* to go yet." She looked up at him. "You said you had to go, and you don't. Not tonight."

"I was trying to do the right thing, Hope." He took a tear from her cheek with a gentle thumb. "If I had anything to offer you, I'd give it to you in a minute, but I don't. Not for a woman like you. I'm just a—"

"Give me the time you have left, Luke." She said it quickly, because she knew how awful it sounded, but she wanted every minute. Every moment they had together was precious to her now that she knew how badly she would ache for him once he was gone.

"A couple of days, honey. That's all." If neither of them had wanted anything more than a good time, a couple of days would have been plenty. But she wasn't thinking that way—he could tell by the way she was looking at him now—and, God help him, he wasn't, either.

"I want as much of that time as you'll give me," she whispered. "I'm in love with you, Luke."

He closed his eyes and touched his forehead to hers. Her skin was warm, and his was cool. How could she love him? She was a princess and he was a tin soldier.

"We've only known each other—"

"Since Christmas," she whispered. "Since the beginning of time."

"I want to make love to you, Hope. I hurt with it."

"Then let's ease the hurt—" their lips met in a brief and tender kiss "—with love."

They went to her room, and she turned the key on the hurricane lamp beside her bed. The small light glowed inside the milk-glass base. Luke tugged at the knot in his tie as he watched her turn down the bed. There were pastel sheets under a white, ruffled spread on a bed big enough for two. A far cry from what he was used to. He wore the only drab green in the room, and he was about to shed it.

She sat on the bed and folded her hands over her skirt. Pausing as he pulled the tie through his collar, he reconsidered. This wasn't the season for shedding. He tossed the tie on a chair and took his place beside her on the bed. She lifted her chin toward him, then her eyes, bright with her faith in him. He moved her hair aside and touched the nape of her neck as he leaned closer. She laid her palm against his cool, starched shirt, and his heart thudded beneath her hand as banked coals burst into flame.

They came into each other's arms as though the lost had been found. The kisses they exchanged lit the dark corners of the night with flashing colors and filled their heads with bells and tambourines. They unwrapped each other, hearts beating wildly in anticipation of gifts that were pleasing even before they were unveiled.

This was Hope, who had braved the high horse in order to spend the day with him. She had opened her mind to customs that seemed different and her mouth for food that looked strange as she made a place for herself in Luke's heart. This was delicate, soft Hope, pale as moonlight. So touchable. So responsive. In her arms he could be more, do more, give more. She filled him with possibilities.

This was Luke, who had brought laughter and tears and kissed her on the heels of both. His body had been honed and shaped to muscular perfection by the job he did, but he took pains to touch her gently. It was his nature to guard and protect, and he was prepared to do that for her. It was his custom and his pleasure to give, and he was prepared to do that, too.

He gave her unexpected joy. She gave beauty he expected to experience this one time and never again.

After the heat of their coupling there was still the warmth of their loving, the time of hazy satisfaction and shimmery wonder. Wrapped together in pastel sheets and soft shadows, they touched, nibbled, nuzzled and sipped, admiring every marvelous aspect of the gifts they shared.

"You must exercise all the time." She watched her fingertips skate over the contours of his chest. "You're all muscle."

"Not all." He chuckled. "Not between the ears."

"You're beautiful there, too." She traced a circle around his nipple with the tip of her fingernail, and he sucked a quick breath through his teeth. "Does that tickle?" she asked.

He cupped her breast in his hand and imitated her teasing, until she groaned. "Does that?"

"Mmm, not exactly."

"Not exactly," he confirmed, and he kissed her eyebrow. "I've never been AWOL, but it's a tempting thought right about now."

She smiled against his cheek. "Why would you want to do a thing like that?"

"I'd like to take you places."

"You took me places tonight, Luke. Places I never even imagined."

He looked into her eyes and touched her face in a way that said he'd been with her all the way. "I want to take you other places, Hope. Places that are always pretty, always..."

"I've been other places," she said, "but never where we went tonight. I don't think anyone else can take me there. Just you."

Holding her in his arms, he rolled to his back, and she ended up on top of him. Her hair brushed over his shoulder, and he smiled wistfully. "The hell of it is, the only other place I could take you when I leave here is Fort Leonard Wood, Missouri."

"I've never been there, either." She offered a teasing smile. "Is that a place where it's always pretty?"

"It's an army post. In the last twelve years I've seen a lot of army posts."

With her thumb she explored the shape of his chin. "Some of them must have been pretty."

"You know what's pretty?" He moved his hand along the slope of her back. "Your face is pretty. Your eyes, your mouth..."

"I've never been to an army post," she told him. "I suppose they have guards at the gate."

"Mmm-hmm. Gotta have a pass to get in."

"What if I went down there and asked to see you?"

He chuckled. "They'd say, 'How could a sweet dream like you be interested in a coldhearted DI like Tracker?'"

"And I'd say, 'We can't be talking about the same man.'" She kissed his chin before she slid down to touch her lips to his chest. "The Sergeant Tracker I know has warm smooth skin all over his sleek... hard... beautiful body." Her foray led her to his abdomen."

"Sweet heaven..."

"And I can make every inch of him—"

"Feels too good to be..."

"—stand at attention."

She had loved him well. He had given her all he had, and it seemed worthless by comparison. He was still a visitor in her bed. He was in the habit of leaving what he loved behind, and he was leaving soon. The life he'd made for himself was fine for him. There were no ruffles or frills, but he told himself he didn't need those things. And he'd gotten over being homesick long ago. He had worked hard at it by stretching the bonds until they were slack. Now he was a visitor in the town where he'd grown up and a visitor in this woman's bed. Hell, he was a visitor in *any* woman's bed. After all, he belonged to the army. He was a soldier.

It wasn't that simple, and he knew it. The truth was that, after all, he was a man, and the woman who slept in his arms was not a ruffle or a frill. He had also loved her well. When he left her, he would carry a gaping hole in his chest.

Hope refused to believe she had made a mistake when she woke up New Year's Day and found that Luke was gone. The note she found in the kitchen said that he'd left before daylight to avoid "embarrassment or complications," but he'd said nothing about seeing her again before he left. Neither had he said goodbye. She'd spent New Year's Day waiting for a call that never came.

Avoiding any mention of Luke to Frances on their first day back in school had left Hope in doubt all day. Was he still home? Had he mentioned any plans to see her before he left? Had he talked about her at all? Why hadn't Frances kidded her a little, or at least dropped a hint about his frame of mind? Why hadn't Hope just leveled with her friend early that morning and spared herself the rest of the day's anguish?

She was a coward, she told herself. That was why. As the doubts tumbled over and over in her mind, she straightened out her desk and gathered her homework into her canvas satchel. She decided that the need to know outweighed the fear of finding out that Luke had left without a word of goodbye. Her shoes followed the papers into her satchel, and she bent over to put her boot on.

A pair of spit-polished black shoes stepped into the doorway of the classroom. Hope lowered her boot to the floor as her eyes traveled up the path of army-green trousers to a brass belt buckle to a narrow tie, a square chin and half-smiling lips. His dark eyes brought her visual travels to an abrupt, breath-stealing halt.

He stood there with his hands in his pockets, his jacket and his overcoat tucked behind his arms, waiting for some sign from her. She left the chair slowly, her heart racing ahead of her inefficient feet. Without taking his eyes from hers, he stepped across the threshold and pulled the door shut behind him.

"My bus leaves Mobridge at seven-thirty." He spoke quietly, but the words seemed to rebound off the high ceiling. It sounded as though he were announcing the scheduled end of the world.

"Tonight?"

He nodded. "I should be able to sleep most of the way. I've been saving up for it."

Her mouth went dry. She swallowed hard. "You came to say goodbye, then."

"I came to ask you to drive me to the station."

"Oh." She took one step closer. "How did you get here?"

"I had Frankie's car. I dropped her off this morning. She'll take me if you'd rather—"

"I'll take you," she said quickly.

"I thought we could have supper together."

"That would be nice. I'll get my—" Her hands fluttered as she thought coat, shoes—no, boots.

"Hope." She turned, and the pain in his eyes immobilized her. "I didn't want to leave you the other morning. I don't want to leave you now."

She went to him, put her arms around him and pressed her face against his neck. His overcoat nearly swallowed her as he wrapped her in his arms, and he had a wild vision of buttoning her up inside his coat and smuggling her past the gate.

"I didn't know what to think," she whispered. "After such an incredible night, to wake up and find you gone."

"I knew that if I woke you, I wouldn't be able to go. God, these last two days have been the longest of my life."

"Then we should have spent them together."

He pulled back from her and took her face in his hands. "I don't like goodbyes, Hope. I thought a clean, quick break would work out best, but...it didn't work at all. I couldn't just leave, and I can't stay. Hell, I don't know what to do. I love you."

The words made her eyes sparkle. "Then you could kiss me."

He slipped his fingers into her hair and slanted his mouth across hers. It felt like a homecoming. Before he let himself get lost in the feeling, he put his arm around her and nodded at the boots on the floor. "Get something on your feet and let's get out of here."

Luke said goodbye to Frances, transferred his duffel bag to Hope's car and got behind the wheel because he had "a couple of quick stops to make." The first was on a hill overlooking the frozen Missouri River. The sun stood low in the western sky, and the clouds were tinged with red. He parked the car near a monument that purported to mark the grave of Sitting Bull, the famous medicine man of the Hunkpapa Lakota.

"I was driving around earlier today," Luke told her, "and I wandered up here. You know, this rock is a hoax. This isn't Sitting Bull's grave."

Hope studied the marker. "It says it is."

"If it's carved in stone, it must be true, right?" He considered the inscription on the marker. "It's supposed to be a tourist attraction. Years ago a bunch of businessmen from Mobridge said they'd robbed the grave the army *claimed* to have put Sitting Bull in up at Fort Yates, which is where they took his body after he was killed. Alive, you can bet those same businessmen would have had no use for that foxy old man, but dead, they figured he might be worth something."

"People can't just go around digging up—"

"People can do anything," Luke argued. "And even if they don't succeed, they can claim it's true, and pretty soon they even believe it themselves. The army claimed that lime was poured into the casket before Sitting Bull was buried because they thought the Ghost Dancers might try to resurrect him somehow. So, according to them, there weren't any remains. But these guys said they stole some bones, and here's the monument to prove it." He raised a gloved index finger as if to scold the rock for its lie.

"Now the Lakota people say that Sitting Bull's family claimed his remains in secret, and that the army made up the lime story to save face for losing the body." Luke scanned the distant hills and the sky. "The people say that he rests near his home in Little Eagle, north of here."

"Which story do you think is true?"

"The truth is that Sitting Bull is home." He smiled as he shifted his gaze back to the river. "Even if they found some bones, those businessmen probably wouldn't have known the difference between a hand and a hoof unless there was meat on it. And the lime wouldn't have changed anything, either." He looked at Hope. "Those ties are too strong for the army to break. There are times when a man has to be home."

Hope turned her face toward the window, but, with a gentle hand under her chin, Luke brought her back. "It must be true for a woman, too," he said.

"If she has one."

"If she doesn't, she needs to make one. That's what women do." He smiled. "What do you think of my family?"

Her eyes softened. "They made me feel welcome in their home. They gave me the nicest Christmas I've ever had. I love them for that."

"It would be easier to come back from time to time if I knew that, each time I left, I'd be taking you with me." He saw something like disbelief in her eyes, and it scared him. "We could make a home, Hope. You and me. We love each other. We could start with that." The look was still there, and he rushed on. "I know we haven't had much time to get to know each other, but we'll work on it. We'll—"

Suddenly she was in his arms, and she was up to her eyebrows in the sting of bittersweet joy. "I'll come and see you," she promised. "Easter break, summer— whenever you think—"

"I want to buy you a ring before I leave." He kissed her hair, her temple, her cheek. "I want you to wear my ring. Will you do that?"

"Yes, Luke. Oh, yes, yes."

"You're my road back home, honey. I need a home. I need family. I need you to root my seed and make my love grow."

"Where will our home be?" she asked.

"Here, for starters. We won't live here, but it'll always be home to me. I understand that now." He laughed. "Beyond this, it'll be wherever the army sends us." He thought about cots and lockers and army blankets, and decided it was time for something else, if what he was held enough promise for the woman he loved. "I'm a soldier, honey, and a good one. I believe I can be a good husband and a good father, but I'll always be a soldier."

"Then I'll always love a soldier. And wherever you do your soldiering, I can teach."

He kissed her, and the temperature that dropped with the setting sun had no effect on the warmth they shared. "It was stupid of me to waste these two last days brooding over all this. I want to give you Christmas every day. We can still make it to the jewelry store and ring in the new year."

She laughed and covered the back of his hand with hers. She ran her little finger along the callused edge of his hand and wondered at the contrast of this hardness with the gentle way he touched her. "I'll take one Christmas a year if I can spend it with you. Just love me, Luke, and make every season feel this beautiful."

"How extended are we going to make this engagement?" he asked. "Give me something to circle on the calendar."

"Circle the Twelfth Moon."

"Aw, Hope," he groaned. "That's a year away. How about July, the Cherry Ripening Moon? Or August, the Moon of the Ripe Plums?"

"Do you think I'll be ripe for the picking then, too?"

"I think you're ripe right now," he teased, touching her soft brown hair. "But I'll marry you whenever you're ready. The Twelfth Moon is a nice time for lovers."

"With all that frost inside the tipi..."

"And that cozy pile of buffalo robes," he added. "A perfect time for planting a seed in a warm, deep place..."

"It's always supposed to be warm inside at Christmas," she mused, loving the warmth in his eyes. "No matter how cold the weather gets."

"Then we'll keep Christmas inside you," he promised, his mouth hovering over hers, "all year long."

* * * * *

A Note from Kathleen Eagle

"The Twelfth Moon" is really my husband Clyde's gift. It takes its special flavor from his childhood memories. Many stories get started with an author's "what if..." but this one was born with the author's husband's "I remember when..." As I worked, he would pop into the office every now and then with "I just remembered something else." It might have been an anecdote or the detail of a remembered image. As often as not, I'd have to wait until he got the laughter out before he could tell me about it.

Much of the life of the small community Clyde grew up in centered on St. Elizabeth's Mission. In fact, that was where we first met. When we moved to Bismarck a few years ago, our need for an extended family was met within our church of St. George's. We share most of our holidays with those good friends, rotating the hosting responsibilities and sharing the cooking. I'm not a keeper of prize recipes, so I'm usually assigned ordinary dishes, like candied sweet potatoes, winter-squash casserole and the children's favorite, gelatin fruit salad. One woman is our special dessert maker, and her Sin Pie is just that. Another always takes a ribbing for "stealing" recipes and "publishing" them as her own. Lest I be accused of the same, let me share a nonfood family tradition with you.

I'm a collector of Christmas ornaments, and bears are my special favorites. (Until recently the Bismarck Zoo's main attraction was Clyde the Kodiak bear.) Several years ago I decided that my collection seemed lost in the greenery of a traditional tree, so we switched to our "bear" branch trees, which are spray-painted white and planted in clay pots filled with gardening rock. I usually put up two or three and string them with miniature white lights. One tree is reserved for the bears. Another holds ornaments made over the years by our children, David, Elizabeth and Christopher. I have no needles to vacuum up, and my trees can stay put until I get good and ready to take them down—usually by Valentine's Day.

My own family is scattered across the country, but I wrote "The Twelfth Moon" after spending a memorable holiday in Orlando with my mother, my brother, Dan, and his wife, Donna, and my sister, Jill. It had been seven years since we had all been together.

The renewal of family, friendship and faith is, to me, the spirit of Christmas. May you carry Christmas in your heart throughout the year.

Kathleen Eagle

EIGHT
NIGHTS

Brooke Hastings

POTATO PANCAKES [Latkes]

3 to 4 large potatoes,
    peeled and diced
1 large onion, diced
2 eggs
4 tablespoons flour

1 teaspoon baking
    powder
1 teaspoon salt
Vegetable oil
Apple sauce or
    sour cream

Place onion, eggs, flour, baking powder, salt and half cup of diced potatoes in a blender jar. Grate, using five-second bursts; you don't want the mixture to become too watery. Add remaining potatoes a third at a time and chop, also in short bursts. The blender jar should be almost full when you're done. The consistency should be like hand grating—not too fine.

In an electric skillet, add oil to measure about one-half inch; heat at 425°F until oil is bubbling. Pour batter onto hot skillet using a ladle, and cook the pancakes, turning once, until they're brown on each side. Drain them on paper towels. You can serve the pancakes at once with apple sauce or sour cream, or save them; they refrigerate or freeze beautifully and can be reheated in a 400°F oven.

Chapter One

Sometimes Rebecca wondered how long it would take before they stopped running the stories. Five years? Ten? More? She looked away from the row of newspaper boxes in front of Macy's, already knowing what it said above the *San Francisco Sun*'s masthead: Coming Sunday...Dick Lehman, A Remembrance. She'd given the reporter an interview shortly before Thanksgiving.

Her husband had died three years ago, the victim of irrational hatred in a city that prided itself on its tolerance. The gunman, a neo-Nazi madman who'd hated everyone who wasn't exactly like himself, had been angry about a piece of legislation Dick had introduced. He'd opened fire while Dick and a fellow congressman, Otis Lincoln, were speaking in a local church—a *church*, of all places! Otis had lost a kidney; Dick had lost his life.

The city's Christmas celebration had been subdued that year, a combination of lowered flags and soaring evergreens, of black bunting and silver tinsel. The gunman had gone on trial a year later, eventually receiving a sentence of life without parole, and Rebecca had lived the tragedy all over again. Now, though, the only reminders of Dick's death were the annual memorials in the papers and on TV. Rebecca cooperated out of a sense of public duty; as Dick's widow, she was an icon in this city. Besides, the two or three weeks before Christmas were her busiest time of the year.

She worked as a concierge in one of the city's swankiest office buildings now. After Dick's death, she'd created the job from scratch, determined to live her life the way she wanted. Whatever the top officers of Stern Tower's corporate tenants requested, she did. In December that included providing a personalized shopping service in addition to wheedling hard-to-get tickets and reservations, picking up stray children, in-laws and pets, waiting in posh suburban homes for servicemen to show up and running minor but necessary errands. Although the position hadn't existed until she'd walked into David Stern's office and sold him on the idea, the executives in this building considered her one of life's necessities now.

After five hours of shopping, she dumped a final batch of packages into her limousine and told the driver to meet her at Stern Tower. The streets were so clogged with traffic that walking was faster than riding. Her office, a spacious room off the lobby, was empty when she returned, but her assistant, a student named Jeff McCray, had left a stack of messages on her desk. She quickly flipped through them.

Jeff was at the airport, picking up an executive's in-laws. There were requests for tickets to a hit musical, a New Year's Eve show at Lake Tahoe and Sunday's 49ers game. A suit needed to be returned to Wilkes Bashford, a jade statue had to be retrieved from Gump's and Mr. Stern wanted to see her at five o'clock.

She picked up the phone, using the contacts she'd made during eight years in politics to obtain the unobtainable. Her driver arrived with the packages and delivered them to the appropriate executives, Jeff got back from the airport and saw to the suit and statue, and her children walked in after school and zeroed in on the box of candy a tenant had given her for the holidays.

"One piece each," she said, and added into the phone, "Not you—my kids. They're attacking the See's truffles on my desk. Thanks for the lead on the tickets. Right. You, too. Bye now."

"Who was that?" Danny asked. Her ten-year-old son thought he could do her job better than she could.

"Billy in the 49ers office. I need six tickets for Sunday's game with the Rams." She grimaced. "Six, for Pete's sake. The president of Calmac has a group of relatives in from L.A., and he only has two season tickets."

Her seven-year-old daughter nibbled on a truffle. Sarah was quiet and shy, especially with men. "You could ask Mr. Stern," she suggested.

"Mom doesn't like to do that," Danny said.

"Why not?"

"She saves him for emergencies."

"Like when I cut my lip and he took me to the hospital?"

"Not that kind of emergency. If she ran to Mr. Stern every time she needed something, he'd get sick of her bugging him and he'd fire her." There was a devilish look on Danny's face. "And then she wouldn't have any money, and we'd all starve to death."

Sarah's eyes widened in alarm, but Rebecca assured her Danny was only teasing. After chatting with them about their day, she told them they could watch TV and got back to work. Eight calls later she hung up the phone and checked the time. "Four seats down, two to go. I have to see Mr. Stern now. Don't attack the truffles while I'm gone."

"What does he want?" Danny asked.

"I don't know. He didn't say."

Sarah slid out of her chair. "Can we come?"

The kids were obviously restless, and Stern seemed to like them well enough. "Okay, but just to say hello. You'll have to go back outside when we start talking."

David Stern was a commercial real-estate developer whose company had built some of the biggest projects in northern California. He always seemed to be in the middle of six different deals, so Rebecca wasn't surprised to find him on the phone when they entered his office. He crooked his finger at Danny and Sarah, handed them some chocolate coins wrapped in gold foil and motioned them to the couch.

Rebecca sat down between the two children and tried not to fidget. She liked David Stern—he'd been exceptionally generous both to her and to her pet charities—but he made her nervous. Like so many other men in this city, he wanted to sleep with her. While he wasn't one of the creeps who figured her for a sex-starved widow or wanted to possess the woman who'd once been married to a martyred hero, she still wasn't interested. David was a Presence in San Francisco, a charming man-about-town who kept a high social and civic profile and did more running around than a marathoner. She'd led that type of life during her marriage and had no intention of resuming it.

He hung up the phone and swung his chair toward the couch. "I'm looking really hard, Sarah, but I don't see a scar. Is it gone?"

"You have to be closer." She hesitated, then walked up to him. When he lifted her onto his lap and peered at her face, she stretched her lip against her bottom teeth to make the scar more visible.

She'd hurt herself about a year before, falling off a swing at school and knocking her top front teeth through her bottom lip. David had been standing by his secretary's desk when Rebecca had called to say she'd have to leave for the day. He'd driven her to Sarah's school, arranged for a plastic surgeon to repair the gash and waited with her at the hospital while Sarah was in the operating room.

Later, after they'd returned to her apartment and she'd put Sarah to bed, she'd impulsively thanked him with a peck on the cheek. His arm had circled her waist and he'd cupped her chin, but she'd backed away before anything could happen. She'd taken to calling him David by then, but had immediately reverted to a polite Mr. Stern. Every couple of months he asked her out, always to fabulous places, and she always turned him down. If her refusals bothered him, it didn't show. Other than the warm way he looked at her, he was the perfect boss.

He inspected Sarah's lip. "It's looking better all the time. You'll have to come by my office more often so I can keep tabs on your progress."

"Okay. Mommy needs tickets to the Niners game. Danny says you'll fire her for bugging you if she asks you for them."

Rebecca reddened. "Sarah, you shouldn't—"

"It's okay." He smiled at Danny. "Your mom is too good at her job to fire. How did your soccer team do this year?"

"Pretty good. We only lost twice."

"Because you're such a great goalie!"

Danny broke into a grin. "Yeah."

David's memory for details, even small ones such as what position Danny played, was part of the reason for his success. Still embarrassed that Sarah had mentioned the tickets, Rebecca pointed to the door. "Mr. Stern is a busy man. Go along outside now, you've taken up enough of his time."

He set Sarah on her feet. "You can have my extra tickets, but I have a favor to ask in return. I'd like you and your kids to come to my place at Tahoe next Friday and stay with Joey and Mike for a week. Linda and Phil were supposed to take them skiing, but they have to go to Tokyo."

Linda was David's ex-wife; Phil Harris was her second husband. Joey and Mike, David's sons, lived with the Harrises in the suburbs but dropped by Stern Tower every couple of days to spend the night in San Francisco. Since Rebecca's office had a TV, a refrigerator and adult supervision, David usually sent them there to wait. They were good kids, but, at ten and thirteen, too active to sit still for long.

Danny and Sarah begged Rebecca to say yes, but she hesitated. She had the time off, there was nothing to keep her in San Francisco and her kids hadn't played in the snow since they'd left Washington, but there were problems. "I need to talk it over with Mr. Stern," she said. "In private." They took the hint and trotted out of the office, glad to cooperate if it would mean a trip to the mountains.

"Now that you've put me in a position where I can't possibly refuse without seeming like an ogre..." she began.

He lazed back in his chair and folded his arms across his chest. "Did I do that, Rebecca?"

"You know you did. I haven't skied in years, and my kids don't ski at all. Other than that, I'd be glad to help out."

"I'll take Mike and Joey skiing. Of course, if you want to rent equipment and take some lessons—"

"You're going, too?" She hadn't expected that.

"Me, the boys and the Hanukkah presents. I might have to make a few quick trips to the city, but otherwise I'll be there all week."

"You want someone available in case you have to leave?"

He nodded. "It's easier than dragging the kids back and forth, and I hear you make great potato pancakes."

Rebecca wasn't dense; she realized there must be more to this than baby-sitting and cooking. "Give me an honest answer, Mr. Stern. Are you going to try to get me into bed?"

"Would it do me any good if I did?"

"You didn't answer the question."

"Yes."

She was momentarily nonplussed. Honesty was one thing, bluntness another. He smiled at her, watching her with warm, appreciative eyes, and she nervously looked away. He was a handsome, dynamic man, with dark curly hair, teasing gray eyes and a strong lean body, and she was more attracted to him than she wanted to be. "Maybe you should find someone else," she finally murmured.

"I don't want someone else. I want you. The boys like you. *I* like you. You can cook. You can get me tickets to Liza Minnelli's New Year's Eve show." He sighed. "You're the perfect woman, Rebecca. Is it any wonder I love you?"

He could get the tickets more easily than she could, but that was beside the point. "If you would stop joking—"

"Who's joking? Tell me something. Would you go out with me if you didn't work for me?"

"No."

He mimicked a missile crashing back to earth, complete with sound effects and appropriate gestures. "Shot down again. Okay, then, I won't try to get you into bed. Now will you go to the lake? Before you say no, picture your children frolicking happily in the snow. Should I call them in for a vote?"

"My vote is the only one that counts. I'd like to pay you back for all you've done, but if you're going to make me uncomfortable—"

"That's the last thing I'd want to do." He was suddenly serious. "You asked me to be honest, and I was, so don't punish me for it. I understand your position, and I respect it, okay?"

She relaxed a little. "What time do you want to leave?"

"Around noon. About the football game—"

"I still have a couple of people to try."

"Who wants the tickets and how many?"

She stood up. "Have a nice weekend."

"Fine. I'll ask your kids."

Who would promptly tell him. "Hank Reynolds of Calmac—he needs two more—but I'll take care of it. It's my job."

"And I'm your boss. I'll leave the tickets at the box office. Say no and you're fired."

"Thank you, Mr. Stern." It had been too long a week to argue. She let herself out of his office, relieved that she didn't have to disappoint Danny and Sarah but dreading January's credit-card bills. She spent a fortune every year on Hanukkah presents in order to compete with Christmas and compensate her children for not having a father. Buying snow gear wasn't going to help.

David waited until she'd closed the door, then phoned his ex-wife and suggested she join her husband on his business trip to Tokyo. It wasn't hard to talk her into it; she'd only planned to stay home because of the holidays and was glad to have David take the boys. Mike and Joey had argued with Phil from the beginning, but the fights had grown worse as they'd gotten older, and it was putting a strain on Linda's marriage.

After hanging up the phone, he stretched contentedly, pleased with the way things were shaping up. Hiring Rebecca Lehman had been strictly business—amenities like concierge service had helped make Stern Tower one of the most desirable locations in the city—but he couldn't pretend that was true of what had followed. He'd knocked out a wall to enlarge her office and bought her a refrigerator and TV so her kids would be comfortable when she had to have them there after school. He'd put a limousine at her disposal eight hours a day. He'd told her to set her own hours and hired her a part-time assistant to pick up the slack. Some people would have done those things because she was the widow of a man who'd been loved deeply in this city, and others would have done them because she was so good at her job, but David had had an additional motive. It seemed to him that he'd wanted her forever.

He wasn't sure when the wanting had turned to loving, but he'd first become aware of it after they'd brought Sarah home from the hospital. An innocent kiss on the cheek and he'd been lost. Rebecca was a pretty woman, with thick dark hair, gentle brown eyes and a soft, desirable body, but the attraction had been more than physical even in the beginning. She was a wonderful mother and, in her own quiet way, a force for progress and understanding in this city. She was honest, valiant and sweet. He'd felt comfortable with her from the moment they'd met.

He'd been immensely frustrated when she'd withdrawn that afternoon, but he'd told himself to be patient. Obviously she liked him, so maybe she was still bereaved. Maybe she was shy or simply cautious.

Three months later she'd started dating again, and he'd realized she was none of those things. He didn't know what the problem was, but a week in the same house would give him a chance to find out—and change her mind.

Chapter Two

They flew to South Lake Tahoe in David's private jet, the first time Rebecca had been in a plane since wrapping up her affairs in Washington after Dick's death. The life she led now was a far cry from the days when she'd zipped to Dick's district in San Francisco at the drop of a hat or joined him on only a few hours' notice for meetings and speeches in places like Los Angeles and New York. The only trips she took nowadays were by car—modest vacations to Southern California and visits with Dick's parents in Redding and her own family in Fresno.

She was close to all of them, especially to her older sister, Emily, who'd provided unstinting comfort and solace these past few years. Rebecca hated to burden people with her problems, but when things got really tough, Emily was the one she turned to. They weren't just sisters by now; they were best friends.

Rebecca much preferred her life now to those fast-paced days as a congressman's wife and aide, but even if she hadn't, there wouldn't have been anything she could do about it. Dick had been a public defender before his days as an assemblyman and congressman and hadn't left much in the way of assets—only a heavily mortgaged house near Washington that she'd traded for an apartment in San Francisco, and some insurance money that she'd lived on while she was picking up the pieces of her life.

She was happy with the choices she'd made, even proud of them. Many of Dick's colleagues had admired her political savvy and offered her jobs after his death, but she'd turned them down. A delegation from the party had approached her about filling his seat, but she'd declined. Any number of his supporters would have created positions for her if she'd asked them to, but she hadn't. Instead, inspired by an article about an office-building concierge in Dallas, she'd drawn up a list of possible buildings in San Francisco, eliminated the ones owned by people she knew and sent out letters of application under her maiden name. David Stern had been the only one to grant her an interview.

He'd recognized her the moment she'd walked in, but she truly believed he would have given her a chance even if she hadn't been Dick Lehman's widow. Things had worked out well; he had a more desirable building and she had a job that was flexible enough for the mother of two small children. In fact, she saw more of her kids now than when Dick was alive. She felt a stab of remorse whenever she thought about the years she'd spent fewer than half the eight nights of Hanukkah with them, but those days were behind her forever.

Janet MacDonald, the teenage daughter of David's next-door neighbors, met them at the airport, driving a Ford Bronco David kept at his house in the mountains. His home wasn't the lakeside showplace Rebecca had expected or even a condo near one of the ski areas, but an unpretentious house in an ordinary residential area. There was a snow-covered hillside across the street, and since school was out, it was dotted with children and sleds. David's sons had barely gotten inside before they asked to go out to play. He agreed, then added, "If anyone mentions Santa Claus, remember to keep your mouths shut about the fact that he doesn't exist." Christmas was on Sunday, so it was bound to come up.

Joey, the ten-year-old, rolled his eyes. "We know that, Dad. We're not *idiots*!"

"Tell that to the MacDonalds. They still like to remind me about the time you almost ruined Patty's Christmas."

"I was only six then. I didn't know any better." He looked at Danny. The two boys had always liked each other and had chattered nonstop about sports on the way up. "You wanna come? You can share my sled."

"Can I, Mom?"

Rebecca unzipped a suitcase. "Sure. Sarah? Do you want to go, too?"

She shook her head and sidled closer. "I want to stay with you."

"Your mom and I need to go shopping," David told her. "Why don't you help us?"

"I could take you sledding when we get back." Rebecca pulled out the kids' snow gear, realized she hadn't removed the tags yet and fished a pair of embroidery scissors out of her purse. "We could ride together. Would you like that?"

Sarah smiled and nodded, captivating David completely. He liked the idea of becoming a father to this fragile, red-haired child and her mischievous older brother.

His sons went upstairs for their boots and parkas while Danny and Sarah dressed in the living room. The tags on their clothing told David that Rebecca had gone shopping especially for this trip, and he felt guilty and frustrated about it. In a city as costly as San Francisco, her budget was bound to be tight, but she had a streak of pride a mile wide about accepting what she considered to be charity. He couldn't even pay her more than a fair-market salary without insulting her, so reimbursing her for the clothing was out of the question.

He asked Mike to keep an eye on the two younger boys, then led the way outside. The shopping center was only a few miles from his house, the stores crowded with shoppers searching for last-minute Christmas presents. David walked up and down the supermarket aisles with Rebecca and Sarah, talking about their meals and deciding what to buy. Divorce had forced him to learn how to shop and cook, but it had never been this much fun before.

Rebecca was having fun, too, enjoying the unexpected vacation, the respite from the pressures of daily life and the special Christmas feeling in the air. This wasn't her holiday, but she liked the bright decorations, the beautiful carols and the friendly, giving spirit of the season.

She took out her wallet at the check stand, but put it away when David insisted he would accept her money only if he could pay her for helping with the kids. Once the order had been rung up, the checker smiled at Sarah and handed her a candy cane. "Have you been good this year?" he asked. "Is Santa going to bring you lots of nice presents?"

Sarah looked at Rebecca uncertainly. Although this had happened before, she never knew how to answer. Rebecca was about to rescue her when she giggled and told the checker, "I've been *very* good. Have you?"

"Not as good as you, I'll bet." He finished packing their bags and wished them a Merry Christmas.

As they left the store, Rebecca remarked, "That was an interesting answer you gave the checker."

"It was quicker than explaining why we don't have Christmas, and anyway, it made him feel good." She paused. "Was that okay, Mommy?"

"It was fine." Rebecca didn't care whether Sarah explained or played along as long as she was clear in her own mind about who and what she was. When you were only seven, and bombarded with Christmas by music on the radio, specials on TV, art projects and pageants in school and the frantic excitement of your friends, it could be difficult.

Back at the house, David put the groceries away while Rebecca unpacked the suitcases. There were only four bedrooms, so she and Sarah were sharing a room while Danny bunked in with Joey. Afterward she took Sarah sledding. After several runs together on Mike's Flexible Flyer, Sarah asked to try it on her own; she was flushed with pride when she reached the bottom of the hill successfully. That moment alone was worth the trip to the lake.

David had been on the phone when they'd left the house but showed up half an hour later carrying a large metal saucer that looked as if it had crashed over one too many rocks. He attracted the attention of the four children and some of their friends from the neighborhood, who teased him about what a wreck it was. "Kids were tougher in my day," he retorted. "We couldn't afford fancy sleds. Isn't that right, Rebecca?"

"I wouldn't know. I'm from Fresno." It didn't snow there.

"You've never ridden in one of these?"

She might have in Washington if she hadn't been so busy being Mrs. Dick Lehman. "No," she said.

"There's a first time for everything." He grabbed her hand. "Come on."

"I get dizzy—"

"Chicken."

The kids repeated the accusation, teasing her until she gave in. She didn't realize David planned to join her until they reached the top of the hill, and then it was too late; the kids were watching and hollering. She sat down first; David wrapped his arms and legs around her and squeezed in behind her. She was intensely aware of his warmth and strength—aroused by it, frightened by it, annoyed by it. Her heart began to race. If this was his idea of not making her uncomfortable...

He pushed off with his heels, and the saucer slid downward. As they picked up speed, the exhilaration of falling and spinning crowded out every other sensation. Then David leaned to his right, sending them whirling off the well-worn path toward some trees, and they careened out of control.

The child in her took over. Shrieking that he was crazy, she leaned into the security of his arms as he rocked to make the ride wilder. Finally, when the trees were looming ahead, he stuck out his feet to slow the saucer down. The pressure he applied wasn't even, so they jerked sideways. David tumbled backward onto the snow and slid downward a few yards, taking a laughing Rebecca with him, her back flush against his chest.

A moment later he sat both of them up. "That was great. How about another run?"

She wriggled off his lap and grinned at him. "It was suicidal, and no thanks."

The sky was a light cloudless blue with snow-dusted evergreens in the foreground and ice-capped mountains beyond. He stared upward, smiling. "It's so beautiful up here.... When I stand on top of the mountain and look out over the lake, I feel as if it's the closest I'll get to heaven on this earth. I'll rent you and the kids skis tomorrow morning and sign you up for some lessons. I want you to see for yourself. And before you start arguing about who should pay, remember that it would have cost me hundreds of dollars to bring a baby-sitter up here this week, assuming I even could have found one."

Rebecca knew he was right, but skiing lessons were outrageously expensive. When she didn't reply, he stood up and pulled her to her feet. "Your kids will have a great time," he said. It was the ultimate bribe.

She returned to the house to make dinner while David stayed with the kids. By the time they came in, the table was set, a roast was in the oven and she was mixing up *latkes*, or potato pancakes, a traditional Hanukkah treat. The secret to good *latkes* wasn't just in the recipe, but in frying them in plenty of oil. If you were worried about calories, it was better to eat something else.

The kids washed and changed, then fetched a box of Hanukkah decorations out of a closet and began putting them up. They were positioning a menorah lit by electric candles in the kitchen window when David strolled in, his hair damp from the shower. He sniffed appreciatively, then remarked that the table looked very nice.

It was Friday night, the beginning of the Sabbath, so Rebecca had set out candlesticks, a silver wine goblet and a tray and embroidered coverlet for the Sabbath *challah*, a braided egg bread. Everything was hers, even the *challah* and kosher wine; she'd brought them from home in case David didn't have them. As far as she could tell, he didn't.

He filched a potato pancake that was draining on some paper towels. "I didn't realize you were so religious. I hope it isn't a problem for you to be here."

"It's okay—I don't keep kosher. There are just certain customs I like to observe, like saying the blessings on Friday nights." It was something she'd done far too seldom when the kids were little.

Although David wasn't used to that, he certainly didn't object. On the contrary, he liked the way Rebecca was turning this house into a home, even if it was only for a week. He finished the potato pancake and reached for another. "These are terrific."

She slapped his hand. "The rest are for dinner."

She looked so adorable guarding the pancakes that he wanted to grab her and kiss her. It was a feeling he'd had repeatedly, especially when they'd tumbled into the snow and she'd wound up on his lap. Given how well they got along and how she'd trembled in his arms when he'd sat behind her on the saucer, he was sure she'd eventually stop running. If he was lucky, it would happen before the week was out.

Before they started eating, Rebecca and Sarah lit the Sabbath candles. Rebecca was surprised when David offered to chant the kiddush over the wine; although he belonged to a San Francisco synagogue and supported a variety of Jewish causes, he obviously didn't say Shabbat blessings every week. He'd probably learned them in religious school—everyone did—but she figured he'd forgotten them by now. Afterward Mike blessed the bread.

David helped her bring the food to the table, then carved the roast. Watching him, she mused about how nice it was to have a man at the head of her table. The thought surprised her, as did the sudden lump in her throat. This was crazy—she wasn't pining for another husband.

Sarah lit the Hanukkah candles as soon as dinner was over—first the shammes, or servant candle, and then, using the shammes, one candle for the first night. Sundown was the more traditional time for this ritual, but they'd wanted the kids to be able to enjoy their presents without having to sit through dinner first. They chanted three blessings, the first two specifically for Hanukkah and the third for the onset of holy days and festivals. It gave Rebecca great joy to share these occasions with her children, but the third blessing, the Shehecheyanu, was always difficult for her. Although they sang it in Hebrew, which she read but didn't understand, she knew what the words meant.

Blessed is the Lord our God, Ruler of the universe, for giving us life, for sustaining us and for enabling us to reach this season.

She knew what usually happened and was determined it wouldn't happen again, but it was hopeless. Her voice was husky with unshed tears by the middle of the blessing; by the end, the tears were rolling down her cheeks. She threw her napkin on the table and ran upstairs.

David, who'd never known Rebecca to be anything but efficient and even-tempered, was stunned. Not only was he concerned about *her*, he was worried about her children, who were sure to be upset by the way she'd broken down.

He glanced at them apprehensively. Sarah looked a little sad, but Danny, who'd put his arm around her to comfort her, seemed unfazed by the incident. When he realized David was watching him, he said nonchalantly, "It's the Shehecheyanu. It always gets to her—ever since Dad died. You know. We're here and he's not."

David struggled for something safe to say. "I understand. It must be really tough . . . on all of you."

"I guess." Danny paused, then added with the innocent candor of childhood, "To be honest, he wasn't around all that much. Sarah doesn't even remember him very well, but it upsets her when Mom cries. I'm used to it, though. If I give her a hug, she always snaps out of it."

"Then maybe you should go upstairs."

Sarah looked at David shyly, her sadness fading. "I think you should, Mr. Stern. You're the adult."

"Yeah, Dad. Why don't *you* go up and hug her?" Mike gave David a typical teenage smirk. He seemed to know exactly what his father was up to, and judging by the look Danny and Joey exchanged, so did they. Even Sarah smiled.

It was pointless to take offense. "It sounds as if the four of you have been talking."

"A little. We figured out that you didn't even offer to take us skiing until Mrs. Lehman said she would come along." There was an eruption of knowing looks and smothered giggles. Playing to his audience, Mike drawled, "Are you in love with her, Dad?"

"That's none of your business—"

"I knew it! Didn't I tell you, Joey?"

It was either admit the truth or live with giggles and whispers for the rest of the week. "Okay, yes. I'd marry her tomorrow if she were willing, but she's going to take some persuading. What do you guys think about that?"

They thought it was fine. His kids liked Rebecca, her kids seemed to like him, and most important of all, Sarah and Danny hadn't been as close to the saintly Dick Lehman as David had feared. He was only human; he couldn't compete with a legend.

It wouldn't always be this easy—there would be doubts, fears and resentments along the way—but for the moment, David had four powerful allies in his corner. They seemed to consider it a wonderful conspiracy and promised not to breathe a word to Rebecca. Not counting on it, he winked at them and headed up the stairs.

Chapter Three

Rebecca felt like a fool. Crying was one thing; running upstairs and shutting herself in her bedroom was another. She didn't understand why she'd gotten so unhinged, especially when she'd made it through the Yom Kippur memorial service this year with only a few tears.

She sighed and reached for a tissue. David walked in as she was blowing her nose, neither knocking nor asking permission. She told herself that was only to be expected. He hadn't made a fortune by being shy and retiring.

He sat down on the bed. "How are you doing?"

"All right. It's the time of year, I guess, and the Shehecheyanu and—I don't know. I just felt so—it just hurt so much." Her eyes filled with tears. "I don't know what's wrong with me. I thought I was doing fine, and then this happened...." She sniffed and shook her head.

He put his arms around her, settled her against his chest and rubbed her neck, treating her with such gentleness that she started crying all over again. Her thoughts were disjointed. She was here and Dick wasn't.... David felt so solid and safe.... It was Hanukkah, the children were waiting downstairs, and she needed to get a grip on herself.

"It's okay," he murmured. "That prayer—when you've lost someone you were close to, it's so wrenching and poignant. Every Passover..." He took a deep breath. "It reminds me of my older brother. I understand your reaction."

She'd read somewhere that his brother had died in his teens, but she didn't know the details. "You lost him around Passover?"

"The cancer was everywhere by then, but Mike was determined to have one last seder with us, and he did." He smoothed her hair. There were things he wanted to tell her about Mike, but this was the wrong time. "December must be tough on you—the holidays, the stories in the paper and on TV.... People loved Dick. They don't want to forget him."

"He was a wonderful man," she agreed softly.

It killed David to admit it, but it was true. Lehman *had* been wonderful—the champion of the poor, the protector of the helpless and the defender of the sick. Half the city was waiting for the second coming.

"There's so much about him I miss," she added. "The work we did together, the talks we had..."

"Mmm." He kept rubbing her neck.

Rebecca relaxed in his arms. She'd never discussed her marriage with anyone except Emily, who'd listened sympathetically and encouraged her to follow her own instincts, but suddenly she wanted to talk about it with David. He hadn't been one of Dick's supporters—he wasn't even a Democrat—so he wouldn't be offended by how she'd really felt. And maybe she needed him to understand that a certain type of life wasn't for her.

"There are some things I *don't* miss," she murmured.

That was the best news David had had all year. Treading carefully, he said, "Tell me about it."

"I was so young when we met—only a college student." She'd been a junior at Berkeley, just twenty-one. "I never even thought I'd meet him when I started working on his campaign, much less that he'd notice me and ask me out. He was so much older—almost forty—that I refused, not because I didn't want to but because I thought it would hurt his public image. He talked me into it, though." She sighed. Dick had talked her into lots of things, including quitting school, getting married and going to work for him. "I was so in love I was thrilled to do whatever he asked, but once we had children things got complicated. Dick wanted me to keep handling constituents' problems for him. He'd gotten used to having me at social events. It meant leaving the kids with a housekeeper a lot of the time, and that wasn't my idea of how a family should be. I hated being away from them so much."

David nodded, picturing the life she must have led. Lehman's national reputation would have put him on everyone's list for receptions and conferences. He'd probably gone out several nights a week when he was in town and traveled extensively in between. It was little wonder he'd wanted Rebecca with him; with her flawless political instincts and her ability to charm everyone she met, she'd been a tremendous asset. Between work and Washington's social whirl, there wouldn't have been much time for a family life.

She obviously felt guilty about that, so David did his best to reassure her. "Sarah and Danny are great kids. You're a wonderful mother."

"I try my best, but when I was married... I insisted on cutting back on the time I spent in the office once the kids were born, but it was hard to make up for..." She hesitated.

"For what?" he prompted softly.

"For—for the fact that they barely had a father." He could hear the defensiveness in her voice. "You'll probably think I'm awful for saying this, but it was hard to be married to a saint. He had plenty of time for the tired, the poor and the huddled masses, but when it came to his wife and children—to *our* problems, to *our* hurts and pains . . ." She swallowed hard. "I did love him. I admired him so much, and his work was so important, but damn it, David, the kids should have been important, too."

"And you."

"And me." It was a relief to admit her feelings. She should have mattered more. She'd deserved more of Dick's attention.

Still, he'd done so much good in his life, and he'd been so busy with the awful problems in this benighted world. . . . She pulled out of David's arms. "Maybe it was my fault. Things might have been different if I'd fought harder for the kids—made him understand their needs."

David doubted it. Men like Dick Lehman believed too strongly in their own ideas and goals to worry about other people's opinions. They seemed more comfortable with the troubles of strangers than the problems of those closest to them. Still, Rebecca had loved the man. Only a fool would have criticized him to her face.

"You did the best you could," he said. "It was a tough situation with no right answer for everyone." She looked at him gratefully and excused herself to wash her face.

Having been married to a woman whose moods could last for days, David expected a difficult evening, but by the time they got downstairs and the children fetched their presents, Rebecca was animated and smiling. Hanukkah had its serious side, but the gift giving was primarily for children, and she obviously took enormous pleasure in their excitement.

The presents Danny and Sarah opened—baseball cards of two Hall of Famers and the season's hottest new doll—weren't as expensive as Mike's sweater or Joey's computer game, but to David's relief, the disparity wasn't glaring. Children traditionally gave their parents presents as well, but only one or two rather than one for each night. Rebecca got a pair of earrings and David received some sheepskin slippers.

Afterward they sang traditional songs and played dreidel. The dreidel is a four-sided top with a Hebrew letter on each facet, and players take turns spinning it, losing or gaining pennies or nuts depending on which letter comes up.

After Sarah had spun, Rebecca said to her, "What letter is that? I've never seen it before."

She rolled her eyes. "Yes, you have. That's a *pay*."

"A *pay*?" Rebecca pretended to be stumped. "It's supposed to say *nun, gimel, hay* and *shin*, for the first letters of the phrase *Nes gadol haya sham*, which means—"

"A great miracle happened there," Sarah translated with exaggerated patience. She'd learned all this in Sunday school. "This is an Israeli dreidel and it has a *pay* instead of a *shin* and it means 'A great miracle happened *here*.' *Nes gadol haya po*." She looked at David. "Did you get this in Jerusalem?"

He nodded. "I went there a few years ago."

"I want to go someday. You can take me." She gave the dreidel to Joey. "It's your turn."

"You didn't put any pennies in," Danny pointed out.

"I forgot," she said, and giggled. Rebecca decided there was a streak of larceny in the child, not to mention an incipient case of Jewish princessitis. Where had she gotten the idea that everything she wanted was hers for the asking?

"Just because Mr. Stern invited you to Lake Tahoe, that doesn't mean he'll take you to Israel," Rebecca said. "It's much farther away, and it costs a lot more to go there."

"I know where it is. I found it on my globe." She gave a penny to each player. "Hurry up, Joey, or my mother will ask about Hanukkah." Although Joey could have no idea what she hoped to avoid, he spun right away.

"You won't escape indefinitely," Rebecca teased, but let them continue playing. The children always grumbled when she asked what Hanukkah was all about, but they always learned something new, too. The message behind the holiday was relevant to anyone's life.

An hour later David went to make some phone calls while Rebecca cleaned up the kitchen and got the kids to bed. The next morning they drove to a ski shop so she could rent equipment for the week and then backtracked to a ski area near the house. Rebecca, Danny and Sarah took a lesson on the bunny hill at the base of the mountain while David and his sons headed for the more challenging runs higher up.

It was a glorious day, sunny and crisp but not too cold. Having skied in college, Rebecca found the techniques came back to her quickly. Danny was brash enough to zip down the hill right away, but the ski instructor persuaded him to take things step-by-step. Sarah watched five- and six-year-olds giggle after spills and make it to the bottom in one piece and decided she could, too. After the lesson she snowplowed slowly down the hill while Danny planted his skis parallel to each other, got into a crouch and went as fast as he could. They practiced a while, then met David and his sons in the base lodge and ate lunch.

In the afternoon David, Mike and Joey headed back up the mountain while Rebecca and her children took another lesson. She was amazed by how quickly the kids improved; a few more lessons and they'd be doing parallel turns. They practiced for the rest of the day, eventually graduating to harder terrain higher up the mountain.

She was tired when they got home, but so exhilarated by the exercise and beautiful surroundings that she insisted on cooking and serving dinner. Her exhaustion finally caught up with her after the Hanukkah candles had been lit and the presents opened. David and the boys cleaned up while she and Sarah showered and went to bed.

She awoke the next morning feeling as if she were swathed in gauze. She looked blearily at the other bed. It was empty. Sarah was already up.

She checked the time, then closed her eyes. The clock said nine o'clock, but it was too early to move. She slowly became aware of muscles she'd forgotten she had. So much for the assumption that she'd been in good shape.

She was fantasizing about hot baths and massages when someone knocked on the door. She turned toward the sound as David walked in with a breakfast tray. "Rise and shine," he said cheerfully. "It's time to hit the slopes."

She looked out the window. It was another beautiful day. "I'm going to die," she moaned.

"It's unhealthy to die on an empty stomach." He settled the tray on her lap as she struggled to sit up. "You can't be sore, can you?"

Only a sadist would have asked a question he already knew the answer to. "After walking up and down all those hills in San Francisco? Of course not."

"You use different muscles." He pulled over a chair and helped himself to coffee. "The juice is fresh-squeezed and the pancakes are made according to the secret Stern-family recipe. Eat, Rebecca."

"Yes, Mother." She tasted a pancake, told him it was very good and continued eating. After a few minutes she felt human enough to remember she was wearing ancient flannel pajamas and hadn't washed her hair since Friday. She was conventional enough—or vain enough—to be embarrassed.

"Thanks for breakfast," she said. "It was sweet of you to bring it up." Instead of taking the hint and leaving, he nonchalantly topped off his coffee. "Where are the children?" she finally asked.

"With the MacDonalds, checking out their Christmas presents." Rebecca had met the MacDonald clan the previous day; in addition to Janet, who'd picked them up at the airport, and Patty, who no longer believed in Santa Claus, there were two teenage boys. "Their living room looks like a bomb hit it—toys and clothes all over the place." He grinned at her. "The kids'll be there for hours."

She couldn't tell whether he was teasing or serious. "If you're thinking what I think you're thinking, stop thinking it."

"I can't help it, Rebecca. Those pajamas are so sexy they're driving me crazy." He tugged at the covers, forcing her to grab her breakfast tray to keep it from falling off. "Stop being so paranoid. The only thing I had in mind was a mission of mercy."

She clutched the covers. "Airing me out?"

"Massaging your aching muscles. Let go of the covers. You can finish breakfast while I do your calves."

"You're sure you have no ulterior motives?"

"Would it get me anywhere if I did?"

"No, and haven't we had this conversation before?"'

"Yes, and I'm a realist. I don't waste my time wanting what I can't have." David wasn't going to tell her she wasn't in that particular category. "What's it going to be? Terminal misery or blessed relief?"

Rebecca felt as if she'd been trampled by oxen, but it was stupid to borrow trouble. "You promise you're only doing this because you're a nice guy?"

"Absolutely," he said, reasoning that only a nice guy would put himself through the agony of touching her without making love to her.

He pulled the covers aside and sat down on the bed. As his hands circled her left calf, Rebecca told herself that the firm but gentle pressure of his thumbs felt soothing and nothing else. In fact, it was sheer bliss. If she hadn't been so sore—if it hadn't been such a relief—she would have told him to stop. Something this nice had to be bad for you.

When she ran out of food, he set the tray on the floor and settled her legs on his lap. Whatever thoughts she had of pulling them away went straight out of her head when he massaged the backs of her knees. Never mind bliss; this was paradise. Besides, she was perfectly decent—the pajamas covered everything essential. She lay down and closed her eyes, murmuring that he was a miracle worker.

David smiled and moved his fingers higher. Touching Rebecca's legs was arousing the hell out of him, but it was worth it. All that mattered was that she was letting him closer. He worked his way upward, kneading her muscles until they were warm and loose, enjoying her soft sighs of pleasure. There was no question that the massage was having the effect he wanted; he could see her erect nipples, even through the flannel of her pajamas.

When he reached her thighs, her eyes drifted open. "David . . ." His name was a drowsy, sensual murmur that went straight to his loins.

"What's wrong?" he asked. "Am I hurting you?"

Rebecca looked away. He was turning her on, not hurting her, but if she encouraged him by admitting it, she'd never get rid of him. "No. You're just—this is getting too intimate."

"Intimate is unbuttoning your pajamas and kissing your breasts. This is a therapeutic massage." He kneaded her thigh. "How does that feel?"

"Wonderful, but—"

"So relax and enjoy it. I won't make a pass at you."

"You'd like to, though, and that makes it a bad idea."

"Somehow I'll manage to control myself," he said drily, and kept massaging her. "Besides, I don't have time to make love to you. I have to leave soon."

"Leave?" She felt a stab of disappointment totally at odds with her protests.

"I have to go back to San Francisco. There's a deal I need to work on."

"People are meeting you on Christmas?"

"If it makes them money, they'd meet me on Mars. It shouldn't take more than a few days. You want me to massage your thighs or don't you?"

Maybe it was his offhand manner and maybe it was the fact that he'd be gone for the next several days, but the massage suddenly seemed to be exactly what he'd claimed—therapeutic. "All right. Maybe just a little more." She closed her eyes again.

David finished her legs, then coaxed her onto her stomach and massaged her back and shoulders. His reward came after he'd finished, when she looked at him and sleepily thanked him. The unwitting desire in her eyes took his breath away. He meant to take full advantage of that look as soon as he got back from San Francisco.

Chapter Four

The house was empty and quiet by the time Rebecca dressed and went downstairs. She felt both guilty and relieved when she realized David was gone—guilty because she'd lingered in the shower when she could have been driving him to the airport and relieved he'd be in San Francisco for the next several days. Somehow, in the space of only forty-eight hours, their relationship had changed.

She called him David now, as did the kids. She'd let him pay for their lunch yesterday without a word of protest. He touched her with casual familiarity and strolled into her room whenever he felt like it, and she didn't object. Other men she knew—her relatives, her old friends—might have done those things, too, but David wasn't in either category.

Her problem was that she kept forgetting that. She allowed him to comfort her, pay her bills and massage her calves and told herself he was simply being nice—a chum, a pal—but a pal didn't look at a woman the way David looked at her. A pal didn't leave a woman languid, confused and aroused. And he didn't have a history of going after what he wanted not necessarily in a straightforward manner.

It was ironic, but the very thing that made her reject David also protected her. He was as obsessed with business as Dick had been with politics, so he was always making phone calls, attending meetings and going on business trips. She knew better than to become involved with another man who would put her second in his life, but there was no danger of getting in too deep with David. He was too busy with the next three business deals to pursue her seriously.

In the meantime there was enough dirty clothing around the house to wash and open a store, and the kids had left toys, papers and dishes on almost every available surface. They needed to shape up, but it was Hanukkah and she didn't mind spoiling them a little longer. She did the housework, then went next door to fetch them home.

The MacDonalds were openly curious about her, perhaps because she was Dick Lehman's widow, perhaps because they'd known David for years and would have wondered about any woman he'd brought to Lake Tahoe. Ellen MacDonald asked Rebecca and the kids for Christmas dinner at three o'clock, and Rebecca accepted, but they left immediately after the meal despite Ellen's coaxing to stay. Sarah was tired, Mike looked bored and Danny and Joey were getting rowdy.

A weekend together was generally as much as two ten-year-old boys could tolerate, so Rebecca wasn't surprised when a fight erupted in the middle of a computer game. She ended it by sending Danny to his room with a book and telling Joey to stay where he was. He edged forward defiantly, then thought the better of it and returned to his computer. Mike, meanwhile, was down in the master bedroom talking on the phone, and Sarah was asleep on the living room couch.

Rebecca had twenty quiet minutes with a magazine before Mike wandered into the kitchen and began rooting around in the refrigerator. He was probably more bored than hungry—he'd shoveled in an amazing amount of food at the MacDonalds' house—but she joined him in the kitchen and asked if she could fix him something to eat.

"There's nothing good in this house," he said glumly.

He meant there was no junk food. David had indulged the kids and bought some, but it was long gone. "I could make you a chicken-salad sandwich," she offered.

"I had turkey for dinner."

Not to mention two different kinds of pie and ice cream, but she tried again. "How about some potato pancakes?"

"I'm sick of them. Let's go to the store."

"It's Christmas. Everything's closed."

"Not everything. There's a store on Highway 50—" The phone rang, distracting him. He brightened and lunged for it, probably hoping it was one of his friends. "Hello?" His enthusiasm faded. "We're fine. How's Tokyo?" He turned to Rebecca. "It's my mother. Could you ask Joey to pick it up?"

Since the upstairs phone was in the room where Danny was reading, Joey took the call in David's room. Rebecca returned to the living room and picked up her magazine. With the exception of the master bedroom, the first floor of the house was completely open, so she couldn't help hearing Mike's end of the conversation.

Looking less sullen, he told his mother how well he'd done skiing and described what the MacDonald kids had gotten for Christmas. Rebecca turned to the article about New Year's resolutions and how to keep them.

Several minutes went by. Then, howling like a tornado that had just swept in, Mike said, "I'm not gonna go! No way! It's not fair!" His shouts roused Sarah, who yawned and asked why he was screaming. Rebecca answered that she had no idea.

After a brief respite, he started yelling again. "I don't have to if I don't want to. I can stay with Dad." There was another pause. "I can take care of myself. I'm not leaving my friends and my school...." He listened for a moment. "Dad will if we ask him to. He likes Sausalito."

Obviously the Harrises planned to move, and Mike wasn't happy about the idea. "There's nothing to talk about," he shouted. "I don't want to go, and you can't make me. Anyway, all you care about is Phil, and I hate him!" He slammed down the phone and ran upstairs.

Joey emerged a minute later, looked around for Mike and ran upstairs, too. "Maybe they're moving to Tokyo," Sarah said. "They told us their stepfather goes there all the time. They don't like him because he always yells at them."

"About what?" Rebecca asked.

"He says they have awful taste in music and don't help enough around the house and that they'd rather play ball and watch TV than do their homework."

In other words, they were typical kids. Rebecca was torn between wanting to comfort them and feeling this was none of her business. In the end her maternal instincts won out, and she went upstairs. All three boys were in Mike's room, talking softly. They clammed up when they noticed her in the doorway and exchanged incomprehensible looks.

"Are your mother and stepfather leaving California?" she asked Mike.

He nodded. "They're moving to Japan. My stepfather's bank is putting him in charge of its operation there. I called Dad to tell him about it but he wasn't home. I left a message on his answering machine to call us back."

Rebecca sat down between Mike and Joey and put an arm around each of them. "I know you're upset, but maybe you'll feel better once you have a chance to talk to your dad. How about a movie tonight? Would that cheer you up?"

Mike shrugged, Joey mumbled, "Maybe," and Danny said, "Their stepfather's a real jerk, Mom. If you marry anybody that bad, I'm leaving home."

"I'm not going to marry anyone, period, so you don't have to worry." Rebecca didn't want to be drawn into a conversation about Phil Harris—she'd never even met the man.

"How about marrying David? He's—"

Mike poked him. "Danny..."

"I was just kidding. Can we see that new science-fiction movie where aliens take over the earth?"

"You can if it's playing here. Let's check the paper."

The movie was being shown in the theater complex near the supermarket, as was an animated feature Sarah wanted to see. Mike left a second message on David's machine, saying they were going out and would be back by nine, and then everyone piled into the Bronco. The same four children who had picked at the hamburgers Rebecca fixed for dinner claimed they were starving when they reached the theater, so she bought them popcorn and sodas. Mike and Joey were so subdued she would have done anything to put smiles on their faces.

They were happier after the movie, but when the time came to open their Hanukkah presents, she noticed they chose gifts from David. They played Monopoly afterward, repeatedly checking the time, waiting to hear from their father. When he hadn't called by eleven, Mike tried him again, and this time he was home. Joey got on the extension in the kitchen, saying very little but finally smiling. David had apparently reassured them, but Rebecca was annoyed with him for not calling back.

Joey held out the phone to her as Mike walked out of the bedroom. "Dad wants to talk to you." She turned around so the children couldn't hear her.

"I'm sorry you got caught in the middle of a family crisis," David said. "It was obvious Phil's bank was grooming him for Japan, but I thought the move was a few years away. I also figured they'd give him more notice."

She frowned. "Mike didn't mention a date. I didn't know there was one."

"I don't think Linda got to that—they didn't give her a chance. It's February first."

She'd been speaking softly but lowered her voice still more. "You've spoken to her?"

"She left a message on my machine after she called the boys, complaining about how they'd reacted."

"You knew about the move and how upset the boys were and you still didn't call, even though you'd gotten Mike's messages?"

"I listened to the tape when I got home, but I had five people in the house and we were about to start a meeting. I couldn't tell them to wait while I spoke to a hysterical teenager. Besides, what was I going to say? That I'd move to Sausalito so he could stay in the same school district? I happen to prefer San Francisco, and for all Linda's complaints about the boys being lazy slobs who are rude to Phil, I doubt she'd give them up without a fight." He sighed. "Hell, Rebecca, I don't know what I'm going to do."

"What did you *say* you would do?"

"I promised them they wouldn't have to move to Japan if they didn't want to. Look, I was making some phone calls when Mike reached me, and I need to finish them before it gets any later. Take the kids skiing tomorrow. The boys can go off by themselves as long as they stay together. I'll be back on Tuesday."

In other words, he'd made a promise he might not keep and he was too busy with business to waste any more time on the matter. "Don't hurry on our account," she said coldly. "We're doing just fine."

"Rebecca—"

"Goodbye." She hung up the phone, plastered a smile on her face and turned around. The children were engrossed in their Monopoly game again. "If you want to go skiing tomorrow, you'll have to go to bed now," she said.

She expected wheedling and stalling, but they told her they would finish the game tomorrow and put it away. Since they were in a cooperative mood, she added that she'd appreciate more help around the house, especially when it came to keeping their rooms clean. Without her asking, they collected the dirty dishes and put them in the dishwasher and threw away the wrappings from their presents. It reaffirmed her impression that Mike and Joey were just like Sarah and Danny—a little messy and lazy at times, but good kids who helped when you reminded them to. They deserved better than a mother who sided with her second husband whenever they were less than perfect and a father who considered business more important than their anger and tears.

The casual affection Rebecca had always felt for David's sons had grown into real fondness in Lake Tahoe, and the phone call from Linda Harris added a strong element of protectiveness to her feelings. Joey and Mike were only ten and thirteen and victims of a divorce that had dragged on for months due to a dispute over the property settlement. It must have taken years for the world to seem like a safe place again, and now their mother was pulling the rug out from under them by moving to Japan. Maybe Linda had no choice but to go with Phil, but a decent father would have fought tooth and nail to keep his sons in California if that's what they wanted. When David returned to Lake Tahoe, she was going to make sure he knew that.

In the meantime she wanted to take their minds off the future and show them a good time. She was a little nervous about letting them go off on their own the next morning, but they claimed they'd done it before, talked her into taking another lesson and promised to meet her for lunch. Afterward they insisted on skiing with her and her kids on the easier intermediate runs. They were such good skiers, she thought they'd be bored, but Mike helped Sarah with her turns and seemed to enjoy himself enormously, while Joey stuck faithfully by Danny. Rebecca saw the view David had mentioned and decided he was right—this was as close to heaven on earth as you could come. It was only as they trudged wearily back to the car that she realized that Mike and Joey had wanted *her* to have a good time, too.

They stopped at the house to change, then picked up some groceries and had dinner at the boys' favorite pizza place. Rebecca let them rent some movies afterward, even though they looked too tired to watch them. They didn't so much walk into the house as drag themselves.

She was still putting the groceries away when the doorbell rang. Mike answered it, returning with a bouquet of roses. "The florist left these at the MacDonalds' house. Todd brought them over. They're for you."

All four kids gathered around as she slit the envelope open, Mike peering over her shoulder. Although she was five foot six, he was already an inch taller than she was.

"How about a little privacy?" she said.

Sarah stood on tiptoes, trying to see the card. "Who's it from?"

"David. Do you mind if I read it?"

"What does it say?" Danny asked.

The card read:

I'm sorry I was such a jerk last night. I could use someone to talk to. Please have dinner with me when I get back.

David.

Rebecca was trying to decide how much to repeat when Mike asked what his father was apologizing for.

She shoved the card in her pocket. "You're nosy."

He grinned at her. "I know. What did he do to get you mad? Are you going to have dinner with him?"

"I don't know." She found a vase in one of the kitchen cabinets and filled it with water, thinking the kids wouldn't give her a moment's peace until she provided an explanation. Choosing her words carefully, she said, "Sometimes I'm too emotional. I expected him to call you last night, and I was upset when you had to call him."

"He's in the middle of some big deal that he won't talk about. He had to set up meetings for today and tomorrow, but he would have called us when he was done. He said he was sorry for not getting back to us sooner." Mike paused. "We really don't need a baby-sitter, but if you want one, Janet could probably do it."

"Or Todd," Joey said. "Did you yell at my dad?"

"Of course not." She'd hung up on him but she hadn't yelled.

"Are you still mad?"

She ruffled Joey's hair. "I'm not if you're not, and anyway, I'm a sucker for flowers. Where do you think I should put them?"

"On the dining-room table." Joey carried them over while Mike fetched the menorah and a box of matches. After the kids had opened their presents, Rebecca made popcorn and put a movie on the VCR. Everyone fell asleep but her and Mike, who helped her put the younger kids to bed. That night she kissed all of them good-night, not just Danny and Sarah.

She was grateful for the unwatched movies the next morning; it was snowing so heavily there was no question of leaving the house. According to the radio the storm had moved in around 2:00 a.m., deposited six to eight inches by dawn and was due to blow out that afternoon.

The kids watched two movies, ate lunch and begged to go outside. The storm had tapered off by then, but the wind was blowing briskly and the temperature had dropped. Rebecca walked them to the hillside, saw half the children in the neighborhood either sledding or making snowmen and let them stay.

She was restless herself, so she shoveled the front walk, even though Mike had said he'd do it, and then mixed up some dough for Hanukkah cookies. As she worked, her eyes repeatedly strayed to the roses on the dining-room table. David should have returned Mike's call, but at least he'd admitted he'd been wrong. She wasn't annoyed anymore, and the house felt a little empty without him. Life was more fun when he was around.

She'd just put a sheet of cookies in the oven when he called to tell her he'd be leaving San Francisco around four. "Is everything okay there?" he added.

"Everything's fine. It was snowing hard before, but it stopped about an hour ago. The roads have been plowed, and so has your driveway, but it's still cloudy out. You might want to check the weather up here before you leave." She looked at the roses. "Thank you for the flowers. They're beautiful."

"Am I forgiven?"

"It's not my place to tell you—"

"Am I?"

Rebecca's hand tightened on the phone. "You should have called them right away. I don't care *how* important this deal of yours is—your kids should come first."

"I know. I was just—" He cut himself off. "I want to tell you about it, but I don't have time right now. Can we have dinner tonight?"

"Are you looking for a sounding board?"

"Something like that. I need to get things in perspective—to talk to someone about what I should do. You've been through so much.... You'd make a good counselor, Rebecca."

She smiled to herself. "You must be a mind reader. That's what I'd like to do eventually. When the kids are older, I'm going to finish college and get a master's in social work."

"You can practice on me anytime. I'll see you about five-thirty, okay?"

Rebecca said she would meet him at the airport and hung up, then went next door to ask Janet Mac-Donald to baby-sit. She was so preoccupied with where David would take her and what she should wear that the cookies in the oven looked like charcoal by the time she remembered them and dashed back to the house to take them out.

Chapter Five

The kids were soaked and hungry when they returned, but their appetites didn't extend to the pot roast Rebecca had made. With very little effort, they talked her into putting it in the refrigerator and taking them to Harrah's for dinner. It was only when she led them through the casino to the coffee shop that she discerned their real motive—they wanted to play the slots.

A law-abiding woman would have refused, but Rebecca was a soft touch. She gave each of them some nickels and let them pull the one-armed bandits while she kept an eye out for the security men whose job it was to kick out minors. Everyone lost but Sarah, who won twenty cents and decided she preferred slot machines to dreidels. Having learned absolutely nothing, the kids begged Rebecca to play keno in the coffee shop. She made them chip in their own money, thinking it would teach them a lesson when they lost. Inevitably perhaps, they won eight dollars.

They got to the airport ten minutes early and sat down to wait for David's jet. Five-thirty came and went, then six o'clock. Rebecca started to fret. South Lake Tahoe wasn't the easiest place to fly in and out of even in good weather, and it was cloudy and blustery out.

"Is your father usually on time?" she finally asked Mike.

"Not when he's working. Five-thirty could mean six or six-thirty. He always calls when he's going to be late, though."

Maybe he had, but they hadn't been home to answer. By the time fifteen more minutes had gone by, she felt as if a lead weight were sitting in the pit of her stomach. Danny put his arm around her and told her not to worry—David would be there soon. "She hates it when we're late," he explained to Mike and Joey. "She always thinks something terrible's happened."

"It's part of motherhood," she said.

Sarah looked at her quizzically. "You're not David's mother. You must like him a lot or you wouldn't be worried."

"Of course, I like him. I like all my friends." The truth was that she wouldn't have been half this upset about a friend, and the kids knew it.

Ten more minutes went by. Finally Mike said he would check with the MacDonalds to see if his father had left a message *there*. It was embarrassing to realize that a teenager had more presence of mind than she did. When he returned, he told her David had called the MacDonalds around five to say he was just leaving; he would probably arrive within the next several minutes.

Even so, Rebecca was relieved when he walked in. Looking at him, she felt such a surge of physical and emotional longing that it was hard to smile casually and say hello. He hugged Mike and Joey, tousled Danny's hair and swept Sarah up in his arms, perching her on his hip. "I'm sorry I'm late. I got tied up in a meeting."

"We know," Mike said. "Rebecca was totally panicking, so I tried the MacDonalds' and got your message."

"She was, huh?" David looked pleased. "It's nice to be missed. Come on—let's go home."

Janet MacDonald had obviously been watching for them to arrive, knocking on their door moments after they walked into the house. It was the fifth night of Hanukkah and Sarah's turn to light the menorah, but when Rebecca suggested it, she shook her head solemnly. "David looks hungry. He should eat first. We can do it when you get back."

"A lady after my own heart. My stomach thanks you." He put his arm around Rebecca's waist and led her to the car.

She was troubled by the way he kept teasing and touching her—it was giving the kids the wrong impression—but he looked so exhausted she didn't have the heart to scold him. As they drove to the restaurant, she told him what she and the kids had been up to, adopting a nonchalance she didn't feel. It was bad enough that she'd missed him and worried about him; now that they were alone, she wanted him in a way that would lead to heartache if she were foolish enough to act on it.

The restaurant was one of those Italian places so dark you can hardly see the menu, but he assured her the food was good. It didn't matter; she wasn't hungry. "So tell me about this deal of yours," she said once their salads had come.

"It's a football stadium in San Jose. Mel Kempner wants to move his team out of Texas, and he's willing to go to whichever city gives him the best package. We've got more people involved in this than I want to think about—bankers, lawyers, accountants, politicians, other NFL owners..."

"And you. Stern Development is the prime contractor."

"Yes, but I feel more like a juggler than a developer at this point—holding politicians' hands, reassuring environmentalists, getting Kempner to bend a little.... Josh called me Christmas morning to tell me Kempner had threatened to go to Baltimore unless I could talk everyone into sweetening the deal." Josh Heller was his cousin and chief lieutenant. "The two of us were about to meet with some officials from San Jose when I got Mike's message. Kempner flew in with his lawyers yesterday morning, and we signed an agreement with him late this afternoon."

It had never occurred to Rebecca that David had been working on such a tight deadline or that such a sensitive project might be at stake. With half a dozen squabbling factions to bring together, he must have had an aggravating, draining few days. His failure to call Mike didn't seem so neglectful now; he would have gotten around to it as soon as he had the time. "I shouldn't have jumped all over you before I knew what the situation was," she said. "I'm sorry."

"Don't apologize. You were right. I should have called Mike up, explained what was going on and told him I'd get back to him when everyone left. He would have understood—he wants to go into the business eventually, and he knows how crazy things can get. The truth is that I didn't want to deal with it." He sipped his wine. "In a way I still don't."

It wasn't what Rebecca wanted to hear. "How can you say that? Mike and Joey are your sons. You *should* want to deal with their problems."

David saw the reproach in her eyes and sighed. The past few days had been hectic, but he'd thought of her constantly and missed her more than he'd dreamed possible. For the first time in his life, he'd been in the middle of an exciting, lucrative deal and wished he were somewhere else. Now she was looking at him like he was scum, and he was almost desperate to explain himself.

"They're Linda's sons, too, and the thought of another battle with her..." He shook his head. "I don't want to sound like an embittered ex-husband, but it's a toss-up as to which was worse—the marriage or the divorce. I thought we'd finally gotten to the point where we could discuss things rationally and even amicably, but when I called her yesterday afternoon and mentioned that the boys might want to stay in California, she went totally berserk. First she accused me of poisoning their minds and then she said that with the amount of supervision I'd give them, they'd wind up flunking out of school or spaced out on drugs."

Rebecca felt downright guilty now. David *had* asked for the boys, but Linda had refused. She kept jumping to conclusions based on gossip and newspaper stories when all she knew for sure was that he and Linda had lived in high style while they were together and fought bitterly over the community property when they'd split up.

"Linda sounds awfully angry with you," she said. "Do you know why?"

David had a good idea, but before he admitted anything he wanted Rebecca to understand him. Linda never had, and it had cost him dearly. Of course, when he and Linda had met, he hadn't really understood himself.

He began with his brother Mike, explaining that Mike had been the golden boy of the family, an outstanding student and athlete who'd been raised to turn a modest family business into a huge success. "There was nothing my parents wouldn't have done for him; they were crazy about him. I was jealous of him, but I also idolized him. Then he got sick and died, and their expectations fell on me. I felt guilty I was still alive, but I knew I could make up for it if I was enough of a success."

He'd met Linda in college, and they'd fallen in love and married. Their first son, whom they'd named after his brother, had been born a year later. During the early years of their marriage Linda had stayed with the kids while David had concentrated on building up the family business, and they'd been fairly happy. Although he'd worked long hours and traveled extensively, he'd enjoyed his work more than he'd ever expected to. "I'm not sure whether Linda was a compulsive spender, bored or wanted to get back at me for working so much, but once the money started rolling in, she went through it like water—furs, jewelry, antiques, a huge house, fancy cars.... I didn't give a damn about those things, and I resented her extravagance, but it was easier to let her shop than to argue. Then she decided to crack San Francisco society, and large donations to socially correct charities got added to the tab. We had less and less to do with each other the longer we were married, which wasn't surprising, because we had very little in common. I had the business, and she had the kids and her charity work. Finally she met Phil, who gave her the attention I couldn't. Six months later she hired an aggressive lawyer and filed for divorce. Even though she got the house, I had to sell a lot of assets to buy out her share of the business. We're still not back to where I'd like us to be."

Rebecca could understand David's preoccupation with business now—his need to prove himself to his parents and his determination to rebuild the company after his divorce—but nobody had forced him to put Stern Development ahead of his wife and children. "From your point of view, Linda was extravagant and unfaithful, but from hers she was married to a man who ignored her and left her to raise their kids on her own. I don't think much of how she retaliated, but I can understand why she doesn't want to give the kids up. Either she's punishing you or she genuinely doesn't trust you."

David reddened, aware that he hadn't been blameless in the divorce, embarrassed that Rebecca had seen it so clearly. "You're saying that Linda replaced me with Mercedes-Benzes and Phil because I wasn't much of a husband, but that's not entirely fair. I took her to Europe every year, attended her fund-raisers, went to the opera with her.... The problem was, even when we spent time together, we bored each other. She wasn't interested in the business, and I wasn't interested in the details of her shopping sprees." He paused. "As far as the kids go, Linda was a better mother than I was a father, but I tried to be around for back-to-school nights and soccer games...to play ball with them...to take an interest in their lives. I know I didn't do as much as I should have, but I did try."

"And now? Is Linda right when she says they won't have any supervision if you take them? How much of a father are you prepared to be?"

David planned on having Rebecca around to look after the boys, but he couldn't admit that. Besides, he meant to be a better husband and father this time around. He *had* learned from his mistakes. "Phil doesn't have much patience for kids to begin with, even his own grandchildren, and the boys give him a hard time, so there's a lot of tension in the house. Over the past six months they've spent almost as much time with me as with Linda. Things have worked out okay. They're not babies. Plenty of kids their age have working parents and are on their own a lot of the time."

"So you don't plan to make any changes."

"If you're asking me whether I'm willing to move to Sausalito and spend two hours a day commuting, the answer is no. I'll get a bigger place in San Francisco, maybe hire a housekeeper. And I'll try to be around more."

"You'll try to be or you will be?"

She was making him uncomfortable, pressing him this way. "I will be. I love my sons. I think I have a good relationship with them."

Rebecca didn't doubt that, but David seemed terribly ambivalent. Although he'd said the right things, she couldn't help thinking he didn't so much want the boys as feel obligated to take them. "You seem to be happy with your life. You enjoy your work, you like being a major player in how the city is run, you know everyone there is to know.... Do you really want to upset all that just so your kids won't have to go to Japan?"

"I want to do what's right," he answered.

"Even if it means a court fight?"

He stared at his plate. "I don't have much choice."

"But do you *want* to?" she persisted.

David didn't know what he wanted beyond having Rebecca share his life. Until a minute ago everything had been simple. They would marry, operating as a team in a way he and Linda never had. She would encourage and support him in his work, just as she had Dick Lehman. She'd probably want to return to school for her MSW, but she was strong and loving enough to make time for all four children as well, even if Mike and Joey stayed in California.

Now he realized she would expect *him* to take primary responsibility for his sons. He'd have to work less, travel less and go out less, and he wasn't sure how he'd manage that, or even if he wanted to. He knew only that he wanted Rebecca as much as ever, and that he wouldn't have a prayer of getting her unless she respected him as a man and a father.

"I can't pretend I'm enthusiastic about having my life turned upside down," he said, "but I don't want my sons to be miserable, either, or see them for only two weeks in the summer every year. If they want to stay in California, I'll do whatever I have to to keep them here. And I'll be as good a father as I possibly can. If I didn't want to do all that, I probably wouldn't. Does that answer your question?"

Rebecca leaned forward. She'd never known David to look so tense or sound so lost, and her heart instinctively went out to him. What he really wanted was to have the boys in San Francisco without changing his life, but to his credit, he seemed to realize that adolescents needed supervision and that a housekeeper was no substitute for a father. Maybe he wasn't thrilled about the sacrifices he would have to make, but he was willing to make them.

"Yes, and I think you're going to do just fine." To her surprise, he looked relieved, as if she'd given him a reprieve rather than reassurance. His vulnerability touched her; she'd always thought of him as confident almost to the point of arrogance. Cupping his hand with her palm, she said gently, "Linda will come around if you talk to her the same way you've talked to me. I'm sure she loves the boys and wants what's best for them, so if you can convince her you'll take proper care of them... that they'd be happier in California... And then there's the problem with Phil.... She can visit them as often as she wants to and have them for part of the summer."

David took her hand in both of his, keenly aware that she'd willingly touched him for the first time since they'd brought Sarah home from the hospital. "Thank you for listening. It's helped me put things in perspective. The more we talk about the boys, the more I realize I really do want them to live with me." He didn't add that she was a large part of the reason why.

She smiled at him. "I've eaten as much as I can. Let's go home and light the menorah."

David was full, too. He threw a couple of bills on the table and walked Rebecca out of the restaurant, thinking that Hanukkah could wait till later. He had a better place to take her than home.

Chapter Six

When David made a right turn out of the restaurant parking lot instead of going left toward his house, Rebecca assumed he was taking Highway 50 home rather than the back road they'd come on. At the highway, though, he turned right again, toward Stateline. "Is your sense of direction addled or do you feel lucky tonight?" she asked.

He smiled. "I do feel lucky, but I wasn't heading for the casinos. I promised a friend I'd check on his house. He was worried about damage from last night's storm. Do you mind?"

"Of course not. Where is it?"

"A few miles north of here, on the Nevada side of the lake." He added that the place was spectacular, a redwood-and-glass chalet with a private beach and dock. It belonged to Roger Carey, the attorney handling the stadium deal.

"I hope it's been plowed out," Rebecca said, thinking that even a Bronco with chains on might have trouble in all this snow.

"We'll see in a few minutes." David *knew* it had been. He and Roger used the same plowing service, paying a yearly fee to have someone come after every storm. Sometimes the service took an extra day or two when they knew the owner wasn't around, so he'd called to ask that the driveway be cleared and the walk shoveled.

Rebecca couldn't see the house from the street; it was down by the lake at the end of a long private road. David parked opposite the front walk, took a flashlight out of the glove compartment and asked if she wanted to look inside. From what little she could see in the moonlight, the place was as impressive as he'd said. She hopped out of the Bronco and followed him up the walk.

The house was chilly but not really cold; the thermostat had been set at fifty-five so the pipes wouldn't freeze and the interior would warm quickly once the heat had been turned up. David clicked on the light in the entry hall, revealing a twenty-foot ceiling and a staircase leading to a railed-in upper story. "You're right," Rebecca said. "It's spectacular."

The water she'd sipped all through dinner had caught up with her, so she asked if she could use the bathroom. David told her where it was, adding that he had to check a leaky window in the kitchen. "Roger was having a problem with it the last time he came up," he explained.

The picture window in the powder room overlooked the lake, but Rebecca couldn't make out more than the outlines of a redwood deck and the silhouettes of trees. She wondered if there were lights surrounding the house, and if so, whether David could turn them on so she could see the view.

He was in the hallway by the time she left the bathroom, waiting to show her around. They started in the kitchen, went through the dining room, family room and office, and ended in a huge living room. The decorating job had obviously cost a fortune, but Rebecca found the place stark and impersonal.

"I expected you to have a house like this," she said.

"So did Linda, preferably in Aspen, but I told her my parents' place would have to do. Actually, I like it better than this. It's comfortable, I have nice neighbors and I get a kick out of seeing my sons do the same things I did as a kid."

She hadn't realized the house belonged to his parents, who had retired to Palm Springs, or that he'd vacationed there as a child. Whatever else he was, he wasn't pretentious. "That's nice—to have a home with some family history behind it. This place is a little cold. Stunning, though. If we opened the shutters, could we see the lake?"

"The view is better from upstairs." He put his arm around her and turned her toward the door.

There were three surprisingly charming guest rooms on the second floor along with a master suite with the same exposure as the living room. As she walked into the master bedroom, she absently noticed that it was warmer than the rest of the house. The wall facing the lake had two large windows on either side of a stone fireplace; David opened the drapes, turned on the outside lights and clicked off the ceiling fixture. The snow-covered deck was bathed in light now, and the surface of the lake glistened beyond. A three-quarter moon was hanging in the sky, illuminating the snow stirred up by the breeze. Rebecca stared out the window, entranced.

Although she sensed David behind her, she wasn't aware of how close he was until his arms slipped around her waist. She started in surprise, then felt his fingers on the zipper of her jacket, smoothly pulling it down. Dumbfounded, she asked him what he was doing.

His hands slid to her shoulders and grasped the fabric of her jacket. "Taking off your parka." He pulled it down, tossed it on the floor and put his arms around her again.

Her heart started hammering. "David—"

"Hmm?" She felt his lips against her neck and his fingers on her waist, slipping under her sweater to fondle her breasts. She wasn't shocked that he'd made a pass at her; it was probably inevitable. She'd simply expected more warning, or at least less audacity. He was acting as if he'd done this a hundred times before and had every reason to expect her to welcome it.

The hell of it was that she did, at least physically. The teasing sensuality of his touch...the quiet, moonlit room...the gentle but confident assault on her senses... The eroticism of it took her breath away. Her response was immediate and intense; she could no more control it than she could control the feelings that had made her so vulnerable to him in the first place.

Her face grew flushed, her skin prickled under his lips, and her nipples hardened against his light but firm caresses. Pressed close to his body, she could feel heat, muscle and urgent male desire. She shut her eyes and took a sharp breath. Dear God, the things he was doing to her...the way he was making her feel...

She tugged at his arms, but he refused to remove them. "Don't, David. Let's go home."

"Home, huh? I'm glad you think of it that way." He kissed his way to her ear and nibbled the lobe. "Did I ever mention that I love the way you taste and smell?" Her bra hooked in the front; he unfastened it and ran his palms back and forth over the warm, bare flesh. She shivered, not from the cold but from excitement. "And feel. You're like satin." He took her nipples between his thumbs and forefingers and massaged them. "Most of you, anyway."

Rebecca wasn't used to this sort of verbal and physical seduction; Dick's idea of foreplay had been twenty seconds of kissing. Either David was awfully good at making love or she was awfully susceptible, but either way the effect was overpowering. The more he touched her the more excited she got, and the more excited she got the less she cared about being rational and cautious. The raw pleasure—the growing need for satisfaction—made her want to fling herself into his arms and blindly seek his mouth.

She leaned against his shoulder instead, too aroused to pull away but trying to be sensible. "That's enough. We have to leave now." Her voice was soft and husky, as if she wanted the exact opposite.

"Really?" He sounded amused. "Why? Don't you like it?"

"That's not the point. It's a bad idea."

He gently turned her around. She took a step backward, bumped into the window and stared at him blankly. The determination in his eyes destroyed what little resistance she had left. He'd only demanded what she ached to give.

"On the contrary, it's a good idea." He cupped her chin. "We should have done it a long time ago." His mouth was only a fraction of an inch above hers, and she wanted it so much she was shaking. She closed her eyes and waited.

He ran his thumb over her mouth, then slipped it between her lips. She moaned softly, put her arms around his waist and tasted him. His skin was salty and callused. She wondered how the rest of him would taste, especially his mouth.

"So?" he said softly. "Is it still a bad idea?"

"Yes, but I don't care." She pressed herself closer, moving her hips restlessly. He cupped her buttocks to fit her intimately against his body and toyed with her mouth until she couldn't stand it a moment longer. "Oh, God, David... Please..." She sought his lips in helpless agitation.

The kiss started with a gentle nip of her upper lip; within moments it had exploded into a passionate and entirely mutual exploration. Rebecca clung to him, feeling as if this were happening to someone else. She'd never savored a man's mouth so possessively or clawed her way under his shirt because she was desperate to touch him...not her, not careful, rational Rebecca Lehman.

It was only when he lifted her into his arms and carried her to the bed that her head cleared a little and she began to panic. Necking in the moonlight was one thing, but this... Things were happening too fast. "David, I'm not—I don't—"

"Trust me, sweetheart. You're dying to." David swept aside the covers and laid Rebecca on the bed. He knew he was pushing her hard, but if he waited for her to figure out that she loved him and make the first move, they would be on Medicare by the time they got together. Besides, if she hadn't wanted to sleep with him, she would have done more than murmur weak objections.

Even now she was watching him intently, showing no inclination to leave. He clicked on the electric blanket and sat down beside her. Everything about her was exquisite—her breasts, her mouth, her wild, sweet response—and he wanted her with an intensity that stunned him. There was only one thing he wanted more, and that was to arouse her so fiercely she'd forget every other man who'd touched her.

Rebecca didn't have to think about what David had said—she knew he was right—but you could want something desperately and realize it was dangerous. "You and me—it's never going to work...."

"Sure it is." He slid his hands under her sweater and caressed her breasts. "You know what your problem is? You think too much." She shuddered and watched, mesmerized as his mouth moved closer, and finally she closed her eyes. "Don't think," he murmured against her lips. "Just feel."

Within seconds she was too aroused to do anything else. His deep, erotic kisses and gentle caresses were only the beginning of a long, sensual campaign to obliterate her objections. The feel of his mouth on her breasts, the teasing touch of his fingers on her belly and loins, the patient way he encouraged her to touch him back and the wild pleasure she felt when she did so...nothing had prepared her for his fiery, tender lovemaking. He stripped her bare in every way possible—not only physically, but emotionally. Not only was she naked in his arms, burning with excitement and desperate for his touch; she longed to give herself however he asked. When he moved away, she felt bereft.

He stroked her hair. "If I stop to take my clothes off, are you going to bolt off the bed?"

She shook her head and said thickly, "No. I want you so much I can't think straight."

David smiled and got up, feeling as if he could conquer the world. He stripped off his jacket, tie and shirt, then reached into his pocket and tossed some foil packets on the night table. His slacks were half off thanks to Rebecca, who'd burrowed under his briefs and done such provocative things with her fingers that he'd finally pushed them away. She didn't seem to realize the effect she had on him.

She looked at the night table. "You think of everything."

"You're damn right I do. I've waited over two years for this." He pulled the rest of his clothes off, got back into bed and grabbed a foil packet. A moment later he took her in his arms.

Rebecca didn't want to wait even a second, but David slowed her down, caressed her until he was sure she was ready and then carefully entered her. His tender, controlled lovemaking quickly gave way to reckless passion and shattering pleasure. The sheer intensity of it left her stunned. Never in her life had she lost control so totally. She'd never even come close.

She lay in his arms afterward, confused at first, then agitated and upset. How could this have happened? How could she have *permitted* it to happen? And why had it been so perfect? He was as wrong for her as he'd ever been.

"I don't have affairs," she said, as if that would somehow negate what had taken place.

"So when do you want to get married? Tonight? One of the chapels might still be open." He fondled her breasts with absent affection. "Did I mention how much I love you? How beautiful you are? How much you excite me?" His touch grew more insistent. "On second thought, let's make love again. We can get married tomorrow morning."

She squirmed out of his arms. "We have to talk, David."

He sighed. "I should have known it was too easy. Just because we like each other's kids, have a great time together, drive each other crazy in bed and love each other to distraction—"

"Who says I love you to distraction?"

"I do. You missed me while I was in the city, you panicked when I was late and you worry about my problems. Besides, look how easy you were to seduce."

It was true, even the last part. As she brooded about how to answer, she suddenly noticed the sound of a fan blowing. There was a portable heater in the room. She frowned. Now that she thought about it, things had been awfully convenient for David. Roger Carey was rich enough to own this house and pay people to look after it in his absence, so why would he ask a friend to check on a leaky window?

Suspicious now, she said slowly, "I should strip the bed and take the sheets to the house to wash."

David had more important things on his mind than laundry. "Don't worry about it. The maid will do it."

"The maid? When does she come?"

"A couple of times a week, just to check..." He clamped his mouth shut, wondering how he could have been so stupid.

"So *you* didn't need to come here. You got the key from Roger so you'd have someplace to take me and turned on the heater while I was in the bathroom and lured me upstairs to get me into bed—"

"To make love to you," he corrected. There was no point denying it. "It was a little manipulative, but—"

"A *little* manipulative?" She thought it was outrageously manipulative. She moved farther away. "Did it ever occur to you that it wasn't fair to take advantage of the fact that I was attracted to you? That I might have had a good reason for saying no?''

''You only think you did. It was the only way I could prove to you that—''

''For heaven's sake, David, you're the Fortune 500 version of Dick Lehman! Instead of politics, you eat, breathe and sleep business. I'd have to be crazy to get involved with you.''

''Is *that* the problem? You think work is more important to me than you are?'' He shook his head. ''It isn't. I love you very much. I want to make you happy. I'd have to be a fool to marry you and then spend all my time on business. Besides, I have the boys to consider.''

Rebecca wasn't a naive coed anymore. She knew people didn't change so easily, especially when a part of them didn't want to. ''In the beginning you might cut back on your work, but the next big deal would always be waiting around the corner to tempt you. Eventually the temptation would be too great, and you'd give in. With me around to run your home and look after your children, it would be easy to work half the night and fly to out-of-town meetings. Then there are all the civic and charitable commitments you accept. Naturally you'd want me to share them. I'd be back where I was with Dick, except that I'd be responsible for *your* kids as well as my own, and I'd wind up shortchanging all four of them.''

Several seconds went by. ''I notice you haven't tried to tell me I don't love you,'' he finally answered.

''No.'' She was a fool not to have seen it sooner. It was obvious from his kindness and generosity.

''And you're not denying you love me.''

She hugged the blankets to her chest, knowing she did. The last half hour had demolished the pretense that her feelings were shallow enough to be withdrawn or even contained. "I can't—not after the way we made love."

That was precisely why David had done it—to force her to confront her feelings. She was too honest to respond so emotionally and then claim it was merely physical; it was one of the things he loved about her. She hated deception, she didn't give a hang about social status or fancy possessions and she was as discreet as a Philadelphia lawyer. In other words, she was nothing like Linda.

"Then try to trust me," he said. "I know you wouldn't be happy with another husband like Dick and that I put business first when I was married to Linda, but credit me with having the brains to learn from my mistakes. Things will be different with you because I *want* them to be different."

He'd been thinking about their life together for a long time now and considered them so perfect for each other that he couldn't understand how Rebecca could fail to see it. Moving closer but not touching her, he spoke in a soft compelling voice about why he loved her, what a wonderful team they would make and how happy they would be.

Rebecca wanted to be convinced, but the more David said, the more uneasy she got. She couldn't forget the frenetic life he led, his obsessive drive to succeed and, most important of all, how ambivalent he'd been about fighting for his sons. Equally disturbing, he seemed to have a vision of the two of them side by side, dazzling all of San Francisco. "I know you believe what you're saying," she said, "but your feelings could be different in a year or two, once your physical infatuation with me wears off. And you seem to have this picture of being married to Dick Lehman's widow—of taking me places and showing me off.... It's the ultimate coup, something even Mike might not have accomplished.''

"I admit it's crossed my mind—how people would react to our marriage," he said, startling her with his honesty. "But it's you I love, not some idealized image of courage and virtue. As for changing my life, it scares the hell out of me in a way, but it's something I want to do. Whether that's because of you, the boys or because I'm ready for different priorities, I don't know. I don't see what difference it makes.''

"The difference is that if you do it for the wrong reasons, you'll wind up resenting it," she said. "Both of us will be miserable. You can't base a marriage on sacrifice.''

"What sacrifice? If you're happy, I'll be happy. That's all I care about.''

Rebecca of all people knew that you couldn't ignore your deepest principles and desires and still be happy, no matter how much you loved someone. David was allowing emotion rather than logic to rule him. Still, he'd been honest about his feelings. He hadn't tried to con her. If he had, she wouldn't have trusted him enough to take him seriously.

"Someday, maybe in six months or a year, after you've had a chance to live with the changes you say you'll make..." She paused. "If you still want to marry me—if you come to me and tell me it was the right choice—I'll say yes. In the meantime, I think we should just be friends.''

David agreed only because it was pointless to argue. He'd gotten his way once and planned to do so again . . . and long before six months had gone by. It would take a little persuading, but he was very good at that.

Chapter Seven

The kids were giggly and exuberant when David and Rebecca returned, but she doubted it was because they'd had such a good time playing Pictionary with Janet. Their parents had been gone for hours, much too long for dinner in an informal restaurant. David looked at Rebecca differently now—the way a man instinctively looks at a woman he's made love to. The situation made her uncomfortable, and she supposed it showed. Even a child as young as Sarah was capable of sensing something had changed, although the details were probably a mystery to her.

The boys were more worldly, especially Mike. Although he didn't say anything when they walked in, he grinned at David so knowingly that it was obvious what he was thinking. Even more unnerving, once David had returned from walking Janet home, Mike remarked nonchalantly that his mother had called, was sorry she'd missed him and would try again tomorrow. Rebecca couldn't believe how calm he was. Was this the same adolescent who'd slammed into his room after Linda's last call and then moped for hours?

"Did you talk about moving to Japan?" she asked.

"Yeah. We should light the menorah now." He started toward the table; the rest of the children followed. "Sarah's really tired."

Something was definitely going on. She turned to Joey. "Did you talk to your mom, too?"

Joey looked at Mike, repressing a smile. "Uh-huh. She says we can probably stay in California."

"Just like that. She changed her mind."

"I guess so. Press harder, Sarah," Joey instructed. She was having trouble lighting a match. "Do you want me to do it?"

"No, I can." She struck another match, successfully this time, and added, "We never talked about Hanukkah, Mommy. We have to tonight."

"I thought you didn't want to. You wouldn't be trying to change the subject, would you?"

"We always do, and we just have to." She started singing the blessings, neatly sidestepping Rebecca's question.

Rebecca decided there was more to the kids' good mood than giggly speculation over her relationship with David; something had happened during Linda's phone call that they didn't want to talk about. As soon as they'd opened their presents, she tried again. "Mike, do you have any idea *why* your mother changed her mind?"

"She probably just came to her senses," David said, staring hard at Mike and Joey. "Isn't that right?"

Mike nodded, Joey blushed and Sarah giggled.

"Do you want me to tell you about the Maccabees?" Danny asked innocently.

"I want you to tell me about the phone call." She looked at David. "Everyone in this room seems to know what happened—except me."

"We should talk about Hanukkah first," Danny insisted. "Sarah will fall asleep and miss it if we don't do it now."

Sarah promptly yawned. Sighing, Rebecca bowed to the inevitable. It didn't matter whether they discussed it now or later as long as she found out what was going on. She had the uneasy feeling it concerned *her*.

They sat down in the living room, and Danny began to explain the events the holiday commemorated. With occasional questions and comments from Rebecca, the story gradually unfolded....

Over three hundred years before the birth of Christ, Alexander the Great of Greece conquered the ancient world, and the splendors of Hellenic culture—its art, science, philosophy and physical comforts—spread to the East. Greek culture had one glaring deficiency, however; it lacked a system of religious and moral ideals. The old faith in Olympian gods had decayed into cynicism, superstition and cultism, and the same society that championed artistic and intellectual freedom also tolerated slavery, sexual excess and contempt for the poor and the weak.

Alone in the ancient world, Judaism offered a monotheistic, ethical basis for daily life. Still, the mixture of Hellenic and Eastern culture was dazzling, and its pull was strong. Even many Jews embraced aspects of it—not only Jews who'd settled outside the Holy Land and were more distant from their roots, but the affluent, assimilated aristocracy in Jerusalem and the surrounding province of Judea.

In about 200 B.C., Palestine was conquered by the hellenized Syrians, who saw themselves as the rightful heirs to the glory of Alexander. After about thirty years of Syrian rule, Jerusalem's ruling aristocracy pressed for self-government and the social and economic advantages it would bring. The Syrian price was further hellenization; the Jewish aristocracy willingly paid it. They ousted the High Priest, who'd resisted hellenization, and replaced him with his more tractable brother Jason. The common people—farmers, shepherds and laborers—were antagonized by the aristocrats' lack of religious piety and the use of Temple money to promote Greek customs, but they considered themselves powerless to change things.

Three years later the Syrian king, Antiochus IV, took the next logical step; he installed his own man, Menelaus, as High Priest in order to procure Temple money to finance his foreign conquests. Not only did Menelaus have no proper hereditary claim to the office, he sold sacred Temple vessels to raise money, outraging even hellenized Jews. A civil war erupted between the followers of Jason and those of Menelaus, and Antiochus responded with stern repression. He prohibited circumcision and adherence to Jewish dietary laws, placed a statue of Zeus on the Temple altar and sent Syrian soldiers from town to town to root out any vestige of Jewish observance. The penalty for resistance was death.

Many peasants fled to the hills of Judea to hide, and a grass-roots resistance movement developed. A group led by Mattathias, a priest, eventually assumed leadership. Two things distinguished them: they insisted that fighting on the Sabbath was permissible if it was in self-defense, and one of Mattathias's five sons, Judah the Maccabee, was a brilliant military leader. He won several battles over forces dispatched by local administrators, then defeated a larger army led by two Syrian generals.

Antiochus, with his tremendous superiority in numbers and weapons, might have quelled the rebellion at this point, but instead, he decided to lead his forces on a campaign to Parthia, to the east. Judah and his followers marched into Jerusalem, purified the defiled Temple and rekindled the sacred lights. An eight-day celebration was held—the Feast of Hanukkah, the Feast of Rededication.

While Antiochus was still in Parthia, his regent back in Syria decided to send troops to subjugate Jerusalem; they succeeded in surrounding the city and holding it under siege. But just when things looked darkest, a treaty was offered guaranteeing the Jews religious freedom. Political freedom was won later on the battlefield.

"So what does the story have to teach us?" Rebecca asked, when Danny was finished.

"That it's important to fight for what you believe in. It was the first war in history for religious freedom, and we won it."

David had learned more about Hanukkah in the past fifteen minutes than in seven years of religious school, but the tale seemed incomplete. "Wait a minute," he said. "Whatever happened to the cruse that contained enough holy oil to burn for only one night but lasted eight?"

"It's not mentioned in any of the books of the Maccabees," Mike said, looking pleased that he knew something his father didn't. "The oil only came into it hundreds of years later. The story is in the Talmud."

David glanced at the younger children, afraid Mike might have done the Jewish equivalent of announcing that Santa Claus didn't exist. None of them looked surprised. "You've all learned that?"

"You can believe the part about the oil if you want to," Danny said reassuringly. "Orthodox Jews do, but most scholars don't."

Danny obviously didn't, either, nor did the rest of the kids. A little bemused, David asked, "So why did the Maccabees celebrate Hanukkah for eight days?"

"Probably because they were fighting during Sukkot and missed observing it," Mike said. Sukkot, the Jewish harvest festival, was celebrated for eight days. "Either they were observing it late or copying some of the customs to celebrate their victory over the Syrians."

"So much for miracles," David murmured with a smile.

"The real miracle was that Judah won at all," Rebecca pointed out. "The Syrians were powerful enough to crush him, but first Antiochus decided to go to Parthia, and later, after he died there, there was such a fierce power struggle in Syria that the regent for his young son decided to sign a treaty with the Maccabees so he could bring the troops home to attack his rivals. Otherwise Judaism would have been eradicated and there would have been no Christianity or Islam. It was either luck or the will of God—take your pick."

"And you? What do you think?"

"I'm not sure. I only know that time and again our enemies have tried to annihilate us, and they've never succeeded. When I think about those four thousand years of Jewish history, I feel very humble and very awed." She looked at Sarah. "What about you? What do you think Hanukkah teaches us?"

"That nobody should be able to make me do what I don't want to." She giggled. "I don't want to go to bed, Mommy."

"Very funny. Do you want to know what I think?"

"Is it different from last year?" Danny asked.

Rebecca smiled and rolled her eyes. She didn't mind the kids' teasing; it was a family tradition by now. "A little different. I always thought of Hanukkah as being about religious and political freedom, but something happened this year that gave me a new idea about the holiday. Maybe it's not so far from what Sarah said." She looked at David, making it clear that the "something" had to do with what had happened earlier, then continued in an unsteady, impassioned voice, "Maybe Hanukkah is about having the freedom to be yourself—to do what you feel is right for *you*, whether you're Judah Maccabee and you want to worship in a certain way, or Sarah Lehman and you want to be friends with someone everyone else makes fun of, or Mike Stern and you want to play basketball after school instead of going drinking with the guys. You have to look inside yourself, find the truest, best part of yourself and honor it. Because if you don't—if you let somebody else run your life or you do things that violate your deepest convictions—you'll lose all respect for yourself and you'll never have any peace. Never."

Nobody said a word. The kids didn't even look at one another, much less smirk or giggle. Rebecca knew it wasn't the brilliance of her rhetoric that had gotten through to them—she wasn't that eloquent—but the passion in her voice. They weren't used to her talking so emotionally. Her lectures were seldom so deadly serious.

The silence was broken by the ringing of a telephone. As David walked over to answer it, the kids mumbled good-night and slipped away. They seemed a little shaken, but if she'd given them something to think about, that was good. Children's lives were full of insecurity, conformity and careless cruelty, and she wanted them to be confident and compassionate enough to resist.

In the kitchen, David listened with a growing sense of dismay as his cousin Josh described the latest hitch in the stadium deal. An environmental group had reconsidered its agreement to a key aspect of the proposal and was threatening to seek an injunction delaying the start of work. Mel Kempner wasn't about to get involved in a project that might get tied up by lawsuits, so a delay would kill the deal. Josh offered to explore the possibility of a compromise, but at twenty-eight, he lacked David's extensive experience in such matters.

David cupped the phone and said softly, "Have Frank bring the plane back up tomorrow." Frank was their pilot. "Let's shoot for ten o'clock. Contact Mel in the morning to let him know there's a problem and schedule a meeting in the afternoon with Citizens for Controlled Growth. Tell Mel I'll give him a call as soon as I have a sense of whether this can be resolved to his satisfaction."

"Right." Josh paused. "I'm sorry about this, David. I know you wanted to stay with Rebecca."

"CCG's timing was great. I got lectured tonight about what a workaholic I am. I'd almost rather face a firing squad than tell her I'm leaving again."

"You're sure you don't want me to—"

"No, I'll do it. You've learned a lot, but you're a few deals short of being able to handle this sort of thing the way both of us would want you to." He added that he would come directly to the office in the morning.

After he'd hung up, he poured himself a glass of juice and steeled himself to talk to Rebecca. He hadn't realized the strength of her feelings about her marriage until she'd spoken about the meaning of Hanukkah, but the pain in her eyes and the agony in her voice had finally gotten through to him. She wasn't simply feeling guilty about spending too little time with her children; she felt she'd broken faith with herself—disregarded the truest, best part of herself, as she'd put it—in order to accommodate Dick Lehman. And in three long years, she hadn't been able to forgive herself.

He saw now that he hadn't given nearly enough thought to the situation. He'd unconsciously assumed that if he tried his best to do what she asked and failed, it would be okay. She'd compromise. She'd nurture and support him. That was what wives were *supposed* to do. But now, for all his sweet talk and promises, he was running back to San Francisco and his latest deal, and he had no right to expect her to sympathize.

He turned away from the refrigerator, saw her sitting alone on the couch and realized the kids had gone upstairs. He carried his juice into the living room and sat down next to her. "That was Josh. There's a problem with the stadium deal. I have to go back to the city tomorrow morning."

Rebecca told herself there would always be problems with deals and he would always put them first, but he looked so despondent she couldn't bring herself to say so. Instead, she asked him what was wrong and tried to cheer him up. She couldn't.

He finished his juice, set down the glass and lightly stroked her cheek. "You know, I was looking at life like it was...fruit salad. If there was too much of this or not enough of that, you could tinker with the quantities and the recipe would be fine. But when I listened to you just now, I realized that changing the recipe won't be enough. You want a whole different dish.''

Rebecca stared at the floor. David had finally understood the point she'd tried to make, but he hadn't said anything about what he planned to do about it. It hurt so much she felt as if there were metal bands tightening around her chest, squeezing the life out of her. Even though she'd meant every word of what she'd said tonight, she didn't want to lose him. She wanted him to miraculously change so she could have it all.

"I suppose I do," she said.

"And if I make promises I don't—or can't—keep, I'll put you through hell. You'll be forced to choose between me and your own convictions."

She nodded. The first time, when she'd been younger and less sure of herself, she'd chosen her husband. She wasn't so sure she would make that choice again.

"So the priorities have to be *my* priorities. The commitment has to be *my* commitment, because otherwise I won't keep it. Even though I love you very much, I'll backslide into doing what *I* want to do."

"That's how it seems to work."

"Then I have some thinking to do." He put his arms around her, and she tensed, but he seemed content simply to hold her. "I'm beginning to hate this damn stadium deal. I wish I didn't have to leave."

"You've put too much work into it not to try and salvage it." She settled against his chest, then added quietly, "You know what *I* think? That you *haven't* been doing what you want...that it was for your brother or your parents at first, and then for Linda, to prove to her that she couldn't destroy what you'd accomplished, but never really for you."

"I've been at this so long I don't know *how* I feel anymore," he said, "but the power I have...the recognition I get...I like those things."

Liked them and needed them, she thought. More than her. The pain was unbearable. She hugged him hard, then pulled away and ran upstairs.

Chapter Eight

After her husband's death, Rebecca had wanted to crawl into bed and never come out. She hadn't been able to, not with two young children to raise, but somehow, with the love and support of her family, she'd managed to clean, shop and cook, to take the kids on outings . . . to resume the patterns of ordinary life. After that, she figured she could survive anything, even David Stern.

The two of them barely spoke the next morning. David refused to let her drive him to the airport, insisting he could take a cab; feeling rejected, she made sure she was in the shower when he left. The kids reacted with whispers and pregnant looks, but no questions.

It was an effort even to dress, but she'd learned that keeping busy was the best therapy. She went sledding with the kids in the morning, treated them to lunch in the deli near the supermarket and took them snowmobiling in the afternoon. She hadn't slept well the night before and didn't feel like cooking, but fortunately the pot roast was still in the refrigerator. She knew the kids were worried about her when they ate it without complaint.

They lit the menorah and opened their gifts, then went to the MacDonalds' to watch a movie. Alone now, Rebecca took a hot bath and got into bed with a book. She couldn't concentrate on it, but she couldn't fall asleep, either. When the phone rang, her pulse rate jumped. She wanted it to be David, telling her he'd been a fool not to realize that nothing was more important than family and friends, saying he couldn't live without her, proposing again.

Instead, a woman responded to her husky hello. "Is this—you must be Mrs. Lehman."

"Yes..."

"It's nice to finally meet you, even if it's only on the phone. This is Linda Harris. How are you coping?"

The connection was so clear that Linda might have been in Stateline. "Fine. Please, call me Rebecca. Are you still in Japan?"

"Yes, but we're leaving tonight." Linda added that she'd been calling since early morning—it was noon on Thursday in Tokyo—and finally had decided they might have gone home. "I tried David's office and got Josh. He sounded frazzled. He said he doubted David would get back to the lake before the weekend, and I really would like to spend the last night of Hanukkah with the boys. I've bought them the cutest things here! Would you mind putting them on a bus Friday morning and sending them home? I'll call tomorrow night from Sausalito to find out what time they'll be in."

Rebecca said she'd be glad to, thinking that if David was staying in the city there was no point remaining at the lake. She could take the kids skiing tomorrow, then drive back early Friday in the Bronco.

"That's settled then," Linda said. She paused, "Rebecca, I can imagine the things David must have told you about me, but there are two sides to the story."

Rebecca had been so wrapped up in her problems that she'd forgotten the kids' evasiveness the night before. Now, though, she realized that Linda wouldn't have spoken so personally if her change of heart hadn't been due to *her*, Rebecca. "There usually are," she said uneasily.

"You've worked for him for two and a half years. You know how he—how busy he sometimes is. And I just felt I couldn't possibly leave the boys in California when he might not take proper care of them. With all the drinking, drugs and gangs out there . . . You're a mother. You understand."

"Yes," she murmured.

"What I'm trying to say is, I'm thrilled with the way things have worked out. I'll miss the boys every moment, but I realize they'll be happier in California. David is lucky to have found you, and I'm sure he knows it. I admire you so tremendously—everyone in San Francisco does—and I'm just delighted the boys will be in such good hands. And I was thinking—if you can drag David away on a honeymoon before Phil and I move to Japan, I'll be glad to look after your children while you're gone." She laughed. "That's the modern American family for you—his, hers, her ex-husband's new wife's . . ."

Since Linda had talked to Josh rather than David, her information could only have come from the boys. Yet last night, even David had seemed to know why Linda had dropped her objections. The conclusion was obvious: he'd encouraged the kids in their thinking, and not just by the way he touched Rebecca and looked at her.

The logical course of action was to set Linda straight, but Rebecca couldn't do it. Why spoil the rest of Linda's trip? Why upset the boys and ruin the rest of their vacation? She could explain the situation to Linda on Monday morning, once the boys were back in school.

"Thanks for the offer," she said, "but I honestly don't know what's going to happen. That is, it's all so sudden . . . we haven't made any plans—"

"He *is* taking you on a honeymoon, isn't he?" Linda's tone said she didn't put anything past her ex-husband.

Rebecca fell back on a tried-and-true method of ending an awkward conversation. "I'm sure—oh, dear, Linda, I think I hear my daughter crying. I'd better go see what's wrong. I'll speak to you tomorrow evening, all right?"

"Yes, of course." Linda repeated that it was nice to have met her and rang off.

Rebecca put down the phone and stared at the wall. Who was she kidding? She hadn't lied because of Linda and the boys, but because the truth was so damn painful. It was easier to hope things would work out than to face the fact that David was too busy avoiding her even to inform her about his plans.

She considered calling him, but it was pointless. She had nothing new to say. She thought about phoning Emily—talking to her sister always made her feel better—but Emily and her family were vacationing in San Diego, and Rebecca hated to intrude with her problems. Even television reruns were better than lying in bed looking at the same two pages of a book, so she pulled on a robe and went downstairs to the couch.

When the kids got back, she told them that she'd spoken to Linda and would be driving Mike and Joey home Friday so they could spend the last night of Hanukkah with the Harrises. The four of them exchanged uneasy looks, probably wondering what else might have been said, then squeezed onto the couch and watched a movie with her. For a few hours, she was surrounded by their warmth and love, and the pain faded.

They skied till midafternoon the next day, then took back the rented ski equipment and returned to the house to clean and pack. The kids were so helpful it was unnatural. It brought back memories of something Danny had said after Dick's death: "If I'm good enough, Mommy, will he come back?" The kids seemed to think that if only they were good enough, Rebecca's and David's problems would vanish.

Linda called around eight, spoke briefly to Mike and asked for Rebecca. "I hear you plan to drive the boys home," she said drowsily. "You're a doll to offer, but I wouldn't want to inconvenience you."

It was only an extra half hour. "It's no trouble at all. Besides, you sound exhausted. It will save you a trip into San Rafael to pick them up."

"Then thank you." She yawned. "Excuse me. It was an awful flight, and they lost one of our bags. I'll look forward to meeting you in person. I'll just say hello to Joey..."

"He's right here." Rebecca handed him the phone.

As soon as he'd hung up, she went into the master bedroom to call David, to tell him about the arrangements she'd made. She was hoping she'd reach his machine, but he was home. Talking to him made her nervous, so her explanation was brief and a little choppy. "I'll leave the Bronco in the garage under your building," she finished. "I hope it won't be too much trouble to get it back to the lake."

"There's no reason for you to drive," he said. "Hire a limo. I'll pay for it."

It was a good idea, but it had never occurred to her. She couldn't afford things like limousines. "All right. I'll see you in the office—"

"I've missed you."

She swallowed hard. "Me, too."

"I've been doing a lot of thinking—or trying to. It's hard. When I'm not in a meeting, I'm on the phone."

"And?"

"The only promise I can make is not to make promises I might not keep." He paused. "I love you, Rebecca. I don't want to hurt you."

"I know." She started shivering. "Linda thinks we're getting married. She offered to take the kids while we're on our honeymoon."

He cursed softly. "Look, I'm sorry about that—it's all my fault. I told the kids . . . Hell, the details don't matter. I'll straighten it out when I'm done with the stadium deal, okay?"

In other words, his work was more important to him than she was—still. She desperately needed to be with people who loved her, to soothe the pain he kept inflicting. She said goodbye, then called her parents in Fresno and told them rather shakily that she planned to visit. Her mother urged her to come as soon as she could; Emily and her family were due back in the morning, and it would be nice if everyone could get together for Shabbat dinner and the final night of Hanukkah. The night after that was New Year's Eve, a time of hope and promise, and Rebecca was suddenly relieved she wouldn't have to spend it alone with the kids.

The limousine was a lifesaver. Since the driver had passengers to pick up in San Francisco, he couldn't afford to stay in Sausalito for more than a few minutes. Rebecca was spared not only the long, tedious drive west, but also embarrassing questions from Linda Harris. Within an hour of getting home, she'd fed the kids, watered the plants, packed for Fresno and loaded the car. Even so, she wasn't quite fast enough to avoid the Friday traffic across the bridge.

The kids spent the first couple of hours talking, napping, squabbling and listening to their Sony Walkmans. Finally, halfway through the trip, Sarah tapped Rebecca on the shoulder and asked timidly, "Mommy, why are you and David mad at each other?"

The question was inevitable, but it still caught her off guard. "We're not mad. We just disagree."

"About what?" Danny asked.

"It's pretty complicated." How did she explain it to a seven- and ten-year-old? "Remember what I said the other night about being true to what's most important to you? Well, you two kids are the most important thing in my life, and I want to give you as much time as you deserve." She paused, then added softly, "I didn't do that when I was married to Daddy. I wasn't home enough. I wasn't a very good mother."

"Yes, you were," Danny said. "You're the best mother anyone could have."

Her eyes filled up. "Thank you, honey, but—"

"And anyway, what's that got to do with marrying David? He loves you a lot. He told us he did."

"You can go out with him all you want," Sarah said. "We won't mind."

There was no way to convince them they *would* mind, just as they had with their father, or to explain that you needed more than love for a successful marriage. "I do care what you think," she said, "but this is between me and David. I want a husband who comes home every night. I want someone who likes doing things as a family. David has to decide if he wants those things, too."

"But—"

"The subject is closed, Danny." He muttered something to Sarah about how grumpy Mom was, but she let it pass. Between the trip to San Francisco and this one, they'd been traveling for over six hours. Everyone's temper was a little short.

They arrived in Fresno just after her family had given up waiting and sat down to dinner. Within minutes of joining them, Rebecca began to relax. She loved the gossip, teasing and joking of these holiday celebrations.

The evening passed quickly; one moment the kids were lighting the menorah and the next, in what seemed like an hour but was actually three, Rebecca's parents yawned and headed upstairs. Emily's husband promptly got up, and so did all four children— Danny and Sarah were spending the night at their cousins' house, a few miles away—but Emily didn't budge.

Once everyone had left, Rebecca smiled at Emily and murmured, "Talk about a mass exodus! Why do I have the feeling it was planned?"

"Because it was. I hadn't been home for more than half an hour before Mom called and told me you seemed to be having a crisis. I thought you might want to talk.''

Emily knew so much about Rebecca's life that it didn't take long to relate the latest chapter. Emily had even met David a couple of times, when she'd come to San Francisco to visit and shop.

In the past she'd never criticized or pushed her point of view; she'd simply listened and comforted. Because of that, Rebecca had assumed Emily would agree with whatever she said, but instead, her sister replied gently, "Isn't it time you stopped punishing yourself for what a lousy mother you were when Dick was alive? What good is all that guilt?''

"No good at all, but that's not the point. I don't want to make the same mistake twice.''

"What mistake? Leading a full life?" Emily put her hand on Rebecca's shoulder. "You've cared about making the world a better place since you were eight years old and marched around the neighborhood with campaign literature. You still do, or you wouldn't give speeches and sit on boards of directors no matter who you were once married to. As for David, you're talking as if you expect him to drop everything he cares about and sit around darning socks. I wonder...does that include the waterfront project you keep raving about or the AIDS hospice you talked him into building? He still chairs their board, doesn't he?''

Emily knew perfectly well that he did. "I don't expect him to drop everything, and I'm sure he realizes it," Rebecca said. "His projects are an asset to any city he builds in, and I admit I've gotten him involved in a few charities. But there's a difference between going out one or two nights a week the way I do and five or six the way he does. I want a real husband and father this time around.''

''And you deserve one. I'd be the last one to argue with that.'' Emily sighed. ''I don't mean to nag, but you're not seeing that *you* have a problem, too. You spoke about Hanukkah and being true to what's best in you, but what is that, really? What are going to be the driving forces in your life? Love and generosity or anger and guilt? Why do you keep punishing yourself and resenting Dick when it's obvious to anyone with eyes that your kids are doing fine?''

Rebecca was a little stunned. ''You honestly think I'm being driven by guilt rather than concern for the kids?''

''In part, yes. From what you've told me, Danny and Sarah aren't worried about the marriage, and believe me, kids are selfish. If they felt threatened, you'd know it. Maybe they see David more clearly than you do.''

Rebecca shook her head, confused now. ''But he's never around, Emmy!''

''I'm not saying he doesn't need to make some changes, but between you and his sons, he's been hit with an awful lot. Give him time to adjust. Let him know you're flexible—that when you talk about commitment, you don't mean prison. Forgive yourself for the past; your kids have. And if you love him, Becky, for heaven's sake, compromise!''

Rebecca gave Emily a hug and promised to think about what she'd said. She went upstairs expecting to toss and turn for hours, but felt an unexpected sense of peace once she'd curled into bed. *Be true to what's best in you.* How heartening and inspiring that was!

* * *

David was tired of doing things he didn't want to do. He'd spent three solid days renegotiating the stadium deal—and salvaging it, thank God—but he'd felt more relief than triumph at the end. He was happy about it, naturally, but it wasn't the same without Rebecca. He missed talking to her, holding her, making love to her. The moment they'd wrapped up the deal, he'd picked up the phone and called her.

She hadn't been home, so he'd tried again...and again and again. He'd wanted to ask her to go to a New Year's Eve party with him. He hadn't reached a decision yet, but he would have admitted that. He'd simply wanted to see her...desperately.

Now he was at the party, standing in a glorious mansion with the most powerful people in the city, drinking splendid wine from the host's Napa Valley winery. An invitation to this annual party was one of the most coveted in town. Six years ago, when he'd finally made the list, he'd grinned like a kid. These people were his friends now. By any standard one could name, he'd made it.

He took his wine outside and leaned against a tree. Okay then, he had it all. He'd accomplished everything he'd set out to, maybe even more than Mike could have. It didn't matter why he'd worked so hard; the fact was that he'd always enjoyed it. He enjoyed his *life*.

On the other hand, the people inside might be his friends—movers and shakers whom he ran into constantly at parties and fund-raisers—but only a handful really mattered to him. They liked one another and cultivated one another for their money and influence, but there were few emotional connections.

If he'd dropped off the face of the earth, few of them would have mourned him, and vice versa. The party bored him, his work didn't excite him as much as it used to and his life felt a little hollow. If he had it all, it wasn't enough.

He thought about what Rebecca had said Tuesday night, trying to fit his life into her framework. He'd never violated his deepest convictions, and nobody else told him what to do, but something was still missing. It shouldn't have been, not if he was doing what he really wanted—what was right for him. So either he hadn't noticed the empty spaces all these years or something had changed. He didn't know which or particularly care; he knew only that he wanted far more from and with Rebecca than he ever had from Linda.

A minute later he was sitting in his car, calling Rebecca for the fifth time. He felt like kicking the dashboard when there was still no answer. It was almost eleven. Where in hell was she? Could she have left town, gone to visit her parents? The number was in his secretary's Rolodex, in case they needed to reach her when she was in Fresno. He started the car and pulled into traffic.

Rebecca knew it was crazy to rush back to San Francisco after dinner—David was sure to be at the Chappelles' party—but she couldn't stop herself. She was so eager to see him she would have camped outside his house if it hadn't been for all the drunks and crazies out tonight. As it was, she'd have to settle for calling him after midnight.

She stifled a yawn as she reached her street, slowing as she approached her building. There was a private garage underneath, and as she turned to enter, she saw a man in formal dress standing under the light by the gate. David.

She unlocked the door, and he slid into the car. She noticed he was holding a bottle of champagne. "What are you doing here? How did you know—"

"I called your mother. She told me you were on your way home." He put the car in park and took her in his arms. "God, I've missed you."

His kiss was sweet, passionate and emotional, and it told her everything she needed to know. She responded ardently and joyfully, trying to tell him the same things. Their hands found their way under each other's jackets, oblivious to the fact that the car was blocking a public sidewalk. They might have kissed indefinitely if it hadn't been for the eruption of giggles in the back seat.

Smiling, they broke apart and looked over their shoulders. The kids, who'd fallen asleep on the way home, were now awake. "Does this mean you're gonna get married?" Danny asked.

"I think that's what it means," David answered.

"And Mike and Joey will live with us, too?"

"It looks that way." He put his arm around Rebecca. "I've been thinking about moving to the suburbs. The commuting won't be that bad—not with a chauffeur to do the driving. Besides, I'll be spending fewer evenings in the city. What do you think?"

"I don't care where we live, as long as I have my own room," Danny said.

Sarah smiled sweetly. "Can I have a canopy bed, David?"

He laughed. "Ah, fatherhood!"

Five minutes later, as they entered the elevator, Rebecca whispered to David that she didn't care where they lived, either, as long as she shared *his* room. Inside the apartment she got some glasses for the champagne and settled the kids in sleeping bags on the living room floor. She'd promised them they could see in the new year.

She and David sat down on the couch. Midnight came, with the tape of the ball dropping in Times Square. And somehow, even though the holiday had ended at sundown, she knew exactly what he meant when he kissed her gently and whispered, "Happy Hanukkah, sweetheart" rather than "Happy New Year." They hadn't had a chance to talk, but neither of them would have been here if they hadn't learned something from the spirit of the holiday—and acted on it.

The children were fast asleep now. "The happiest one I've ever had," she said, and kissed him back.

* * * * *

Hanukkah is pretty low-key around our house. I put up decorations that my teenagers insist are silly looking, we light candles and exchange presents, and we eat entirely too many *latkes*. When the kids were smaller, they enjoyed playing dreidel, but now they think it's boring. My son still helps me make Hanukkah cookies—butter cookies cut out in the shapes of dreidels, menorahs and Stars of David—but that's mostly because he likes to eat the dough.

Rather like David Stern, I learned more about Hanukkah in the course of researching this story than in seven years of religious school. Our primary historical source for the holiday is the Books of Maccabees, especially I Maccabees, written around 120 B.C. Although the original Hebrew versions have been lost and are not part of the Jewish Bible, the Greek translations have come down to us as part of the Roman Catholic Apocrypha.

For that reason, nobody knows the Hebrew origin of Judah the Maccabee's surname, *makkabaios* in Greek. It might have come from the Hebrew word for hammer, *makkeb*, or from *makabiah*, "named by the Lord." In any event, while I learned as a child that Judah led a war to preserve our religious freedom and some oil miraculously burned for eight nights, I was told nothing about Hanukkah's historical background or populist roots. To me, as to my heroine, the real miracle is that the Maccabees won at all.

I'm indebted to my rabbi, Dr. Lester Frazin, for discussing the holiday with me and for suggesting a theme that fit in perfectly with my characters...that the underlying message of Hanukkah is having the freedom to be ourselves. Additional information came from the book *Hanukkah*, edited by Emily Solis-Cohen, Jr.

As a minor festival, Hanukkah doesn't exert the same powerful emotional pull as Passover, Rosh Hashanah (New Year) and Yom Kippur (the Day of Atonement), which are not only fundamental religiously but are also the major family holidays of Judaism. For two reasons, however, Hanukkah has gradually become more prominent. First, we live in an age when personal and religious freedoms are singularly precious to us, so Hanukkah and the events it commemorates speak to us in a special way. And second, assimilated Jewish parents feel a need to "compete" with Christmas that our ancestors surely didn't.

To kids, though, the grass is always greener on the other side of the fence. Jewish kids may envy the magic of Christmas morning, but I've heard several stories about Christian kids thinking this one-present-a-night thing is definitely the better deal. Whichever holiday you celebrate, may the season bring you joy and peace.

Brooke Hastings

CHRISTMAS MAGIC

Annette Broadrick

*To Nancy, who has a
special magic of her own*

SWEET POTATO-BERRY BAKE

2 17 oz. cans sweet potatoes, halved and drained
1 cup of fresh cranberries
¼ cup chopped pecans
½ cup orange marmalade

Place the sweet potatoes in a 10″ x 6″ baking dish and top with the berries and nuts. Dot with the marmalade. Bake for 30 minutes in a 350°F oven. Serve piping hot.

Chapter One

Natalie Phillips patiently made her way through the crush of Christmas shoppers in the large department store. The store and the mall surrounding it had been built during the six years since Natalie had left Portland, Oregon. This was the first time she had returned to the city where she'd grown up, and thus far she had found the visit to be as painful as she had feared it would be. Poignant memories kept intruding on the present.

In quiet desperation, Natalie had borrowed her brother's car that afternoon and had gone shopping at the Clackamas Town Center, a large mall near I-205. Surely she would find nothing there to remind her of other times—of happier and more innocent times.

Natalie had learned a great deal about people in the six years she had been gone. Never would she be so gullible again, so willing to believe in fantasies—in happy-ever-after.

She could sense the anticipation and excitement in the very air she breathed. Christmastime—a time to spend with loved ones; a time of suppressed excitement and secrets; a time of smiles and laughter, of family warmth and giving; a time of peace.

Unfortunately Natalie hadn't been able to find much peace. Not in Portland. She had another life now and no longer wanted any reminders of the past. She had left the unhappiness of six years ago behind her and was determined not to allow it to influence her future.

Natalie watched as a young child paused to exclaim over a Christmas display at the store's wide entrance to the rest of the mall. The excited child pointed, calling his mother's attention to the glitter and animated figures.

Natalie glanced around, unconsciously searching for someone with whom she could share the small scene. Her gaze caught and held for a moment, and she stared at the broad back of a man standing in front of a jewelry display counter.

There was something about the wide shoulders, the confident stance and the way he held his head that reminded her of the one man she had worked hard to forget.

Tony D'Angelo.

Surely not. She must be imagining a likeness that wasn't there. After all, she hadn't seen him in six years. No doubt the Tony she remembered no longer existed. He had probably never been as attractive as her memory had recalled during the many nights she'd lain awake thinking about him.

Natalie moved closer, drawn to the man who seemed to be intently studying the jewelry beneath the glass display counter. He turned his head so that she saw his profile, and Natalie froze, no longer able to deny what her senses were telling her.

There was no mistaking that beautiful profile that looked as though it belonged on an ancient Roman coin. Black curly hair fell across his forehead, and he impatiently shoved it back, a familiar gesture that almost brought tears to her eyes.

Hesitantly, Natalie cut through the crowd toward him. Should she speak to him? Would he even remember her? Wouldn't it be better to leave all of her fantasies and memories intact? Surely speaking to him would only destroy any of her remaining illusions.

But could she walk away and not at least give herself the opportunity to speak to him once more? While part of her seemed to be in a perpetual debate, her feet continued to move toward him until she stood an arm's length away.

"Tony?"

She watched as he seemed to tense, then slowly turned to face her.

"I wasn't sure it was you," she said, trying to smile. "Hello, Tony."

The six years had been more than kind to him. His body had matured and filled out. At twenty-two he had been tall and slender with a wiry strength that she'd found impressive. Now his arms and chest were wide, tapering down to a narrow waist and hips.

His face looked more chiseled. There were lines around his mouth and eyes that hadn't been there before. And his eyes—those beautifully expressive black eyes—no longer told Natalie what he was thinking. He stared at her with no discernible expression.

"Don't you remember me? I'm Natalie—"

"I remember you," he broke in. "I was just surprised to see you."

"Yes. It's been a long time, hasn't it?"

"Has it?"

His gaze flickered over her as though automatically registering any changes in her. She wondered what he would see. She had just turned eighteen the last time she had seen him. She'd been so young then—too young to have known how to handle the situation she'd found herself in. Would she ever be able to forget the last time she'd seen him? He'd been angry then, watching her with snapping eyes as she'd walked away—out of his life and away from the future that they had naively planned together.

It was obvious he'd never forgiven her for her behavior. Those expressive black eyes were now shuttered, reflecting nothing of his thoughts or feelings.

"Do you live around—" Natalie started to say when someone brushed heavily against her and knocked her off balance and against Tony. She stumbled, and he automatically put his arms around her to keep her from falling.

Being suddenly jarred was not responsible for the way her body reacted to his touch. How many nights had she dreamed of being in Tony's arms once more, of having him hold her close, murmuring soft love words in her ear? How could she ever forget the hard-muscled length of him, the familiar scent of his after-shave lotion that continued to haunt her whenever she caught a whiff of it being worn by someone else—and the way she fit so well against him, her head nestling into his shoulder?

Natalie placed her hands on his chest and tried to collect herself. "I'm sorry," she muttered breathlessly. "I'm afraid—"

He cut her off by growling, "Let's get out of here." Taking her arm he guided her out of the store and across the mall to the ice-skating area. Food franchises circled the upper level, and he moved with her toward the small tables and chairs that overlooked the rink. Motioning for her to sit down, he asked, "What would you like to drink?"

In some respects Tony hadn't changed. He was still in charge, not even asking if she wanted something— just giving her a choice. Six years ago he probably wouldn't have bothered asking that—he would have known her so well he would have automatically ordered for her.

"A hot chocolate, please," she said, and met his gaze.

She saw his eyes flicker briefly at her familiar selection, then whatever emotion had washed over him was gone. "I'll be right back."

Natalie watched as Tony weaved his way through the crowd to the nearest window and ordered.

Now that she could catch her breath, Natalie observed other changes in him, changes that surprised her.

His clothes, for one thing. Tony had always worn jeans, motorcycle boots and a black leather jacket, only one of the many reasons her father had disapproved of him. She smiled at the memory. She remembered how her heart would race whenever she heard the sound of his motorcycle pulling into the driveway.

Even then Tony hadn't cared what anyone thought of him, not even her father. He had dressed the way he wanted.

He'd worked in construction back then, and his wardrobe hadn't lent itself to formal attire. Tony had worked hard—doing heavy physical labor, taking on tasks that others shirked.

Whatever he was doing now for a living was certainly not hard on his clothes. He wore well-fitting slacks that accented his hips and thighs and a pull-over sweater that made a pleasing contrast to the long-sleeved shirt he wore.

But no tie.

That was in keeping with the Tony she remembered. She continued to watch him through the crowd as he patiently waited in line. Patience had never been one of Tony's biggest virtues, either.

But then she'd never considered patience particularly appealing herself. Yet now she was content to sit and watch him, speculating on his life in the past few years.

Was he married? He didn't wear any rings, but then he'd once explained to her that rings were dangerous in his business. Maybe he'd never gotten into the habit of wearing one.

Natalie had long ago convinced herself that she would not get upset when the time came that she heard Tony D'Angelo had married someone else. How could she possibly blame him? If she hadn't been so frightened and so unsure of herself, perhaps she could have better withstood her father's terrible anger.

She shook her head. Dwelling on the past was such a waste of time. There was no way to go back to undo the damage that had been done. Instead she forced herself to bring her mind back to the present and to the fact that, despite everything that had happened between them, she could think of no one she'd rather be with. For a short space out of time, Natalie was reminded of the magic of Christmas, the magic that Tony D'Angelo had brought into her life so many years before.

To most people, Natalie Phillips's childhood would have seemed to be blessed with a plentiful supply of wealth and advantages. Her brother, ten years older, had never had much time for her, and her mother had been very cautious about her playmates.

Consequently she had been a rather lonely child. She'd learned early in life to amuse herself by reading or playing with her dolls. Later she had enjoyed swimming and tennis, whenever she could find someone who was willing to play.

Natalie could remember exactly when she first laid eyes on Tony. She'd been ten years old.

It was summertime, and she had spent the morning in the house. She'd been upset that day, she remembered, because her parents had refused to allow her to go to summer camp. Or more precisely, her father had refused. Her mother had acquiesced to his decision as she always had, even though she had better understood Natalie's desire to go.

Henry Phillips had learned early in life that his only vulnerability was through his family, and he guarded them jealously. He knew that he'd stepped on many people getting to the top. He'd made enemies. He didn't care, but he wasn't going to take any chances that his family would suffer for any of his decisions. Consequently, Natalie was given very little freedom.

That day she had felt rebellious at her father's restrictions and had stomped outside, looking for a way to vent her anger and frustration.

Instead, she had fallen in love.

Fourteen-year-old Tony was riding a large lawn mower in the area behind her home. Two men were trimming the hedge that surrounded the swimming pool, but she never even noticed them.

He wore a pair of cutoffs that left his bronzed body bare. A red bandanna tied around his head kept his hair and the perspiration out of his face. He was so intent on what he was doing that he was oblivious to the people around him.

He looked like Adonis to the impressionable Natalie. She lost track of time as she watched him. Eventually the heat of the day penetrated her preoccupation. That's when she came up with the idea of bringing the gardeners something to drink.

Natalie rushed into the house, made a pitcher of ice water, found some freshly baked cookies and hastily returned to the back lawn.

Tony had stopped the mower and was checking the grass catcher when she came out.

"Hi! I bet you're thirsty, aren't you? I brought you some water and some cookies," she said.

She would never forget the way he had turned around, looked at her standing there so eagerly holding the tray and smiled.

"That sounds great. Thanks." She watched him untie the bandanna and rub it over his face before retying it around his forehead. Then he walked over to where she had set the tray on one of the tables by the pool. "What's your name?" he asked with a grin, after promptly emptying one of the glasses.

"Natalie."

"Thanks for the water, Natalie. That was very thoughtful of you." He glanced over at the house. "You live there?"

She nodded.

"Nice place," he said, studying the lines of the house as though they meant something to him.

"Would those men like something to drink?" she asked, nodding to the men who were at the far end of the pool.

"I'm sure they would." He raised his voice. "Say, Uncle Pietro, do you and Grandpapa want some water?"

The younger man glanced up. "We have a jug of water, Tony, and you know it. Don't bother the little girl."

Natalie flushed.

Tony glanced around and grinned. "He's right, but the ice has long since melted. And we certainly didn't bring any cookies!"

His black eyes danced mischievously as though she would understand and share the joke.

"How old are you, Natalie?" he asked, after he'd finished off two of the cookies.

"Ten."

"Ah, that's a good age."

"How old are you?"

"Fourteen."

"I'll be glad when I'm fourteen!"

"Why?"

"Because then maybe my father will let me do more things. He never lets me go anywhere!"

Tony smiled. "Maybe he just wants to protect you."

"From what?"

"From the world. From life. You're a very pretty girl, Natalie. If you were mine, I'd want to protect you, too."

His flashing smile in his dark face caused her breath to catch in her throat. He thought she was pretty? He would want to protect her, too?

She smiled, unable to think of anything to say.

"Get back to work, Tony. We don't have all day," one of the men hollered.

Tony shrugged and grinned. "I gotta run. Thanks again, Natalie."

She had watched him as he'd walked away with a spring to his step. She remembered thinking that day that she had never met anyone like him. She found him fascinating.

Nothing had ever caused her to change her mind.

"Here you are."

Startled, Natalie glanced up to see Tony sitting down across from her at the table. He carried two steaming insulated paper cups.

"It's good to see you again, Tony," she managed to say, her voice sounding husky to her ears.

He sat there for a few moments in silence, studying her. Finally he spoke. "Six years is a long time, isn't it?"

"Yes."

"You look very different from the young girl I watched grow up. I didn't think you could ever be more beautiful than you were at eighteen. I was wrong."

He spoke in a quiet, matter-of-fact tone, as though he were discussing the weather or skiing conditions on Mount Hood. He was making it clear that no matter how he'd reacted to her in the past, she had no effect on him now.

"How have you been, Tony?"

He took a sip of his drink. "You're a little late in asking, aren't you?"

"Yes, I suppose I am. I have no excuses to make for my behavior back then. I behaved very badly."

"Not really. You were young. You'd been sheltered all your life. Your actions were predictable."

"Perhaps. But I can see that you never forgave me for leaving."

"It wasn't a matter of forgiveness. You made your choice, that's all."

They sat there for a few moments in silence, sipping their hot drinks. Natalie discovered that she couldn't meet his gaze. She recalled that he had always had a direct gaze. He'd stood up to her father and brother, never showing any sign of being intimidated by them. Natalie had always felt as though Tony had the ability to look deep inside her, to see her innermost thoughts and feelings.

If only she had the knack of doing the same thing with him.

"How's your family?" she finally asked.

"Fine. Mama is busy cooking and baking for the holidays." He shook his head. "Now Angela is working right along with her. They could feed everyone around us for blocks."

"Is Angela married?"

He tilted his head slightly. "As a matter of fact, she is. Why?"

"I just wondered. I wrote to her a couple of times after I went back East to school. But she never answered." Natalie shrugged. "I've wondered if she decided to go on to school."

"Yes, she did. She met Paul in one of her classes. They were married two years ago."

"I think of Christmas and remember your family, Tony. I always thought they had such a wonderful way of celebrating—all the cooking and preparations and the fun they always had with the younger children." She shook her head. "I used to envy you your family."

"You envied us? That's funny, with your back-ground."

"Everything was always so formal at our home. The traditional tree and trimmings, the carefully wrapped gifts for Tom and me. The formal meal. There was never any laughter, any surprises. We seemed to go through the motions without experiencing any of the feelings of Christmas."

"And what feelings were those?"

She sighed, and her expression became wistful. "The love, the laughter, the sharing, the giving. All the wonderful things that your family seems to take for granted."

He shook his head. "Never for granted. We've always known what we had. I suppose I never realized before that you could see and appreciate all that we shared." He studied her for a moment, then asked, "When did you arrive in town?"

"Last night."

He glanced around the busy mall. "And now you're trying to get your shopping done, I take it?"

She shook her head. "Actually, I've already done that back in Boston. No, I just wanted to get out of the house today."

"How is your mother these days?" he asked politely, ignoring the undercurrent between them.

"Busy, as usual. She's so pleased that I decided to come to Portland for Christmas. She and Tom have always flown East each year, since my father died."

"I'm sure your brother was just as pleased that you came home."

"I suppose. Tom and I don't talk much."

"I see."

There were so many questions she wanted to ask him, so many things she wanted to know. But how could she? It was none of her business. Tony D'Angelo was no longer a part of her life. It was obvious that he had accepted that. Natalie had thought she had accepted it years ago. And she had. Of course she had. But only when she had the entire continent between them.

"How long are you going to be here?" he was asking her, and she forced herself to concentrate on his question. "I'm leaving the Monday after Christmas."

"Then you won't be here for New Year's."

"No. I have to get back."

How was it possible that they could be carrying on this perfectly normal conversation, like old friends who had been out of touch for a while, as though there was nothing between them?

But of course there *was* nothing between them now. Her father had seen to that—six years ago.

Chapter Two

Look, I've got to go," Natalie said, gathering her purse and packages. "Mother will be wondering about me. I borrowed Tom's car, and he's probably irritated that I've been gone this long."

Tony got to his feet. The smile he gave her didn't quite reach his eyes. "I'm sorry you have to rush off. I was rather hoping to hear about your life since we last saw each other."

She looked up at him, surprised by his interest. "Most of the time I was in school."

He seemed to hesitate. "I'm sure my family would be pleased to see you again. Would you like to come over some evening while you're here? I could pick you up."

Natalie's pulse began to race. Was this actually happening? Did Tony D'Angelo want to see her again, to spend additional time with her, after all that had happened between them?

Was there such a thing as a second chance?

"I'm not at all sure that you're right, Tony. I doubt that they want to see me after all this time."

"You might be surprised. Of course, it's up to you."

"I'd like to see them again, Tony. I'd like that very much."

His slow smile set up a vibration within her that caused her to almost visibly tremble. "Good. When could you go?"

"I really don't have anything planned."

"Then how about tomorrow night? I could pick you up at seven, if that would be convenient."

"That would be fine," she heard herself saying, as though from far away.

They parted, and only after Tony disappeared in the crowd did Natalie face the fact that except for the time when she'd been accidentally knocked into him and when he'd guided her through the crowd, Tony had carefully refrained from touching her.

What was she doing to herself? This was going to be some kind of refined torture, to become a part, once again, of the D'Angelo gathering at Christmastime.

Torture or not, she couldn't resist. How could anyone resist magic?

That night Natalie disgustedly punched her pillow and tried to straighten her rumpled bedclothes. She was tired. Fighting holiday crowds and traffic was always wearing, and she had gone to bed early, hoping to get some rest.

It was no use. Every time she closed her eyes she saw a pair of black eyes watching her. Sometimes their expression was warm and loving. At other times they held no expression at all.

Tony had handled their unexpected meeting today so well, without showing any shock or surprise. Was that an indication of how little his emotions had been affected by their meeting?

Natalie reminded herself that he had been standing at the jewelry counter—the *women's* jewelry counter, which strongly suggested there was definitely a woman in his life.

What else did she expect, anyway? Tony was extremely attractive. He always had been. She smiled, remembering...

She would never forget the summer she first met Tony, when he came to help his family take care of the sloping lawns and gardens of her home. Natalie had counted the days in between.

Not that she got to spend any time with him. That part didn't matter. It was enough for her to be able to watch him as he worked. As the weeks passed, she managed to find out more things about him.

He was the oldest of five children. She discovered that he had three sisters, one of whom, Angela, was Natalie's age, and a brother who was only a few months old. It was plain to Natalie that he loved his family very much.

By the time Natalie started high school she knew that there would never be any man who could possibly take Tony's place in her heart. In six years she had watched him become a man. He'd stopped working at her home after a couple of summers, but Natalie was able to see him occasionally because of Angela.

She had met Angela her first day of high school. The school was large, covering a vast district. As soon as she saw Angela she knew that the girl was related to Tony, with her curly black hair and dark eyes.

Angela had been shy but pleasant. Natalie and she quickly became friends. Although she could never convince Angela that she would be welcome in Natalie's home, eventually Angela had begun to invite Natalie to the D'Angelo home.

Natalie didn't deliberately lie to her mother about her whereabouts. It was true that Natalie was busy with school-related activities. However, there were times when meetings and other activities ended early, and luckily for Natalie the D'Angelos lived close to the school.

Not that she was ashamed of Angela or the D'Angelo family, but Natalie had learned early in life that her family had decided ideas about who she should spend time with. Her father, especially, had set stringent rules about her dating and the young men who he would consider worthy of her attentions.

Because of Natalie's shyness, most of those young men soon lost interest and went in search of more lighthearted friends. Natalie was content to help Angela with her younger sisters and brother. And when Tony happened to come home while she was still there, Natalie's day was complete. She lived for the times when she happened to see him.

Even the fact that he treated her much in the same way he treated Angela made no impression on her. He was Tony, and that was enough. His flashing smile and teasing remarks were cherished like a priceless treasure.

It was the summer between her junior and senior years, when she was seventeen, that everything changed between them.

Natalie had finally coaxed Angela into meeting Natalie's mother. Her mother seemed relieved that the two rather quiet girls had formed a friendship. She had heard enough stories from her friends about some of the wild parties and problems occurring around their children.

Consequently Natalie spent most of her summer at the D'Angelos' home with her mother's silent blessing.

She would never forget the first time that Tony asked her for a date. She and Angela had just come from swimming at Natalie's home. They were late and rushed back to the D'Angelos' because Angela had promised to cook dinner for Tony since the rest of the family had gone out of town for the weekend.

Tony was working full-time in construction, his only means of transportation a rather beat-up motorcycle. They had just gotten home and hadn't had time to change out of their suits when he walked into the house, looking hot and very tired.

"Oh, Tony," Angela wailed, "I'm sorry. The time just slipped away from us. I'll make you something to eat right away."

He sat down at the table. "Don't worry about it, Angie. It's too hot to eat right now, anyway." His gaze slid from his sister to Natalie, who was self-consciously tugging at her suit. Why hadn't she worn the new one she'd purchased the week before? This one was last year's and too small. It hadn't mattered to her when they'd first gotten the idea to get some relief from the unusual heat of the day.

Now she wished she'd taken the time to have searched for the new one instead of standing there wishing she could disappear.

Tony grinned, the mischief in his eyes apparent. "Hi, Natalie. That's a lovely shade of red you're wearing."

She glanced down at her faded blue suit, then looked up, puzzled.

"I'm talking about the color in your cheeks. No doubt you got too much sun today. You'd better be careful with your fair skin."

His eyes seemed to assess the condition of her skin, from her face down to her toes, lingering along the length of her legs.

"Uh, Angela, I'm going to go change clothes. Then I'll help you with dinner."

"I have a better idea," Tony said. "Why don't both of you go change, and I'll take you out for pizza."

"Oh, but Mama said that I was supposed to feed you," Angela replied.

"She won't care, as long as we eat. And it's too hot to cook."

Angela didn't need much coaxing, and the girls scurried to Angela's room.

Natalie could still remember that night. They had laughed and talked. Tony had seemed content to listen to their chatter. He'd subtly questioned Natalie about her activities, her interests and the boys in her life.

Angela had embarrassed her by pointing out that Natalie showed no interest in the boys *at school*. The emphasis was made for Natalie's benefit, and was the closest that Angela would come to letting Tony know where Natalie's affections lay.

It hadn't taken Angela long to discover Natalie's secret crush on her older brother. Since she quickly learned to love Natalie, Angela could think of nothing better than for her to love Tony. Angela worshiped her brother and always had.

But she had been zealous in never alluding to Natalie's feelings for Tony. Until that night.

Natalie retaliated by kicking her under the table, which elicited a spate of giggles from Angela. Tony looked mystified.

And later it was Tony who insisted on taking Natalie home—on the back of his motorcycle. He found her a helmet and made sure that she had a good grip around his waist before they left. Angela's sparkling smile when they drove off was filled with glee.

Natalie had never been that close to Tony before, and she reveled in it. He'd showered before taking them out for dinner, and she could distinguish the slight scent of soap and after-shave. She rested her head against his back and closed her eyes. Natalie didn't care how long the trip took. She could have stayed that way forever.

When they pulled into the driveway, Natalie noted that her parents were gone. Tony followed the driveway to the back, coming to rest near the garage.

After he helped her off, Tony turned as though to get back on the motorcycle again. Natalie found herself saying, "Do you have to go?"

He looked up, surprised.

"I mean, well, it's such a beautiful night and all. Wouldn't you like to sit out here and talk for a while?" She gestured toward the tables and chairs by the pool.

He glanced around. "Where are your parents?"

"They were invited to a dinner party tonight."

"And they left you here alone?"

She laughed. "Hardly. Charles and Harriet live up there." She pointed to the apartment located over the garage. "Charles always waits until my parents are home before making sure the house is locked and going home."

"What does Harriet do?"

"Cooks and does some of the light cleaning."

"Is that why you're always over at our place, learning to cook?"

She nodded, shyly. "Yes. Harriet doesn't like me messing around in her kitchen. Besides," she said with a toss of her head, "she doesn't know how to cook Italian."

Tony stroked one of the loose blond curls that lay on Natalie's shoulders. "And you want to learn how to cook Italian?"

Natalie was thankful that the moonlight concealed her blush. "Yes, I do."

"Why?" he asked bluntly.

She shrugged and glanced around, desperately looking for another topic of conversation. Spying the pool, she blurted out, "Would you like to go swimming?"

He laughed. "Sure. Unfortunately I don't have anything to swim in."

"That's no problem. We have extras." She grabbed his hand. "I'll show you." She led him to the cabana at the end of the pool. Holding up her bag, she said, "I'll slip my suit back on and meet you out here in a few minutes."

Natalie was trembling so, she could scarcely get undressed. Tony was there, and they were going swimming together...in the moonlight. It was the most romantic moment she could possibly imagine.

By the time she came out of the dressing room, Tony was already in the water, swimming laps. The moonlight glinted off the water, bathing him in a glow of light as he moved rapidly through the water.

Natalie quickly joined him, and he began to pace her, matching his strokes to hers. When she could not swim another stroke Natalie grabbed the edge and gasped, "I give up! I'm going to drown if I don't stop!" Her breath came in short pants.

Tony laughed. "I'd never let you drown, Natalie. You know that." He placed his hands on the side of the pool, one on each side of her, so that she was boxed in.

Her heart was racing so fast it was almost painful in her chest, and Natalie couldn't seem to get her breath. Tony was no longer smiling. In fact, she had never seen him look at her so seriously.

"You are so beautiful, Natalie, you seem almost unreal to me. Those silvery-blue eyes staring at me so innocently almost unman me completely." His voice was low, and he spoke haltingly, as though the words had been dragged out of him.

"I'm real," she managed to say softly.

He groaned. "Don't I know it." He glanced around. "I don't think this was such a good idea, after all."

"Why not?"

He shook his head. "Come on, let's get dressed."

Tony was only a few inches away from her, and Natalie couldn't resist the temptation to find out what it would be like to kiss Tony D'Angelo.

Before he could pull away, she let go of the side of the pool and placed her hands lightly on his shoulders. Then she leaned over and kissed him very softly on his lips.

She felt his start of surprise, then her body floated against his, touching his bare chest and legs. His mouth opened slightly, and he began to return her kiss without ever letting go of the side of the pool.

Natalie felt safe in the circle of his arms, and she relaxed more fully against him. Tony deepened the kiss, nudging her lips apart with his tongue. Natalie thought she would faint from the joy of sharing this intimate act with him.

When he finally pulled away, they were both breathing hard. Tony grasped her firmly around the waist and lifted her to the side of the pool, then vaulted up beside her. Without saying a word he pulled her into his arms again, this time holding her tightly against him as he repeated the lesson he'd just given her.

Natalie was eager to learn all that he taught, and she wrapped her arms around his neck, luxuriating in the feel of his crisp curls beneath her fingertips.

Tony's hand eventually slipped from her back to her breast. Natalie couldn't conceal her gasp, and Tony abruptly let go of her.

"What am I doing?" he muttered. "I must be insane." He glanced down at her. "I'm sorry, Natalie."

"I'm not," she replied. "I've dreamed of kissing you for years." Then she realized what she'd admitted to him and covered her face with her hands.

"Natalie?" he said in a wondering tone.

She refused to look at him.

"Natalie?" he repeated. "What are you saying? That you want to go out with me, spend time with me? What?"

Slowly she removed her hands from her face and looked at him. "Only if you want to be with me."

He shook his head. "I've spent years reminding myself that you aren't for me, that I shouldn't show my interest in you, and now you're telling me that—"

"You mean you don't think of me as just another sister?"

He almost choked with his laughter. "Hardly."

They stared at each other in silence. Then Tony brought his hand up and rested it against her cheek. She felt the tremor in his fingertips and vaguely recognized the restraint he was placing on himself. "Oh, Natalie. Do you have any idea what you do to me?"

She shook her head.

"I've got to go. Now." He stood up and strode to the dressing room. She sat there and stared at the door that had cut off her view of him until he reappeared. Then she slowly came to her feet. He walked over to her. "Against my own sense of self-preservation, I'm going to call you for a date. I'll borrow Dad's car. We'll go to a movie or something. We'll go someplace where there are people and where I'm not so tempted. But I've got to see you again, Natalie. Do you understand?"

She smiled. "I'm glad."

He ran his hand over her damp curls. "I've got to be out of my mind."

"If so, then I've joined you," she said with a shy smile.

He pulled her to him and gave her a brief, hard kiss, then set her away from him. "Good night," he said, and turned away. The sudden sound of his motorcycle in the quiet night seemed to bring a touch of reality to the fantasy evening. Natalie watched Tony pull away. She stood there until he disappeared down the driveway, then turned away to go upstairs to relive the past few hours.

For the next two and a half months she saw Tony every day. She no longer cared what her mother thought, or her father. When her father made his disapproval of their relationship clear, she ignored him for the first time in her life.

She loved Tony. She had loved him for years. And now she had the opportunity to be with him as much as his work schedule would allow. Natalie refused to think of the future. She wanted to enjoy her time with Tony that summer. In her mind's eye each day spent with him was another pearl of memories that she collected until a beautiful strand of shared moments linked them to each other.

Natalie floated through the summer in her own dreamlike state of contentment, until the end of August when her father announced that she would not be returning to the public high school for her senior year. She would be going back East to a private girls' school.

Chapter Three

Tony D'Angelo lay awake for hours the night he saw Natalie at the mall. He went over each and every word that was spoken, looking for clues to how she felt about him.

The changes in her were not surprising. Six years was a long time. Was it too long for feelings to last? She had loved him at one time, that much he was sure of. But what about now?

She had seemed glad to see him, hadn't she? He wasn't sure how he had appeared to her. He'd been too busy guarding his reaction to the sudden, unexpected sight of her.

After six years, he had given up hope of her returning to Portland. He had known that sooner or later he would have to make the effort to contact her one last time, but he had continued to put off that inevitable meeting for as long as possible.

Now he had no choice. She was back, and he had to talk with her. He owed her some explanation regarding his silence for the past six years. Would she understand? Would she even care?

She hadn't asked him why he hadn't attempted to contact her nor had she given any explanations for her silence. He wasn't sure he was ready to hear that she had long ago dismissed him from her life. But then, what could he expect from her?

Six years was a long time. But he had kept his word to her father, long after the man was gone. Tony considered his word his honor. Her brother, Tom, had kept her family's side of the bargain.

Now was the time to bring their situation to an end and hopefully use it as a new beginning.

Tony turned over and lay on his stomach, his thoughts full of memories.

He would never forget the first time he'd ever laid eyes on Natalie. She'd been a shy little girl who looked like an angel to him, the kind that always sat at the very top of the D'Angelo family Christmas tree. She'd worn her hair long, the golden curls cascading down her back in a saucy ponytail. But it was her eyes that had drawn him to her. Those clear blue eyes that seemed to be the window of her soul, as though she had no secrets to hide. The dark fringe of thick lashes had appeared to be almost artificial with her light hair and fair skin.

Tony knew that he'd fallen in love that very first day, when she'd shyly offered him something to drink and some cookies.

How old had she been then? Ten or so, probably. She'd looked like a little porcelain doll, and he'd wanted to wrap her up and take her home with him, to protect her against all the hard knocks that life had to offer.

He still felt the same way. He just wasn't sure what course to take. Perhaps she only needed protection from him. At least her father had always felt that way. Perhaps he had been right.

Well, now she was back in Portland again, and she had agreed to visit his parents with him the next night.

That was a start, anyway. He would just have to play it by ear.

He fell asleep thinking about her clear-eyed gaze smiling at him with love.

"Mama, look who I found out shopping yesterday," Tony said, motioning for Natalie to join him in the hallway of the family home. He had kissed and hugged his mother when she opened the door.

"Natalie! What a surprise! Come in, come in. You must be freezing out there." Serena D'Angelo waved her arms and hurried Tony and Natalie into the other room where a merrily dancing fire in the fireplace added to the warmth of the atmosphere.

"Hello, Mrs. D'Angelo. I hope you don't mind that I came along."

"What nonsense. Of course I don't mind. You have been a part of this family for years. Besides, you know me. I always cook enough to feed a couple dozen people." She turned and hurried out of the room. "Papa, you will never guess who Tony brought home with him!"

They stood and listened to the voices from the other room. "What did I tell you?" Tony asked with a grin.

From her place in the center of the room, Natalie slowly turned, taking in everything. Tears filled her eyes. So much was familiar—the decorations and ornaments, the Nativity scene on the mantel, the gaily decorated fir tree in the corner that she knew the family had found and cut down as part of their traditional Christmas celebration.

And yet, she saw signs of change as well—new drapes, a new sofa and chair. The place looked homey and lived in—in addition to being well loved.

For the first time since she'd arrived in Portland, Natalie felt as though she had finally come home.

"What's wrong?" Tony asked, concerned.

She shook her head. "Nothing. It's just so good to be here. I didn't think I'd ever see any of this again."

He held out his hand. "Let's go find the others. I forgot to ask if Angela and Paul were coming."

Natalie soon found herself accepted into the laughing circle of the family as though she had never been away. The changes were more apparent at the dinner table. There were only two children still living at home, and they had changed so much that Natalie wasn't certain she would have recognized them. Tony's brother was now fourteen and bore a distinct resemblance to the boy she'd met so many years before.

The D'Angelos were such a warm, loving family. She enjoyed watching the banter and teasing that seemed to be a part of their conversation.

At one point, Serena turned to Natalie and said, "I called Angela and told her you were here. She said that Paul was working late tonight but they would try to come over in time to have coffee and dessert with us." She patted Natalie's hand. "Angela was very excited to know you were here. She has lots of news for you."

Natalie had missed Angela. She had never made another friend who had been as close to her as Angela. Natalie felt as though she'd lost so much that was irreplaceable when she moved back East.

She wondered how Angela would treat her now.

"So tell us what you've been doing, Natalie," Serena continued after making certain that everyone had all that they wanted to eat.

Natalie glanced around and saw that the whole family was waiting for her answer.

"Mostly going to school. I've been doing some graduate work, learning how to help children who have learning disabilities."

"Where do you intend to work when you're through with your schooling?" Serena asked.

Natalie shook her head. "I don't know."

"I'm sure you could find something in the Portland area if you wanted," she pointed out.

Natalie's gaze met Tony's intent one. "That's true," she said softly, wondering what would happen if she were to move back to Portland. Two days ago she would never have considered the idea. Now that she had seen Tony again, her mind seemed to be coming up with some rather unusual ideas.

Serena went on. "I know you must be proud of Tony. Hasn't he done well?"

Natalie looked at Tony sitting there so relaxed beside her. His hand rested alongside hers, and she had an almost uncontrollable urge to touch him. "What do you mean?" she asked, reluctantly forcing her attention toward Serena.

"Hasn't he told you?" Serena asked, beaming. "Tony has his own company now."

Natalie looked at him once more. "Your own company? I don't understand."

He shrugged. "Construction is what I know. I've been going to night school, learning the technical information I needed to build. I started remodeling old homes until I got enough capital to buy one. After that it became a matter of selling the remodeled homes and buying more. I've been doing some new construction as well."

"Oh, Tony. That's wonderful."

"I doubt that your father would have been impressed."

His words seemed to echo and reecho around the room. Her father. Yes, her father's influence on her life still lingered. How different things would have been now without his interference.

"Natalie! You're really here!" Natalie glanced up in time to see Angela rushing toward her. "I couldn't believe it when Mama said you had come to visit." She hugged Natalie, then whirled around. "Paul, come meet Natalie."

A tall blond-headed man had followed the diminutive brunette into the room and had stood there watching the reunion with a smile on his face. "Hello, Natalie," he said with a nod. "I'm glad to finally meet you."

Serena motioned to two empty chairs and said, "Sit! Sit! You're just in time for some cake and ice cream."

"Oh, no, Mama, I can't. I'm having to watch everything I eat these days."

Natalie looked at her slim friend in surprise. "Surely you're not dieting, Angie?"

Angela chuckled. "Not exactly. But I'm still having trouble with nausea in the morning, and I've discovered that it's much easier to eat lightly the night before."

Natalie looked from her friend's face to those seated around the table. "Is this news to anyone besides me?"

They all burst out laughing. Serena explained, "Angie insisted that she wanted to be the one to tell you. I thought we managed to stay off the subject very well, didn't you?"

"Oh, Angela. I'm so happy for you." Flashes of previous conversations they had had over the years came back to her. They had both wanted large, happy families. It looked as though Angela was well on the way to starting hers. Natalie felt a flash of envy at her friend's good fortune. She glanced at Tony and found his intent gaze on her. She dropped her eyes, unable to face him.

Once upon a time she and Tony had talked about the family they wanted to have some day. That was another life ago, before she had decided to train to help other people's children.

She looked at Serena. "So you are going to have a grandchild, are you?"

Serena laughed. "Yes. I can hardly wait."

No one mentioned that Tony, being the oldest, had been the most likely candidate to produce the first grandchild. Natalie glanced down at her hands, which restlessly twisted in her lap.

Tony reached down and touched her hands lightly, as though gently soothing her. She looked up at him, startled by the gesture. What she saw in his face made her realize that he, too, remembered their plans.

The conversation continued with numerous interruptions and hilarious anecdotes as each family member shared with Paul some of the situations that Natalie and Angela used to find themselves in while trying to learn to cook.

Natalie couldn't remember the last time she had laughed so hard nor felt so loved and accepted. After clearing the table and cleaning the dishes, the family returned to the living room where Natalie found herself sandwiched on the small sofa between Tony and his younger brother.

Tony had pulled Natalie against his side with his arm around her shoulders as though it were normal and a routine they had established in front of his family. She smiled at the thought. He had always treated her with such careful distance whenever they'd been around the family in the past, making sure that they understood he was taking no liberties with her.

Now he seemed to be making a silent claim on her, one that was deeply affecting her. How had she possibly stayed away from him this long without making some effort to know if what they had once shared was salvageable? Because if it was—if his body language this evening was any indication—Natalie knew that God in His mercy was willing to give her another chance at happiness.

"Are you ready to go?" Tony asked Natalie some time later, after Angela mentioned that she needed to get home and get some rest.

Natalie smiled. "I'm never ready to leave this place," she said, coming to her feet and hugging Serena. "But I do need to get home. It's been so wonderful, seeing everyone again and sharing one of your marvelous meals. Thank you so much for dinner."

"You're quite welcome," Serena replied, hugging her back. "What are you planning to do for Christmas, Natalie?"

"We haven't discussed anything, actually. My brother's tied up in some big business negotiations and is seldom home. Mother's been busy with Christmas plans for some of the organizations she works with, but she hasn't said anything about our family plans."

"Well, you're welcome to come over here. You know we still have the open house on Christmas Eve, and we all go to the church services at midnight."

Serena glanced at her oldest son. "You were planning to come, weren't you, Tony?"

"Of course, Mama. I've never missed spending Christmas with you, now have I?" he said, giving her a hug.

One of the many things that Natalie had always admired was the freedom the D'Angelo family had with each other to express their affection. She had never seen her father, or even her brother, hug her mother. She couldn't remember the last time either her mother or brother had touched her.

There was so much she missed about this family. Watching Tony she knew that she would give everything she owned to be a part of it now.

Tony was quiet during the drive to Natalie's former home located in the west hills overlooking Portland. Natalie wanted to say something, anything to break the silence.

"I take it you're no longer living at home," she finally said.

Tony glanced at her, then returned his gaze to the road in front of them. "No. I'm living in one of the houses I'm currently remodeling."

"Would it be possible for me to see it?" she asked. "Now?"

Her heart seemed to be thundering in her chest. What did he think she meant? She wasn't sure, herself. She'd just been trying to fill in some of the silence between them, trying to overcome the tension that had appeared as soon as they were alone.

"I don't think that would be a very good idea," she said, knowing that she was admitting a great deal more than she'd wanted to by her statement.

Tony didn't reply but continued toward her home.

They pulled into the long driveway that followed the hillside up to the large home. Instead of parking in front, Tony continued around to the back entrance. He turned off the lights and engine of the car, then turned to her. "If you really want to see my place, I could take you over there after I finish working tomorrow."

The light over the garage created shadows across his face, and she couldn't read his expression. "I'd like that," she admitted softly.

Tony looked at the garage, the house, the swimming pool, then back at her. "This feels very familiar, doesn't it? Bringing you home like this? Wondering if we woke up your parents?"

She smiled. "You have to admit that this car is considerably different from your old pickup or the motorcycle."

He grinned. "True. I doubt that anyone in the neighborhood heard us drive in this time."

They stared at each other in silence. Tony placed his hand on her cheek and gently brushed his thumb across her slightly parted lips. "I've missed you," he finally said in a husky voice.

"I missed you, too. I guess I just assumed that you never wanted to see me again."

He stroked along her ear and down her neck as though relearning the shape and feel of her. "Why would you think that?"

"Because of what happened. Because I never heard from you after I left."

He tilted her chin so that she had no other option but to look at him, unless she closed her eyes. She was tempted by the thought—to close her eyes and move the necessary few inches to kiss Tony again, to experience the wonderful magic that only he seemed to evoke. But she had to know. Why hadn't he tried to contact her through the years? She had asked Angela to have him write to her, but she hadn't heard from either of them.

He leaned over and placed a gentle kiss at her temple, his touch feeling like butterfly wings brushing against her sensitive skin.

"I couldn't contact you. That was part of the agreement."

She stared up at him in confusion. "What agreement?"

"The one I made with your father."

"I don't know what you're talking about."

"I'm not surprised."

"He told you to leave me alone?"

"What else did you expect from him? He never accepted me in your life. He made his disapproval very obvious, particularly that last time I saw you."

She could feel the heat rising to her face, but could not control it. How many years had she tried to forget that last time she'd been with Tony? She shook her head. "I was so frightened."

"I know. I even understood your reaction at the time. But it still hurt."

She placed her hand on his arm. "I never wanted to hurt you, Tony. Please believe me."

"I know. I understood that at the time. You were very young. You were faced with a decision you weren't prepared to make."

"You're right. I thought I'd made all the decisions that were necessary." She could feel her heart racing in her chest. She wanted him to kiss her and hold her, to reassure her that his feelings hadn't changed for her.

If he were to ask her to stay in Portland, she would willingly do so. But how could she understand how he felt if he didn't say anything?

He leaned over and lightly kissed her on the lips, then pulled away from her. "I'd better get you inside. It's late."

Natalie tried to hide her reaction, hoping that the shadows masked her expression. What had she expected, anyway? They were both too old to sit out in the car like a couple of teenagers.

"Why don't I come by tomorrow early enough to show you the house before dark? Then we can have dinner together somewhere."

She smiled. "I'll be ready whenever you say." Tony got out of the car and walked around to her side. She waited until he had opened her door, then said, "I want you to know how much I appreciated getting to see your family tonight. Being with them brought back so many happy memories."

"Yes, it did. We used to enjoy teasing you and Angela so much. I'd almost forgotten."

They reached the screened porch and paused. The cold night air seemed to move around them in swirls. "Sleep well," he said with a smile, holding the door open for her. "I'll see you tomorrow."

Natalie nodded. "You do the same," she said, and hurried inside to the warmth of the house.

Natalie slowly climbed the stairway to her room. Memories of her last Christmas in Portland continued to stir around her, as though insisting on being recalled and acknowledged.

After going through her nightly ritual of getting ready for sleep, Natalie stretched out on the bed and pulled the covers up around her.

If only she could understand the man that Tony had become. He acted so natural around her, as though he were comfortable with her. Was she the only one feeling the tension that seemed to hold her prisoner whenever he was present?

What had happened to the young man she had known, the one she had fallen so much in love with? Did he still exist somewhere beneath that calm and controlled exterior?

The hovering memories swooped down around her, eager to gain her attention once again.

Chapter Four

After almost four months away from home, Natalie still hated the boarding school. She missed Angela and her friends at school. But most of all, she missed Tony. After having seen him every day during the summer, the sudden jolt of being away from him had been almost more than she could handle. Her father had not even allowed her to come home for Thanksgiving, insisting she take the time to get better acquainted with her new classmates before coming home for Christmas.

With only another week before Christmas, Natalie hurriedly packed so that she would be ready to catch her ride to the airport. She felt like she'd been away from home for years instead of months.

She'd written Tony almost every day that she'd been gone. He had managed to respond to a few of her letters, admitting that he wasn't very good at corresponding, but that didn't mean that he wasn't counting the days until she arrived home for Christmas vacation.

Natalie had kept a large calendar hanging over her desk and had drawn a large X through each day before going to bed. At long last she would be able to see him again, even though she wasn't sure how.

Her father had refused to be swayed from his decision to send her away last September. She had cried.

She had pleaded. Never in her life had Natalie wanted so desperately to stay home, but he would not relent.

He made it clear that his daughter was going to have a proper education and meet the right kind of people. Her summer rebellion was now over.

She hadn't even been given the opportunity to tell Tony goodbye. Instead, she'd had to send a message through Angela.

Natalie had learned a great deal in the past few months. She had learned not to be so open and trusting. She had always thought that her parents respected her, including her beliefs and opinions. She had learned that she was wrong. She would never make that mistake again.

Natalie had no intention of telling her family that she was going to spend any time with the D'Angelos. She had made sure that her letters were full of the new people she'd met and all of her activities. As far as her parents knew, she had forgotten her old friends.

By the time she'd been home for two days, she could tell that she had convinced them of her lack of interest in anyone in Portland. She made a great many remarks about how boring it was to be home and how she could hardly wait to return East. Watching the satisfied glance her father gave her mother convinced Natalie that she could have a career in acting if she chose. She had managed to cover her true feelings.

Consequently she was given a great deal of freedom to come and go as she pleased, which suited her just fine. She spent every available minute at the D'Angelo home.

Tony was the one who wasn't pleased when she refused to allow him to take her home. He was much harder to convince that what she was doing was the only way she could still see him without creating all sorts of difficulties with her family.

They even argued about it.

"Don't you see, Tony? This is the only way I can see you!"

"Don't give me that! We aren't in the Dark Ages, you know. You're eighteen years old, Natalie. Your father has no say-so over you."

She nodded. "But he does. I'm still in school."

"So what?"

"I have no choice but to go by his rules as long as he's taking care of me."

"Then let me take care of you."

They were in his car at a secluded lookout near the Columbia River, and she looked at his shadowed face in surprise. "What do you mean?"

"Marry me, Natalie. I can take care of you. Then you can go to school here. We have the community college and Portland State if you want to go further. Just don't go back East."

"Oh, Tony," she whispered, her heart seeming to pound in her throat. "Do you really mean that?"

He pulled her into his arms. "Of course, I mean it. I can support you. I love you. I want to marry you. I can't stand the thought of your being so far away."

His kiss made it clear to her that he wanted her in every way that a man could want a woman. Natalie surrendered to his touch, trembling in his arms. When he drew away, they were both having trouble breathing.

She shook her head. "You know they'd never allow that," she managed to say.

"They can't stop us."

"What do you mean?"

He nodded to the other side of the river. "We could go over to Washington and get married. They wouldn't have to know anything about it until it was already accomplished."

"Are you serious?"

The kiss he gave her removed any doubt in her mind. When he finally raised his head, his voice was husky with longing. "I've never wanted anything more in my life."

"But what will they do when they find out?"

"What can they do? They'll just have to accept the fact that we're married." He brushed a stray curl away from her brow. "It's the only way I know to keep them from sending you back East after the holidays."

The thought of being married to Tony D'Angelo caused Natalie's heart to triple its rhythm. To actually be married to him, to live with him, sleep with him, have his children was more than she'd ever envisioned.

She couldn't think of anything she'd rather have happen in her life. "All right," she managed to say, her voice quavering.

This time it was Tony who needed reassurance. "Do you really mean it, Natalie?" She nodded her head, and he hugged her to him. "You'll never regret it, Natalie. I promise. I'll make you happy, I swear."

She laughed. "You don't have to do anything to make me happy, Tony. Being with you is all that it takes."

He stroked her cheek. "I love you so much, Natalie. I can't begin to tell you how much."

"I love you, too."

He shook his head. "But you're so young. Maybe we should wait awhile. Maybe until after you've graduated."

She pulled away from him. "You want me to spend five more months away from you?"

He shook his head. "No."

She grinned. "So what do we have to do?"

He was silent for several minutes. "Tomorrow is Christmas Eve. We always have an open house and go to midnight services. Are you going to be able to come?"

"I think so. My parents are having some people in, and I told them I'd be going to church. They probably won't know when I leave."

"If you could get away early, say around noon, we can go to Vancouver, get a license and find a judge to marry us. Then we'll spend the evening with my parents. Instead of taking you home, we'll go to a hotel. I'll take you home Christmas morning, and we'll tell your family."

"When will we tell yours?"

"Not until after we've told your family. We'll go back home and spend Christmas with my folks."

"Your family is going to be hurt at our doing it this way."

Tony was quiet for a moment. "I know. And you won't be having the kind of wedding that you and Angie have always talked about, I'm afraid."

"I don't care," she said, tracing his jawline with her finger. "All I care about is being with you." Her voice broke. "I can't stand being away from you, Tony."

"Then this is the only way I know to keep you here." He held her so close that she could feel his heart beating, its rapid rhythm telling her better than words how she affected him.

Tony had been so careful with her ever since he'd first started seeing her. She had been aware of the tight rein he'd kept on his reactions to her, but she wasn't so naive that she hadn't understood what a strain he'd been under.

By this time tomorrow night, they would be married. He wouldn't have to keep such a rigid control over his actions.

The next day there was talk of snow for Christmas, and her mother warned her about driving in the bad weather. Natalie laughed at the idea. She wouldn't be going far. She explained that she had some last minute errands to run and some gifts to deliver and that she wasn't sure when she'd be home.

She met Tony at noon.

They were in the clerk's office in Vancouver by one o'clock and by two had found a benevolent judge who agreed to marry them.

By two-thirty they were back in Portland. Natalie couldn't believe it. She was actually married to Tony. She was now Natalie Phillips D'Angelo, and she had the ring to prove it. "It's beautiful, Tony," she said, touching the wide gold band on her third finger.

"Not as beautiful as you. Someday in the near future I'm going to buy you an engagement ring to go with it."

"I don't need one, Tony. This is all I need."

He took her hand and placed it on his thigh. "I wasn't sure you'd be there today."

"Why?"

"I thought you might have second thoughts about the idea."

"All I could do was to count the hours."

"Where did you tell your mother you were going?"

"I had some last-minute shopping. If I go home now, she won't think anything of my leaving later."

"I'm not sure I can let you leave me, even for a few hours," he said, pulling up beside her car in the parking lot where she'd left it earlier.

She threw her arms around him. "This will be the last time. I promise."

He hugged her tightly against him. "I'll see you at our place this evening."

"Yes."

"I love you, Natalie."

Those words echoed in Natalie's mind all that afternoon. She hurried home and helped her mother prepare for their guests. She made sure the gifts she'd brought from school were under the tree so that her parents and brother would find them the next morning.

For just a moment she had a strong desire to tell them about her marriage, but Tony had cautioned her against that. He wanted to be with her when they heard the news.

Besides, she wanted this particular night with Tony before they told anyone. For a little while they would share their special secret only between the two of them.

By the time she quietly left the house, her parents' guests had begun to arrive. She had no difficulty in slipping outside with her overnight case.

The sky had cleared, and the twinkling lights from downtown Portland were no competition to the bright stars that seemed to be specially polished for this particular night.

Natalie drove slowly through the streets, enjoying the many decorated homes. The crisp air seemed to shimmer with the echoes of church bells and carols being sung.

Such a special night. One that she would never forget. She and Tony had picked a beautiful time to be married, to share the love they felt for each other with the love that had been brought to the Earth almost two thousand years before.

Tony met her at the door of his parents' home, giving her a brief, possessive kiss before escorting her into the room filled by members of their family and a collection of laughing friends.

"I missed you," he whispered. "Are you sure you want to stay here all evening?" He couldn't hide the desire in his eyes.

"Don't you think we should?"

"Yes. But I don't know how much longer I can be around you without shouting to the world that you now belong to me."

She hugged him tightly, thrilled at the leashed control he was keeping on his emotions. When he finally let go, she would be able to show him how much she loved and wanted him as well.

"None of that, you two," Angela warned with a grin. She was carrying a large tray of food to the buffet table set up near the Christmas tree. "You don't want to be shocking anyone with your behavior now, big brother."

Tony grinned, refusing to remove his arms from around Natalie.

The rest of the evening passed in a blur to Natalie. When it was time to leave for church, she and Tony managed to slip away in his car without offering to take anyone with them. They didn't intend to return to the house. Natalie had placed her bag in his car when she arrived.

The church bells were ringing as family clusters went through the front doors of the church. Once inside each person was handed a candle.

The service, as always, touched Natalie's heart. After the story of the Nativity was read aloud, the lights in the church were dimmed and each candle was lit. The smiles around her were so beautiful. The shared love was so tangible that Natalie felt that she could reach out and almost touch it.

She was so glad to spend this time with Tony, to be reminded of the magic of Christmas, that time of year when people took time out of their busy lives to remember the wonderful gift they had been given, the example they had been shown on how to love one another. It was a gift that could be carried with them throughout the new year.

After the service Tony quietly took her hand and led her out of the church. Silently they walked to the car and drove to one of the luxury hotels downtown that overlooked the Willamette River.

He carried their small cases and went inside. Without pausing at the desk he walked over to the elevator.

"Don't we have to register?"

He glanced down at her. "I checked in earlier."

"Oh."

When he opened the door to the room, Natalie walked in and stopped, awed by the view.

The moonlight shone brightly over the city and highlighted the snow that coated Mount Hood in a pristine white blanket.

"I left the drapes open. I thought you might appreciate the view."

"It's beautiful, Tony," she murmured, moving over to the window and staring outside. The lights along the many bridges spanning the river were reflected in the water, so that the entire city seemed to be a gigantic ornament lit up for their pleasure.

Tony pulled her against him, her back resting against his chest. "I hoped you would like it."

She turned in his arms. "Thank you. Thank you for being who you are, for being so thoughtful and considerate. Thank you for loving me."

"You don't owe me any thanks, love. I got to marry the Christmas-tree angel. What more could any mortal ask?"

His kiss was gentle, as though he didn't want to frighten her. At last, after all these months together, there were no more restrictions between them.

Natalie felt so loved and protected. She had loved this man since they had both been children. Now they were grown. Now they were married.

Now they belonged to each other.

Tony dropped his arms and stepped back. "I don't want to rush you. I want this night to be special."

"It already is."

He nodded to the bathroom where the only light they had glowed. "You can change in there if you'd like."

She could feel herself blushing, despite everything she could do. Why should she feel shy with Tony? She loved him. She wanted him to show her how to express that love physically.

Somehow he must have known how she felt. He touched her cheek softly and smiled. Turning away, she opened her case and pulled out her gown and robe. "I'll only be a few minutes," she whispered, picking up her bag of toiletries.

"There's no rush. We have the rest of our lives together."

When she came out, she turned off the bathroom light. Moonlight poured through the large expanse of glass, illuminating the room so that she could see Tony was already in bed, waiting for her.

Natalie moved silently toward him. She let the robe slide from her shoulders and fall to the floor beside the bed. Then she shyly slid under the covers beside him.

Tony turned onto his side and leaned on his elbow. "You are so beautiful, I'm afraid to touch you for fear you're not real."

She rested her hand on his bare chest. "I'm real enough." She could feel the heat of his skin almost burning her fingertips.

He touched her hair lightly, brushing it out over the pillowcase. Then he traced the shape of her ear with his forefinger.

Natalie turned her head so that she could see him. His dark eyes glittered in the moonlight, and she could see the tension in his face.

For the first time, Natalie realized that he was as nervous as she was. Recognizing that fact helped her to relax. She tilted her head so that she could kiss him.

His mouth felt so familiar, so dear to her. She remembered the months that she had lain awake at night, wishing he were there to kiss her good-night. Now her dreams had come true on this most magical of all nights. Tony was there to share his love with her.

As the kiss continued, the soft gentleness began to change. It became heated, moist and more demanding. Natalie felt as though she were igniting. Everywhere he touched, Tony's caressing hands seemed to set off tiny explosions of excitement within her.

He began to explore her face with his kisses while his hands followed the contours of her body. Although he had never taken such liberties before, Natalie felt no qualms about allowing the intimacies. This was Tony, and he was turning her into an inferno.

She could no longer lie still and restlessly began to trace the well-developed muscles of his shoulders and back.

When his kisses moved down along the low neckline of her gown, Natalie shivered. He raised his head and looked at her. "Did I hurt you?"

She shook her head. His hand cupped her breast. "Would you rather I not touch you?"

"I love you to touch me, Tony."

He slid his hand under first one strap, then the other, then slowly pushed the gown down until it was around her waist.

Natalie had always been shy, and yet she loved the expression that Tony had on his face when he looked at her. When he leaned over and kissed the rose-tipped surface of her breast, she almost cried out with the pleasure of his touch.

She ran her hands restlessly across his chest, then around his back and up through his hair. The curls clung to her fingers as though returning her soft caress.

Natalie clung to him as he worshiped her body. By the time he moved so that he was lying between her legs, she was almost whimpering with longing without understanding what it was she needed.

He showed her—with infinite gentleness he showed her the beautiful ecstasy that two people can share. With patience he allowed her to adjust to him before he began the age old rhythm that brought them ever closer to each other and to the pinnacle of sensation.

His murmured love words filled her mind and heart. She clung to him as though he were the only thing that prevented her from being swept away with all the new sensations. He waited for her to respond, to ignite, to take the lead in finding their goal.

His patience was rewarded. When she gasped, he felt the contractions begin deep within her and could no longer postpone his own reaction. With a soft cry he gave a convulsive lunge and held her as though he never intended to let her go.

"Oh, Tony," she whispered when she could get her breath. "I never knew it could be like this. I never guessed making love would be so wonderful. How could we have waited so long?"

He had rolled to his side, holding her tightly against him. "I had to wait, love. I could never have loved you so intimately, then walked away from you. I had to know you were mine to hold all night, every night."

She smiled, kissing him. "If only I'd known."

"I'm glad you didn't. You were enough of a temptation as it was."

They lay there, sharing memories of the separation they had just gone through, planning for their future, talking about their family. He had been careful to protect her from pregnancy, and they had discussed the need for waiting until she was through with school before starting a family.

Then they had made love once again. This time they took their time—the urgency was gone. There was time for exploration and experimentation. Natalie was eager to learn all about him and what affected him. When they finally fell asleep it was almost dawn, and they were exhausted.

Which was why they did not hear the key in the lock or the door being opened the next morning.

The first thing they heard was the sound of Natalie's father demanding that they get up, get dressed and get ready to leave.

Chapter Five

With a sob Natalie came awake, shaking. She sat there for a moment, trying to get her breath. She'd been dreaming again, the same dream that had haunted her for years. Why did her subconscious persist in reminding her of the past when she'd worked so hard to forget it?

Instead, she continually relived the nightmarish feeling of waking from a sound sleep to find her father yelling at her and Tony, calling them names she'd never heard coming from her father.

She could still remember the horror of that moment as she scrambled to find the robe she'd discarded the night before beside the bed. She could still hear her father's angry words, threatening Tony.

She had tried to explain that they were married, that they had done nothing wrong, but instead of appeasing him, her explanations called forth an even louder denunciation, most of it aimed at Tony.

Her father had reminded Tony of her youth, her lack of education, her family's plans for her. Then he told them that he intended to have the marriage annulled and that if either one of them gave him any trouble over it, he would see that not only Tony but his entire family would never be able to find work in the entire Pacific Northwest.

Then he'd demanded that Natalie get dressed and come home with him, that her brother was waiting downstairs.

Her humiliation was complete. She felt like a rebellious runaway as she ran into the bathroom to get dressed. She could still hear her father's voice as he continued to roar at Tony. She could hear Tony's attempts to break into the tirade, but without success.

When she had replaced the clothes she'd worn the day before, Natalie had reentered the bedroom. The first thing she noticed was that Tony was up. He wore the pants he'd had on the day before, but was still barefoot and without a shirt. In the bright morning light streaming through the window he looked like a marble statue that could be found in Rome. She was forcibly reminded of the night they had just shared, the intimacies, the passion, and she found herself moving toward him.

"Leave him alone!" her father ordered. "Go on downstairs and wait for me, Natalie."

Tony's calm gaze met hers. "You don't have to leave, Natalie. There's nothing he can do to us, you know."

"The hell there isn't!" her father interrupted to say. "You don't know what trouble is, young man, until you've tangled with me. I've got enough clout in this area to see that you and your father are hounded out, forced to move clear across the country. I'm telling you to leave my daughter alone!"

Tony continued to watch Natalie, waiting for her response.

All she could think about was what her father was saying. It was true. She had seen what he could do. She knew how he had destroyed competitors. What could he do to the D'Angelos if he really set about bringing them down? It didn't bear thinking about.

"Tony?" she whispered, uncertainly.

"Don't go, Natalie. He can't hurt us. You belong to me now!"

Her father blew up with that remark, shouting words that made Natalie cringe. Tony didn't understand. He didn't know the kind of man that her father was capable of being.

But Natalie did. How could she do something that would hurt not only the man she loved but his wonderful loving family as well?

She began to cry. "Oh, Tony."

Tony started toward her, but her father blocked his way.

"Go downstairs, Natalie. Now!" her father said. He looked as though he were ready to strike Tony. "I want you out of her life, D'Angelo. Do you understand? Completely and totally out of her life. I don't care what sort of ceremony you think you went through, there is no marriage. I'll see to that!" He turned to Natalie. "Now get out of here."

Years later, Natalie could still feel the awful pain in her chest. She remembered starting to the door and looking back. The anguish in Tony's eyes was unmistakable. His murmured, "Don't go, Natalie," as she slowly went out of the room continued to haunt her all these years.

She had never seen him again. Not until two days ago when she'd recognized him at the mall.

Her father and brother had driven her home. She'd been hysterical. Her father had told her to forget about Tony and any marriage. The marriage was no longer in existence, he would see to that.

He had sent her back to school the day after Christmas. She had never talked to him again. Three months later her father had had a sudden heart attack and died before they could get him to the hospital.

She had flown home for the funeral, but hadn't attempted to contact Tony or his family. After three months of silence in response to her letters, she had gotten her answer from the D'Angelos. None of them wanted anything more to do with her.

Now, here she was, six years later, back in their lives. They had all been kind to her, including Tony. He had treated the past as though it had never happened, as though they had never spent that marvelous night together, as though he hadn't taught her so much about his own sexuality and hers.

She had stayed in the East once she finished school for the year, taking summer courses and planning her college curriculum. It was as though she could bury herself in a heavy schedule so that she wouldn't have time to think about what she had given up.

Natalie knew that she was responsible for the present situation. The choice had been hers, and she'd made it. If she had it to do over again, she would probably have done the same thing. Even with her father gone, it was too late to go back and attempt to make amends.

She knew that walking out on Tony at that vulnerable time in their relationship had been a betrayal of all that they had shared.

Now he was treating her like a friend. He was relaxed and easy around her. And it was slowly killing her. When she had attempted to discuss what had happened, he had excused what she had done as though it were no longer important.

She glanced at her bedside clock. It was almost four o'clock in the morning. He was coming by later that day to take her to see his home. What did it mean? Why was he willing to spend time with her without discussing anything personal between them? Natalie wondered how she could possibly continue to be around him without betraying her feelings.

She felt as though the past six years had been wiped away and she was once more the eighteen-year-old girl whose bones seemed to melt whenever he appeared.

Some things never change.

When Tony arrived to pick her up, both Tom and her mother were there. Natalie brought him into the living room with her.

"Mother, Tom, I believe you remember Tony D'Angelo, don't you?"

Natalie was surprised to see Tom promptly get up and stride over to Tony. "Hello, Tony. It's good to see you. It's been a while," he said with a smile.

Tony nodded. "I've been busy."

"So I understand. I read in the paper that your company won the bid on the Crandall property."

"That's right."

"Congratulations. Your growth in the industry has been phenomenal."

Natalie could scarcely believe her ears. Tom was talking to Tony as though they were old friends, although Tony was much more reserved. And it was obvious that Tom had been keeping tabs on Tony's company. Why?

"Hello, Tony," her mother said quietly. "How is your family?"

"Doing very well."

"Would you like to join us? We've been having coffee in front of the fire and enjoying a quiet moment. We don't seem to have many of them these days."

He smiled at the older woman. "Not today. I promised Natalie I would take her over to see my latest project, then we're having dinner."

"Yes, she told me. I know she's enjoyed seeing her old friends after such a long absence."

Tony glanced at Natalie from the corner of his eye. "I've enjoyed seeing her as well," he offered in a noncommittal tone.

After Natalie put on her coat, they left the house and walked down the steps to the curving driveway where his late-model sports car waited.

"Quite a different reception than I'm used to from your family," he pointed out quietly after they'd started down the driveway.

"I don't think either my mother or brother shared my father's animosity toward you, Tony."

"So I noticed."

"Tom seemed to be very interested in you."

She noticed that he hesitated a moment before answering her. "Yes, well, we've run into each other occasionally over the years."

"He's never mentioned you whenever we talked."

"There was no reason for him to, was there?"

She shook her head, trying to pull her thoughts away from the past.

She noted that Tony was headed south along the Willamette River, toward Lake Oswego. After several turns and winding streets he pulled into a driveway that was marked Private. They followed it through the dense trees until the driveway split, forming a circle in front of a large home.

Natalie looked at the two-story structure, then back at Tony. "This is where you're living?"

He nodded. "It had been neglected for several years and needed some major renovation. I decided it was worth saving. I've finished up most of the inside work. Now all that needs to be done is cosmetic repair to the outside."

Natalie slowly got out of the car and walked to the door. "This is beautiful, Tony."

And it was. It looked like an English country home, with weathered red bricks and large windows with small panes of leaded glass. She could almost feel the warmth that seemed to radiate from the place.

"The house had been tied up in probate proceedings for years with no one taking proper care of it."

"It has such a happy feel about it, as though you can almost hear the laughter of children," she said as he opened the door into the wide foyer.

He pointed to the curving staircase. "I'm certain that more than one person slid down that railing, aren't you?"

"It certainly is tempting, isn't it?" she said with a grin, running her hands over the smooth-grained surface.

Each room was open. Tony had done an excellent job of lightening the look of the place, painting pastel colors on the walls and refinishing the hardwood floors.

When they walked into the breakfast room, Natalie paused, touched by the view from the multipaned windows. A garden sloped down to the edge of the lake. The profusion of rhododendrons, azaleas and rosebushes told her that the spring and summer would be filled with riotous colors. An arched trellis indicated climbing roses made their home there during the blooming season.

"Oh, Tony," she whispered, enchanted.

"Do you like it?"

"I love it. I've never seen a more homey, comfortable place."

He took her hand and led her through the kitchen that had been thoroughly modernized, then back into the hallway. "Let me show you upstairs."

The upstairs contained four large bedrooms. The master suite had a built-in bath and dressing area that had been completely modernized.

The furniture in the room was distinctively masculine, but not heavy. She caught herself staring at the massive bed that was located on a dais. How many women had shared that bed with Tony? Of course she didn't want to know. It was no longer any of her business. She had walked out of his life.

She turned away, trying to cover her reaction to the room. "This is marvelous, Tony. You've done a wonderful job. Do you intend to put it on the market now that you've completed most of the work?"

"I'm not sure at this point what I intend to do."

"I see."

She wished she did. Tony had not mentioned another woman in his life, and yet she knew that he was entirely too attractive not to have someone. She had listened carefully to his family's conversation, hoping a name would be dropped in the conversation that would give her a clue to his personal life.

If she were more brave, she could question him, but she knew it was none of her business, and she wasn't sure she would be able to handle his answer when she heard it.

"Are you ready to go? I have reservations at one of the restaurants overlooking the river."

She nodded and started toward the door.

"Natalie?"

She turned. He still stood there in the middle of the bedroom, watching her.

"Yes?"

"Do you think I should keep this place?"

She attempted a casual shrug. "I can't really say, Tony. It seems to be a rather large home for one person to occupy."

"I don't intend to live here alone."

A lump seemed to form in her throat, and she had trouble swallowing. "Then you need to ask the woman you intend to share it with."

He was by her side in a few long strides. Gripping her forearms he gave her an intense look. "I'm asking *you*."

Before she could form any words, he pulled her up against him and kissed her, a long, slow, mind-drugging kiss that took her far back into the past to other times, other kisses and to the one unforgettable night they had spent together.

Her arms curled up around his neck, holding him close. She had never forgotten the feel of Tony's arms around her, his powerful body molded tightly against hers. His kiss revealed that the restraint he'd shown around her was merely a facade, and Natalie reveled in the knowledge that she could still affect him so strongly.

When he finally raised his head, his face was flushed and his eyes glittered.

"Let's get out of here now," he muttered, "or I'll never be able to let you walk out of here."

Without looking at it, Natalie was aware of the presence of the large bed waiting only a few feet away. It would be so easy to let him know how much she wanted him again, after all this time.

But giving in to her feelings wouldn't solve anything. After a few hours with Tony in bed, she would once again be faced with a life without him. She didn't need the reminder.

They walked out to the car in silence. When Tony slid behind the steering wheel beside her, she glanced at him and smiled. "You're wearing more lipstick than I am at the moment," she said, handing him her handkerchief.

He glanced in the rearview mirror, then took her handkerchief and slowly removed the color from around his mouth.

"I'm sorry. I didn't mean to do that," he said without looking at her. He returned the handkerchief and started the car.

Natalie decided to be honest. "I'm not. I've wanted to kiss you like that since I saw you the other day in the mall."

He glanced down at her in surprise, then a smile slowly spread across his mouth. "No kidding?"

"No kidding."

He began to laugh. "And here I've been trying to be so careful with you."

"Why?"

"I didn't want to scare you away."

"Tony, there is nothing you can do that would scare me away."

She watched his reaction to her statement. He reflected on it for several moments in silence. Then he spoke. "We need to talk."

"Yes."

"But not tonight. I wanted a quiet evening with you, a chance to get reacquainted." He paused, as though searching for words. "Tomorrow is Christmas Eve."

She knew that they were both remembering what that day meant, but she could find no words to express what she was feeling.

"Natalie, would you spend tomorrow evening with me? We could go to my parents' open house and to church...." He paused, as though unsure of himself.

"I'd like that."

"Would you come back to the house with me, afterward?"

Her heart felt as though it was going to rocket out of her chest at his words.

"We need to talk. There's so much to say, but I'd rather wait until we have enough time and privacy."

He waited, and Natalie knew that a great deal rested on her response. "Yes, Tony. I'll spend as much time with you as you'd like me to."

They both knew what she was agreeing to without further words. He took his hand from the steering wheel and without looking at her, brushed his knuckles gently against her cheek. "Thank you."

How could he possibly be thanking her for agreeing to something she wanted so badly? She was the one who had walked out on him.

When they arrived at the restaurant they were immediately shown to their table. She had never been there before but was impressed with the decor and the privacy afforded each table. They were seated near a wide expanse of glass so that they could see the river and a nearby bridge. A fat candle in an oval glass holder flickered on the table, casting a warm light that created a halo effect to enfold them.

After they had ordered, Tony took her hand in both of his. Looking deep into her eyes, he said softly, "Tell me about you, Natalie. About school, about your friends, your hobbies. Help me learn about the woman that has grown from the young girl I once knew."

Haltingly at first, Natalie described her life. Tony quietly asked probing questions that she answered easily. Her life was open, free of secrets, almost boring.

By the time she had answered all of his questions, they were being offered dessert. She shook her head, sighing. "I couldn't eat another thing." They both ordered coffee, and when the waiter left, she said, "How about you? When are you going to tell me about you?"

"I will. Tomorrow night. I promise." He glanced away for a moment, and once again she was aware of the perfection of his profile. Then his dark eyes met hers once more. "It's getting late, and we both need our rest. I'll pick you up tomorrow to go to the open house."

She nodded, her thoughts flying ahead. Their plans for the next day were so similar to that day six years ago that she had a frightening sense of déjà vu. This time her father wasn't around to make changes in any of their plans. This time Tony was not suggesting marriage. This time she was not a foolish girl with stars in her eyes.

She knew he wanted her, there was no way to miss that. She wanted him, too. If this was all she could have, she was determined that it would be enough.

After all, the Christmas season was once more with them. During that magical time anything could happen. Love could grow and become whole once again.

When Tony took her home he walked her to the front door, refusing her invitation to come in. "They're predicting snow tomorrow. I hope not. There'll be so many people traveling."

"Drive safely," she said, going up on tiptoe and kissing him softly on the mouth. "Take care of you for me."

He grinned. "Always. I'll see you tomorrow."

When she walked inside the house, Tom came out of the living room. "I thought I heard you."

"Where's Mother?"

"She went up to bed. She's tired. Would you like a glass of sherry or wine before going to bed?"

"Sure, why not? Sherry would be nice." She wandered into the living room behind him and walked over to the fireplace. "The fire feels good tonight. I understand there's a chance of snow."

"Yes." He handed her a glass, and she sat down opposite him in one of the chairs in front of the fire. "Did you enjoy dinner?" he asked, watching her.

She nodded.

"Do you intend to spend tomorrow evening with him?"

"Yes, why?"

"I just wondered. You've never talked about Tony to me since you left Portland. I wasn't sure you'd even see him when you came back."

"I probably wouldn't have. We ran into each other accidentally."

"I don't believe in accidents."

"What do you mean? There's no way either of us could have known the other was shopping at the mall that day."

"But you would have seen him, sooner or later." He took a sip of his drink. "I know that you think Dad was very harsh with you and Tony back then."

"'Harsh' isn't the word. He was brutal, and you know it."

"He was concerned about you."

"He had no reason to be."

"Dad loved you very much, Natalie. He wanted what was best for you."

"Except he seemed to think he was the only one who knew best."

Tom shook his head. "Getting married in the middle of your senior year didn't make much sense, did it?"

She looked away from him, watching the fire dancing along the logs. "I loved him. It was the only way we could be together. Besides, I would have gone on with my schooling."

"Unless you had gotten pregnant. There's always that chance."

She shrugged. "What difference does it make now?"

"Do you still love Tony?"

She looked at him, surprised at the personal question. "Of course I love Tony. I always have. I always will. That isn't the issue."

"And what exactly is the issue?"

"Tony has put me out of his mind and life. He doesn't even bring up what happened, as though it means nothing to him."

"Natalie, he's right. You can't continue to live in the past or let the hurts of the past hang around you today. What happened, happened. You can't undo it or change it."

"I know. I really thought I had put it all behind me until I saw him again. I lost so much."

"I don't think 'lost' is the proper word. 'Postponed,' perhaps, would better describe the situation. You're both young yet. You can have so many happy years together, now that he's successfully established in business and you have your education."

"Except for one minor detail."

"What's that?"

"Tony never brings up a future for us. He talks as though we'll both continue on our separate paths."

"He's never suggested that you consider moving back to Portland?"

"Not once."

"Interesting."

"What do you mean?"

"Nothing. I just find Tony D'Angelo an interesting character study." Tom finished his drink and stood. "Then you won't be home tomorrow evening?"

She shook her head. "Not until very late, anyway. I'm not sure what time I'll be home." She couldn't quite meet his eyes. How could she tell her brother that if Tony suggested she spend the remainder of Christmas Eve with him, she would do so, without any qualms?

Natalie set her glass down and got up from the chair. "I'll see you in the morning, Tom. Good night."

His murmured good-night was barely audible as she walked out of the room.

Chapter Six

When Natalie came downstairs the next evening she discovered that Tony had already arrived. He and Tom were standing in the foyer in the midst of a discussion when she came out of her room and started down the stairway. Both men stopped talking and looked up.

She caught her breath. Tony wore a black suit that fit him like a glove, the white of his dress shirt showing up in a splendid contrast, emphasizing his tanned skin, black hair and eyes.

He looked wonderful to her, and from the look on his face as he watched her descend the stairs toward him, he was having a similar reaction to her.

She had chosen to wear a white dress with silver threads interwoven through the fabric so that the dress sparkled with every move she made. The style was simple so as not to detract from the beauty of the cloth. It swirled around her legs as she moved toward the two men.

"I'm sorry to keep you waiting, Tony. I wasn't aware you were here."

He glanced at Tom. "I just arrived. You look beautiful, Natalie. All you need are your angel wings."

She looked at Tom and winked. "I'm not sure I'm ready for my halo just yet. What do you think, Tom?"

In an unusual gesture, he put his arm around her and hugged her close to him. "I have to admit there's a glow about you, sis, that I haven't seen in a very long time. Who knows? Maybe the halo comes next.''

Surprised at his show of affection, she kissed him on the cheek. "Where's Mother?''

"She hasn't come downstairs yet. I'm taking her over to some friends' home a little later.''

Tony picked up her coat and laid it across her shoulders, carefully lifting the hood so that it protected her head.

"I'm not sure when I'll be home, Tom,'' she began when Tom interrupted her.

"Don't worry about it. Just have a wonderful Christmas celebration, all right?''

She smiled. "I will.'' Glancing at Tony, her smile widened. "I know I will.''

It was already dark when they stepped outside. Once again a sense of déjà vu swept over her. The night was so clear that the stars seemed to be within reach. The air felt clean and fresh, and Natalie took a deep breath, as though to draw in some of the magic of the night.

Tony tucked her into the car before closing the door and joining her.

"Mama is so excited. She and Angela have been baking all day. Several of my aunts and uncles came over from the coast to join us. So the house will be full.'' He glanced over and grinned at her. "As usual.''

They had to park several houses away from the D'Angelo home. Every window was brightly lit, and as they approached the front porch they heard the music, voices and laughter of happy people.

Just before he opened the door, Tony paused and placing his hands lightly on her shoulders, he leaned down and kissed her softly on the lips.

"Merry Christmas, Natalie."

She knew her face was flushed when they walked into the house. Everyone greeted them boisterously, teasing them unmercifully about arriving late. Within minutes Natalie felt as though she'd been embraced by every member of the clan as they hugged and kissed her, exclaiming how beautiful she looked. Tony never loosened his hold on her hand as they moved through the crowded rooms. Instead, he stood beside her grinning, refusing to respond to the teasing they were receiving. To his father he shrugged and said, "I was late getting away tonight."

His father patted his shoulder. "I know. This is a busy time for you."

The hours seemed to run together as the family gathered around the old upright piano while Serena D'Angelo played. Tony's father had a rich baritone voice and led the rest through several carols.

Even the small children joined in, their treble voices occasionally off-key but always enthusiastic.

Before Natalie realized the time, Tony was placing her coat around her once more. That was when she saw that the rest of the family members, Angela and Paul included, were gathering up coats and hats in order to go to the midnight services at the church.

There was no question about anyone riding with them, since the sports car only contained two seats. Tony wrapped his arm securely around Natalie, and they hurried to the car. Snowflakes had begun to fall all around them.

"The children will all be happy if this stuff sticks," Tony said as soon as they were on the way. "But right now it's fairly slick to be out driving."

The peaceful serenity of the night seemed to surround them as they drove slowly through the residential streets. Most people had gone to bed by now. For a moment Natalie felt as though she and Tony were the only people awake. The illusion dissipated when they pulled into the full parking lot at the church. Many people had chosen to spend this night in quiet contemplation of the meaning behind all of the festivities.

Tony and Natalie found places toward the back of the church and sat close together to give room to others arriving behind them.

Natalie had never dreamed that she would be able to reenact that night with Tony once again. Looking at him, she knew that there were vital changes now. They were both adults. They knew what they wanted in life. At least, she did. What Natalie realized as she sat there through the moving story of the very first Christmas was that what she wanted more than anything was to spend the rest of her life with the loving, tender, compassionate man beside her, to share many more moments like this one with him.

She could visualize the years to come when they would have children who would participate in the observance of Christmas, a family they would be able to share with and teach to appreciate what it meant to have been blessed with such love from God.

When the service was over they left the church without speaking. They drove to Lake Oswego in silence, although Natalie felt as though there were unseen carolers singing in the far distance, just out of range of her conscious hearing.

When they pulled up in front of the house, Natalie noticed that the snow had dusted the shrubs around the doorway, as though even they needed to be decorated in order to fully celebrate the occasion.

They entered the hallway, and Natalie noticed a light coming from upstairs. She looked around at Tony. "Did you mean to leave a light on?"

He helped her out of her coat and then took her hand. Leading her toward the stairway, he nodded. "Yes." When he started up the stairs, she followed.

He paused in the doorway of his bedroom and motioned for her to go inside.

A small Christmas tree sat on a table between the large picture windows that overlooked the lake. Twinkling lights blinked on and off. Gaily colored decorations hung on the tree. Perched at its point, a tiny angel with long blond hair and a white gown waited for them.

"When did you do this?" she asked in surprise.

"This afternoon. I wanted us to have our own special tree."

"What a lovely idea."

He walked over to the tree and picked up a small package. Without saying anything he handed it to her.

Natalie's hands were shaking so hard she wasn't sure she was going to be able to pull off the paper. When she finally did, she almost dropped the small case. Inside was a glittering ring, a sparkling blue stone surrounded by diamonds.

"Oh, Tony. It's beautiful."

"The color matches your eyes. I was told that it's called a London blue topaz. All I know is that I thought of you when I saw it."

He lifted it from the box, then slipped it on the third finger of her left hand. "Merry Christmas, love," he whispered, and kissed her.

When he loosened his hold a few minutes later, Natalie couldn't hide the tears in her eyes.

"What's wrong?"

"Nothing's wrong! Everything is so right I can't believe it. Tony, does this mean you want to start all over again? That we have a chance to build a life together?"

"Is that what you want?"

"More than I've ever wanted anything."

"Do you mean you're willing to move back to Portland?"

"I want to be with you, Tony, wherever that might be."

"Would you want to live here in this house?"

"If that's what you want."

He picked her up and carried her to the side of the bed. "That's what I want."

She watched as he loosened the unaccustomed tie around his neck and slipped off his suit jacket. Then she glanced down at the ring. "This time we're doing everything in order."

"What do you mean?"

Holding up her hand, she said, "The engagement ring first."

Tony paused as he unbuttoned the top two buttons of his shirt. "Well, not exactly." He turned away and walked toward the windows. "Do you remember that I told you I made an agreement with your father six years ago?"

"To leave me alone?"

"Yes. To let you get on with your life and your education. I promised him that I would not do anything to influence you to come back to me." Without turning around he added, "I believe I kept that promise."

"Yes. You did. I never expected to hear from you again."

"You would have, at least indirectly, if at any time you had made any indication to your family that you were interested in another man."

"I don't understand."

Tony continued to stare out the window. "I agreed to leave you alone. In exchange, your father agreed not to have our marriage annulled."

She stared at his back in astonishment, trying to make some sense out of what he was saying.

"You mean—" she walked over to him, trying to see his face "—there was never an annulment?"

"That's right."

What he was saying was unbelievable. Did he mean that during all this time—while she was away at school and he was here—

"Tony?"

Slowly he turned to face her, his hands in his pants pockets, his expression guarded. "The marriage was valid, Natalie. Your father made sure of that. He hoped to find some way to get out of the agreement we made, so he had it all checked out."

"Then you and I are married."

He nodded.

"And no one ever told me."

"Your mother doesn't know. Only your father, Tom and I. Then after your father died..." His voice faded off.

"All this time Tom knew, and he never said a word?"

"No. He wanted to see if it was an infatuation with you. I promised him that if you ever met anyone else,

I would immediately start proceedings to dissolve the marriage."

"I was never interested in anyone else."

"That's the only thing that has kept me going all these years, love. I got reports third hand—through your mother to Tom, then to me."

"So that's why you seem to know him so well."

"Not well. But we've stayed in touch. You see—" Once again he turned away, this time to the little tree that blinked so merrily beside the window. "You were my wife, and I wanted to be responsible for you. I insisted on paying all of your school expenses."

"You what! But that wasn't fair. My family had the money. You didn't."

"Maybe not at first," he admitted wryly, "but I was determined to show your family that I could do whatever it took to take care of you." His grin slowly appeared. "The hours I put in at work and school kept me too tired to think about anything else—like the fact that I had a wife that didn't know she was my wife. Like the fact that I didn't even know if you'd ever want me again. Like the fact that your refusal to return to Portland had almost convinced Tom that I was wasting my time and money in hopes of your wanting me."

"Oh, Tony," she cried, throwing herself into his arms. "If only I'd known! All these years we could have been together. All of these years so wasted."

"Not wasted. We both needed some time. Proving myself to your family made me more determined than ever to succeed. You had never treated me as the gardener's grandson, someone to look down on. I wasn't going to tolerate that treatment from your family."

She hugged him tightly, her cheek resting against the softness of his silk shirt. "Oh, Tony, I love you so much."

He sighed, his arms going convulsively around her. "There were nights when I would lie in bed wondering if I'd ever hear you say that again." He tilted her chin so that his mouth found hers, and all the longing, the uncertainty, the love that he'd carried within him for her all of these years seemed to pour from him, filling her heart and soul with gladness.

When the kiss could no longer properly express what he was feeling, Tony picked her up once more, this time laying her tenderly on the bed without breaking the kiss. He came down beside her, his restless hands exploring her, loving and adoring her.

All of the uncertainty she had experienced since seeing him that day at the mall disappeared in the passionate intensity of his kiss. She couldn't seem to get close enough to him, and Natalie hastily tugged at the buttons on his shirt, trying to reach the warm flesh hidden beneath the silk.

She felt the zipper at the back of her dress move down, and she willingly moved away from him long enough to remove the beautiful gown. Tony pulled away from her in order to slide the silken underwear from her body, so that she was bathed in the twinkling light coming from the tree.

"My Christmas angel. Happy anniversary, darling," he whispered. He quickly dispensed with the remainder of his clothes and stretched out beside her once more.

Natalie could more readily see the changes that had taken place in his body—the wide chest and heavy shoulders were revealed to her in all their silken splendor. She followed the curve of his chest down to his waist, then smoothed her hand across his abdomen and down his thigh. His skin rippled beneath her touch, and he pulled her over until she lay on top of him.

"Do you have any idea what you're doing to me, woman?" he groaned.

"I seem to be having a similar reaction," she admitted.

"Six years is a long time to wait, you know."

"I know that. I'm not asking how you spent those years, love. How can I possibly ask?"

"But I can answer. I didn't want anyone but you, Natalie. My thoughts and dreams have always been filled with you. I never wanted anyone but you. Never." His hands encircled her head and gently brought it down to him so that his mouth could touch hers. He ran his tongue along the surface of her lips, then plunged deeply inside—taking possession.

There was never any doubt how his body reacted to her nearness, and Natalie could no longer ignore her position on top of him. Raising herself slightly, she moved so that she could enfold and absorb him, her action causing him to gasp at the pleasure of joining with her once more.

Fiercely he held her as she moved over him, at long last able to enact some of her many fantasies over the years.

Eventually she collapsed on his chest, too weak to continue. Tony rolled so that she was tucked beneath him, bringing her to repeated peaks until at long last he joined her in that wonderful feeling of total satiation.

Not wanting to crush her, he stretched out beside her, holding her close. Her eyes drifted shut, then popped open again. She didn't want to waste a moment of this time.

The Christmas angel kept a watchful eye over the proceedings, her kindly smile indicating that all was well. Once again the magic of Christmas had brought to Natalie her heart's desire.

This time she knew it would last forever.

"Are you awake?" Tony whispered a few minutes later.

"Mmm-hmm."

"Are you hungry?"

"Not really, why?"

"I thought we could raid the refrigerator. I stocked up on everything I could think of before I left here today."

"Do you think I should call Tom so he and Mother don't worry about me? The roads are going to be treacherous tonight."

With his forefinger, Tony traced a trail from her chin down her throat, between her breasts and finally paused at her abdomen. "Tom knew you weren't coming back home tonight."

"Is that what you two were talking about in the foyer?"

"Yes. He told me that there was no reason not to tell you the truth now. I'd already decided I couldn't wait any longer, anyway. Whatever the outcome, you had to know."

"I can't believe that both of you kept this from me all these years."

"Your mother is going to be the one in shock. She never knew what had happened. Your father told her that he had found you at my parents' home, that you'd stayed overnight with Angela.''

"And she believed that, as upset as I was?"

"I suppose. So now we're going to have to explain to her why you aren't going to be home until a few days after Christmas."

She ran her fingers through his black curls. "A few days?"

"I don't intend to let you out of my bed any longer than I can help it. Why do you suppose I'm offering food? I want you to keep your strength up."

"What about you?"

"I've been doing that for six years, love." His slow kiss made it clear that he was more than willing to demonstrate.

Natalie settled contentedly into his arms. In a contest of this nature, there were definitely no losers.

With Christmas magic, anything was possible.

* * * * *

What Christmas Means to Me

Whenever I think of Christmas, my senses become involved.

I hear:
Sleigh bells, church bells, voices caroling, children giggling, lovers whispering and that special hush that sometimes heralds a truly magical time.

I smell:
Pine trees, bread baking in the oven, spices simmering, crisp cold air, scented candles, hot coffee, burning logs and that peculiar scent of winter that defies description.

I see:
Flickering flames dancing around the logs in a fireplace, houses trimmed in twinkling lights, red ribbons and green foliage, a bright star shining in the heavens, a church spire silhouetted against a midnight-black sky, snowflakes drifting downward to lay a gentle mantle across the countryside, making everything look brand-new.

I taste:
Homemade cookies and candies, all brightly decorated, fruitcake that has matured to its richest flavors, roast turkey with all the trimmings, chocolate-covered cherries, because someone always remembers that they are a favorite of mine.

I feel:
The anticipation of those around me waiting for loved ones to arrive from far away, the eagerness of the children to find out what is in that package under

the tree, joy in the ability to share all of these things with my loved ones, grateful that we have been shown what love is, what it can be and how important it is to each and every one of us.

Annette Broadrick

MIRACLE
ON I-40

Curtiss Ann Matlock

NEVER-FAIL PIE CRUST

Pies are my favorite sweet in the entire world. To me they're not only dessert but country-style home decoration, as well. I take great satisfaction in placing a just-baked pie smack in the middle of my table—just like a vase of flowers—to pause and admire throughout the day.

But until ten years ago I couldn't even bake a pie because making the crust would frustrate me to tears. My dough tore, stuck, wrapped around the rolling pin and my hand, but never made it as a whole piece into the pie plate. Then my friend Cleo gave me this recipe.

It makes four to five crusts, depending on diameter. It rarely tears, but if it does, simply roll it back into a ball and start again. You can do this numerous times, and it will still bake up deliciously, so it works great for trying out the fancy crusts in the cookbooks. It also freezes well.

4 cups flour
2 cups shortening (yes, that much!)
1 egg
1 teaspoon baking powder
1 tablespoon white vinegar
Cold water

Directions:

In large bowl mix together flour and shortening, using pastry cutter or 2 forks, until mixture is crumbly. Break egg into a measuring cup, beat, then add enough cold water to measure three-quarters cup liquid. Add baking powder and vinegar, blending well. Then add liquid mixture to flour mixture and blend well. Dough will be quite moist. For best results, cover and refrigerate for at least thirty minutes before rolling out. Follow baking directions for your favorite pie recipe.

Chapter One

Lacey paused at Web Connor's table and swirled the steaming coffee around in the pot. "More coffee, Web?" she asked. Web had already downed five cups and by all rights should have been swirling himself.

Web shook his head and smiled. "No, gotta get going. Thank you just the same." He began to slide his hefty frame from the red vinyl seat. "Gerald outdid himself on that pie today."

"Glad you enjoyed it, Web. See you soon," Lacey called after him as he wound his way among Formica-topped tables to the door. She began stacking the dirty dishes, and beneath Web's plate she found a twenty-dollar bill.

She stared at the bill a moment, then jerked it up and pivoted. Web was just pushing through the glass doors. "Web!" she called, waving the bill in the air. "Wait! This is a twenty."

He turned and called back gruffly, "I can see that. You think I haven't noticed how you always cut me the biggest piece of pie and make sure my steak's done just right?" He raised a hand. "Merry Christmas from me and Milly." Then he was out the door.

Lacey watched him walking rapidly away toward the tractor-trailer rig he drove for Inman Trucking, the wind tugging at his red-plaid jacket. Turning again to the table, she blinked to clear her vision and slipped the bill into her apron pocket, then finished gathering the dishes.

Lacey Bryant waited tables at Gerald's Truck Stop Restaurant, part of a large complex that served truckers and other drivers from nearby Interstate 40, which cut right through Albuquerque, New Mexico. A mix of modern efficiency and homey friendliness, Gerald's did a thriving business with the locals, too. Lacey was on a first-name basis with many of her customers.

The restaurant was a gay place at Christmastime, with so many people bustling in—families heading home or to visit relatives, truckers trying to make as many hauls as possible before Christmas Day, women taking a break from their shopping. Christmas songs played from the jukebox. Silver garlands swooped over the windows and doorframes. Tiny multicolored lights blinked on the green plastic tree. Shiny stars and bright Mexican piñatas hung from the ceiling. Already Gerald had allowed a few small children the treat of breaking a piñata and gathering up the candy that rained across the floor.

Lacey loved the way customers acted at this season. Everyone seemed to smile for no particular reason—didn't matter whether they knew each other or not. Folks chatted freely, confided their holiday plans. Even Harry Cummings smiled, and he was about as sour as they came.

Lacey just plain loved Christmas. She had ever since she could remember. It was as if magic descended on her world at this time, swelling her heart with invincible joy.

One hand balancing the dishes from Web's table, the other bearing the coffeepot, Lacey headed behind the counter. She dumped the dishes into the waiting plastic pan and glanced at the clock. Four-ten. She would be off at five, making it a ten-hour day. She'd been glad for the extra hours; it was her last day before taking off for two weeks, and she needed all the money she could earn.

Lacey had been putting in lots of overtime for the past three months. There were Christmas presents to buy for her children, and like the singer now crooning from the jukebox, she was going home for Christmas.

Thinking of the trip gave her pause, and she stood for a moment with a wet dishrag held in midair as her thoughts traveled across miles and years. There was a distinct possibility that she might not be welcome at the home where she'd grown up, that her father might turn her away. But she refused to dwell on the possibility. It was Christmas, after all. And Lacey considered it her greatest strength, the thing that enabled her not only to survive but to enjoy life, that she never, *never* dwelled on the less than best that could happen.

The swinging door to the kitchen burst open.

"Doin' okay out here?" Jolene asked. She was the only other waitress on duty through the quieter afternoon hours between the lunch and dinner rushes.

"Doing fine," Lacey said. Giving Jolene a wry smile, she added, "Someday you'll have to teach me your trick for keeping all the customers away from your tables and sitting at mine."

"It's a secret I shall never reveal." Jolene pranced away to the jukebox. Thirty seconds later Glen Campbell was singing about Santa coming to town.

"Does that guy always slide his cup back and forth like that?" Jolene asked when she joined Lacey behind the counter. She inclined her head toward the booth where a lanky J. B. Hunt driver sat.

Lacey nodded and slipped the funnel from the coffee machine. "He has ever since he came in."

"Glad he's over there. If he was any closer, I think I'd scream at him." Jolene reached into the cabinet for the coffee filters and plunked the box onto the counter. "Your eyes are lit up like Christmas trees."

Lacey couldn't help smiling broadly as she discarded the used filter. "I've made enough in tips to get Jon the remote-control car he wants for Christmas—the exact one! I've been putting off buying another model, hoping I could get the real thing."

"That's good, honey. How *are* the kids? Are they getting excited about the trip?"

"Anna has a cold. And yes and no to excitement," Lacey answered. She sloshed the plastic funnel around in the soapy water, then rinsed it. "I didn't bother with a tree this year, since we're not going to be home, and the kids were none too happy about that. But on the whole, they see the trip as an adventure. They've told everyone—and I mean everyone, including the UPS delivery man—that they'll be riding across country in a big eighteen-wheel truck, and they keep asking all kinds of questions about their grandparents and what things were like when I was a kid." She dried the funnel.

"Did you ever tell them about the problem between you and your parents?" Jolene asked.

Lacey sighed. "I tried, but every time I lost my nerve. I was afraid of prejudicing the kids against their grandparents or making them disappointed in me. I ended up saying that Grandma and Grandpa didn't know we were coming and it was to be a surprise."

Jolene gave a nod of understanding. "I guess it would be a pretty touchy subject, especially for Jon. You all set for the trip?"

Lacey filled the filter with fresh-ground coffee. "I have a few last-minute things to get tonight—Jon's car, nose drops for Anna and new underwear for me." She jammed the filter into the machine. "Why is it that women's underwear doesn't seem to survive more than a few launderings these days?"

Jolene shrugged and studied her bitten-off fingernails. "Pate still picking you up at six tomorrow morning?"

Lacey glanced at the clock and felt her stomach tighten. "I guess so. I was sort of expecting him to call or drop by today, he hasn't."

"If Pate told you six tomorrow morning, he'll be there at five to," Jolene assured her. "He's as punctual as the sunrise."

"I know." Lacey nodded.

She thought about Pate and all his kindnesses, the latest being his offer to drive her and the children all the way to North Carolina and back on his truck route. Without that ride, she and the kids would not be making the journey. She was a single mother, the sole support of her two growing children. She already had to stretch the budget for clothes, dentist's visits, school field trips and to try to put a little aside for a rainy day. Due to a hefty and unexpected car repair bill, her rainy-day money at the moment was all but nonexistent, and she simply had to count on sunshine.

"You know," Jolene mused, "Pate's a lot like my Frank. You could do worse."

"Oh, Jolene!" Lacey laughed and adjusted the glass pot beneath the stream of steaming coffee. "It's not like that with us. Pate's more like a father to me."

"What do you think Frank is to me? That and a lot more. Older men can give you what younger ones never can—in more ways than one, if you get my drift." Jolene gave her a knowing look. "It's a thought."

"No, it's not," Lacey said firmly.

"Okay—don't get touchy." Jolene's gaze moved past Lacey's shoulder, and a slow, welcoming smile slipped across her face. When her friend lifted her hand to wave, Lacey turned to see a regular customer they all knew simply as Cooper pushing through the glass doors.

"Mmm, he's a sight to warm a woman's heart," Jolene said in a hoarse whisper. "And he'll sit at your table, of course." She winked and pushed away from the counter.

Knowing Jolene intended to retreat to the kitchen again, Lacey reached for the coffeepot. "Since I've got a new customer to take care of, you can refill coffee cups," she said sweetly.

Jolene gave a throaty chuckle and took the glass pot. Lacey walked over to grab a menu, even though it was probably a waste of time. Cooper would either order the Texas T-bone or the Piping Hot Chili. For the past four years she'd been serving him, it had been one of the two. Of course, there *had* been that time he'd ordered breakfast.

As she turned, she was surprised to see that Cooper had slipped onto a stool at the counter. It struck her as strange; Cooper always sat in a booth, usually the front corner one with a good view of the parking lot. Equally unusual, he was watching her expectantly.

"Good afternoon." She set the menu in front of him and looked into his dark eyes, finding an odd expression there. A hesitancy, a nervousness.

Cooper extended the folded piece of paper Pate had given him and said, "From Pate." The note would explain, so he didn't think he needed to say more at this point.

Lacey's pale, slim, feminine fingers seemed a stark contrast to his large, rough, dark ones as she slowly took the note. Confusion and apprehension clouded her eyes. Cooper noticed they were the color of spring grass just before she lowered them to the paper.

He ran his gaze over her curly brown hair and ivory cheeks and for the hundredth time asked himself how he'd gotten hooked into doing this. Maybe he would escape his own foolish sentimentality; maybe she would simply refuse to go now.

Either she was a slow reader or she couldn't comprehend the words the first time, because it seemed to take her an inordinately long time to read the few words. Cooper knew what was in the note; he'd read it, unashamedly.

Dear Lacey,
    Cooper will explain about me. He will also take

you to North Carolina right along with hauling my payload on up to Washington. Cooper is a good man. I trust him with my life. So I can trust him with yours, too. Have a good Christmas. Hope everything turns out the way you want.

Love,
Pate

Cooper felt a bit of embarrassment over the high praise. And he wondered about it. He didn't think anyone, even a friend like Pate, knew him well enough to form such an opinion.

After what seemed like a very long time, Lacey raised her eyes to him. Her face was white, her green eyes filled with confusion. "What…" She stopped the question and waited.

Just as Cooper opened his mouth to explain about Pate, a tall, good-looking guy appeared at his shoulder, standing in front of the cash register.

"Excuse me," Lacey said.

She stepped behind the register to take the man's payment. The guy called her "honey" and attempted to chat in an overly familiar way. She called him politely by name—Lyle—but seemed to put him in his place by being cold as ice.

Cooper looked at her and couldn't blame the guy for flirting. Lacey was a pretty woman, always friendly, and Cooper chose to sit at one of her tables when he could because she was a damned good waitress.

He recalled several times when he'd considered asking her out. Well, it'd been more than several. Fact was, more than once when he'd looked at her, she'd looked back. There'd been mutual interest. But something told Cooper she could cause him a lot of complications, so he'd never asked her and had kept to himself. He wondered how serious her relationship with Pate was. He knew they were real friendly, spent time together.

"It iced up on us in Santa Fe yesterday evening. Pate slipped and fell down the front stairs of his apartment," Cooper told her when she returned. He watched distress replace the confusion in her eyes. "Broke his leg bad enough to require a hospital stay. I told him I'd haul his payload and take *you* on to this place in North Carolina."

"Pine Grove," Lacey said.

"Yeah. He said west side of Raleigh."

She nodded, a faraway, thoughtful expression on her face. Then she blinked and focused on him. Maybe now she'd say she wouldn't go. Cooper waited.

"Pate's in the hospital?" she asked.

Cooper nodded. "But he should be released day after tomorrow. His son's family is flying out from Richmond to spend Christmas with him and take care of him."

"Oh." Now she was studying him closely. The next instant she turned quickly and reached for the coffeepot. "Want some coffee?" she asked.

Cooper stood and stretched, saying, "That and the chili dinner. I'll sit over there." He inclined his head toward the corner booth. He waited while she poured him the coffee, then he took the cup. For an instant he looked into her green eyes. The way she kept studying him was annoying. Why didn't she just say she'd changed her mind about going East?

Lacey bent to write his order on her pad and listened to his boots scuff the tile as he walked to his usual booth.

What was she going to do now? she asked herself. The children were counting on going. It was way past time they met their grandparents and aunt and uncle and cousins. Her sister was planning on their Christmas Eve arrival, and would be watching, ever so discreetly, out the big front window. And Lacey hungered to see the home where she'd grown up, to see her parents. She longed for the chance to make things right with her father.

"So, what's the big deal?" Jolene asked when Lacey explained the situation to her. They were in the kitchen, where Lacey was putting together a salad for Cooper.

"Cooper isn't Pate," Lacey said. "Pate...well, we're good friends. I wasn't imposing on him—it's not imposing on a good friend. And you didn't see Cooper's face. He doesn't want to do this. He's only doing it for Pate."

"Oh, Cooper always looks grumpy. The man's afraid to be friendly, afraid people will find out he's got as big a soft spot as everyone else."

"Where in the world did you get that idea?"

"I've been out with him."

Lacey stared at her friend. "When?"

"Oh, about three years ago—before I met Frank." Jolene handed Lacey the salad dressing. "Went out with him twice, as a matter of fact. Once to a show, then to a show and dinner. He's a real gentleman— good manners and all—but he's a loner. Not the marrying kind, if you know what I mean. Still, he's a good guy."

"What's his first name?" Lacey asked.

Jolene frowned. "I don't know."

"You went out with him twice and never learned his first name? Didn't you ask?"

Jolene shook her head. "He's just Cooper. Everyone calls him Cooper. Maybe that *is* his first name. And why would I need to know? Two shows and dinner doesn't mean marriage." Jolene pointed a finger at Lacey. "You want to go home—you need to go home. Now's your chance, and my advice is to take it, because you're not going to get another like it. Besides, what will you tell the kids? Sorry, it's all off? Then they'd have to tell their friends, *and* the UPS man, that their bragging was all lies."

"Thanks, Jolene," Lacey said dryly, and thrust the bowl of salad toward her. "You take this to him. I need a few minutes to think this thing through."

Much of what Jolene had said was true, Lacey reflected. She imagined Jon's and Anna's disappointed faces when she told them the trip was off. Lacey herself hated the thought of not going. Beth was expecting her; they would talk and laugh about scrapes they'd gotten into as children. And she missed her mother, who wouldn't be around forever, she reminded herself sadly. And her father—well, it was time one of them made an effort at reconciliation.

Riding back East with Pate had been a perfect arrangement. Pate Andrews was around fifty, widowed and lived alone up in Santa Fe. His job as a trucker brought him into Gerald's on a regular basis, and over the years he and Lacey had formed a special kind of friendship. As Lacey once told Jolene, Pate had taken the place of the father she didn't have, the grandfather the children had never met.

When she discovered he was driving back East for the holidays, she hadn't hesitated to ask him the big favor of taking her and the children along. She'd even explained her intentions. Pate hadn't laughed or told her she was being foolish. He'd told her he'd fix it with his company.

But hitching a ride with Cooper wasn't the same. She had no doubt as to his character; Pate wouldn't have set it up if Cooper wasn't completely trustworthy. It was just that Lacey hardly knew Cooper. He wasn't a friend. How could she impose so much on a man who was almost a complete stranger?

A loud clanging made her jump. The cook had dropped a pan. Needing something to do with her hands, Lacey walked over to stir the chili and the potato and vegetable soups.

She tried to recall what she knew of Cooper. Pate and he were friends; they often ate together at the restaurant. Cooper seemed to be respected by the other drivers; while not overly friendly, apparently he was well-known and liked.

Lacey knew little else, and what little she did know was mostly impressions. She'd been waiting on Cooper since she'd started working at Gerald's four years earlier, yet she didn't even know whether Cooper was his first name, his last or a nickname. He was polite but seemed to wear a big invisible sign that said No Trespassing.

Though, Lacey admitted reluctantly, she'd felt his low-keyed interest on more than one occasion, and she'd be lying if she didn't say she found him attractive. But she'd never considered Cooper a man to get involved with.

The qualities that made him extremely attractive to women, including herself—a rugged handsomeness, an aura of strength, even a hint of danger—made Lacey equally leery of him. She'd want a gentle, caring man—if ever she got around to having time for a relationship. It wasn't easy, what with raising and supporting two children.

Jolene burst through the door, bearing the big plastic dishpan. She set it on a counter and whirled to hold out several bills toward Lacey.

"Here's your tip from that man who favored sliding his cup around. He was right nice, too," she said. "Now, you'd better get Cooper his chili. It doesn't take long to eat that small salad. And no, I'm not taking it."

Absolutely no closer to a decision, Lacey grabbed the big plate of thick chili and cheese the cook had prepared, took a deep breath and pushed through the swinging door.

As she walked toward Cooper, her heart thudded within her breast. In an instant she noted his thick hair and coarse mustache, both so dark brown they were almost black. That he was a lean hard-muscled man was plainly evident, even though he wore a flannel shirt over a long-sleeved undershirt. He had to have heard her footsteps, but he didn't so much as lift his head from his newspaper. The austere impression again came to the fore, and Lacey liked neither of the choices she faced.

She stopped at his table and waited for him to look up at her. Slowly he raised his gaze to meet hers. His dark brown eyes reflected curiosity.

His gaze dropped to the plate she held. Quickly he folded his paper and put it aside. Lacey set the plate before him, hesitated, then slipped into the opposite seat.

"How did Pate seem when you left him?" she asked as she folded her hands and forced them to rest quietly atop the table.

Cooper shook dried hot pepper atop his chili and cheese. "He was wide awake and flirting with the nurse." He didn't look up at her.

Lacey stared at him. It was either go with him—or not go at all. The latter would mean she didn't know when she would get to see her family or when the children would meet their grandma and grandpa.

"You going or not?"

Cooper's voice startled her, and Lacey blinked, realizing she'd been staring at him without really seeing him. Now his dark eyes seemed to bore into her, demanding an answer.

She licked her lips. "I hate to bother you...."

"Look—" he held his knife like a pointer "—I told Pate I'd take you. The deal is still on, just like before, and I'll probably get you there a bit faster than Pate would have. It's not like it was with Pate—I ain't Pate—but it is a ride. Now, do you want to go?"

Lacey stared into those dark, forbidding eyes and felt the squeeze of being caught between the proverbial rock and a hard place.

"I'd be very grateful for the ride," she said.

Something flickered in his eyes. Surprise? Dismay? Lacey wasn't certain, and immediately the cold, blank expression reclaimed his features.

"Okay" was all he said before returning his attention to his chili.

Lacey shifted in her seat. She was reluctant to pressure him about particulars, such as the time and place of pickup. It seemed rude of him not to volunteer the information. She stared at him, but he didn't lift his gaze.

"Pate was going to pick me up at home at six o'clock tomorrow morning," she said at last. She felt ridiculously like a beggar and hated it. Why in the world was the man so purposely disagreeable? Was common cordiality against his principles?

"I'll meet you here at the restaurant at five," Cooper said without looking up. "I like to get an early start."

Lacey opened her mouth in surprise, then closed it and quickly masked her dismay. "Fine," she said with a brief nod. She rose and walked stiffly away.

Perhaps she should simply not go, she thought, her mind whirling. But the results of such a decision were even less appealing than driving sixteen hundred miles with a rude lump of a man.

She sighed. She had chosen the lesser of two evils, she supposed. And now she'd have to spend three whole days in the confines of a tractor-trailer rig with two active children and Mr. Delightful. She might spend most of that time keeping the children and herself out of his way. What fun!

Chapter Two

Lacey's shift ended before Cooper finished his dinner. She stopped by his table, braving the tight-lipped dragon, to ask the name of the hospital Pate was in.

When she said, "See you in the morning," he gave a short nod and a grunt.

He wasn't all that handsome a man, Lacey decided. Looks weren't everything.

She drove through the heavy traffic, mentally reviewing the details that needed to be taken care of before morning. She'd pretty much cleared out the refrigerator; what was left could be tossed out. The newspaper had been stopped...mustn't forget to turn down the furnace.

The shopping mall was packed, the store's shelves emptying rapidly. There was only one Tough-Stuff radio-controlled car left at the hobby shop. Lacey spotted it and at that same instant saw another woman heading directly toward it.

With a burst of speed, Lacey sprinted and reached the car first, snatched up the box and held it close. The woman glared at her, and Lacey's cheeks burned from shame. Still, she bit her lip and held the car tightly.

Her embarrassment eased into pleasure as she handed her hard-earned money to the cashier. Jon hadn't asked for another thing, and getting the Tough-Stuff remote-control car would surprise and delight him; he had so few lavish toys. Lacey couldn't help the fact that Anna would not get her longed-for puppy for Christmas, but doing this for Jon helped some. And when they got back home after Christmas, she promised herself, she would see about getting Anna a puppy—even though the thought of such a troublesome critter made her wince.

She laid her packages on the car seat with an audible "Phew!" Her feet and back ached, her hands were stiff and dry, and before her lay dinner still to be prepared, two children to wash and packing to do.

As she drove home, Lacey worried about having overspent. But Anna had really needed socks, and that fancy hair clip hadn't cost *that* much. And Jon's present shoes were disreputable. But she really hadn't needed to buy that belt buckle for Cooper. It'd been a silly, extravagant thing to do. Fifteen dollars. For fifteen dollars she could buy dinner on the trip for her and the kids. Just once, she thought, for an entire month, she'd like to have enough money not to have to scrimp and calculate all the time.

It was spilled milk now, she told herself as she pulled the car into the drive of her duplex apartment. As she opened the front door, both of her children burst from the adjoining apartment, where they stayed with Susan Price during the school holiday break. Lacey called a greeting to Susan, who stood in the doorway. Jon and Anna surrounded her, pretending to try to peek into the bags as they entered the apartment.

"You'll spoil your Christmas," Lacey cautioned.

"Not me. I won't see my puppy until Christmas morning after Santa brings it," Anna said flatly.

Jon switched on the table lamp and held the door for Lacey. "I've told her and told her that Santa won't bring her a puppy this year because of the trip," he said.

"He might." Anna jutted her chin, sniffed and shook her short straight hair.

"Pate won't want a noisy, messy puppy riding all the way back here from North Carolina in his truck," Jon argued.

"He won't care."

"That's enough," Lacey said as she headed down the small hallway to her bedroom. "You two get washed up so you can help with dinner. We've all got a lot to do tonight." She laid the bags on her bed and paused, worrying about how the change in plans might affect the children. It would be best to tell them about Cooper right away and give them as much time as possible to get used to the idea, she decided.

She managed to convey the information, soothe their disappointment about not riding with their friend Pate and get them into bed by eight-thirty.

"What will we do with the puppy Santa brings, Mama?" Anna asked as Lacey tucked the covers around her. "Will Cooper let us bring him home in his truck?"

"Blow," Lacey instructed, holding a tissue to Anna's tiny nose while searching her mind for a response to the question. She stroked the fine hair from her daughter's forehead. "Anna, I told you that your puppy would have to come later, even if we were riding with Pate. A puppy is a delicate thing for Santa Claus to haul around, especially from the cold North

Pole. Why, I can't think of anyone who ever got a puppy for Christmas.''

"Tammy Henderson did.'' Anna's big brown eyes dominated her face.

"Well, we'll see.'' It was one of those situations where a mother couldn't win, Lacey thought. She hated disappointing her daughter, but there seemed no way around it.

In the kitchen she poured a cup of coffee, then called Information for the number of the Santa Fe hospital where Pate was recuperating. She was relieved when his voice, sounding perfectly normal, boomed across the line.

He was obviously surprised and touched to hear from her and kept repeating that he was fine. His son and son's family were due in the following morning, and they were going to have a grand old time.

"And I want you to have a good time, too, Lacey. I'm really sorry to disappoint you, but Cooper will see you and the children safely to Pine Grove. I've known Cooper for nigh on to twenty years now. He's a good, reliable driver. A good man. You can depend on him. I wouldn't have recommended him if I didn't know that.''

"I know, Pate,'' Lacey said. "Thanks for taking care of us.''

"Well, I know Cooper can seem a mite disagreeable,'' Pate drawled. "I know, too, that you'd rather not go with him, but I'm awful glad you are. You need to see your folks, and, Lacey... well, Cooper needs your company on this trip. Holidays are a mighty lonesome time for him.''

Lacey silently thought that Cooper didn't seem like the type of man to want, much less need, anyone, but she kept the thought to herself. It would only distress Pate, and that wouldn't change the situation. She hurried to assure him that she and the children would be fine and to wish him a Merry Christmas.

As she replaced the receiver, she realized with chagrin that she'd forgotten to ask Pate what Cooper's full name was.

With a large sigh she reached for the gift she'd bought Pate, a leather tobacco pouch with his initials embossed on it. She would have to save it for after Christmas.

Shaking away the melancholy that suddenly engulfed her, Lacey briskly began wrapping the few remaining packages. She'd sent some gifts on ahead to her sister's house, but these precious things she wouldn't have entrusted to the mails.

There was Jon's car and the battery charger that went with it and the soft baby doll for Anna. On the doll's wrist Lacey fastened a real Mickey Mouse watch. Would the doll and the watch make Anna forget about a puppy? Lacey frowned as she smoothed down the doll's hair. No, probably not even a trip to Disney World would do that.

As she wrapped, Lacey's thoughts turned to her own childhood. Though their father had been strict, he'd always seemed to mellow at Christmastime. He'd take Lacey and Beth out to a friend's land and be uncharacteristically patient while they tramped for acres, searching for just the right tree. Then he'd chop it down and haul it back to the house.

The shiny green leaves and red berries of holly gleamed from the mantel and tabletops, and the pungent smell of pine filled the rooms. She missed those things here in the drier, more rugged climate of Albuquerque. She missed sharing the holidays with her family. For the past four years every Christmas Eve had been spent as this evening was: alone.

It was Lacey who picked out the gifts, who wrapped them, who drank warm apple cider and listened to Christmas carols and hummed along, no other voice echoing with hers. And, though she treasured the presents she received—two nonsensical things made by childish hands, and a lovely gift from Beth every year—she sometimes longed for a special present from a person who knew her well. A treat bought for herself simply wasn't the same.

She unrolled red elf-print paper and placed on it the gift she'd put together for her parents—a photo album chronicling the young lives of Jon and Anna.

The first pictures were of Jon when he'd been only weeks old. A tightness gripped her heart as she paused to look at them. She'd been oh, so foolish, and she fervently hoped she could put things right now.

Lacey had been nineteen and had been going with Shawn Bryant for six months when she got pregnant with Jon. The old saying had been that you couldn't get pregnant on the first experience with sex, but Lacey had.

Her parents had been furious. She could still see her father's face, red with anger and scorn. She'd needed his love and support and had been so bitterly disappointed.

According to her father she'd committed an unpardonable sin and had brought terrible shame upon the family. Her parents had insisted she give the baby up for adoption—something Lacey couldn't bring herself to do. Trying to force her, her father had demanded she follow his edict or get out and fend for herself. She'd left that very afternoon, screaming from the yard that she would never return.

However, pride didn't pay the bills. So she and Shawn had started out like a million other young couples in the world—broke, and with a family on the way. To Shawn's credit, he'd married her without a grumble. He'd enlisted in the air force, a good, steady job, and in the early years they'd moved a number of times. Anna had come along, and they'd become a family of four.

But domestic life brought a sense of confinement rather than contentment to Shawn. There were too many experiences calling him, experiences in which a wife and children had no part. He simply got tired of bills and responsibilities and sleeping with one woman, so four years ago he'd left.

Lacey looked at the picture of Anna's last birthday, her sixth, and smiled sadly. She felt more pity for Shawn than anything else. He'd missed out on so much by not being able to give of himself. And not only didn't he give of himself, but he provided no financial support, either. Though her friends had suggested going through legal channels to get money from him, Lacey had learned that the legalities would end up costing her more money than Shawn would be able to give.

Lacey closed the album and began wrapping it. She thought of Beth, who was expecting her.

Over the years she'd stayed in contact with her sister. During most of those years Beth had urged Lacey to return and attempt a reconciliation with their parents. Lacey had often considered it, but she'd never had the money for the trip. Beth didn't have it, either, and Lacey refused to approach her mother and father for a loan. When she did return, it had to be under her own steam. And of course, there was still that stubborn pride. Why couldn't her parents *ask* her to come home?

Then, two months ago, a letter had come from her mother, at long last. In the letter, her mother had asked Lacey to consider coming home; she'd expressed love for the first time in almost eleven years and a great desire to see her grandchildren. Lacey knew the time had come for going home and rebuilding burned bridges.

But the letter had been from Emily Sawyer alone. Leon Sawyer, Beth admitted, had seemed to grow harder over time. He hadn't spoken Lacey's name since she'd defied his wishes and left, and he grew angry when any other member of the family mentioned her.

Lacey had decided, and Beth had reluctantly agreed, that the best approach to her father was surprise—which meant not telling even her mother that she was coming. She intended to show up on the doorstep with their grandchildren in the flesh. Whether or not it angered her father, she knew he would never do anything to hurt the youngsters, and she hoped with all her heart that her act would tumble the giant wall of bitterness the past had wrought between her and her father. The photo album was a means toward this end as well.

The last gift to be wrapped was the one she'd bought for Cooper in a weak moment that evening. She looked at the shiny metal buckle nested in its small box. It was cast with images of trucking: a smoking tractor-trailer rig, exaggerated tires and highway signs.

For a moment Lacey considered setting it aside. Giving such a personal gift to a man whose full name she didn't even know seemed awfully silly. No doubt she would feel odd when she gave it, and he would feel odd taking it.

But she again cut the elf-print paper to wrap it. The buckle was a token of appreciation. She needed to express that. And it was Christmas, a time for giving, no matter the motive or the relationship.

The final bag to be packed was her own. Lacey found herself pulling everything out of her drawers and closet, despairing over the lack of suitable outfits. All her clothes seemed so worn and out-of-date. And suddenly, looking her best was very important.

She did have one pair of fairly new blue jeans—designer ones bought on sale—and there was the mauve sweater that brought out her skin tones. They would do for the first day. And it wasn't too much trouble to roll her hair. A fleeting anticipation touched her spirit. Would Cooper possibly think her pretty?

She didn't sleep much, tossing and turning, the rollers poking into her scalp no matter what position she tried. And they were the supposedly painless foam ones.

But the next morning her hair looked great—soft, bouncy and shiny. She decided she looked pretty good in her jeans, too, and her efforts served to make her feel confident about the trip ahead as she got herself ready before waking the children.

Maybe yesterday had been simply a bad one for Cooper, making him abnormally grumpy. Maybe today he would welcome them, even be glad to have their company.

"It's a thought," she murmured to the skeptical-looking image in the mirror.

Lacey parked out of the way at Gerald's lot and tucked the key beneath the mat for Jolene, who would return the car to Lacey's duplex later that day.

"Middle of the damn...darn night," Jon grumbled.

Lacey silently agreed as she settled the children in a front booth where she could watch for Cooper's arrival through the big front window. With the night's blackness broken only by the building's silvery outside lights, the window reflected her family's faces.

As often happened, her reflected image startled her. Was that really her with the nice curly hair? Was that woman's figure—shapely and feminine—really hers? She didn't feel like that inside. Inside she felt quivery and sort of small and uncertain, though she was careful to hide those emotions from her children.

And she wouldn't spend one more second wondering if she were right or wrong in making this trip, she told herself as she tugged a tissue from her tote bag for Anna. She'd gone too far to back out now. And it *was* Christmas season, not a time for fretting.

"Order anything you want, kids," she said, checking her watch. "We have over half an hour."

"It's too early to eat," Jon said.

"Try."

"Three days until Christmas," Anna piped up out of the blue, and gave a bright smile.

Lacey had to smile in return. Things were going to be fine, she told herself. The trip would go well, be an adventure, and at the end her father would open his arms wide for them. She hoped. What would she tell her children if he didn't?

For the next twenty-five minutes Lacey's heartbeat gradually picked up tempo, and her insides began to quiver like a bowl of gelatin, so that when Jon, who'd been craning his neck to peer out the window for the past ten minutes, said, "Did you say Cooper's truck was red?" she almost jumped out of her seat.

"Maroon," she answered, purposely glancing outside with a casualness she didn't feel.

A big, shiny, top-of-the-line Kenworth truck pulling a silver trailer rolled to a stop several yards away. It gleamed in the fluorescent lighting.

Lacey's heart hammered, and a distinctly sinking feeling claimed her when her gaze fell to the Christmas lights draped across the Kenworth's grill. In merry greens, reds and yellows, the lights crudely spelled out Bah, Humbug. She had to stare at them for approximately thirty seconds to be certain, but that was what they said.

She grasped at the idea that maybe it wasn't Cooper. Plenty of drivers drove such trucks; maybe it was someone else.

Then a figure dressed in a thick vest, shoulders hunched against the cold, with a black Stetson on his head, strode around the front of the truck toward the restaurant. It was Cooper.

When Lacey turned to look at her children, Jon's eyebrows were raised in silent question.

"It's Cooper," she said, stifling a sigh.

"What do those lights say, Mama?" Anna asked.

When Lacey hesitated, Jon filled in. "Bah, Humbug—like old Scrooge." Then he muttered, "I get this funny feeling...." He stopped at Lacey's sharp look.

"Here, Anna, let's get your coat on," she said, casting both children a bright smile. "It's time to go."

Without looking, she mentally pictured Cooper striding into the restaurant. She knew exactly when he entered; she felt a cold breeze—and his gaze. She looked up and across the room.

Cooper was frowning—in fact, his expression was thunderous—as he approached. In the process of zipping Anna's coat, Lacey's fingers stilled. She could do no more than stare at him and wonder what she'd done, because it was obvious he was furious with her.

Cooper knew he'd been hornswoggled. A small voice in the back of his mind told him that it hadn't been by Lacey. It'd been Pate. Pate had neglected to tell him about the kids, and the old guy had done it on purpose. He'd known Cooper wouldn't have gone along with the idea—not at all.

But at the moment Pate wasn't there. And Lacey was. And she should have said something yesterday about there being kids!

"Good morning."

Cooper heard her gentle greeting and fleetingly took in her curling, shiny hair and the softness of her being before turning his gaze to the two pint-sized kids beside her. He didn't say good morning, hello or anything. He didn't know what to say and was afraid of letting the anger within him explode. He returned his gaze to Lacey.

"I'd like you to meet my two children, Cooper," she said, her voice polite and soft, just as if nothing was wrong. "This is Jon—" she touched the boy's shoulder "—and this is Anna."

"Pate didn't say anything about kids." Cooper spoke low, an inner caution clamping down on his vocal chords. But he wanted out of this, and he intended to get out. He wasn't spending three days in the cab of his truck with two wet-nosed kids.

Lacey's eyes widened. She glanced nervously past Cooper, reminding him they were in a public place, then met his gaze again.

"Pate didn't..." Her green eyes searched his. "Pate didn't tell you I had two children—that he was taking all of us to Pine Grove?" Her voice came out hoarse, as if forced from her throat.

"No, ma'am, he didn't." Cooper ground the words out, though he wanted to shout. "And neither did you." So now she would apologize, he thought, and know the trip was off.

"Well, I'm sorry...."

Her eyes were extremely dark against the paleness of her face. She looked confused and apologetic, and a shaft of disappointment touched Cooper. Why did she have to go and have kids? He'd sort of been thinking it might be nice to drive east with her, that having her along might make the stretch ahead seem shorter. A stupid thought that had been.

"I had no idea," she said, seeming to grow taller and straighter right before his eyes. Her voice was soft yet perfectly distinct. "I simply assumed you knew. Pate's note said it was all arranged, and last night when I spoke to him, he didn't say anything."

"No, I guess he didn't," Cooper allowed, his gaze dropping again to the children in front of him.

One was a little girl, about five, a replica of Carla from the vintage Little Rascals shows, with her short, straight brown hair and wide brown eyes. She clung to her mother's leg and regarded him as she would a horned devil. The boy standing next to her was about ten or eleven, with tousled light brown hair and eyes and a body stance that indicated he knew all there was to know in this world.

"Well," Lacey said, "as I said before, these are my children, Jon and Anna." She rested her hand atop the little girl's head and smiled at Cooper. "Kids, this is Mr.—this is Cooper, who's generously agreed to take Pate's place and drive us to Pine Grove."

It wasn't what Cooper had expected. He stared at her, feeling the tables had turned, because now he was the uncertain one. How had she done it? Only seconds ago she'd looked hesitant, vague and definitely on the verge of running. Now she was acting as if everything was going perfectly smoothly, like a blacktopped highway snaking off into the prairie.

What could he say? Cooper thought as he stared into her clear eyes. He'd told Pate he would do this favor for him; the older man was relying on him. Even though he had been devious, Cooper still owed him. And he was a man to pay his debts.

"Come on. We got three days to get there, and I'd sooner make it in two."

He pivoted and strode toward the restaurant doors, the sound of "Jingle Bells" following him. Some jerk had punched the tune into the jukebox, regardless of it being five o'clock in the morning. *Bah, humbug!* Cooper thought fiercely. Three days in the cab of his rig with a woman and two wet-nosed kids.

A *beautiful* woman and two wet-nosed kids, he thought as he paused at the truck's passenger door and turned to watch Lacey and her children approach. The thought rubbed salt into the wound. Though Lacey carried a bulging bag in each hand and another hung from her shoulder, she walked straight and with firm steps. The cold breeze blew her hair back from her face; small gold hoop earrings caught the fluorescent lights.

"Five bags aren't going to fit," he told her when she came abreast of him. He knew his words were prodded by a strange desire to rock her self-confidence. If he felt off-balance, he wanted her to, as well.

"This is a tote bag," she said, indicating the large one hanging from her shoulder. "And Pate said we could bring four suitcases."

Cooper was rewarded by the slight quaver in her voice and the uncertainty that glimmered momentarily in her eyes. "I ain't Pate," he reminded her.

"You want me to leave one behind?" she said, anger slipping into her eyes. "Where should I leave it?"

"Here is fine with me."

"I need all four bags—and everything in this tote. There *are* three of us."

"Rearrange things. There isn't room."

A movement drew his gaze, and Cooper glanced down to see the little girl gaping at him. She looked on the verge of tears, and a twinge of remorse pricked him.

"Okay, fine!" Lacey plunked the two bulging bags onto the black pavement. Kneeling, she unzipped one of them and began jerking clothes from it. A blue sweatshirt flew to the pavement. "I can do without this . . . or this. . . ."

A flutter of white followed the sweatshirt, then several frilly pink things that resembled a nightgown and underwear, giving Cooper an uncomfortable feeling in the pit of his stomach. Suddenly he was aware of the cold and of several curious faces peering through the restaurant windows. He knelt and quickly grabbed the scattered clothes, catching a pair of panties that came sailing his way.

"All right!" he said, doing a peculiar bellow through clenched teeth. He thrust the clothes at her. "Put these back in there, and let's get going. At this rate it's going to be six before we get out of here."

Adjusting his hat low on his brow, he strode around the front of the truck, leaving Lacey and her kids to get inside as best they could.

Chapter Three

Lacey watched Cooper disappear around the front of the big truck and contemplated words too ugly to speak. She was embarrassed by her actions and didn't know what to do about the entire situation. Cooper had said he would take them for Pate, yet he wasn't Pate, as he'd reminded her, and he didn't *want* to take them, though he wouldn't say so.

"I don't like him, Mama," Anna said, slipping an arm around Lacey's leg.

"You sure you still want to do this, Mom?" Jon asked.

Lacey looked at him. "Yes." Turning from her son's gaze, she grabbed hold of a handle and hoisted herself up into the vibrating truck. She pulled the two children after her.

In all her years of working at the truck stop, watching the rigs come and go, Lacey had never been inside one. She'd heard of the renowned Kenworth truck, but her imagination hadn't done it justice.

Though the big engine ran, it sent only a gentle, even pleasant, rumble into the truck cab itself. It was cozy, warm. The two high-backed seats were upholstered in thick gray velour and resembled living-room recliners, complete with armrests. Tufted gray vinyl lined the door panels and roof and thick gunmetal-gray carpeting covered the floor.

In the center, behind the chairs, was the opening to the sleeping compartment. Jon could stand in the compartment and move about easily. Lacey paused to stare at the padded vinyl lining the walls and ceiling, the bed that was larger than a double, the luxurious blue bedspread.

"There's a TV!" Jon exclaimed, drawing Lacey's gaze to the small portable on a shelf. Color, no less. There were also speakers in the wall, indicating a stereo system somewhere.

Lacey opened what she thought to be a cabinet, finding a refrigerator instead. Straightening, she came face-to-face with a microwave oven. In a narrow closet hung several pairs of jeans and numerous shirts, a pair of gleaming boots sitting beneath them.

"Where's the shower?" she quipped to Cooper.

His answer was a low grunt. He sat in his seat behind the wheel, apparently engrossed in checking the numerous gauges on the dash, acting as if he were alone in the rig, as no doubt he wished to be.

Lacey squeezed three of their bags into a large, only partially filled cabinet beneath the bed. She was standing in the narrow compartment opening, debating about what to do with the fourth bag, when Cooper appeared at her side.

"All set?" he asked.

Lacey caught the sudden scent of his sweet-musky after-shave. He turned to look at her, his face, lit by the golden glow of the interior lights, only inches away. His eyes were deep and dark, his eyelashes long, his mustache slightly bristly. She realized for the first time how wavy his hair was. His arm came around in

front of her, causing her to pull back, as he tossed his
hat onto a hook above the television.

"I don't know where to put this bag," she said.

Without a word, Cooper squeezed past her, his
thighs rubbing hers, his belt buckle pressing her arm.
Lacey felt an odd tingling in her breasts and a flutter-
ing in her stomach and was suddenly very aware of
being a woman—and that Cooper was very much a
man.

Bending at the knee in order to fit into the compartment, Cooper opened a cabinet above the end of
the bed, pulled out two blankets and tossed them beside Jon and Anna, who were sitting on the bed. Then
he took the bag from Lacey, placed it into the cabinet
and shut the door with a hard snap.

He looked at her, and she looked at him. Realizing
that she was in his way, she searched for somewhere to
go. The only place was the passenger seat. She sat
down immediately.

Cooper took his seat, flipped switches and turned
on the headlights. Anna came quietly to wiggle onto
Lacey's lap. Lacey held her close and worried if it
could possibly harm her children to take this trip with
a man who so obviously didn't want them around.
What if, at the trip's end, their grandfather did reject
them, just as their own father already had? How
would that make them feel about themselves?

"Can I watch the television, Mr. Cooper?" Jon
called from the back. Obviously Jon wasn't bothered
by Cooper's rudeness. But then, Jon could generally
return as good as he got.

"Yeah," Cooper said. His hand on the stick shift, he looked at Lacey. "She can't stay here," he said, inclining his head toward Anna. "It's not safe."

Anna gripped Lacey and wasn't about to let go.

"I'll get in the back with her," Lacey said.

Cooper nodded and turned his attention to getting underway. As Lacey cleared the pass-through, the truck gave a gentle jolt of forward motion. Cooper jerked the curtain across the opening, enclosing her and the children in the cozy confines of the sleeper—and himself up front, alone.

Lacey gratefully stretched out beside Anna beneath the bedcovers. She was exhausted and quite chilled. Jon propped himself against her feet, avidly watching a cartoon show, the television providing the only light in the compartment. It was a comfort to have both children physically touching her.

"This is nice," Anna said softly, her eyes wide with wonder. "It's like being rocked."

"Mmm," Lacey answered. For some reason her daughter's innocent fascination touched a raw spot in her heart.

She mused over the idea of spending the entire trip in the sleeping compartment. Surely that would make Mr. Delightful happy. How in the world could Pate think Cooper needed company?

The headlights illuminated the concrete ramp leading down to Interstate 40, and Cooper shifted gears, feeling the big Kenworth easily gain speed. He watched for oncoming vehicles—there was a surprising amount of traffic for so early in the morning. People trying to get home for the holidays, he thought, half bitterly, half wistfully.

The road passed beneath the rig at sixty-five miles an hour. Nearly three days stretched ahead of him before he dropped his load—Pate's load—up in Washington, D.C. He could have made it in less than three if he drove as he usually did. But with the woman and two kids with him, he probably wouldn't.

Cooper turned up the volume of the radio to drown out the murmur of the television. He gave thanks for a foot-stomping Mel McDaniel country tune without a hint of Christmas in it.

Thirty minutes passed, and the sky began to glow with morning. Cooper enjoyed the feeling of the steering wheel in his hands and the smooth rumble of the truck pushing through the wind.

Was that woman going to spend the entire trip back in the sleeper? he wondered. Now that she was here, the least she could do was get up front and fill his coffee cup from his thermos. A fool in a red Corvette pulled dangerously close in front of him, and he let up on the accelerator. He was suddenly very aware of his passengers.

He frowned, thinking of the fear in the little girl's face when she'd looked at him. Was he really so much of a monster? Well, he couldn't pretend to be something he wasn't. He was thirty-eight years old, a bachelor for all intents and purposes, no kids, and he didn't much like them. They reminded him of Martians, a little species with customs and language all their own.

He began to sing along faintly with the radio. The cab didn't seem so empty then.

Minutes later Lacey parted the curtain behind him. He met her gaze in the mirror and stopped his singing. She smiled. She had a rare kind of smile that lit up her entire face and reached out to touch a person. Cooper wanted to smile in return—only he didn't. He didn't want her to get the idea she was welcome or anything. But he had to admit to himself that he didn't mind looking at her, not at all, and that he felt a certain lightness all of a sudden.

Without invitation, she slipped into the passenger seat. Out of the corner of his eye, he noticed her move the armrests up and down, then give a little bounce, like a kid testing the seat.

He stretched out his arm and moved the lever to activate the seat's air cushion. She jumped, and her eyes widened.

"The air," he said, quickly returning his hand to the wheel, "for the seat." What did she think—that he was trying to cop a feel?

He returned his strict attention to the road ahead. It felt odd to have her beside him. He'd never had a woman in his rig, had always purposely avoided it.

Lacey didn't realize she was studying Cooper until he glanced over at her. Self-conscious, she jerked her head to look out the side window and folded her hands in her lap. She wasn't nervous, she told herself, and she didn't care what Cooper thought of her. There was no reason to.

It was cozy in the cab. The change in the seat when he'd moved that lever had surprised her. And now it was like an easy chair at home, though it rocked a bit more. She loved the lordly height of the truck. They passed a Toyota, and she looked down to see the driver's knees, which seemed an intimate observation.

The eastern horizon stretched orange. The shadowy woods and pastures they passed showed signs of heavy frost.

"Looks like a sunny day," Lacey commented. She loved sunny mornings.

"Radio says clouds," Cooper said.

"Oh."

On spying a slowly pumping oil well draped with colorful Christmas lights, she felt a pleasurable warmth flash within her.

"Look! Aren't they pretty?" she cried before she thought. She glanced at Cooper, and he grunted, keeping his eyes on the road.

A man of few words, Lacey thought, feeling self-conscious and childish—and irritable because of it.

He pushed in the lighter, pulled a cigarette from his shirt pocket and tucked it between his lips. For all the attention he paid her, she might as well not be there. Lacey's irritation grew.

Well, they had hours and hours ahead of them, she told herself. Jolene had said Cooper had a softer side, and Pate had said Cooper needed people at this time of year. Maybe he was just sour and distant because he was shy. She could try harder to extend a friendly hand.

"What's a Jacob's Brake?" she asked.

Cooper gave her a lazy glance. "What?" he drawled.

"That." She pointed to the switch labeled with the odd name.

"A brake's all," he said. "I got a lot of wheels to stop." He jerked his thumb back toward the trailer.

Obviously it was something he felt that she, a woman, wouldn't understand. Lacey took a deep breath and pushed away her irritation.

"I had no idea these trucks were like this," she said brightly. "So luxurious. It's really a work of art."

He grunted around his cigarette.

Lacey refused to give up. There'd been few people in her life she couldn't relate to, make friends with. All it took was being friendly first, and that didn't cost much.

She continued to ask questions, and he answered— with one-and two-word sentences or the familiar grunt. He was hauling computer printers for Pate. He'd known Pate for twenty years. He lived not far from Pate in Santa Fe. When he showed no inclination to continue polite conversation, Lacey fell to silently staring out the window.

For some unfathomable reason, she wanted to smack him. Didn't he know that no one liked being treated as if they were less than a speck on the windshield?

Face it, she told herself baldly, you're miffed because he doesn't take notice of you. You want him to treat you like a pretty—even desirable?—woman.

"Would you pour me some coffee?" His voice startled her. He handed her the cup from the nearby holder. "The thermos is right behind my seat," he said.

"Oh..." She smiled. "Sure." So the silent man had finally spoken—and had asked for something, no less. She filled his cup with hot coffee, replaced the thermos and handed him the cup, along with a smile. He didn't smile in return.

"Thanks," he said, and retreated back into his own world.

The only sounds in the cab for the next fifteen minutes were the engine's low rumble and music from the radio. When there came a loud, crackling static and a man's voice calling out for the Snappy Maroon Kenworth, Lacey jumped. The call came again. "Got your ears on, Kenworth?"

She listened in fascination as Cooper spoke into the CB radio microphone and identified himself as the Solitary Man. He exchanged information with the unseen driver, who was heading west, about conditions on the interstate. Lacey heard some terms she understood, some that baffled her. "Bear in the air" which meant police in a plane; "pedal to the metal" which meant going as fast as possible; something about a "rocking chair heading west," which she didn't understand. Then "five byebye," as a sign-off.

Cooper had actually carried on a friendly conversation—with a total stranger. Something he apparently didn't want to do with her.

Jon poked a bright face around the curtain and said he was hungry. Cooper gave his familiar grunt. Lacey dug into her tote bag and handed Jon a snack cake.

"You know, the danger of cancer is about tripled for passive smokers," Jon said, waving at Cooper's cigarette smoke.

"Then sit in the back so you won't suffer," Cooper drawled.

Lacey vowed to curtail her son's television news watching and had the urge to stuff a sock in his mouth. Lord, how she hated discord in any form. She avoided it religiously; even her divorce had been amicable. Yet never had she been in such close contact with a person who plain didn't like her. It hurt and confused her.

"Mama, I have to go to the bathroom." Anna's young voice squeaked as she poked a sleepy-eyed face beside Jon's.

Cooper turned to Lacey and looked as if he wanted to scream. Very quietly he said, "There's a rest stop up the road about ten minutes."

"That will be fine," she said, equally quietly.

A little past nine o'clock Cooper stopped at a familiar truck stop for breakfast and refueling. Lacey and her kids went on ahead to the restaurant, while he lagged behind to give his brakes a thorough inspection. They'd been performing okay, but he'd sensed something not quite right.

Besides, he'd just as soon be on his own for a few minutes. Nothing in his deal with Pate said he'd have to do anything but give these people a ride; he didn't have to eat with them.

After the inspection revealed nothing amiss with the brakes, Cooper headed for the restaurant, his stomach anticipating a plate of ham and eggs and a cup of scalding black coffee.

The restaurant's entryway was strategically placed right through the trucker's store, and a display of the latest in compact disc players for vehicles drew Cooper's attention. He paused to look at one.

"Pretty slick machine," came a voice from beside him. "Maybe Santa will leave one in your stocking."

Recognizing the smart tone of voice, Cooper slowly turned his head to see the kid, Jon, at his elbow. He'd slicked his light brown hair back from his face and had his hands stuffed into his fashionably baggy denims.

"Listen, kid," Cooper said, feeling an unexplainable annoyance. "You have to work for what you want in this life. There's no free ride. I learned it by the age of five—there is no Santa Claus."

The boy's easy grin seemed to melt and slide right off his face. Shifting his gaze, Cooper experienced a sinking feeling. Peeking around the boy's side was his sister. Her lower lip trembled.

"Anna . . . Jon." Lacey appeared from the nearby ladies' room doorway. Her gaze moved quickly from the children to Cooper and back again. The little one, Anna, ran to clutch her around the leg.

Cooper looked down at little Anna, who was looking at him as if he had horns again. He'd never felt so completely in over his head; he had no idea what to do.

"Better get some breakfast 'cause I'm leaving here in thirty-five minutes," he said, making an immediate retreat toward the dining room.

Puzzled, Lacey watched Cooper walk away. She looked down at Anna.

"Mama," Anna said, her lower lip trembling as she tightened her grip around Lacey's leg, "he said there's no Santa Claus."

Oh, no, Lacey thought. "I'm sure he didn't mean exactly that, Anna."

"He said it," Anna pronounced logically.

"Aw, Anna," Jon said, "you know some people like to say stuff like that. Cooper, he don't know. He's just like that Scrooge guy in the movie we saw. He can't enjoy Christmas. Now, come on—I'm starved."

Anna went along quietly, and throughout the meal Lacey could practically see the thoughts revolving in her young daughter's mind. Though Lacey considered it cowardly on her part, she was terribly glad Anna didn't ask her straight out about Santa, because she didn't want to tell her daughter the stark truth. Not one bit. She wanted her daughter to hold the magic as long as possible.

Cooper ate alone at the bar, and Lacey found it distinctly awkward. How odd it felt to look at him across the room and know they were traveling in the same vehicle but weren't friendly enough to eat together. And she wasn't friendly enough even to ask him his whole name. Did they *have* to be friends for her to ask that?

It wasn't going to work, Lacey thought starkly as she helped Anna blow her nose. The situation wasn't fair to the children, nor to Cooper. And she didn't think she could remain all sweetness and light for the remainder of the trip, not to mention coming back. Her mind leaped ahead, counting money as usual. She could just barely swing it, though she might need to borrow some money from Beth in case of emergency. She and the children could return to Albuquerque by bus. It was the best way, the only way.

As they finished their meal, Jon talked about Christmases past and the favorite things Santa had brought him, and Lacey sent her very verbal son a grateful smile. He was doing it because he loved his sister.

Later Anna and Lacey were alone in the truck while Cooper saw to the refueling and Jon followed at his heels. Though Lacey knew Cooper probably didn't appreciate it, she didn't forbid Jon; he needed an outlet for his boundless energy.

"Mama, why is Cooper so grumpy?" Anna asked.

Lacey sighed. "I'm not certain, honey. A lot of times a person gets like that from sad things that have happened in his life." She frowned. "Then again, some people are just born grumpy."

"Maybe he doesn't believe in Santa Claus because Santa doesn't bring him anything—because he's too grumpy all the time," Anna said.

"Oh, Santa brings everyone presents, but maybe Cooper just can't see them."

Anna gave a puzzled frown. "That's one of those things I'll understand when I'm older, right?"

Lacey laughed and hugged her. "Right."

Thirty minutes later Lacey told Cooper her intention to make the return trip by bus. She expected her announcement to put him at ease. After all, he could look forward to having them out of his hair.

He didn't smile. "Pate said the trip was both ways."

"I think returning by bus will work out better," she said.

He shrugged. "Suit yourself."

The miles rolled along beneath the massive Kenworth wheels, and they pushed on across the Texas panhandle. Anna had just required her second rest stop in two hours, and Lacey was handing each of the children a juice drink she'd purchased from a machine when Cooper took the cans right out of her hands.

"If we continue to make every rest stop between here and North Carolina, we won't get there till Easter," he said.

"When are we going to get some lunch?" Jon asked. "I'm hungry."

"We don't get lunch," Cooper said. "We'll eat dinner tonight when we stop."

Lacey swiftly reached out and retrieved the drink cans from Cooper. "If you're not planning to stop for lunch, these children need something to drink." She fixed her eyes on him and silently dared him to argue. He didn't.

Reminded ten minutes later by Jon about a growing boy's hunger, Lacey produced homemade cookies and pumpkin bread from her tote bag. As she passed the sweets back to the children, she considered offering some to Cooper. But *he* was the one who'd refused to stop for lunch, she thought smartly. Let him smell the goodies and drool. Minutes later she was shamed by her own six-year-old daughter.

"Mr. Cooper, would you like some of my cookies?" Anna asked in a hesitant voice as she extended two cookies as far toward Cooper as she dared.

Cooper amazed Lacey by taking the cookies and thanking Anna politely.

He likes sweets, Lacey thought, watching him out of the corner of her eye. When he'd finished the cookies, she offered him a slice of the pumpkin bread, feeling almost as if she were offering a bribe. No, she thought as he took the sweet bread, a distinctly sheepish expression on his face. She was trying to build a bridge.

* * *

Gray clouds closed in as the afternoon wore on. Cooper learned from fellow truckers on the CB that north of them a storm was wreaking havoc, covering everything with a thick layer of ice and dumping snow in the mountains. So far it looked as if the storm would stay to the north; he hoped so.

The kids retired again to the sleeper compartment. "Napping," Lacey said tersely. Though she sat up front in the cab, she said little and didn't have that friendly air she normally did.

He guessed he couldn't blame her. He had been anything but polite. Before, when she'd said she and the kids would return to Albuquerque by bus, he'd been half relieved, half angry. Now he had this foolish feeling of disappointment and the urge to make friends.

"You going to see your folks in North Carolina?" he asked.

She looked surprised at the question, then pleased. She nodded. "Yes, the children have never met my parents." Lord, her eyes were green. And shimmery.

The silence seemed awfully loud. As he searched for something to say—because he suddenly wanted to talk to her—Cooper had the oddest sensation of being aware of Lacey's breasts gently moving as she breathed.

"Cooper?" Lacey wondered if she really wanted to ask him.

"Yeah?" The interest in his tone gave her courage.

"Is Cooper your first name, your last or what?"

His lips split into a wide grin, his teeth a startling white beneath his dark mustache as he chuckled. "You been wondering about that, have you?"

"Yes, I have."

"Barry B. Cooper is the name."

He sent her a long glance. His eyes twinkled, then changed, as if he was looking deep into her soul. Heat flashed up from the feminine recesses of Lacey's body and filled her cheeks. He seemed, wonder of wonders, to like what he was looking at.

"Nice to meet you, Barry."

"Call me Cooper. I hate Barry."

They'd made an unspoken truce, and gradually that truce mellowed into companionable conversation. Lacey told Cooper she'd been divorced four years and that she hadn't seen her parents since before Jon was born. The main reason for the trip was for the kids to meet their grandparents. They talked of Gerald's restaurant, and Cooper said he'd been stopping there somewhere around ten years; he'd begun driving a truck twenty years before, at the age of eighteen. He'd known Pate almost that long and mentioned "owing the old man," which Lacey interpreted as his reason for giving her and the children a ride.

He was originally from Texas, a million years ago, and had been married once, about that long ago, too. He was also divorced.

Lacey wanted to ask about his family, but an inner instinct kept her quiet. Listening to him, she had a glimpse of a very lonely man, and she saw a reflection of her own well-deep loneliness. It was like that for a lot of people, she thought sadly.

The tires hummed along the highway, soft country music played in the background and they talked of baseball, thick pizzas and dog breeds. Lacey looked at Cooper's profile, which resembled sculpted bronze.

She watched his capable hands caress and maneuver the steering wheel and imagined what those hands would feel like on her body. In a flash of keen awareness, she realized she hadn't thought of a man in such a way since well before Shawn had left.

Then she found herself staring into his dark eyes. And she had the uncomfortable inkling that he knew exactly what she'd been thinking. Had perhaps been thinking along the same lines himself.

They were one third of the way across Oklahoma when they stopped for dinner, and this time Cooper sat with them. He appeared only mildly ill at ease as he sat across the table from Lacey. Every time he looked at her, Lacey felt a jangling sensation.

Jon and Cooper actually carried on a conversation about engines and racing, and things seemed to be going great for the first time since they'd started out that morning—until Anna spilled her cola down the back of a man in the adjoining booth. She had been trying to move across the seat on her knees while carrying her glass. She'd bumped her elbow, sloshing the crushed ice and cold liquid in a neat arc through the air and down the man's collar.

The man let out a resounding holler. "What the hell!"

Lacey's waitressing instincts set her to grabbing napkins from the stubborn dispenser that insisted on hanging on to them. "Oh, I'm so sorry," she said when at last she could hand the man a wad. She extended them, then let her hand drop as the man rose from the booth, shaking the back of his shirt.

She found herself looking up into the face of a crazed red-haired giant, who was bellowing words fit only for ships at sea. Anna cowered behind Lacey's leg, sobbing. Then a hand pressed Lacey's shoulder, and she found herself being pushed aside, Cooper's taut back coming between her and the giant.

"That's enough." Cooper's command cut the air. "It was an accident." Having to look up at the red-haired man didn't seem to bother him. "You owe these ladies an apology."

"Me?" The man clamped his jaw tightly, then glanced around the restaurant, seeing all the faces staring at him. A final look at Cooper must have decided him. "My...apologies, ladies," he muttered, squeezing back into his seat and hunching his massive shoulders in disgust.

Cooper lifted a wide-eyed Anna into his arms and carried her grandly from the dining room. "Stop in the bathroom," he said in the lobby as he lowered the little girl to the floor.

"Cooper—" Lacey began, but Cooper interrupted.

"Go on. I don't want to have to stop again ten minutes down the road."

Chapter Four

Cooper blamed his preoccupation with both the truck's brakes and Lacey Bryant for his overlooking the good probability that the red-haired hulk would come after him, seeking satisfaction for the small fracas in the restaurant. If Cooper had been thinking at all, he told himself, he would have been ready and waiting.

As it was, he was bending over near the trailer, checking the cables and tires, when he heard the man's shout. He barely had time to straighten and get a bead on the guy before the man swung, his fist plowing neatly into Cooper's cheek.

It didn't last long, and Cooper got in a few licks of his own before the hulk sent one final blow that knocked Cooper to the ground. Satisfied, the man hitched up his pants and lumbered away.

Cooper was picking himself up from the blacktop when he heard Lacey's voice and running footsteps. "Cooper? What—"

He quickly tried to straighten his shoulders, though it hurt like hell. Tentatively, he felt the already swelling skin beneath his left eye. He licked blood from the corner of his mouth.

"Oh, Lord..." Lacey, hovering, pressed a tissue to his cheek. Her womanly warmth drifted out and around him. He enjoyed her ministrations for a brief moment, then came to himself and pulled away.

"It was that big guy from the restaurant, wasn't it, Coop?" Jon said. "How'd you do?"

"Well, he doesn't look too good, either," Cooper said, taking the fresh tissue Lacey handed him and pressing it to a small cut beside his eye. He wasn't about to tell the kid, or Lacey, that about the best he'd done was give the hulk a split lip. "Let's get into the truck."

"Cooper, maybe we should go to the hospital. . . ."

"Aw, Mom, Cooper don't need no doctor," Jon said.

"Just get in the truck, Lacey." Cooper jerked open the driver's side door and hoisted himself up, leaving her standing there. She moved around to her own side.

When Anna passed through to the sleeper, she touched his shoulder. Her brown eyes were large and wet. "I'm sorry, Cooper."

"It's okay, kid." He winked with his good eye. "Everybody has accidents." Then he turned quickly away. No one had cared about his welfare for over fifteen years, and it made him feel as uncomfortable and confused as a bear walking down a city street to see the kind of looks these three people were giving him.

Cooper wasn't about to say he hurt all over, but Lacey saw it—in the way he shifted in his seat to find the most comfortable position, the fleeting wince when he stretched to flip the switches.

She remained quiet. It seemed the safest, wisest course. She felt terrible. It was because of her that Cooper was probably having the worst trip of his entire life. And now, because of her, he'd had his life endangered and was in pain with a hideous swollen eye.

They continued across Oklahoma, through several long sections of cold rain, and stopped for the night at a motel just off the interstate in Henryetta. The clerk assumed they were all together, husband and wife and children. Confusion ensued when Lacey and Cooper, talking at once, with interjections by Jon, tried to explain.

"You want a separate room for the children?" the clerk asked when he could get a word in.

"For the three of them." Cooper pointed at Lacey and the kids.

The clerk shot her a questioning look. Lacey nodded and watched the man's gaze move rapidly from herself to the children to Cooper and settle curiously on Cooper's black eye.

"You got it now?" Cooper said sharply enough that Anna jumped.

"Yes, sir." The clerk lowered his gaze and fiddled beneath the counter. "Just sign in here, ma'am. Room number 54." He slid the key across the counter. "Here you are, sir. Room 55." He appeared thoroughly pleased with himself.

Lacey marched the children down the row of rooms to theirs, which was second from the end. The last one was Cooper's. Right next to theirs.

She unlocked the door for the children, then went to the truck to get their bags. Five minutes later she found herself standing in front of her room, Cooper beside her, in front of his room. For some reason she couldn't understand in the least, it was a very awkward moment.

Cooper twisted his key; Lacey pushed open her door, which had been left ajar. They paused and looked at each other. The flesh surrounding Cooper's left eye was the color of roiling thunder clouds.

"I'm so sorry about what happened," Lacey said. "Does it hurt terribly?"

Cooper took a deep breath. "It hurts—but I'll live." His dark eyes searched hers, as if seeking answers to something that puzzled him.

"Mama, do I have to take a bath?" Anna called, her voice bursting into the moment.

"Good night," Lacey said to Cooper, her gaze still riveted by his. What were the questions? She had them, too, yet she didn't know what they were.

"Good night."

Then they each entered their own rooms. The two doors clicked closed at the same time.

Needing time alone, Lacey got Jon and Anna into bed before taking her shower. After having risen so early, the children fell asleep as soon as they'd settled who got which pillow. The ensuing silence was more than golden; it was heaven to Lacey.

As she leisurely undressed she could hear the muffled sound of the television in Cooper's room. She wondered what he was watching.

Was he a late-night or early-morning person? Did he like showers or baths? She continued to wonder as she stood beneath the massaging heat of steaming water. Would he think she had a good body?

Just as she'd turned off the water, she heard a peculiar knocking. Someone rapping on the wall, she realized as she stood in the tub, rivulets of water running down her skin. Cooper? Knocking out a rhythm on the wall?

Lacey hesitated only one self-conscious second, wondering if indeed Cooper was knocking on purpose or if perhaps it came from something he was doing. Throwing caution to the winds, she rapped back, imitating his rhythm. She held her breath.

It came again. Cooper had knocked in return!

Lacey clamped a hand over her mouth, stifling her laughter for fear of waking the children and having to answer for her actions. But it was hilariously funny. Two grown people engaging in a childish stunt. She couldn't believe Cooper would do such a thing. Not solemn, gruff Cooper, who'd spent most of the day treating her as if she wasn't there.

She knocked again and waited expectantly, but no more knocks came. Only silence.

With a sigh, Lacey pulled a plush towel from the nearby rack and began drying herself. She was suddenly exhausted, and very lonely. When she crawled into the big double bed, she pulled the extra pillow into her arms and held it tight.

Morning came much too early. Immediately upon turning off the alarm, Lacey discovered that the rumbling she heard was the Kenworth engine—already running. How revolting. It was still pitch black, for heaven's sake.

Allowing the children a few minutes' extra sleep, she ran across the parking lot to the large gas station-minimart to get sweet rolls and milk to tide them over until breakfast. At the last minute, she bought a sweet roll for Cooper, too.

Cooper knocked at their door while Jon was still dressing. "Come on, let's go." He definitely sounded testy.

Lacey didn't bother to awaken Anna enough for her to dress but gathered her up in her arms and carried her to the truck. Without speaking, Cooper helped get Anna into the sleeper in the back, then slipped into the driver's seat, leaving Lacey and Jon to cope with their baggage.

When he shifted the truck into gear without as much as a "good morning," Lacey wondered if the knocking she'd heard the night before had happened at all. Perhaps she'd imagined it. When he switched off the radio in the middle of "Santa Claus Is Coming to Town," Lacey figured she had the answer to the question of whether he was a morning person or not. And when he snapped at her to please stop that noise, calling her attention to the fact she was now unconsciously humming "Santa Claus Is Coming to Town," she called herself a saint for buying a dyed-in-the-wool Scrooge a sweet roll.

She gave him the roll, however, with every ounce of pleasantry she possessed. He scowled—but he took it. Heaven knew he needed all the sweetness he could ingest. And she continued to feel overwhelmingly guilty about his eye, which, while less swollen, remained the color of thunderheads.

Cooper stopped a bit early for breakfast and varied his schedule to stop for lunch, too. He didn't know much about kids, but he knew enough about people to tell when two young ones were restless enough to explode. He was experiencing something similar himself. The feelings were unfamiliar and damned annoying. Never had he felt so keenly that he wanted to be anywhere but in the truck, stuck in one position behind the wheel.

He hadn't slept well. His face and various bruised parts of his body had throbbed. And he'd kept thinking about Lacey. She was causing him no end of discomfort. Her green eyes were warm and full to bursting with life. Her scent drew him like a magnet. He couldn't seem to quit sneaking peeks at her body— her sleek thighs hugged by blue denim, her breasts full and round beneath her soft sweater, her creamy neck and chin. Last night he'd imagined what she looked like in the shower, just on the other side of the wall. He'd wanted, for some really weird reason, to communicate with her. After he'd knocked, he'd felt a fool. But it was pleasing that she'd knocked in return.

Lord, she must think him some kind of nut. And he *knew* he was having thoughts he shouldn't be having. Besides the practical side, there was Pate to consider.

"I'm going to go ahead and see about fuel," he told Lacey, leaving the steakburger he'd ordered only half finished. "I'll meet you and the kids at the truck."

He simply couldn't sit still. Besides, he told himself, he was falling further and further behind schedule all the time. Several rest stops this morning, now lunch. Good grief! They'd be lucky to get to North Carolina before the new year.

After paying for the fuel he was stuffing bills into his wallet when he looked through the station window into the small gift shop beyond. The kid, Jon, stood there examining something on a glass shelf—

when he was supposed to have his butt out at the truck.

Cooper strode around the pumps and entered the store. "Come on, kid. This isn't a sight-seeing tour, you know." Something in the boy's expression stopped him. Taking another step forward, Cooper glanced down to see a woman's fancy brush-and-comb set on the glass display shelf. He took a second look at the boy.

"I was thinking of getting it for Mom," the kid said. "For Christmas."

"Well, get it and let's go."

Jon shuffled toward the door. "I'm goin'."

"Hey, you can take a minute to get this if you want."

The kid scuffed his feet. "Naw. I'm a bit short, and she probably wouldn't like it anyway."

Though he acted as if it were of little importance, Cooper suspected otherwise. The kid wanted to get this for Lacey.

"How much short are you?" Cooper asked, pulling out his wallet.

"Six dollars."

"Here." Cooper extended a ten. "I'll advance you this, if you make certain my windshield's clean at every stop and be my general gofer, handling whatever I tell you."

The kid eyed the money, then cast Cooper a suspicious look. "Whatever you tell me?"

"I'm not a slave-driver, if that's what's worrying you. Now, do you want the money or not?"

The kid hesitated only an instant. "You bet!" He snatched the bill and reached for the brush-and-comb set. "I'll be out in just a minute." He'd lit up like fireworks on the Fourth of July—and an unusual warmth spread within Cooper as well.

"What is it?" Lacey asked when he reached the truck several minutes later.

Only then did Cooper realize he was smiling, and for almost no reason. "Oh, nothin'...." He looked at her for several long seconds, and she looked back. Slowly that special smile of hers broke across her face, and Cooper recognized then the one thing that made Lacey Bryant unique. She could smile and laugh over nothing at all.

Lacey knew something had transpired between Cooper and Jon. Jon returned to the truck with a secret smile for Cooper and a bag he immediately hid. Her Christmas present, she guessed. But where did Cooper fit into it? And why was he suddenly smiling, too?

She decided whatever had gone on between the two was definitely welcome, because a mellow atmosphere seemed to permeate the cab. Cooper didn't turn off the Christmas carols when they came on the radio, and he didn't even scowl when Jon and Anna began singing along with "Jingle Bells." Lacey dared to join in, and, lo and behold, Cooper shot them all what could have passed for a grin—at least for him. The next song was "Joy to the World," and they sang that, too, then listened attentively to the weather report. A winter storm was pushing down from the north. Though it didn't look as if it would make it into the states of Arkansas and Tennessee, there was a chance.

"We'll make it to Grandpa's and Grandma's by Christmas Eve, won't we?" Anna asked Cooper, her eyebrows furrowed. "I have to be there to get the puppy Santa's bringing me."

"We'll get there for Christmas Eve, darling," Lacey said quickly.

"Santa's bringing me a puppy," Anna said to Cooper. When he didn't reply, she said, "Cooper, didn't Santa bring you presents when you were a kid?"

Lacey sucked in a breath and sent Cooper a silent warning. He glanced quickly at Anna by way of his rearview mirror, then looked at the road.

"I can't remember that he did," he said slowly. Lacey wondered at his words, at the dead way he said them. It didn't take a lot of imagination to guess his childhood had been bleak.

"You said you didn't believe in him," Anna said quietly.

Cooper looked at a loss—and quite annoyed. "I guess I don't.

"Maybe that's why you never got anything," Anna said.

"Maybe so." Cooper dug into his pocket for a cigarette.

"Anna, that's enough," Lacey said. "You and Jon get in back and take a nap.

They did as she said, though Jon protested all the way. But they were tired from two days of early rising, and even Jon fell asleep within fifteen minutes. Lacey watched the scenery roll past and noted the darkening skies.

"Guess your parents are anxious about you coming," Cooper said after a few minutes, making a surprising attempt at conversation. "They probably weren't real thrilled with how you and the kids are getting there.''

"They don't know we're coming," Lacey said. At his raised eyebrow, she continued. "It's a surprise—a ploy, really. You see, my father and I haven't spoken in eleven years." She went on to tell the entire story of being unwed and pregnant, and of her father's fury, her own resentment. "I'd always been the problem child. My getting pregnant was just the last straw, so to speak."

"The man's held his peace for eleven years. What if he doesn't bend now?" Cooper asked, obviously skeptical of her methods. "Where will you stay?"

"With my sister."

"And what about the kids? How do you think they'll feel if their own grandpa turns them away?" He fired the questions at her.

"I admit, I'm taking a chance," Lacey said, feeling the need to defend herself. "But I really think my father will not only bend but melt when he sees his grandchildren."

"Maybe..." Cooper lit a cigarette and fell into thought. "My mother left me with my grandparents," he said quietly. "They didn't want to be saddled with a six-year-old kid, so they took me to the orphanage—we had them in those days. I bounced around in foster homes, too. Finally, at fifteen, I went back to see my grandpa. He told me they didn't have room for me."

Lacey watched the pain flicker across his profile before it was swallowed up in a calculated blank expression.

"My father and I fought," she said finally, "terribly. But he loved me. And that was the cause of his anger—not uncaring." She paused. "Not everyone in your life could have been like your grandparents."

He shook his head slightly. "They weren't."

"Then why don't you forget them and let yourself enjoy Christmas?"

He gave a harsh chuckle. "I forgot them a long time ago. And Christmas is just a time for a lot of people to make money."

The bitterness in his words took her breath away, and she spoke before she thought.

"Oh, how can you say that? Why, even the most hardened of criminals feels love in his heart at this time of year. Wars have stopped at Christmas," she said, as if that were undeniable proof of her stand. She gestured. "Sure, there's Christmas hype, but only because people enjoy it so much—you know, giving the customer what he wants. Christmas is a time when people can enjoy pure, unadulterated loving without feeling embarrassed or threatened."

"You ought to take off those rose-colored glasses," Cooper said with scorn. "What people call love is just lumps of fears and selfish motives in disguise."

Lacey had never met anyone like Cooper. "You don't believe in Santa Claus, you don't believe in Christmas and you don't believe in love. What do you believe in, Barry Cooper?"

"Myself," he said flatly. "And don't call me Barry."

Lacey felt sorry for him, very sorry. But of course she couldn't say such a thing, and she turned away quickly so he wouldn't see the pity on her face. The

devil of it, she thought, was that underneath, just like
Jolene and Pate had said, Cooper had a soft spot
crying out to love and be loved.

Why did he have to be so contrary? She wanted to
like him. She wanted ... Oh, she thought darkly, cutting off further imaginings in that direction, they were
only foolish impossibilities.

Cooper glanced at Lacey. Her hands lay loosely in
her lap; she looked very small. And as if she'd been
dealt a big blow. Cooper felt he'd been a bit harsh with
his words. Yet he'd been truthful.

She really believed in all those forgiving and forgetting and loving fantasies. He hoped she didn't get to
Pine Grove and suffer a rude awakening. He hoped
doubly so for the kids. The thought that Lacey's father might turn them all away made him flinch. He
didn't want them to suffer that. Suddenly he felt an
overwhelming sense of protectiveness. He'd punch the
man, old or not, if the guy didn't do right by Lacey
and those kids.

When he realized his thoughts, he almost stopped
breathing. What business was it of his? What did he
care if Lacey lived in a fantasy world? *It wasn't any of
his business.*

Traffic thickened the closer they came to Nashville,
and it seemed a goodly number of fools were trying to
kill themselves by pulling over in front of Cooper's
Kenworth. Again he had the sense of trouble with the
brakes, and this sense was confirmed when they locked
on him for several seconds. Ten miles farther down the
road, he pulled off the interstate to a familiar truck-
stop-and-motel complex on the outskirts of the city.

Cooper was out and around to Lacey's side of the truck, checking tires as he went, before she made it out of her seat. When her door swung open, it seemed the natural thing to raise his arms and help her down.

His hands slipped up beneath her short coat and closed around her waist. It was warm. She pressed her hands to his shoulders for balance, and Cooper lowered her slowly. A sweet fragrance floated from her hair. Then her thighs were brushing his, and he was looking into her eyes.

"Thank you," she said softly.

"Sure."

A movement from above caught his attention, reminding him that he remained with his hands at Lacey's waist. He jerked them away and looked up at the same time, finding Jon staring down at him with a curious and guarded expression. Cooper had the uncomfortable feeling the kid had read his mind.

"I'll follow you in a few minutes," he said to Lacey, keeping his gaze on his pack of cigarettes. "I want to see if a mechanic here can take a look at the brakes."

"There's a problem?" she asked, her voice breathless.

He glanced up to see her keeping silken strands of hair from blowing into her eyes. He shook his head. "Just a small one. Nothing to worry about." He turned, feeling her gaze on him as he walked quickly away.

Though the mechanic corrected the problem with the brakes in short order, causing no delay, after dinner Cooper elected to stay in the nearby motel. It was a neat, clean place, yet very inexpensive, which he knew would be a help to Lacey. From a couple of remarks she'd made, he knew she supported her kids alone, without any help from her ex-husband. Ordinarily on a haul like this, Cooper would have spent every other night in his truck, but riding with Lacey, he preferred to get a shower and not appear so rumpled.

"What about the storm?" she asked him over their coffee. "Several people here have said it isn't looking good."

Cooper nodded. "Driver over at the garage said up north the highways were closing. But it hasn't turned south yet, and it may not. No sense worrying about it beforehand, but I'll keep a watch, and if the storm looks like it has turned this way, I'll get you and the kids."

This time the room he was given was four doors away from Lacey's. They were lucky to get rooms at all with the heavy holiday traffic.

When Lacey had said her good-night and closed the door, Cooper experienced the oddest sensation of abandonment.

His room was immaculate and modernly stark— bed, dresser, small portable television. He tossed his coat onto the bed, then turned on the television. Absently he watched *The Beverly Hillbillies* and smoked a cigarette. Then he examined his face in the mirror. His eye looked a bit better now, he thought, though he couldn't swear to it. It didn't hurt so much anyway. Lacey must have gotten used to it, because around lunchtime she'd quit getting that expression of guilt every time she looked at him. She'd smiled a lot during dinner.

He'd bet she was having some of the same thoughts he was having, and he didn't think the assumption was all ego on his part. If they'd been alone on this trip, Cooper wondered if he'd be in this room right now— or down in hers.

Stupid thought! he raged at himself. She wasn't a woman to fool around with under any circumstances. And there was Pate to consider.

Suddenly Cooper didn't want to be in the room another minute. Grabbing his coat, he headed out the door and strode along the road toward the shopping center that was just across the highway overpass. The wind was sharp, and passing cars made it sharper. It felt good to be out in the open.

At a discount department store, where he'd come for a carton of cigarettes, Cooper found himself musing over an array of stuffed animals. He chose a wrinkled puppy with a vest and bow tie for Anna. It didn't cost all that much, he told himself.

But of course he couldn't buy that and not get something for Jon, so he wandered over to the toy section. It was bleak, with most of the toys sold out. Unwilling to give up, he meandered back through the boys' clothing department and spied a bright red jacket with black Corvette insignias on it. Guessing at size, he picked one and headed for the checkout counter before he could do anything else foolish. He'd left the store before he realized he'd forgotten his cigarettes and had to return for them.

On his way out of the mall, he glanced into a gift shop window and spied a crystal-ball snow scene. The ball was a bit larger than his gear-shift knob, sat atop stained oak and had a miniature Christmas tree inside. After only a second's hesitation, he went in to buy it. Lacey might like it, he thought. It was something, anyway.

He headed back to the motel. When he entered his room, he set his packages on the bed and wondered what in the world had gotten into him.

Well, he told himself, he hadn't gone out of his way. He'd been at the stores; he'd had the money. Probably the kids would enjoy some extra things. Couldn't get kids too many gifts.

Lacey had said she would return to Albuquerque by bus, and she probably couldn't afford it. Well, he thought almost angrily, she was an adult. She knew what she was doing.

Still restless, Cooper watched television for the weather report, then walked outside and down the row of rooms to the soft-drink machine at the middle of the building. He saw light showing at the edges of the heavy drapes as he passed Lacey's room. Was she up, or had she just left the light on?

On his way back, cold soft-drink can in hand, Cooper stopped in front of Lacey's door. He had the oddest feeling of certainty and uncertainty warring within him. The image of the stark room waiting for him flashed through his mind. The next instant, almost without choosing, he raised his hand and knocked softly.

He immediately thought he needed to have his head examined and was about to walk away when the curtains moved and Lacey peered out at him. Then the curtains fell back into place. He heard her fiddling with the lock, and anticipation mixed with the impulse to run. He'd never felt so screwed up.

The door opened, and Lacey stood silhouetted against the soft light from the room.

"Hi," she said.

"Hi."

She was still dressed, her hair fluffy, like she'd been running her hands through it. She stepped forward and quietly pulled the door closed behind her.

Chapter Five

Kids asleep?" Cooper asked.

Lacey nodded. "They were exhausted." She folded her arms and hugged herself. The north wind was bitter. "Hear something about the weather?"

Cooper looked puzzled, then understanding dawned. He shook his head. "Oh, no...no." He raised the can in his hand. "I'd just come out for this."

Though she couldn't clearly see his eyes or assess his expression because of the dim light on the porch, she felt the warmth of him. She told herself it was because he'd shifted to where he blocked the wind. And she scoffed at the idea he could be attracted to her.

Cooper cleared his throat. "Look, Lacey, you'd arranged to ride back to Albuquerque with Pate. I'll be going back just like he would. You and the kids might as well come along."

She had to smile. "Think you could stand the kids?"

"Hey, it's only a few days," he answered with a hint of a smile.

His eyes were very dark as he stared at her, his smile fading. The wind snatched at his thick hair, and the yellow glow of the porch light magnified the bruise around his eye. Lacey caught the scents of cigarette smoke, leather from his coat and faint male cologne.

His gaze moved from her eyes to her lips, then back up to her eyes again. He leaned very close, and Lacey didn't want him to go away. Attraction, vibrant and undeniable, filled the air.

"Here, take my coat," he said in a husky voice.

Automatically she shook her head. "No...then you'll be without..." But he was already shrugging out of it. "You'll be cold...."

He slipped it around her awkwardly, one hand still holding the soft drink. The back of his hand caressed her neck, and she knew without doubt that he'd done it on purpose. Her breathing became shallow. His gaze never wavered.

"The first time I saw you in Gerald's place four years ago, I wanted to kiss you," he said.

Lacey's heartbeat rushed like water downhill over pebbles. "The first time I saw you, I wanted to touch your cheek to see if you were as cold as you looked."

He gave a guttural chuckle, his black eyes boring into her.

"I didn't want you to come on this trip."

"I know."

"Pate never said... Is there anything between you and him?"

She shook her head. "Not like you're thinking. He's a good friend."

He nodded and seemed to be mulling over her words. "I haven't meant to be an ass—I'm just not good with kids."

"It's okay. I know we came as a big shock to you...."

Her voice drifted off as she looked at him. Slowly she raised her hand to touch his cheek. She felt the stubble of a beard on his warm skin. Heat flooded her, and she forgot the cold wind. She became aware only of his eyes hot upon her and of the deep longings bubbling up and seeping through every cell in her body. He bent close, his arms closing about her, capturing her own arms within his coat.

Then he was kissing her. Hard and demanding, he forced her lips to part. His lips were hot and velvet and magical upon hers. She savored the waves of heat and pulsing energy that washed over her, the sweet weakness in her knees, the warm male smell of him and the strength of his arms supporting her.

It had been so long since she'd been kissed, so long since she had returned a kiss, totally, fully, with no reserve. And it had been a long time since a man had made her feel so completely and wonderfully a woman.

She gasped for breath when he pulled away. Though his face remained shadowed, she knew instinctively his silent questioning. No words were needed, just as she needed no time to decide. But she remained in his embrace, loathe for the wondrous moment to end.

Then slowly, and so gently that a throbbing ache opened up within Lacey, he kissed her again—a kiss of goodbye. He pulled back and looked at her. She wiggled her hand up to touch his cheek one last time. He reached behind her and pushed open the door to her room.

"Good night," he said, breaking away. He gave a lopsided grin, and the familiar coldness came over him.

It was a long moment before Lacey could find her voice and force it past the lump in her throat. "Good night," she managed as she handed him his coat. She turned and entered her room so that she wouldn't see him walk away.

Sleep was next to impossible. Lacey tossed and turned, trying to be rid of the ache of longing that filled her. She clutched the spare pillow but found it a poor substitute for the warm arms of a loving man.

Had he expected her to go to his room with him? She sincerely doubted it. And it was only carnal instinct between them, she thought. They were both lonely. The attraction had always been there between them; now it had a chance to be acknowledged.

To cause them no end of trouble, Lacey thought irritably. She punched her pillow, thinking that he'd certainly been a cold fish when he'd left her. He'd probably had a hundred women react to him the way she had. And right now he was probably sleeping peacefully, having forgotten all about their little encounter. Damn him for that!

Lacey was awakened by a loud pounding on the door. "Lacey...Lacey!" While she struggled to find her way from beneath the covers, she heard the door open and Jon's voice.

Freed at last from the blankets, she stumbled to the open door, finding Cooper filling it. "What time is it?" She had trouble getting her eyes to focus, but she could see it was still black outside. She was tired of getting up before the chickens, and her irritability focused on the man before her.

"Four-fifteen," Cooper said. He allowed his gaze to run up and down Lacey once, seeing the outline of her curves beneath her soft flannel gown. Her eyes were heavy with sleep, her hair like it'd been in a tornado, her cheeks a warm blush. "The storm's turned," he ground out. "It's on its way, and we'd better be on ours if we want to get to Pine Grove by evening."

He turned and slammed the door behind him, retreating to the familiar comfort of the Kenworth. Christmas Eve had arrived, and he was supposed to deliver Lacey and her kids to their family tonight. The sooner, the better, he told himself, munching on a sweet roll.

He hadn't expected her to come with him to his room last night, though, to be honest, maybe he'd hoped. But hell, she couldn't do that—she had the kids to think of. And what was he to her? What was she to him? Nothing.

The way he was thinking was crazy. What had happened to him? He'd barely dozed two hours the previous night. With intimate thoughts of Lacey plaguing him, he'd finally given up on sleep, dressed and returned to the restaurant, downing cups of coffee while he kept an ear out for the road conditions. Thirty minutes ago he'd heard that the storm had not only turned but had picked up fury as it blew across the plains. Within two hours, Interstate 40 to the west across Oklahoma and Texas had been closed because of snow.

And now they had to get on the road or they'd be stuck. Which meant he'd be stranded with Lacey and her two children. And something told him his very life was threatened by that prospect.

* * *

Within twenty minutes Lacey had herself and Jon dressed, their bags gathered, and Cooper was helping a sleepy Anna into the sleeper. Cooper had thought to buy coffee, milk and sweet rolls for the early hours, and at eight they stopped just long enough for a quick breakfast and to refuel the truck. It began to snow then, big heavy flakes. East of them icy rain had fallen, coating the road. Behind them snow pushed from the west.

Lacey found it difficult to meet Cooper's eyes and was glad he had to keep sharp attention on the road. Still, her gaze kept straying to his profile, then down to his hands on the wheel, her mind remembering the feel of his lips on hers. It probably hadn't meant a thing to him, she told herself. She recalled Jolene's comment: Cooper wasn't the marrying kind. And he wasn't *her* kind, either.

Her insides became tighter and tighter as she sat and watched the outside world grow whiter. When she cautioned the children to be quiet, she had to grit her teeth to keep from yelling. The worries piled up in her mind. Would they make Pine Grove by evening? Somehow she wasn't in as much of a hurry now. She dreaded saying goodbye to Cooper, even though they'd hardly said five words to each other all morning. Would her father accept them? Would she be able to borrow enough from Beth to get them home again? No way could she ride with Cooper; he'd know how she felt, and she'd feel a fool. Would Cooper ever be just another customer to her again?

The traffic thickened in the mountains, as did the falling snow, piling up inch by inch. Repeatedly

Cooper swore under his breath at vehicles pulling in front of him, slamming on their brakes, slowing dangerously. He commanded the children to get into the bed of the sleeper and stay there, and he checked twice to make certain Lacey had her seat belt buckled.

Just past noon they were forced to leave the highway. It had been closed ahead because of drifting snow, though it was expected to be cleared within the hour.

"Good a time as any for lunch," Cooper said, bringing the big truck to a stop in a restaurant parking lot.

He stretched his arms, and Lacey saw the lines of strain around his eyes. For a brief moment she dared to meet his gaze. Surprised, she saw an unusual softness in his dark eyes as they met hers. An intimate smile, all for her, quirked his lips.

"Are we gonna make it to Grandpa's by Christmas Eve, Cooper?" Anna asked in a worried voice as they trudged through the wet snow to the crowded restaurant.

Cooper paused and looked down at her. "I'll get you there, squirt, if I can at all." In a fluid, surprising motion, he swooped Anna up into his arms. "Let's keep your feet dry. Don't want to make your cold worse on vacation."

When word came that the highway had been opened to eastbound traffic, Cooper turned to Lacey with a raised eyebrow. "We can go, but it's one lane, and it's slick out there. There is danger."

Lacey appreciated Cooper's consideration of her and the children. In fact, his consulting her came as a warm surprise.

"We have to get to Grandpa's, Mama," Anna said. "Or else Santa won't know where we are."

"Cooper can handle it, Mom," Jon said.

She touched her son's arm. "Of course we're going on."

Lacey struggled to peer through the windshield. The wipers thumped rapidly as the Kenworth pushed through the swirling white gloom, and the hard north wind made a muffled roaring sound. The CB radio crackled occasionally; Cooper left it on to listen for word of highway conditions to the east and to pass along information to drivers heading west. Music from the radio provided a low background to it all. Twice, on two different stations, they heard "White Christmas."

The snow was blowing back onto the road faster than the plows could keep it clear. Repeatedly, the truck plunged through drifts that completely obliterated the pavement. Lacey caught occasional glimpses of two other semi rigs up ahead. Directly in front of them was a red station wagon, a blessing to follow with visibility so poor.

Though she could feel the tug of the wind and the frequent sliding of the truck's wheels, she was confident in Cooper. All his attention was focused on his driving, and it was as if he were attached to the truck, anticipating its every movement. And she suspected, by the rapt look on his face, that he secretly loved the challenge of driving in such abominable weather.

It had begun to grow quite dim when it happened. A brownish sedan came pushing around them in a rare wide spot in the road. As Cooper braked slightly and struggled to keep the Kenworth on the road, he said something under his breath that Lacey couldn't make out but knew was foul. The sedan's taillights disappeared immediately into the gloom. Lacey strained to see, expecting to find the sedan nose first in a snowbank on the shoulder, as they'd seen many others.

She glanced to Cooper and saw a worried frown crease his brow. He let out a curse, and Lacey looked again out the windshield to see red lights, taillights, getting rapidly larger.

Cooper reacted immediately, but he had to be careful. Coming down on the brakes too fast could jackknife the trailer and even overturn the entire rig. The red lights seemed to grow larger right in front of his eyes; the damned car ahead was stopped in the middle of the road!

He applied the brakes as hard as he dared. The trailer began to skid back and forth across the narrow strip of road, dragging the truck with it. Then, in frustrating slow motion, despite Cooper's frantic turning of the wheel, the truck left the highway and pushed its way down the sloping ground. It came to rest quietly, snugged all around in snow.

"Lacey... you all right?" Cooper ran his gaze over her, and relief surged through him when she appeared to be only mildly shaken.

She nodded and jerked around. "Anna? Jon?"

Assured that everyone was in one piece, Cooper reached for his coat and, with Jon's eager assistance, got out to have a look. He knew beforehand, though, that there would be no getting the truck up on the road again without help.

Cooper and Jon reentered the cab along with cold wind and swirling snowflakes. Lacey knew at once by Cooper's expression that they were quite stuck. "What about that car in the road? Are they all right?" she asked.

Jon answered. "The stupid car's gone, Mom."

Looking thoroughly disgusted, Cooper reached for the CB radio microphone. The crackling answer came: help would be sent as soon as they could get through. For now, wait.

"I'm hungry, Mom," Jon said.

"I'm cold," Anna said.

"Guess I agree with both," Cooper said, a grin twisting his lips.

Lacey experienced the sudden absurd feeling of being free and happy. They were all safe and comfortable, the truck's engine continued to purr, putting out heat, and Lacey had plenty of sweet rolls and cookies left in her tote bag. And for the first time in over four years she was spending Christmas Eve in the company of a handsome man she'd come to care a lot about.

After they'd all eaten sweet rolls warmed in the microwave, Lacey tucked herself and the children into the warmth of the bed. When Anna began worrying about Santa Claus, Lacey tried to divert her by telling stories about both children when they'd been babies. Soon Anna and then Jon fell asleep. Lacey laid her head back, lulled, and idly looked at Cooper smoking a cigarette up in the driver's seat.

When she noticed him rubbing his arms as if cold, she said, "Might as well join us. There's room." She wriggled herself and Anna over, indicating the empty space at the end of the bed.

Cooper looked at her, then quirked his mouth. "Think I will. We've got a long night ahead."

Lacey leaned toward Anna, trying not to get too familiarly close to Cooper. It was impossible, of course.

Cooper slipped an arm around her shoulder. "It's okay. I promise I'm not a man to take advantage." He stroked her arm lightly with his thumb.

"Oh, no?" She couldn't keep the smile from her lips.

He grinned. "No...at least not in front of witnesses."

After a moment's hesitation, Lacey decided she wasn't a person to *miss* an advantage, so she leaned back into Cooper's offered shoulder. It felt so good. She wondered what he felt, if anything. What was he thinking? His heart beat against her arm, and he was so wonderfully warm. She drifted off into the sweetness of the moment.

Motion and hushed whispers awoke Lacey. She thought she heard jingling. "Mama..." Jon shook her leg. "Santa..." That was Anna. Then Cooper said, "I'll be damned...."

Lacey rubbed her eyes and poked her head around Cooper and Jon to see what everyone was staring at out the passenger-seat window. She saw Santa Claus highlighted in the glow that spilled from the truck. Light snow fell on the red knitted cap on his head.

She blinked, thinking it was a dream.

But the smiling Santa remained. Anna rolled down the window. "Hi, Santa! Hi! Do you have my puppy?"

"Oh, missy, it's too cold out here for a puppy," the Santa said, never missing a beat. Lacey would have bet a month's tips that his beard was real, as was his nearly shoulder-length white hair. His coat was black, but the pants beneath were bright red.

The wind had stopped, and the snow fell softly now. Road crews were working hard, Santa told them, offering them a ride to the Mountain View Lodge up the road about three miles. Oh, he had some time, he assured a most concerned Anna. Several yards away sat Santa's odd-looking wagon-sleigh, pulled by two draft horses, bells jingling on their harness.

Cooper got out first, and for some odd reason he and Santa walked to the back of the trailer. Lacey scrambled to get herself and her impatient children bundled up and gather their bags. Anna would hardly be still and kept straining to see Santa.

Cooper and the Santa Claus took the children over to the sleigh, then Cooper returned to get his own things and to shut down and lock the truck. Santa helped Lacey with her bags.

Lacey paused in the shelter of the truck doorway. "Who are you?" she asked the pink-cheeked Santa.

"Just a retired old cabinetmaker who looks forward to a lot of fun every Christmas," he answered, a storybook twinkle in his eye. "For six years now I've been bringing gifts to the children here in our hollow. Some's free to the tykes who won't get anything else. Some's bought by parents, who also give a donation to our volunteer rescue squad as payment for me delivering. I was on my way home when I thought I'd better check out this stretch of highway. I've already hauled five people on up to the lodge.''

"Busy night for Santa," Lacey said.

"Yep...most fun I've had in twenty years." The man chuckled. "Ain't found anyone hurt yet."

"Would you..." Lacey lifted the travel bag containing her presents. "Could *you* give the children and Cooper their gifts for me? I'll donate to your rescue squad."

"Surely." His cheeks were rosy in the dim light.

"How will we do it without them knowing?"

"Just set the bag down next to mine in the wagon, and leave the rest to old Santa."

"It's these...these three on the top," Lacey said eagerly.

Santa brought his sleigh to a jingling halt beneath the wide portico of the Mountain View Lodge. Then he distributed presents. Cooper felt a rush of pleasure when Anna squealed over the stuffed dog he'd bought her and Jon insisted on trying on his red jacket right then and there. But mostly it was the wonderment in Lacey's eyes as she held the crystal ball snow scene that moved him so. The eyes she turned to him had tears in them and were filled with so much pure happiness that he had to look away.

When Santa began handing out wrapped packages, Cooper realized that there were more presents than the ones he'd given the old man. With amused amazement, he realized Lacey had done the same as he. His amazement tripled when Santa placed a small package into his hands.

Lacey had bought him a present!

He stared at the bright red package with the gold ribbon. He hadn't had a real present for years; there'd been precious few of them throughout his entire life. He looked up to find Lacey gazing at him, a trembling smile on her lips, a warm light in her eyes. Feeling a whole lot the way he had when he'd lost control of the Kenworth, he smiled back and stuffed the package into his coat pocket. He'd wait until he was alone to open it.

"You'll get your puppy a bit later, Anna," Santa Claus promised just before he climbed into his sleigh. With jingles and creaks and a thunderous *"Merry Christmas!"* he drove away.

Cooper stood beside Lacey and watched the sleigh be swallowed up by the night. He felt a tug on his coat. It was Anna.

"I told you there was a Santa Claus," she said solemnly. "Do you believe now?"

"Yes, I believe," Cooper said.

"That's why you got a present," she said pertly, and broke into a run for the lodge's lobby. "I want to open my package!" she cried.

"Watch the steps, Anna!" Lacey called. Then she murmured playfully, "How do you suppose Santa knew where to find us?"

"Santa knows everything," Jon said with his usual know-it-all expression.

Chapter Six

Cooper rose before dawn, located a tow truck and had the Kenworth and Lacey and the kids rolling down the highway toward central North Carolina by nine o'clock. As the truck brought them ever closer to their destination, two things dominated Lacey's mind: greeting her father and saying goodbye to Cooper.

Did he care anything for her? she wondered as she sneaked glances at his profile. He wore the belt buckle she'd given him, had even said a quiet thank-you out of earshot of Anna. Maybe he was a bit mellower—certainly he seemed more familiar in the way he talked to her and the children—but other than that, there was nothing to indicate he held any intimate feelings toward her.

Why did she expect him to—because of the crystal snow scene he'd given her, the gifts for the children? Or because of her own feelings for him?

How in the world had she come to love him in only two short days? If he'd been as cordial during those two days as he was these past several hours, she could possibly understand it. But he hadn't—he'd been about as agreeable as a cactus, yet she'd been drawn to him from the very first moment.

The trip went perversely smoothly. For the first hour they were confined to one lane, but that one lane remained clear, and Cooper kept up almost normal speeds. Out of the mountains, the highway opened to two lanes. They stopped for breakfast and lunch, then spent the remaining hours serenaded by Christmas tunes on the radio and pacifying the two voices that kept asking, ''Are we there yet?''

Lacey's nerves became tighter and tighter, so that when Cooper pulled the Kenworth off the highway exit for Pine Grove and asked which way, she fairly snapped at him.

''Just drop us over at that restaurant. I'll call my sister to come get us.''

Cooper braked and gave her an exasperated look. ''Which way, Lacey?''

''I'll call my sister.''

''I'll take you.''

He stared at her, and she stared back.

''Left,'' she said. ''Five miles.''

A lot had changed in Pine Grove in eleven years. A shopping mall had blossomed where she and her sister once had cut their Christmas trees. Huffner's country market was now a Super Save, and Fowler's TV Repair had become Fowler's Video Rental.

Soon, however, the Kenworth was rumbling its way slowly down the wide street of the graceful old neighborhood where Lacey had grown up. The big truck was definitely out of place, and Lacey worried over Cooper getting a ticket.

''Is this it?'' Jon asked excitedly.

''Which one?'' Anna said, craning her neck.

Lacey's gaze strained ahead. ''There...'' she said, pointing, and Cooper came to a rolling stop at the curb in front of her parents' large sloping yard. The sameness of it all was heartily reassuring.

Suddenly the children had lost their voices. They sat very still, staring up at the house. Lacey felt as if she couldn't move, even when she saw the front door opening, her parents stepping out onto the porch.

When Cooper said, "I'll go up and speak to them," she could do nothing but gape at him in astonishment.

Ignoring Lacey's expression, Cooper got out of the truck, paused and gave his hair a quick swipe with his hand. He felt pretty foolish and out of place, but he didn't want the kids going up there and being rejected by their grandpa right in front of their faces. For an instant the stark, clear memory of his own grandfather's forbidding face filled his mind. He pushed it aside.

Lacey's parents waited on the small front porch as Cooper loped up the carefully tended walk. Two-story, with a brick chimney and green shutters, the house breathed of substance and permanence.

Cooper came to a stop at the porch and took quick inventory of the people staring at him—a stern, no-nonsense type of man with silver hair and deep creases on either side of his turned-down mouth, the woman stylish and petite and standing one step behind her husband. A movement behind the curtains of a nearby window indicated onlookers inside. He returned his gaze to the silver-haired man.

"I've brought Lacey and your grandchildren for a visit," Cooper said. He watched the man's eyes grow small. "Will you welcome them?"

"Who are you?" the man asked after a long, silent moment.

"Just a friend," Cooper replied.

Another long pause, in which the man's expression changed to one of hope, and his eyes turned moist. "Please ask Lacey to come in," he said quietly.

Cooper hadn't known he'd been holding his breath until the man spoke those words.

The both dreaded and hoped-for moment had arrived, and Lacey didn't know how to cope. Her legs shook, and she accepted Cooper's steadying hand in getting down from the truck. Then joy burst within her when her mother came hurrying down the walk with open arms, making it so much easier.

Finally she was facing her father, seeing the changes, recognizing that some things would never change. He had aged but was as stern as always.

"Daddy, these are my children," Lacey said, standing in front of him, her shoulders squared, Jon and Anna on either side of her.

She couldn't remember ever seeing her father cry, but now a tear slipped down his cheek. Lacey blinked, her vision growing almost too blurry to see. When her father opened his arms, she rushed to embrace him, feeling his rough face against hers, his coarse silver hair. "Oh, Daddy, I've missed you," she said in a hoarse whisper, and then she cried into his white dress shirt.

"Welcome home," her father murmured gruffly. He held her tight, then, self-consciously averting his gaze, he pulled away and turned to the children, pure pleasure lighting his moist eyes. "So, these are my grandchildren...."

Then bedlam broke out, with Beth and her husband and children pouring from the house, everyone hugging and talking excitedly. Lacey pulled away from Beth and anxiously sought Cooper, fearful he would slip away in all the commotion before she could speak to him. She had to thank him—and more. She was bursting with passion. For the moment she felt bold and courageous, enough so to tackle the whole world. She could tell Cooper how she felt about him, self-consciousness and fear be damned. She would tell him, and surely he would feel the same. He just had to.

Her anxiousness vanished when she saw her mother had corralled Cooper; Emily Sawyer was never one to forget the propriety of asking a guest to stay at least for coffee.

Lacey stepped over and boldly grabbed Cooper's hand, tugging him forward. She smiled broadly at Beth's raised eyebrows. "Cooper, I'd like you to meet my parents, my family."

Cooper sat talking with Lacey's father, Leon Sawyer, drinking a third cup of coffee and finishing off a second piece of pecan pie—and knowing he had to get gone. The way Lacey kept looking at him—had been looking at him throughout the day—had him all churned up inside, like a wildcat caught in a net.

He felt almost overwhelmed by the rest of the crowd, too. He'd rarely been surrounded by a family like this, showing so much care for one another—and for him, simply because he was a friend of Lacey's. Of course, everyone kept giving him those secretive looks, as if they shared some private joke with him. Everyone except Leon, who looked at him as if he was trying to guess his coat size. Once Leon asked him how long he'd known Lacey. Cooper could tell his answer didn't set too well with the man, and it was as if Leon had to bite his tongue not to speak about it. Cooper saw the love between Lacey and her father, but he saw the personality clash as well.

"You'll stay for dinner?" Emily Sawyer asked him in her pleasantly modulated voice. "We have plenty of leftovers from the big meal at noon today."

That was his out, and Cooper took it. "No...thank you, ma'am." He rose, looking around for his coat. "I have to get this haul up to Washington."

When Jon and Anna heard Cooper was leaving, they raced to get their coats so they could walk him to his truck. Lacey would rather have gone alone with him, but the children had grown fond of Cooper; it wouldn't be fair to deny them their goodbyes. Jon shook Cooper's hand, Anna gave a little wave, then Lacey ordered them back up to the house. "I'll be right along," she assured them.

The clouds had faded, and the sky was a clear, crisp blue fading into evening. Lacey stood in front of Cooper, feeling the buoyant courage that had sprung up so readily in the emotional moments of the special afternoon evaporating like air out of a hot balloon.

She looked at him, then down at the mushy snow. How should she tell him her feelings? What words could she use? Would he think her a fool? Did he care at all? Would she be more embarrassed than she had ever been in her life?"

Cooper opened the truck door and paused.

"Thanks so much for the ride out," Lacey said. She stared up, searching his dark eyes for any sign that she should speak her heart. She found none.

Cooper nodded. "You want me to stop and get you in a week for the ride back?"

Her tongue seemed to swell. "I..." It *is* Christmas, she thought. A magical time. And you might as well tell him because you'll live with regret if you don't. "Do you want us to ride back with you?"

He gave a shrug and looked over her head before looking back down at her. "It's no problem for me. I'll just take a few local loads up around D.C. and start back in a week. I'll be heading to Albuquerque anyway."

"I asked if you wanted us to come."

He stared at her a long time, and the sorrow that came into his eyes stabbed her.

"You're asking me for something I can't give, Lacey. I don't have it in me to give." His words fell as pebbles dropped into a pond, and with each one, Lacey's heart seemed to crack.

She stared into his eyes and frantically sought her mind for words to make him understand, make him see the beauty that could be between them.

"Maybe it's more what I can give you, Cooper." Her heart beat so fast she thought it would jump right out of her chest. "I love you." She watched him, held her breath and thought wordless prayers.

Cooper looked at her. His eyes softened, and Lacey's hope soared. Then his eyes turned bleak.

"Lacey, I'm just a burned-out old driver. You and me... we're like water and diesel fuel, we ain't gonna mix. You don't see things like they are, only like you want them to be. And life just ain't like that."

"It can be, if you let it." Why wouldn't he see? Why did he have to be so pigheaded and cynical?

"No..." He shook his head.

Lacey knew he didn't believe. Hadn't he told her that before? He didn't believe in things like Santa Claus, or Christmas, or love. He didn't believe there could be a "them." Probably didn't even *want* there to be a "them." And here she was, pressing him.

Stop it! she told herself firmly. Shoving her fists into her coat pockets, she stepped back, squared her shoulders and forced a smile. She would not cry; she'd die first.

"Thanks so much for bringing us...and for going up to check out Daddy for me." Her smile felt frozen. "That was very kind of you. We'll be fine...and we'll ride back on the bus."

Something flashed across his face, pain maybe, but Lacey couldn't see very well. It surprised her when he reached out and gripped her arm.

"See you back at Gerald's?" he said.

"Sure...see you then."

Late that night, when everyone was asleep, Lacey slipped down to the kitchen for some warm milk. While pouring it into a cup, she heard her father's footsteps.

"Can't you sleep?" he asked, entering the kitchen.

She smiled. "Too many thoughts about today, I guess." Her father looked at her a minute, then reached for the pan and milk. "I'll make it, Daddy. Sit down. You're not supposed to stand on that leg." At his look she said, "Beth told me about the problem with your veins last week."

"You'd better not have come back just to plague me like the others—to pander to me," he said sharply, but he sat.

"I didn't, Daddy. I came home to make up and to have my father again. And it was big of me, too." She was rewarded by his slow smile.

He hugged her, and she loved it. "Are some of those thoughts whirling around in your head about that young man who brought you here today?" he asked.

Lacey nodded and looked down into her milk. "Some."

"When you were younger," he said, "you never talked to me about the boys you liked. Guess it's a bit late to start."

"Yes, Daddy." She touched his arm. "But I love you."

He looked embarrassed and reached for the photo album she'd given him. He opened it, and as they drank their milk, he asked questions about each picture, as if hungry to catch up on his grandchildren's lives.

"You doing all right out there in New Mexico?" her father asked, turning his attention from the photos. "Do you make enough to support you and the kids as well?"

She looked at him, realizing he'd know immediately if she lied. "Sometimes the money is tight, but we eat well and have a nice apartment in a friendly neighborhood. I like waitressing, Daddy. I'm good at taking care of people that way. The kids have everything they need and plenty of extras. We're doing okay."

"You have to think of the future, Lace...." When he saw her expression, he stopped and raised an eyebrow. "If you'd like to come here to live, you'd be welcome. I'd... I'd like it, Lacey."

Lacey moved to lean against his shoulder. "Thanks so much, Dad. So very much. I'll think about it."

It had been a wonderful Christmas, she thought when she finally climbed into bed. One she would remember for a long time. Sitting cross-legged, she ran the brush Jon had given her in long strokes through her hair. It was a lovely brush-and-comb set, yet what Lacey held most dear was the look of love on Jon's face when he'd presented it, a gift bought with his own hard-earned money.

The crystal ball snow scene Cooper had given her sat on the nightstand. Lacey gazed at the small globe, then lifted and shook it to watch the "snow" fall gently onto the tree. Then she pressed the glass ball to her heart and squeezed her eyes shut against tears.

She'd never forget her time with Cooper and counted it a joy, if a bittersweet one. She wouldn't have missed caring for him for the world. She wondered when the hurt would go away. And how she would face him back at Gerald's.

The days that followed were good. It snowed again, and Anna and Jon spent several afternoons sledding with their cousins at a nearby hill. Lacey's mother threw a party, inviting old friends and family. There were long girl-talks with Beth, companionable walks with her mother and stubborn arguments with her father, although he did most of the arguing. Lacey simply listened. She'd learned a few things in eleven years.

Her father fumed when Lacey decided her family's home was in Albuquerque now. He didn't understand why she wouldn't come home to live, where it would be a lot easier for her. When she explained that she and the children had their own home out west, that she had a good job, good friends, the children's school, he pointed out her lack of money and security, and most of all, family.

"You and Mama are only a phone call away," she told him, to which he grumbled irritably.

He would help with money, he told her, and if she had any sense at all, she would take it. She told him he could begin by lending her the bus fare back, which led to still more raving about how she didn't have a decent savings account. Her mother mentioned that her father hadn't had any savings account at Lacey's age.

Though she knew she was being foolish, Lacey couldn't help gazing out the window, looking for a maroon Kenworth to come rolling up the street. Beth found her at the window on New Year's Eve, a traditionally quiet time at their house.

"You hoping he'll come back?" Beth asked.

At her voice, Lacey turned, somewhat sheepishly. "I guess I am . . . silly of me." She rubbed her arms. "Thanks for this sweater, sis. I love it."

"You're welcome." Beth flopped onto the couch. "It's not necessarily silly. Maybe he will come back."

Lacey shook her head, bent and prodded the fire with the poker. "It would be more probable for it to snow in July," she said.

"It has snowed in July," Beth stated. "In Vermont, I believe, back in the eighteen-hundreds. So you see, miracles do happen. Is he a good man?"

Lacey smiled softly. "Yes, I think so. He's just so...so ornery."

"But you love him?"

Lacey shrugged but remained silent. Somehow it seemed her heart couldn't bear to admit it, for it would make the pain worse.

"Go ahead and hope," Beth said then.

"What good will that do?" Lacey asked, hugging herself.

"It will get you through tonight—and maybe he will come back."

Lacey tried to smile for her sister, who was lovingly and loyally trying to make her feel better. But maybe the only way to deal with her pain was to accept that Cooper could never feel what she did and put it behind her. It was only a fleeting incident in her life. One that touched her deeply, one that changed her, but not one meant to last.

Was it too late? Cooper asked himself for the twentieth time. If it was, he was stuck with this stupid puppy that had chewed up one of his best leather gloves and half of the small basket in which it now slept in the sleeper compartment.

He hadn't even left the Sawyers' neighborhood on Christmas Day when he'd begun wondering about him and Lacey. All the way up to D.C. and during the week, when he found some short hauls to keep him in the area, he'd told himself he had plenty of time to think about it—*it* being his feelings for Lacey.

But for the last two hours, he'd begun to wonder if Lacey might have changed her mind during the past week. She might have met an old boyfriend. She might even have already left for Albuquerque.

He'd feel real stupid if she'd changed her mind. If he'd called her, he could have been embarrassed over the telephone, which was preferable to being embarrassed face-to-face with her. But he didn't think something like this could be discussed over the phone. He had to see her, talk to her and risk feeling a fool. The thought made his palms sweat, his mouth taste bad.

He thought of her green eyes, her contagious smile and the way she'd had the guts to tell him she loved him. She'd spoken the words plainly, not murmured them during the hot seconds of passion, when a person might say anything, truth or not.

She loved him. Lacey wouldn't have said it if it hadn't been true. But then, he'd been fooled before.

Cooper wasn't certain what he was feeling. He knew only that he wanted to be with Lacey, to see her smile all for him. Good grief, he even wanted to see the kids. He wasn't certain as to the why of any of it. Or the wisdom.

All the questions whirled in his mind as he pulled the Kenworth to a stop at the curb in front of the Sawyers' graceful house. The truck's engine purred smoothly; Cooper stared up at the house. Lights shone from every room, and he wondered if they were having a New Year's Eve party. He cursed himself for not thinking of that. But no cars filled the driveway, and everything seemed quiet.

It would help a lot if Lacey would happen to see him and come out to meet him, he thought as he opened the truck door.

A sound drew Lacey from the table where she played chess with her father. The children upstairs, she thought, though she went to look out the window anyway.

When she saw the glimmer of maroon beneath the street lamp, the breath rushed from her lungs. *Cooper!* Thinking maybe it was her imagination, she closed her eyes, then opened them again. Cooper had said she looked at the world through rose-colored glasses, and yes, she did. But even she hadn't truly believed he would return.

Turning, Lacey strode to the door, then ran out into the night, her father's call "Lacey?" following her.

She ran halfway down the walk and then stopped. Maybe Cooper hadn't come back for her. Maybe she'd left something in his truck, or he'd just decided to give her a friendly lift, or...

He'd circled the front of the truck and now stood at the curb. Lacey waited, her heart pounding. Slowly he walked forward across the snow-covered lawn. Then he was walking faster, as if in eager anticipation! Lacey ran toward him, and when he opened his arms, she went to him and buried her face in his jacket.

"Come out of the snow," he said at last, leading her down toward the shoveled sidewalk.

He stopped beneath the streetlight. His arm remained securely around her, and Lacey looked up, wondering at what was happening. She touched his cheek and waited.

"I don't know what's happened to me," he said. The confusion on his face tore at her heart, yet pleasurably so. He moved in front of her and cupped her face in his hands. "I just know I couldn't leave without you and the kids. Yes, even the kids." He gave a hoarse chuckle, then his brow furrowed. "Will you go back with me, Lacey? Can we...can we see about us?"

"Oh, Cooper..." Her words caught in her throat, and she was crying and laughing at once. "What's happened to you is love, darling." She wound her arms around his neck. "And I love you," she whispered just before his lips crushed hers.

When at last he lifted his lips, Lacey had to gasp for breath. She snuggled against him, unwilling to break the contact. Her mind whirled with the wonder of it all. Then she opened her eyes and found herself staring at the front of the Kenworth. The Christmas lights were still there, but they no longer said, Bah, Humbug.

H-O-squiggle-*O*-squiggle-*O*. Why, it said Ho, Ho, Ho, if one was imaginative.

"I had trouble with the letters," Cooper said, stroking her hair.

Lacey, tears of joy streaming down her face, began to pound his chest. "You believe! You believe! You believe in love now!"

Cooper shook his head, as if he couldn't comprehend it himself. "Yes," he said with a slow smile. "I do."

Slipping a hand onto the back of her neck, he held her firmly and brought his lips to hers in a warm, seductive kiss that promised much more to come.

Then he lifted his head and murmured, "Santa sent Anna's puppy by way of me."

* * * * *

A Note from Curtiss Ann Matlock

As often happens with my characters, Lacey Bryan showed me something hidden within myself—my tendency to slip into a very special world at Christmastime. A world where troubles, hurts and disappointments fade before the bright, glorious wonder that is Christmas.

I'm sure I came by this wonderful habit as a child. We were quite poor, and my parents had serious personal problems, as well. But they took great delight in the holiday season and pushed problems aside in their effort to show us kids a good time.

I can remember how Mama loved a tall tree—one that reached the ceiling—and how Daddy always got it for her, even if we could only afford the scrawny kind. But, oh, it looked magical once it was all decorated!

We were never allowed to sneak into the living room on Christmas morning before waking our parents, and then we had to wait still longer while Daddy plugged in the lights so Mama could see the rapture on our faces. Mama wrapped every single gift specially, no matter how tiny, because she knew that so much of the magic is in the surprise.

I, too, love a tree that reaches the ceiling and am blessed to be able to cut nice fat—not scrawny—trees from our small farm. And my son doesn't sneak a peek in the morning before my husband and I are awake, with lights enough to see his face. I sing along shamelessly with Christmas carols and watch all the holiday specials and movies on TV. I bake raisin and pecan pies and enjoy looking at them as much as eating them. And I delight in the giving—of presents, of laughter, of love.

Because, you see, it is Christmas—a time for believing in miracles and experiencing them, a time for forgiving and for loving.

I wish you a very merry Christmas!

Curtiss Ann Matlock

Silhouette Desire®

CHILDREN OF DESTINY

A trilogy by Ann Major

Three power-packed tales of irresistible passion and undeniable fate created by Ann Major to wrap your heart in a legacy of love.

PASSION'S CHILD — September

Years ago, Nick Browning nearly destroyed Amy's life, but now that the child of his passion—the child of her heart—was in danger, Nick was the only one she could trust....

DESTINY'S CHILD — October

Cattle baron Jeb Jackson thought he owned everything and everyone on his ranch, but fiery Megan MacKay's destiny was to prove him wrong!

NIGHT CHILD — November

When little Julia Jackson was kidnapped, young Kirk MacKay blamed himself. Twenty years later, he found her...and discovered that love could shine through even the darkest of nights.

Silhouette Special Edition
is now
more special than ever
with its
sophisticated new cover!

Look for six soul-satisfying novels
every month . . . from
Silhouette Special Edition

SERLB-1R

READERS' COMMENTS ON SILHOUETTE ROMANCES:

"The best time of my day is when I put my children to bed at naptime and sit down to read a Silhouette Romance. Keep up the good work."

P.M.*, Allegan, MI

"I am very fond of the quality of your Silhouette Romances. They are so real. I have tried to read some of the other romances, but I always come back to Silhouette."

C.S., Mechanicsburg, PA

"I feel that Silhouette Books offer a wider choice and/or variety than any of the other romance books available."

R.R., Aberdeen, WA

"I have enjoyed reading Silhouette Romances for many years now. They are light and refreshing. You can always put yourself in the main characters' place, feeling alive and beautiful."

J.M.K., San Antonio, TX

"My boyfriend always teases me about Silhouette Books. He asks me, how's my love life and naturally I say terrific, but I tell him that there is always room for a little more romance from Silhouette."

F.N., Ontario, Canada

*names available on request

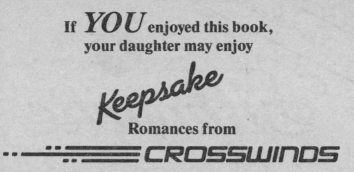